THE
BUTTERFLY
KOI

A. SHERMAN KARLSSON

SYNDICATE HELIOS
MINNESOTA

First Edition: October 2025
ISBN 979-8-9999239-0-5 (paperback)
ISBN 979-8-9999239-1-2 (ebook)

SyndicateHelios.com
SyphonContinuity.com

For all who continue to believe in magic,
even in a timeline of monsters.

SYPHON CONTINUITY *

Map

All locations are estimated in
relative placement to each other.
Not a valid train map for navigation.

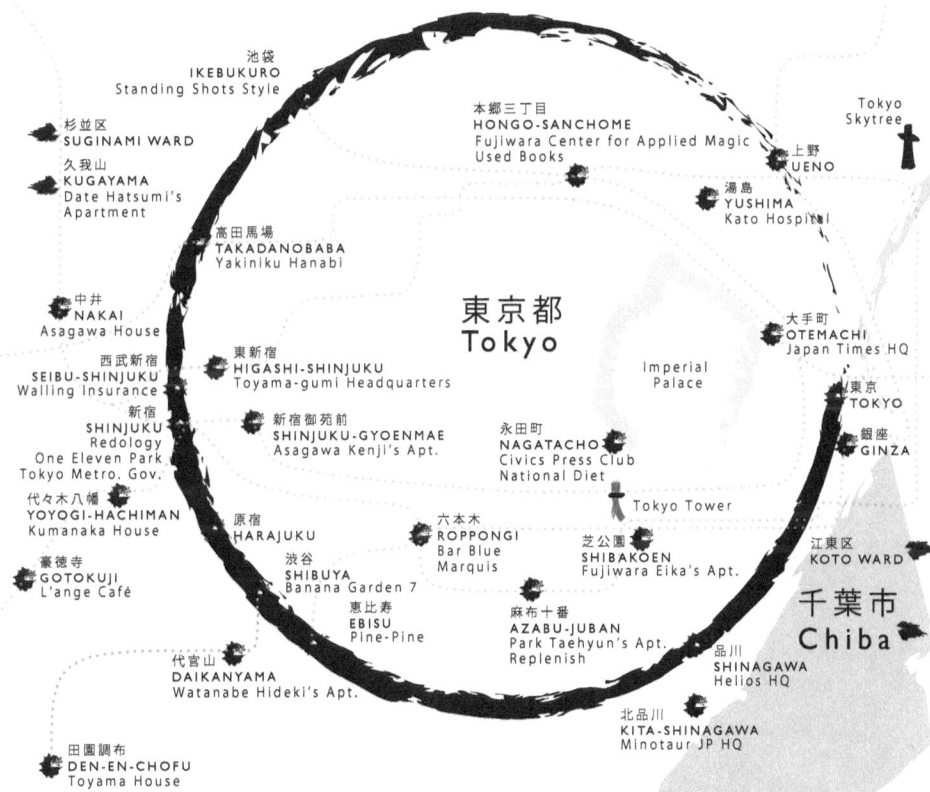

三ノ輪
MINOWA
Cameron Green's Apt.
Ascent Services

池袋
IKEBUKURO
Standing Shots Style

杉並区
SUGINAMI WARD

久我山
KUGAYAMA
Date Hatsumi's
Apartment

本郷三丁目
HONGO-SANCHOME
Fujiwara Center for Applied Magic
Used Books

Tokyo
Skytree

上野
UENO

湯島
YUSHIMA
Kato Hospital

高田馬場
TAKADANOBABA
Yakiniku Hanabi

東京都
Tokyo

大手町
OTEMACHI
Japan Times HQ

中井
NAKAI
Asagawa House

東新宿
HIGASHI-SHINJUKU
Toyama-gumi Headquarters

Imperial
Palace

東京
TOKYO

西武新宿
SEIBU-SHINJUKU
Walling Insurance

新宿御苑前
SHINJUKU-GYOENMAE
Asagawa Kenji's Apt.

銀座
GINZA

新宿
SHINJUKU
Redology
One Eleven Park
Tokyo Metro. Gov.

永田町
NAGATACHO
Civics Press Club
National Diet

代々木八幡
YOYOGI-HACHIMAN
Kumanaka House

原宿
HARAJUKU

Tokyo Tower

六本木
ROPPONGI
Bar Blue
Marquis

芝公園
SHIBAKOEN
Fujiwara Eika's Apt.

江東区
KOTO WARD

養徳寺
GOTOKUJI
L'ange Café

渋谷
SHIBUYA
Banana Garden 7

恵比寿
EBISU
Pine-Pine

麻布十番
AZABU-JUBAN
Park Taehyun's Apt.
Replenish

千葉市
Chiba

品川
SHINAGAWA
Helios HQ

代官山
DAIKANYAMA
Watanabe Hideki's Apt.

北品川
KITA-SHINAGAWA
Minotaur JP HQ

田園調布
DEN-EN-CHOFU
Toyama House

横浜市
Yokohama

お台場
ODAIBA

PRELUDE

This story is supposed to be a puff piece, eloquent prose to permanently elevate the people behind the Daejeon Magical Accords to the top shelf of the shrine of history. Transform unruly pines into heroic bonsai form, any deviation from the abstracted ideal carefully clipped away.

And the truth is it did happen more or less as you would have heard, with the Chiyoda Affair, the IAME white paper, and the Night of Ten Thousand Flowers. We changed the lives of billions, an impact so large I can't comprehend.

But the truth is also that we didn't know what we were doing. We were selfish, short-sighted, and focused on the wrong things for most of the time. We fell together. We fell apart.

The truth is that it was a slow-motion tsunami of cascading trainwrecks from beginning to end.

The first of those, the one that really made the news, was the overdose.

FUJIWARA EIKA

Archival footage: DBW advertisement 1 (15-second clip)

Fujiwara Eika sits up into the frame, her hair disheveled. She puts an elbow over her face and stretches, a baggy blue and white polka dot sleeve falling down her arm.

Cut to her feet sliding across tatami, then onto a wood floor, the hem of matching polka dot pajama pants dragging around her ankles. Finally, she comes to a stop in front of a pair of feet covered in red fabric.

Smash cut to a fabric strawberry that is noticeably taller than her and at least as wide, with no face and with arms completely covered in red fabric. The strawberry is wearing a frilly white apron, and holding out a tray with a full traditional Japanese breakfast. Eika tips her head to the side and smiles broadly.

Red title card that reads "Kinoshita Diet Breakfast Water."

* * *

No matter how often I visit the Helios lab, being here on a Saturday always feels deviant, like I'm trespassing on forbidden ground. The Experimental Magitech team's workbenches, normally littered with tools and half-finished Syphon panels, are clean and dark, standing like sentinels along my path to the damper room. To my surprise, the work-in-progress light outside the carbon-reinforced door is unlit. I slowly edge the door open, wondering if Misora is even here. Did I get my days mixed up again?

"Mi-chan?"

Misora is seated at the conference table in the room's center. Instead of her usual professional attire, she's clad in running tights, a half-zip top, and sneakers. She has access to the Helios car service as well as her father's drivers, so if she chose to come here on foot, it's because she's still stuck. A sheet of magipaper is on the table in front of her, and I can see she's been sketching out designs. She pushes the paper at me.

"It should work. I've gone over it again, I've run the simulations, and everything connects. So why doesn't the power flow? It's like I've built a pile of sopping wet kindling; it looks right, but it can't catch a spark."

I set the basket I'm carrying on top of the magipaper, deliberately blocking the sketches from view.

"How about some sustenance?" I suggest, responding to the frustration in her voice rather than her actual words. "I had a DBW shoot yesterday, and they left all these nice protein bars and fruit in my dressing room."

She plucks a *mikan* from the basket and removes the peel in a single long spiral. "I'm afraid coming here today was a waste of your time."

"Can I top up the powerbanks?" I ask, casting about for a way to be helpful. Misora has her own magic, of course, but it recharges slowly. She's commented more than once that if regular people are gasoline, I'm more like rocket fuel. Then I remember that I was here just yesterday.

"Yes, please do," she replies, much to my consternation.

"Mi-chan! I left you with hours of reserves yesterday. When did you get here today?"

"Early."

"Taehyun is going to think you don't love him, if he's always waking up alone."

"Probably not."

Toyama Misora is one of my oldest friends, but sometimes I feel like I can't read her any better now, after nearly two decades, than I could in kindergarten. I sincerely believe Mi-chan would give her life for me or Ha-chan, but heaven forbid we know her true feelings about her boyfriend.

"Where do we go from here?" I ask.

She sighs as she stands and takes the *mikan* peel over to the airtight compost container. After it decomposes, it will be cycled into food for the plants that fill the damper room, ready to absorb any dangerous rogue magic.

"I'm not sure," she replies, a rare admission of defeat. "I can engineer a battery all day, but getting the body to respond is something else entirely. We need someone who specializes in biology."

"Oh," I say, suddenly understanding her reluctance. A hire requires money. While the Denali project is supposed to be a joint venture between Replenish, my charitable organization, and Helios, only Helios has deep pockets. Unfortunately, as a major corporation, they're also a lot less invested in the idea of a battery that will help people on the low end of the magical ability distribution. Their focus is on the next big Gamestasis hit, not access for the marginalized.

Misora has her head tipped back against the headrest of her chair, eyes scrunched shut in thought. Her portable chimes, the sound that I know, from our years of friendship, indicates a text from her mother, Helios' CEO. She reads the message, then looks up at me, widened eyes gleaming with newfound confidence.

"Mi-chan! I'm dying here, what is it?"

She turns her port toward me, the screen showing a link to a breaking news article: U.S. PRESIDENT SIGNS MAGIC BAN. "They actually did it, the idiots."

"And?" I'm not following why she's so pleased by this.

"Maybe we can pick up an American magitech engineer for cheap. I'll bring it to the board."

* * *

The sun is shining bright in a chill sky on the day my family does their best to co-opt magic.

Like most family appearances, we're all sharply coiffed and perfectly framed as philanthropic for the opening ceremony of the University of Tokyo's new Fujiwara Center for Applied Magic. The classrooms and labs of this building are nothing more than an accessory to the image of it all: a snapshot for the press to sell the story that Fujiwara Heavy Industries is springing into the future of energy.

The auditorium of the new building is a dark contrast, decorated with cedar strips arranged in elegant leaf patterns between columns of acoustic paneling. Warm spotlights along the edges of the room make the space feel cozy. If only Mi-chan or Yuuto-kun had been able to join us today, they would have appreciated the atmosphere. From my front row seat, I discreetly angle my port to snap a photo to share.

My older brother Isao leans over to whisper, close enough that the frame of his glasses touches my ear. "Now is not the time for your self-promotion."

"Today is important for the family," I say softly, responding to the anxiety under his snipe. Then I tap the shutter button.

It's a long opening ceremony, with speeches from the mayor of Bunkyo ward and the president of the university. Next, a lecture on the intersection of magitech and the future of medical research from my ex-girlfriend Sayuri's great-uncle, the one with the Nobel prize. The speeches are similar, about hopes for the future and the joys of collaboration, but there's enough enthusiasm for their words that the audience seems invested by the time Kimiko-*oneesan* and the other representatives get up on the stage to cut a symbolic ribbon.

Afterwards, we all file through the wide hallways and emerge in the atrium, where the windows now show a darkened sky. The lights look like small stars, sparkling in the high space above.

Isao-*oniisan* catches my arm before I can go more than a step inside. "Don't bother anyone tonight. The people here have better things to do than talk about your nonsense."

I keep a pleasant expression on my face, even as the chill in his tone puts tension in my back.

"Don't worry," a voice behind me says. "I'll keep an eye on her for you."

Ahead of us, Kimiko turns back and catches Isao's eye, so he leaves me and my rescuer alone.

"I'm glad I'm not the only black sheep at this event," Johjima Haru says to me, *sotto voce*. He's wearing a suit, but as usual, his tie is loosened, and the top button undone. It gives him a rakish air, and triggers some fond memories, too.

I smile, relieved to see a familiar face. "My younger brother was able to excuse himself by virtue of living in Hong Kong."

Haru grabs two champagne glasses off a passing tray and hands one to me. "Tell Yuuto-kun that if I have to be here, the East China Sea is not nearly enough of an excuse."

"He wasn't willing to buy a ticket for his cello just to be my plus one. But I'm sending him photos of the acoustical set-up in the auditorium to make him properly regret missing out." I show Haru the photo of the room, which came out remarkably clear even with the low lighting causing my port's camera to auto-select a high ISO.

"Nice. I hear you're going by Fujika now."

With a bit of a nudge from my management company, the pop portmanteau of my name has been gaining traction online.

"It seems that typing less is what makes people happy," I reply.

"Hmmph," he says, taking another sip of champagne. "What else have you been up to since I last saw you, Fujika?" Left unsaid: that the last time he saw me, I was leaving his apartment in the wee hours of a Saturday morning. That version of me feels like a lifetime ago.

"Less than you might expect," I say lightly. "Aside from work, just some yoga and mindfulness practice."

Haru laughs, then starts coughing intensely, and his face turns bright red.

"Wrong pipe," he finally croaks out. "You? Fujiwara Eika? Mindfulness."

I turn to catch a passing waiter and request some water. As Haru gulps it gratefully, I lower my voice. "It helps me with—you know." We've known each other long enough, and well enough, that I don't have to spell it out for him. I've always had a hard time staying focused.

"Hmmph," he says again.

"Besides," I continue, flashing him my sweetest and most innocent smile, "the yoga has made me quite flexible."

He grins in delight at this, then downs the rest of his glass. "Well, Fujika, thanks for always being the most interesting thing in the room, but I've got plans tonight. Let's catch up another time, when there's more fun and less"—he gestures at the crowd—"of this."

He pulls out his port, taking a moment to tap something into the keyboard. After a beat, my own port buzzes, and his updated Near Mi profile and contact information—Johjima Haru, Director of Emerging Market Strategies, Johjima Pharmaceuticals—pop up on my screen.

"Just in case you lost my info," he teases.

And with that, I'm alone again.

Around the room, there are so many people I don't recognize, all suits of gray and black gathered in small groups. Kato-sensei, Sayuri's great-uncle, is looking at me when I glance his way, but his eyes slide right off me with disinterest.

The champagne suddenly feels acidic in my stomach as I see myself abstracted out: the scion turned celebrity trying to change herself as much as the world. No wonder Kato-sensei won't meet my eyes.

I take a moment to send the auditorium photo to Yuuto-kun and another message to Mi-chan, though it stays unread like the one I sent earlier today. Since we ground to a halt last month, her focus has been pulled onto another project, and I still haven't heard anything from her about whether she's gotten permission to hire another engineer. She might be in Seoul, too, now that I think about it. When was that trip planned for?

NearMi pings my port again, this time with a foreign name: Cameron Green, Magitech Engineer.

If Mi-chan isn't here to move the project ahead, I'll do it myself.

CAMERON GREEN

I'm in the break room at work, watching the House vote on C-SPAN, when my portable buzzes.

Incoming call: Vanessa Green

"You're up early," I say after the call connects. It's early afternoon here in Minneapolis, which translates to pre-dawn in Tokyo.

"I set a Minotaur alert for when the voting started." She pauses to stifle a yawn. "Drew didn't want to get up, but I felt like I needed to see it live. Not every day that your country steps on a rake in front of the entire world."

True, but my brother-in-law probably still has the right idea. I wouldn't mind going back to bed, either.

"It's only the House," I reply uneasily as the yes tally ticks higher above the chyron HOUSE VOTES ON MAGIC BAN. "Will you have a briefing at work today?"

"Guaranteed. I don't envy the guys in Public Affairs. Oof, even Rep. Wagner? He was part of the congressional delegation that visited us here at the embassy last month. I thought he had more sense."

"Over 200 of them don't have any sense." The door to the break room opens, revealing my labmate, Chuck O'Connell. We exchange nods, and when he sees what's on the TV, he slumps into the chair across from me. The last vote is cast, and the final numbers reflect what most pundits had predicted: the U.S. House of Representatives has passed a bill outlawing magic. The whackjob in the White House is definitely on board, so if it passes the Senate, then I'm out of a job.

You can't research the practical application of magic to human biology when at least sixty senators think it's witchcraft.

"Well, crap," I say, half to Chuck, half to my sister. The possibility of this didn't feel real before, but suddenly it does. It could actually happen. Chuck nods grimly.

"It's only the House," Vanessa says, echoing my earlier words. "Call your Senators."

"Sure, Ness, will do," I reply, with little enthusiasm. She's a federal employee, she has to believe in the system.

"But, Cam—"

"Yeah?"

"You might want to start thinking about a back-up plan, too."

I end the call and turn to Chuck. He's flipped the channel over to CNN, where some talking head is already forecasting how the Senate votes might fall.

"Was that your sister?" Chuck and I have been lab partners for a couple years now, and we've collaborated on a lot of complex, high-stress magic. He knows me pretty well, including the details of my family.

"Yeah. Listen, do you have a back-up plan? For all this?" I gesture at the TV. The anchor is now recapping the events that led to the proposed ban, starting with Wellspring of the People, the pseudo-magic cult who burned down half of Redwood National Park.

Chuck peels open a container of yogurt, then shapes the foil lid into a little ball. "Not really. I'll probably have to retrain in synthetic bioengineering. You?"

"I guess. I don't know. I thought this was going to be a state-by-state thing, not federal." When California and Missouri enacted their bans, I shrugged it off. And even when the Minnesota legislature made some noise about "protecting our state's natural heritage from magical degradation," I figured I could just move. I never mentioned that to Chuck—his ex-wife and kids are here, so he's anchored. But I only have Ingrid, and her job as a financial analyst is flexible. I think she'd be open to Oregon or Colorado, someplace with big trees and clean air, and the kind of outdoorsy culture we're used to. Moving is easier than trying to retrain. My parents already paid for one graduate degree I didn't finish, they won't be keen to fund another.

"Even if it's federal, you could move."

"Out of the country? I don't know. I read that Canada's specialist work visas are totally backed up due to the California exodus."

Chuck flicks the balled-up yogurt lid at me. "Canada? What are you talking about, doofus? I meant Japan."

* * *

Japan.

I'm supposed to meet up with some friends at a tequila bar downtown tonight, but I need to stop by my condo first to let Panzer out. A good run might burn off some of my twitchy energy, too, and get me in a better headspace. As always, Panzer is thrilled when he sees me pull on my running shoes, launching himself into full-on zoom mode. It lifts my mood a bit, buoying me into a swift pace as we head out for a loop around Lake of the Isles.

If I'm honest with myself, I'll be completely fucked if I lose my job. I have 15 months of payments left on my BMW, a mortgage plus HOA fees on a lakeside condo, and this high-energy German Shepherd to keep in kibble. Ingrid has hinted that she'd like to see our relationship get more serious, but I don't think moving in together because I can no longer afford my place was quite what she had in mind.

Japan.

I get why Chuck suggested it. Beyond its powerful magitech companies and plentiful government R&D funding, it's also familiar to me, my home-away-from-home. My siblings and I went to elementary school in Chiba prefecture, a slice of endless concrete suburbia that hangs between Tokyo Bay and the Pacific. Our dad is a civil engineer, and his company sent him there for a short-term build that ended up taking six years. Now my sister is back in Tokyo, newly placed in the Political Affairs division at the U.S. Embassy.

I like Japan, but I never thought I'd have a reason to move back. My life is here in Minnesota. Besides, the law won't pass the Senate. With our huge swaths of prairie preserves and natural forests, U.S. magic is abundant, a precious resource for both the public and private sectors. It would be ludicrous to shut down an industry with this much promise, and though I doubt most Senators care about protecting magic for the sake of science, there are the fat profits to consider, too.

My thoughts have carried me the three miles around the lake, and we're back where we started. I look down at Panzer, who's panting in the unseasonably warm early October air. "It won't pass the Senate, right?"

His dopey doggy grin doesn't dispel the gnawing in my stomach. I open up a text conversation with my sister.

(Would it be crazy if I looked for a new job in Japan? If this magic ban happens } Cameron Green

Vanessa Green { WHAT! No, not at all. Move to Tokyo. Immediately!)

VG { What does Ingrid think?)

(Don't know. Haven't said anything to her yet } CG

VG { Might want to get on that, if you're serious about this)

Am I? Maybe. I am if it turns out to be my only option.

* * *

"You've been watching too much political news lately," Ingrid says, leaning across me to take the remote. "Let's catch up on *The Cartel* instead. We missed last week."

She scrolls through her queue, pausing to delete a soccer match that we watched at my place. The bass thrum of *The Cartel*'s opening theme song starts, and Ingrid settles into her preferred TV-watching position: sideways on the sofa, legs across my lap. We've been together long enough to have this rhythm, and yet—not long enough for me to tell her why I've been watching the news, or for her to intuit the reason.

Ten minutes into the show, an alarm goes off on my port. "Oh, crap," I say when I see the reminder for *Video call: No P in the Gene Ool* on my screen. "I totally forgot."

"Forgot what?" Ingrid asks, pausing the show.

"Sibling chat."

She frowns at the interruption, but she knows I won't miss this. Since we're located on three different continents right now, in wildly different time zones, my brother and sister and I take turns on who gets the worst time. Reilly stayed up late in Europe so that Vanessa could go to a morning appointment in Asia and I could eat a normal dinner in North America. I can't shaft him by skipping.

"Can I use your computer instead of taking this on my port? Keep going with the show, just catch me up later."

Once I'm settled in Ingrid's bedroom, I open up her laptop. The wallpaper is a photo of us on the rooftop terrace here at her condo, backdropped by a sunset over the Minneapolis skyline. How I'd like to be that guy again, tanned and unbothered.

I log into the Minochat, expecting to hear about it for being the last to show when I had the best time, but only Reilly is there. "Hi, Ingrid Nygaard," he says. "Nice throw pillows."

I look over my shoulder at Ingrid's bed, piled high with soft shapes in shades of rose and gray. "I don't know what half of those are even for."

"I'd worry if you did," he replies. Unlike me, Reilly has had the sense to use a background, navy blue with the red-striped shield of the U.S. Men's National Team. He yawns, stretching his arms above his head for a moment, and I try to quash the pang of envy. I swear he's bulked up since the last time we talked. It's a humbling experience to have your baby brother become a professional soccer player. 0/10, do not recommend.

"Remind me what time it is there?"

"Three A.M. Oh, there's Ness." A new block on the screen labeled

"Green-Mukherjee" resolves into our sister, seated at a small table in her Tokyo apartment.

"Late!" Reilly accuses cheerfully.

"Sorry, sorry. My doctor's appointment ran over."

"You okay?" I ask.

"Yeah, it was just a check-up." Like always, we catch each other up on the last couple weeks of our lives: the usual work, relationships, random funny stories. Finally, when I think we're about to wrap up, Vanessa clears her throat. "So, are we going to get to the elephant in this room?"

Reilly crinkles his brow, confused. "Elephant?"

"Whether Cam has thought any more about moving to Japan. It would make scheduling these chats easier."

"Wait, what? Why would Cam go back to Japan?"

I jump in before Vanessa can reply. "Has the possible U.S. magic ban made the German press?"

"Ah," Reilly says. "Yeah. There was a political cartoon about the president in *Süddeutsche Zeitung*—well, it doesn't translate, but it was pretty rough. Is it looking like a done deal?"

"Unclear," I say, drawing on what I've learned from my new nightly hobby of watching *The National Mood with Cara Becker*. "Polls indicate most people don't want a ban, but when have politicians ever cared? A couple senators are being wishy-washy."

"I think it's happening," Vanessa says.

"Insider knowledge?"

"No, and if I had any, I wouldn't tell you. More of a feeling. Cam, you should definitely discuss this with Ingrid."

From the doorway behind me, a quiet voice: "Discuss what?"

From the living room, drums and cello: the ending credits for *The Cartel*.

I guess we're having this conversation now.

* * *

Reilly Green { Do you still have a girlfriend?)

(Er, well. We had a fight. Big fight. But after I explained, she also said she'll think about it } Cameron Green

RG { Thats a good sign)

(Yeah. She started a pro/con list } CG

(Pros: I can work in my field. It's an adventure. We stay together. Cons: she doesn't know the language or culture, doesn't want to sell her condo. No clear end to it } CG

RG { All fair points)

(Yeah. Irritatingly } CG

RG { Is she expecting a ring if she goes?)

(Oh god. It's too early in the day over here for that convo } CG

* * *

The morning of the Senate vote, I start by checking messages in my office. There's one from my boss, Saida, with instructions on things she'd like the team to prioritize today, and all of it is business as usual on our primary project, a magitech-boosted ventricular assist device. If we ever get to submit it for FDA approval, it could save a lot of lives. But if it's banned by this time next week, it will be ten months of hard work wasted.

Chuck is already in the lab when I get there, hold music playing from his port while he cross-checks some of the magic we shaped yesterday. "Morning, Cam," he says, not looking up from his task.

"Does Saida actually think we're getting work done today?" I ask, slouching onto the stool next to him.

Chuck just grunts, eyes still laser-focused on his work. I put on my lab lenses so I can see what he's up to.

"Line A5 has a loop," I say, peering over his shoulder. "It will keep trying to implant in the tissue without moving on to initiate blood flow support functions."

A tinkling chime from Chuck's port, then a soothing feminine voice: "*As a constituent, your voice is important to Senator Thao. We are experiencing a high volume of calls today. If you would like to wait to speak to a staff member, please stay on the line. If you would like your call returned tomorrow, please press 3.*" The message repeats in Spanish, Hmong, Somali, and Vietnamese. The hold music resumes.

"How long have you been on hold?"

"Since eight a.m. Eastern. Thao's supposed to be a no, but it can't hurt to call."

"What about Senator Schmidt?"

"DC office went straight to a full mailbox. I did get through to her local office, though. Her staff said she's still weighing the data and isn't ready to make her decision known."

"Is that code for 'I'll do whatever I want, in spite of my voters' opinions?'" I ask.

Chuck slides a stack of panels my way. "No point in wasting the morning worrying about it. Make yourself useful."

It's hard to see why I should bother. And yet... in spite of myself, I get absorbed in the puzzle of what I'm doing, and the sheer scientific elegance of it.

Magic is a recent phenomenon, and most people don't bother to try understanding it, but it's actually pretty simple. Imagine a river. On its own, the water is already useful for any number of things, from human hydration to industrial processing. However, the river can also be dammed to generate energy. Magic has similar flexibility—it can be shaped to create technology, or it can be used to power it.

So, take your average magitech portable. Your personal magic, which will vary based on where you happen to fall on the bell curve of magic potential, will power up your port every time you slap your palm on the Syphon panel and consent to the transfer. But what you probably don't ever think about is that the port itself was engineered via shaped magic, magic that people like me draw up from within ourselves and arrange into structures that will obey commands. At that point, it's not too far off from computer coding, at least conceptually. Unfortunately for me, the skill set isn't transferable.

"Clear as mud," my Uncle Mitch once said when I tried to explain it all to him.

As I find myself getting engrossed in the structures of the panels I'm checking, I only dimly notice Chuck's call getting answered by a congressional staffer. I'm relieved to overhear that Senator Thao is a definite "no" vote today. Then the work draws me back in, and it's not until my stomach rumbles that I realize the morning has disappeared.

"It's one," Chuck says, either reading my thoughts or hearing my stomach. "We should eat. The vote's in half an hour."

I put away my tools and store the panels in trays above my workbench. I love doing this work. Fuck. I don't want to give it up.

Most of our team, including Saida, is in the break room, the TV already turned to CNN. About ten talking heads are onscreen, each rehashing the things they've been speculating about for weeks. No one is saying anything new.

The energy in the room is weird. Staff from other teams are giving us a wide berth—as the magitech team, we're the only ones who will be affected by this ban. For everyone else, it's just another Tuesday. I reheat my leftover chicken and wild rice hotdish, no doubt a bid from Ingrid to remind me of what I'd lose by leaving Minnesota. She's taped a note to the container: *No matter what happens, I <3 you. -Ing*

She doesn't usually make my lunches, but I was at her place so late last night that I ended up staying over. We talked for hours, mostly in circles, as ineffectual as the cable news pundits. What's becoming increasingly clear: I care about her, but not enough to give up my career. She cares about me, but not enough to give up her life in the U.S.

The infuriating thing about all of this is that it amounts to a branding error. Magitech—the general umbrella field for biokintech, which is my sub-specialty—got called "magic technology" to make it more palatable. To help average people feel more comfortable with what scientists were doing: creating devices that draw on previously undetected, unused human energy. It isn't magic at all, except in the sense of Clarke's third law, that *any sufficiently advanced technology is indistinguishable from magic.* No one is stirring potions or waving a wand around. It's science. Yet the fact that a significant number of my fellow Americans don't get that—well, it's why my whole life is on the verge of getting turned upside down.

To the left of the talking heads, CNN is broadcasting a livestream from the Senate floor. Senators are milling around, shaking hands, sipping coffee. Finally, they gavel in the session, and the pundits are silenced in favor of Senate business.

There are a few impassioned speeches on both sides of the issue, and particularly angry comments from Senator Lee of California, who is so vehemently "yes" that he opposes even the Department of Defense exception that's been added to the bill.

After an agonizing delay, they vote. It's so antiseptic, so anodyne, this moment that might change my life.

The presiding officer calls Senator Schmidt of Minnesota. If she's in favor of the ban, then she's the clinching vote, and SB-114 will be law as soon as it hits President Garcia's desk.

"Yea."

CAMERON GREEN

I turn onto Hennepin Avenue and take the bridge over the river toward Ingrid's. To the east, the lights in the graceful spans of Stone Arch Bridge set it aglow against the inky water of the semi-frozen Mississippi. It's a beautiful view. One I've taken for granted, and I feel a pang of regret.

But it's too late to change things now. I have this last box of Ingrid's stuff to drop off, and all the rest of my belongings are either sold or in storage at my parents' place. The stock market crashed when everyone tried to unload their magitech stocks, and it took the housing market with it. I haven't been able to sell my condo, but at least I have renters moving in on January 1.

In the entryway, I press the button next to Ingrid's condo number; instead of buzzing me in, though, she comes downstairs. So, it's like that.

"Thanks for bringing this," Ingrid says, peering into the jumble of books, socks, travel mugs and other miscellany in the box. All things I'm sure she would have been happy to live without if it meant skipping this awkwardness, but I wanted to see her one more time. The weight of my choices—that I am ending this relationship, moving to Japan, and launching myself into the unknown—settles into the muscles of my neck and shoulders.

I hand the box over, shivering in the cold entryway. Thinking she would invite me in, I didn't wear a jacket over my sweatshirt. The puffs of our breath hang in the frosty air.

"Did you want to come up?" Ingrid asks.

I scan her face, trying to figure out the answer. "Do you want me to?"

Her expression is tight, and I realize her eyes have a glint of tears. She shakes her head. "Not really, no."

It stings, but I get it. I lean down to kiss her goodbye, and she lets me. And then I turn to leave.

"Cam?"

I hesitate in the outer doorway, the December wind whipping into my cheek. "Yeah?"

"Good luck over there. I really mean it." I can tell she does, not that it matters. Ingrid fit so well with the me I was making myself into, the guy with the purebred dog and the European car and the modern loft. But the guy with no job, who has to sell the car and lease the condo just to feed the dog? I should have known there was no way she would move with that version of me to Japan.

* * *

>>>

U.S. PRESIDENT ANNOUNCES MAGITECH BUYBACK PROGRAM
Will Accept Consumer Electronics, Medications, More

CAMP DAVID, MARYLAND, January 2 —In an effort to support Americans in the transition away from magic-powered technology following the passage of a federal ban, President James V. Garcia announced a national buyback program. Beginning February 1, anyone possessing "magic" or "magitech" devices in the United States will be able to surrender these items at their local post office in exchange for a lump sum based on item type, no questions asked. More information on the program, including a list of contraband items and surrender payments, is available at magicbuyback.usps.gov.

The nationwide ban on magitech use by non-Department of Defense entities will go into effect on March 1.

<<<

Under this press release, which my old labmate Chuck has shared on Minotaur Social, he's included an editorial comment: *Humiliation on a global scale, and to add insult to injury, they're only going to give me two hundred bucks for a brand-new port.* Shantel Clark, another former colleague, replied, *They could at least have the decency to throw in a roll of stamps.*

The Syphon charging panel is smooth under my left hand as I scroll through my Social feed, reading all of this from my own contraband port.

"Have you guys heard about this buyback program Garcia announced?" I ask, the question already out of my mouth before I realize how stupid it is when my sister is a literal U.S. government employee.

Vanessa has the grace to ignore this, or perhaps chalk it up to extended jet lag. She grimaces. "Oh, yes. We've already had people try to drop things off at the embassy gate."

"Americans living here in Tokyo?" my brother-in-law, Drew, asks as he stirs cream into his coffee.

"Yep. And one particularly confused Australian who tagged along with his co-workers from *eikaiwa* school."

Drew shakes his head, chuckling. "We're not always sending our best over here, are we?"

"That better not be directed at me," I grumble around a bite of toast.

"Well, you're not going to teach English at a cram school, are you?"

"No, that's a level of desperation I hope not to reach." If that happens, I would have been better off staying at home.

"Are you finding any postings that look promising?" Vanessa asks.

Now that the holidays are over and my brother, his German girlfriend, and my parents have all returned to their respective countries,

I'm the sole guest at Vanessa and Drew's apartment in central Tokyo. Though I'm looking forward to getting Panzer out of quarantine, that will make the clock tick even faster on finding a job and my own place. This apartment is nice enough, but it's still in Tokyo, which means it's also small. Three adults plus a German Shepherd is asking too much.

"One or two. Most places don't want to sponsor a foreign work visa." I haven't actually applied for anything. I have a decent stockpile of cash from selling my car, but it's going to disappear quickly once I pay a real estate agent to help me find a place to live. Apartment hunting in Tokyo, I've already learned, is expensive and frustrating.

Vanessa and Drew glance at each other. I pretend I don't see it, but I know what they're thinking.

"Cam, Drew has an event tomorrow night, the opening of a new research center at Todai. There are a lot of magitech types among the donors—maybe you could go and do a little networking?"

I'd rather do a little root canalling, but I don't have many alternatives. Before my parents left, I overheard Vanessa tell our mom that she and Drew are trying for a baby. I have to get out of here. "Great idea, Ness."

* * *

The brand-new Fujiwara Center for Applied Magic at the University of Tokyo is a monstrous sharp-angled affair, all steel and glass.

"Which window is your office?" I ask Drew as he, Vanessa and I approach the main doors.

Drew chuckles at the question. "I'm a postdoc. We don't get windows."

As we enter the airy lobby, Vanessa starts pointing out people of interest. She has some kind of photographic memory for names and faces, which I guess makes sense, given her career. "That's the PI on Drew's project, Dr. Ichikawa," she says, indicating a diminutive man in an ill-fitting suit. "Oh, and there's Kimiko Fujiwara, one of the center donors."

I know just enough about the Fujiwara family to find their support for this center perplexing. Fujiwara Heavy Industries is one of those old

Japanese companies that was a full-on *zaibatsu* back when they were legal. More than a century ago, they laid waste to a not-insignificant number of mountains in northwest Honshu in their search for copper, and now there are FHI-owned mines all over the world digging for zinc, gallium, tungsten, and god knows what else. As a vertical monopoly on everything related to mineral extraction and processing, why the very public support for applied magic research?

I turn to ask Vanessa this question, but Drew is already leading her away. "Hon, there's Ikumi-san from my project, I wanted you to meet her."

I'm on my own. A twinge—though of what, exactly? —ripples through me as I think of Ingrid. Do I miss her? Yes. At least, I miss the idea of her, and how I felt about myself when I had her as my plus one. A pretty blonde investment banker was good for my ego.

Unsure about how to break into any of the conversations happening around me, almost all of them in Japanese, I drift over to the bar and snag a flute of champagne, then open Minotaur Social again. I don't usually check it this often, but the NearMi feature might help me find someone interesting to talk to.

> *The University of Tokyo has a default ban on all portable device-tracking functions for private citizens. Only results for public figures will be shown. To override this feature and share your profile, please read our policy before consenting to information sharing.*

I tap "consent" and scan the room anyway. While most results are suppressed, a few mini-bios pop up.

Fujiwara Kimiko, chairwoman, Fujiwara Heavy Industries. The woman Vanessa indicated earlier, now engaged in quiet conversation with equally subdued-looking executive types.

Kato Mitsue, Nobel Prize winner and professor emeritus, University of Tokyo Hospital. A stooped man with a few wisps of silver-white hair and a slight paunch.

Fujiwara Eika, socialite and television personality; founder, Replenish

Initiative.

My port indicates a delicate woman standing near the windows. In her blush-colored silk dress, she stands out from the room's mosaic of tan, black, and gray wool. Surprisingly, given her status, she's alone—people nearby keep glancing her way, but no one walks over to chat. Maybe this is my chance.

When my port pings Eika's, she looks my way and smiles brightly. Then she takes a long drink of her champagne, draining the glass. I take the hint. Swapping out my own empty flute for two new glasses, I make my way over to her. Up close, she's even more ethereal-looking, her skin a dewy contrast with this dry, buttoned-up space.

"It's nice to meet you, Cameron Green," she says, taking one of the glasses and clinking it against mine. Our ports have already swapped our business cards, sparing us any awkward fumbling with paper ones. From mine, she will have learned the broad parameters of my skills, including the fact that I speak Japanese, and that I'm looking for a job. "You were working in biokintech in America?"

"Until the new law, yeah. Now I'm hoping to find something here."

"Are you familiar with my organization, Replenish Initiative?"

Not as much as I should be, in order to have this conversation. But I've heard of it before, so I nod. "Environmental clean-up work, right?"

"In part. We believe the data offer ample evidence that environmentally damaged areas are more likely to produce downslope children."

There's some debate in the field of magitech about whether being born in a region of ecological devastation can cause magic-related birth defects—basically, whether it pushes babies further down the left side of the magical ability distribution curve. Some children from these areas do seem less able to use Syphon devices, sucking power out of them rather than recharging them. I'm skeptical but know better than to mention that to Eika.

"It's an important cause," I reply instead. My interest in environmental work doesn't extend too far beyond my personal enjoyment of oxygen and water.

"What kind of projects were you doing in your previous job?" she asks.

"For the past couple years, mostly pharmaceutical and medical. My last one, before I had to shut down my lab, involved creating Syphon-powered cardiac support devices. I'll spare you the details."

A tinkling laugh. "I don't know if I would understand them, anyway. My friend Mi-chan is in this field, too, and most of what she says goes thataway." She makes a gesture over her head, bracelets clinking against one another.

"Where does she work?"

"Mi-chan? She's at Helios." Eika gives me a measured look. "She and I have a collaborative project that has a biological element."

"Oh?" A wan ray of hope.

"Would you be interested in talking with her?"

I was thinking I might end up at a start-up, something small and hungry enough to take a chance on a displaced American. Helios, as one of the biggest tech companies in Japan, is on a plane beyond my most fevered dream. The CEO, Rei Toyama, was an early adopter of magitech, and though Helios has been criticized for creating Syphon devices that aren't universally accessible, her overall gamble paid off. Even the possibility of an interview there—it's like I asked for twenty bucks and got a check for ten grand. This Mi-chan person probably isn't very high up, since Eika looks like she's a little younger than me. But it could be a foot in the door.

"That—that would be amazing," I stammer.

Helios. Holy shit.

FUJIWARA EIKA

Archival footage: DBW advertisement 2 (15-second clip)

Fujiwara Eika leans forward, a look of intense concentration on her face. She is wearing a green tracksuit, reaching for her toes.

Smash cut to her standing, now jogging in place. She stops, then swings her arms over her head and stretches to her left. As she does so, the camera pans out to reveal a person-sized orange with fabric-covered arms mirroring her motions. The two figures stretch in the other direction as Eika smiles.

Orange title card that reads "Kinoshita Diet Breakfast Water."

* * *

The emptiness ahead of my cursor stares at me accusingly, the document refusing to write itself, the page staying stubbornly blank. The future of the world is snagged on a bit of writer's block. I know as much as anyone that telling the story of the thing you're doing is as important as the thing itself. But with Mi-chan still not responding—not even about the engineer I found for her—I'm trying to tell a story that isn't there yet.

Ha-chan wouldn't have any problems with this as a reporter.

"Noah-kun," I call out through the doorway from my office, "do you know what your cousin has been up to recently?"

"I always wish I knew what Hatsumi-san is doing." His tone is light, but I sense there's some history behind that statement.

It's a sentiment I share. Neither she nor Mi-chan have been particularly responsive to my messages lately. Though I shouldn't really hold it against Ha-chan. She's always so busy and it's not like the future of my new organization, the future of magic, is hanging on her response.

Mi-chan on the other hand...should I send her a third message this week?

I close out of the document for now. "Who knew that improving the world would require so many press releases. Righting wrongs shouldn't take so much writing."

Watering can in hand, Noah-kun turns to give me a pleasant but vacant smile from the other room. He didn't quite catch the word play.

Switching partially to English, I clarify, "Sorry, that was 'righting' as in making better, and also 'writing' as in to write. See what I mean?"

"Oh, I do see what you mean!" he says cheerily. "You're adding up all the numbers, and then finding the average."

Now it's my turn to have foreign words wash over me. "Hm?"

"That was the math word 'mean,'" he says.

It's been a long, long time since I had to memorize that definition. It takes me back to nights cramming at my desk in junior high and high school, window cracked to keep myself awake with the cold breeze. "Making jokes that don't translate. Are we being mean to each other?"

He laughs, then holds his free hand up by his chin to strike a studious pose. "Only by means of word play."

Giving him a mock groan, I shake my head in defeat. Back in Japanese, I say, "For that, I'm forwarding you an invoice for the stationery."

"Great! I can take care of that before I leave today."

"You're amazing, Noah-kun," I say, digging for some gloss in my bag. My lips have been getting dry lately. "I don't suppose that, in addition to accounting and word play, you're also proficient at magitech engineering?"

"Is it something I can do in a spreadsheet?"

"I don't think so. Not that I really know," I say, unearthing what appears to be a single sock from deep within the depths of my Celine tote. There are two zipper bags in here. One of them has to have my lip balm. "That was your opportunity to pretend, you know. Your opening for a job at Helios."

"And I missed it."

"They have such a nice dinner out as part of the onboarding. Though you would have to make it through an interview with Mi-chan first."

"What dinner could be worth that?" he asks with mock seriousness.

Finally, I find a tube of lipgloss in the smaller of the two zipper bags. Not my favorite color—this one is a little on the side of peach—but it'll do. "I don't suppose you and Ha-chan have any cousins who are engineers."

"No, sorry. At least not on my side." He peeks his head in around the door, curly black bangs just covering his eyes. "I finished watering all the plants. Do you want to look at the numbers now?"

"The kitchenette could use cleaning," I say with an implied sigh, setting my bag back on the floor.

Noah smiles at me expectantly.

"I know. I know. Okay, let's take a look now. We can sit out there."

I follow him out to the main space of the office and get a bottle of tea from the fridge before taking a seat on the long side of the glass conference table. One more quick look at my port gives me a fresh stab of disappointment—still no message from Mi-chan.

Noah brings his laptop over, the spreadsheet already pulled up. The first tab is a wash of numbers, overwhelming in their uniformity. He switches to a second tab with a graph. This is much more readable, with a line clearly and painfully pointed down.

If only I could say it's a surprise. Replenish has barely gotten started and I'm still sourcing long-term funding. "How long do we have?"

"Um," he pauses, "if we assume that the funding from Fujiwara Heavy Industries is the same and you keep me...?"

"I need you," I say firmly. "And I think my family is going to let us run for a little while. They're trying to improve the company image in any way they can, and canceling Replenish wouldn't help that."

"About a year."

I nod. That's what I feared.

My port dings, the screen lighting up to show that I have a new message. I reach over to look, hoping that it's Mi-chan with the update from the Helios board. It's my agent instead.

Gushiken Hina { Got an interesting invite for you)

(Oh? Do tell } Fujiwara Eika

GH { NHK Discuss! Midswap)

(Oh!} FE

I start to add "why?" but stop myself from sending it. This is exactly what I've been hoping to do—to gain a space in the conversation. To have a voice that can bring attention to the ways that society is creating injustices starting even before birth.

(Is it paid? } FE

GH { No, it's news. They pay in prestige)

GH { We'll talk tomorrow)

Noah is looking glum next to me. He's here from Canada on a working holiday visa, which means that while he's not locked into working at Replenish, it'd be a headache to find something else. And going home has always been his plan, but I expect he'd prefer to decide the timing himself.

Flashing him my brightest practiced smile, I say, "It's okay! I knew that we needed to take a running start, and now we know where the runway ends. It gives us a goal."

I twist open my bottle of tea and take a deep sip, fingers tight around the plastic label, so Noah won't see my hands threaten to shake.

* * *

It might be a staple of Sunday night edutainment, but the styling space for *NHK Discuss!* is a tiny afterthought with block walls.

The makeup artist is working on my eyeshadow, so Gushiken-san leans against the edge of the tiny table to get in last-minute prep. "Kinoshita Group has been relatively open-minded—more fame for you is more for them—but don't push it. Remember, you've got a 'no' on criticisms of bottled beverages, dieting, the health industry, and chocolate, of course. Also, a 'no' on consumer paper products and industrial ceramics. And chopsticks."

I do my best to not ruin my liner by blinking in reaction to that last one. "Disposable chopsticks? Or all chopsticks?"

"Anything related to trees or logging, just to be safe," she says, still focused on her port. "Aviation and bridges too. Oh, and watch your tone. Lately, you've been letting it slide a little high when you're emphasizing a word. We don't want that to be the thing people zero in on."

I give her a thumbs up with a lacquered nail.

The makeup artist moves her attention to my lips, so I shift my port high enough up to be able to review my notes while keeping my head still. A few notifications are on my lock screen, but none of them are Mi-chan. How many messages can I send her before she gets too annoyed, I wonder. But we can't drop this, not after all the work we've done to get where we are.

Anyway, a worry for another time. The topics for tonight are the international magitech market shift and the Hokkaido project, which should be safe for Kinoshita at least.

The Santos and Monteiro study, I repeat to myself, careful to not move my mouth. Santos and Monteiro. Monteiro *et al.* Nkosi.

The make-up artist finishes shortly before an assistant sticks her head in. "On in ten."

I'm a mid-show swap—they're testing my marketability before committing to have me on for the full half hour. One last glance at my notes before I put my port down on the table, and Gushiken gives me an encouraging nod as I leave.

Inside the studio, there's space for a small audience, but it's not in use for this show. Instead, there's just the lights and cameras pointed at a table in front of a large video screen, the walls of the room receding into blackness.

The moderator, Ito Yasahiro, is seated at one end of the table, opposite from the chair that is open for me. His hair is styled into a pompadour and a stack of notecards is in front of him. In the middle, Koike Nenosuke from the governmental Strategic Assets Agency is wearing a stark black suit and navy tie. Both watch me as I walk past them to my chair.

When I sit down, Ito-san taps his index cards against the table and winks at me. "Don't be too afraid. Koike-san only bites occasionally."

This last week, I watched a handful of back episodes, enough to see that Koike-san has become a show regular, and that the reassurance is not exactly true.

I set my hands on my thighs, fingers curled in so my knuckles are resting on my white pencil skirt. "Aren't we lucky, then, to be in a country that is certified rabies-free?"

That earns a chuckle from Ito. Koike keeps a stony face. I cannot let myself be intimidated by him—what I'm trying to do is too important, and there is evidence that backs it up. Santos and Monteiro. Monteiro, *et al.* Nkosi.

Then there's a lighting cue and a countdown, and we're on.

Ito starts the conversation. "We return to our discussion of marketplace disruptions following the U.S. magic ban. Koike-san, before the break, you outlined some of the major shifts in the international market following the American ban. What opportunities do you see for local industry?"

Behind us, the screen switches to a graphic showing the outside of the blunt-nosed Tokyo Stock Exchange building overlaid with an unstable Nikkei index line. Experts lately can't settle on whether Japanese tech companies will benefit from the blow to U.S. magitech competitors like Minotaur and Profuse, or if they're doomed by the loss of American consumers.

"As I said earlier, I can only speak as an outsider since our organization provides limited assistance in the magitech field," Koike-san says, briefly licking his upper lip, "but this does reopen demand for more traditional electronic products. If Americans want to go back to using technologies from ten years ago, Japanese companies certainly have the expertise to produce high quality merchandise to meet the demand."

I really can't imagine the scope of the technological transition that must be happening over there. "Yes, since even companies within the United States are having to switch their focus back to"—I barely stop myself from using the word obsolete—"alternative lines of technology, this is an opportunity for Japanese companies and workers. For example, I know that residents of Ibaraki prefecture are hoping this might cause the local semiconductor plant to reopen."

Ito fixes me with a wide smile. "So, are you saying that you think this situation will come to a happy ending?"

After watching how he treated other women on his program, I'm ready for this kind of comment. If he gets a rise out of me, it will only encourage the behavior, so I keep my smile pleasantly neutral. "I think that there are opportunities, and that Japanese corporations specialize in the type of long-term planning that is well-suited to this situation."

"In the face of such openings, we wouldn't want a quick and dirty resolution, would we, Fujiwara-san? Koike-san, do you agree with that assessment?"

"Industry here is prepared for this shift," Koike says after a moment, his face not betraying any particular emotion.

Ito nods, tapping the stack of notecards between his hands and the table. "There's agreement on one topic, at least. Which brings me to our last point of discussion: the proposed mine near Mikasa, Hokkaido."

Here is the moment I've been waiting for, even though this topic is a field strewn with landmines. Yes, the mine is a Fujiwara Heavy

Industries project, and our environmental track record is far from spotless. Just thinking about what happened in Ashio makes my gut twist. But in Hokkaido, there's an opportunity to do things the right way, to revitalize the local economy and keep people safe. It's a tightrope I feel ready to walk, and the reason I accepted this spot on *NHK Discuss!* tonight.

The screen switches to panoramic photos of Hokkaido mountains interspersed with a shot of the press conference that announced the start of joint efforts. Both Kimiko and Isao are visible on the stage.

Ito continues, "Koike-san, the Strategic Assets Agency has been working to coordinate the purchase, but there has been some criticism of digging a new coal mine when other international corporations have switched to pursuing magic-based energy sources. What are the benefits that your organization sees in this effort?"

"Coal and manganese," Koike corrects. "This mine will have two important outputs, with the manganese especially important for increasing production of NCM batteries."

"Yes, true enough." Ito turns his attention toward me. "What is your opinion? Is this project as fertile as Koike-san implies?"

"I think we're in agreement that those kinds of batteries will be seeing increased demand on the other side of the Pacific," I say. "However, given the widespread domestic use of Syphon, the greater concern here in Japan is that the mine moves forward in a way that ensures the safety of the local people."

"Fujiwara-san, your family's company is behind the mining efforts, and yet your comments now, and press releases from your organization, indicate that you aren't entirely supportive of this work. Do you find it hard to satisfy these two different perspectives at once?"

"Thank you for your concern, Ito-san, but I am always very supportive of the work my family is doing. There are simply some special challenges inherent to a project like this. I know that none of my siblings would want the project to negatively impact the surrounding area. FHI's support for Replenish is proof of this."

A polite fiction, and one that my family may not be pleased to hear on the air, since it creates public pressure to address issues of ecological damage through FHI's direct work, rather than hiding behind my charity. But I haven't been able to get very far by pushing my siblings privately.

Ignoring my statement, Koike backpedals. "By 'keeping the local people safe,' I assume that Fujiwara-san is referring to the convicted criminals."

It's a low blow. Several years ago, FHI was embroiled in a scandal over its use of prison labor on Iriomote-jima during World War II. Our family papered over the controversy with a run of tourism promotion for the island—my first-ever commercial gig.

I turn my attention to the camera and address viewers directly. "The proposed closure of the regional prison is one of the aspects of the planning that needs consideration, yes. But it's not the only part that Fujiwara Heavy Industries is taking care on."

In my peripheral vision, Koike leans back in his chair, a smile stretching his cheeks. "Ah, that famous Fujiwara-san kind heart. What would we do without your concern for even the most hardened of criminals?"

"Prisoners, if you remember, were used for mandatory mining labor as recently as a hundred years ago. All people have a right to basic human dignity, whatever their prior actions. I am more concerned, though, with how strip mining will impact the maternity hospital only a short distance from the proposed site," I reply. Sometimes, the best public relations tactic is radical transparency.

"And yet there has been no reputable study that can prove causation when it comes to the impact of birthplace on magical potential, isn't that right, Fujiwara-san? Isn't it a mistake for your foundation to block these critical financial incentives based on mere theories?"

I start to respond, prepared to state the findings from the studies I've read, but Ito-san cuts me off. "Sadly, we don't have any more time to indulge our imaginations with Fujiwara-san. But clearly this is an important situation to watch. Let's thank both of our guests for bringing their expertise and perspectives to our discussion today. I am Ito Yasahiro and this has been *NHK Discuss!*"

Afterwards, there's a shuffle of bows around the studio. Koike-san walks out in a beeline, looking annoyed, even though he ended up with the better end of the discussion. Maybe that's just how he always looks. Ito-san comes over and thanks me, standing a little too close, the smell of his hairspray strong. I'm all smiles, soft and unthreatening, though I feel a bit sick to my stomach. I had the facts on my side, and I couldn't deliver.

Back in the green room, though, Gushiken has only good news for me. "Well done. Even tone, not too loud, not too pushy. We'll see how the comments are later today, but so far, the immediate reaction on MinoSo is positive. It looks like the Fujika branding is carrying over, too."

She's been with me since the very beginning, that first Iriomote Island campaign, and I trust her instincts. I also want another chance at this.

"Will they call me back for a full episode?"

"I think you can bet on it."

* * *

Since I had to let my full-time assistant go to invest in start-up costs for Replenish, I've been relying on Noah-kun as an intern to handle accounting. I've appreciated his help, but the downside is he doesn't come in on Mondays. So, before I head into the Replenish office for the morning, I have to stop at the Fujiwara Heavy Industries headquarters to pick up our mail. We've been pushing our updated address for months, but people are still sending letters care of FHI.

The headquarters building is expansive, almost completely filling the plot of land, with a small space of green for a line of six emerald trees by the entrance. There's a glass atrium that extends up five floors before dividing into boxy silver windows.

Inside, I wave at the receptionist before taking the escalator up a floor and following the hallway back to the mailroom. There are a few envelopes addressed to me and to Replenish, though they look more like mass marketing than anything.

That reminds me of an email that came in last week: Tokyo Utility has been asking job applicants about their magical ability in interviews. I need to remember to ping Ha-chan about that. But today, I have a meeting with a potential donor, a phone interview with a magazine, and an appointment with my personal trainer. Tomorrow, I'm in a shoot all day, and I'm already behind on my Minotaur Social post schedule for the week. Oh, and I should text Mi-chan again, to see if she wants to set up a meeting with Green-san.

I really do need an actual assistant. Maybe I should sell my car. I barely drive it with the way Tokyo parking goes.

Feeling overwhelmed, I slide the envelopes into my bag and turn to go, just in time to run into Isao-*oniisan*.

Unlike me, he even has assistants for his assistants, which means he came down here for a specific reason. Is my schedule that predictable? Or maybe the receptionist was instructed to alert him if I stopped in.

"You look like you've been working hard, *oniisan*," I say.

"I wish I could say the same to you," he replies, adjusting his cufflinks. "I watched your 'performance' last night."

This was inevitable after I put our conflict about Hokkaido out there so publicly, though the disdain in his voice still stings. "Thank you for your support."

He leans down close to my face, tension around his narrowed eyes. "A bit of advice for you, dear sister," he says. "Marry someone like the Johjima boy, or that Kato girl you used to date. Make some more commercials. Do whatever you need to get the attention you so desperately crave. But stop embarrassing your family with this farce. Our patience—and our generosity—have limits."

I take a step back and bow forward. It's space, both physical and social, but also a way to hide where the color has drained from my cheeks. What to say? "Thank you for your thoughtful advice, *oniisan*."

He turns and strides away, the heels of his oxfords sounding down the hallway.

I stand up straight and adjust the bag on my shoulder, taking a deep breath. There are a few hours this morning before my schedule picks up. Enough time to email someone at the Center for Applied Magic and ask when they're going to start putting real effort into researching the environmental link.

Better send myself a reminder, or I'm going to forget again by the time I get to the office.

As I take out my port, it starts to ring. It's Mi-chan, calling me back.

CAMERON GREEN

"Have you heard from Eika Fujiwara at all since the gala?" Drew is prepping dinner, his grandmother's chickpea curry recipe. Tokyo's restaurants are cosmopolitan, but non-Japanese groceries are tough to come by, so he was pleased to find all the ingredients.

"She sent me a message on Monday asking for my résumé, but radio silence since then."

"Well, that's still promising, right?"

"I guess." I hope so. Desperate to get out of my sister's place, I signed a lease this morning on a place north of Ueno, and the key money cleaned out a good chunk of my liquid cash. I've probably got six months of living expenses if I keep myself to ramen and cheap beer, but I'm going to need a work visa way before that—the tourist visa I'm on right now is only good for ninety days, and I've used up nearly a month already.

"So, what kind of work would it be?" Drew asks as he tears cilantro. The herbal, soapy tang of it fills the small kitchen. I pitch in by working the cork on a bottle of viognier.

"Not sure yet. Hoping it won't be too different from my job in Minnesota, which was mostly R&D on biokintech interaction for pharmaceutical wearables. They're more interested in direct Syphon work here, but that would be fine, it's fundamental to the entire field anyway."

"I understood about half of that," Drew says with a self-deprecating smile. The project he's working on is related to magic prevalence within age cohorts, but it's all statistical. He crunches number sets; he doesn't know the engineering side.

"Biokintech is just shorthand for biology, kinetics, and technology: the interaction between your body, magic, and a device. Magitech stitches and bandages, contact lenses, all that kind of stuff. My last patent was for a delivery system that used a variant of Syphon to draw antibiotics directly to an infected area, so that you're not nuking the good bacteria in your body, too. But it never went past the development stage."

"That all sounds medical." The rice cooker plays "Twinkle, Twinkle, Little Star," indicating that it's done, and Drew starts scooping basmati rice into bowls. "What does that have to do with Helios?"

It's a fair question. Why *would* the company best known for the Gamestasis want to get into biokintech? "They're more diversified than you'd think—"

"Typical Japanese company on that score, I guess."

"Yeah. And from what Eika has said, they're engaged in some corporate image cleanup. Downslope advocacy groups haven't liked their all-in focus on Syphon-powered devices."

"Which explains Eika's involvement with them?"

"Exactly." What I've gathered from my back and forth with Eika is that her friend, the mysterious Mi-chan, is helping her with project development for the Replenish Initiative; in exchange, Helios gets its rep burnished by association. Or, at least, that's the goal.

The sound of a key in the front door: Vanessa's home. "Ooh, my boys made dinner," she says, coming into the main room with a potted fern in her hands.

"*I* made dinner," Drew corrects. "Cam opened the wine."

"A well-known skill of his." Vanessa hands me the plant. "I got you a housewarming gift for your new place. Try to keep it alive. When can you move in?"

"It was vacant, so I took some stuff over there already today. I should be fully out of your hair as soon as they deliver the furniture."

"God, finally," she teases.

I couldn't agree more.

The following Saturday afternoon, Vanessa and I load the last of my boxes into her Toyota hatchback and take them to my new place. I swing open the door to 401. "Ta da."

She slips off her flats in the entry and carries a box to the kitchen table, then slides open the frosted glass door to the balcony. "You have a view of the park across the street, that's not too shabby.... And, hey, a free shoe."

"What?"

She lifts what looks like a man's low black boot, expression bemused. "From the last tenant, I suppose."

"Yeah...." But the leasing agent and I went out on the balcony on our tour. It's small enough that a shoe would be hard to miss. Vanessa shrugs and sets it on one of the kitchen chairs.

"You know, this place isn't bad, Cam. It just needs some personal touches."

I look around at the bare walls and basic Muji furniture. Now that I'm in my own place, I register how much my life has been downgraded. A cramped apartment, no girlfriend, no car. One lead on a job—a dream job, for sure—but I can't pin down a simple informational meeting. And Panzer still has another week in quarantine, so I don't even have my dog.

Vanessa catches my mood immediately. "Hey. I know it sucks, upending your life so much. But you'll find something. And Drew and I are here, just let us know how we can help."

Before I can reply, there's a knock at the door.

"Are you expecting more furniture deliveries?"

"No, the sofa was the last of it." Catapulting myself over the boxes that fill the hall, I open the door to find a Japanese man, probably mid-twenties, standing outside. His hair has been thoroughly dyed a ruddy orange, and he's barefoot. The shoe he's holding looks familiar. He raises it and shrugs.

I could go grab his shoe. But if I do that, I won't get the story of how it ended up on my balcony. "May I assist you?" I ask in my most polite Japanese.

"There's a shoe on your balcony."

Actually, it's in my kitchen, but no need to quibble over details. "Is there?" Behind me, Vanessa stifles a snicker. She knows what I'm up to.

"Yeah. I was doing laundry upstairs and the situation got out of hand."

"Really out of hand, apparently."

"You got it," Apartment 501 replies with a smirk. "So, what's the over-under you're going to release the hostage?"

"Before a hostage is released, there's usually a payment of some kind," Vanessa calls from the kitchen. She's holding his shoe aloft now, almost as if appraising it for value.

"Huh," he grunts. "What's the damage, then?"

"Hmm. This is a nice shoe. Armani should fetch at least—what do you think, Cam? —two trips carrying boxes up from the car?"

501 shrugs, looking amused. "Fine. I'll need the shoe back first, though."

Vanessa tosses me her car keys and the shoe, and I hand the latter over to my new neighbor. "You really don't have to help with this," I say to him as we take the elevator down to the ground level. He has a bandage on his left hand, and I want to give him an out.

"I said I'll do it."

"Well, thanks. What's your name, 501?"

"Asagawa," he replies, omitting a given name. "How about you, 401?"

"Cameron Green." I don't have a card on me, and he doesn't offer one, either. At Vanessa's car, I pull out a paper Yodobashi Camera bag for Asagawa to carry while I heft one of my suitcases. He isn't shy about peering into the bag.

"Is this a Gamestasis?"

My treat to myself. Until I land a job, I won't have much to do besides playing video games and working out. I hear myself invite him to play, and to my surprise, he accepts. He must not have much to do today, now that he's gotten "toss shoe over balcony" checked off his list. I still want the real story on that.

When Vanessa sees me and Asagawa take out the GS and

surround ourselves with game components on the *tatami* room floor, she laughs. "I'll take this as my cue. It was nice to meet you, Barefoot-san."

* * *

Unwilling to pin all my hopes on Eika Fujiwara's mystery opportunity at Helios, I apply for other jobs. A few weeks in, I finally get an offer with a decent salary. It's a small company, but they want me to start right away. It's only when I re-read their email that I see the catch: they can't sponsor a work visa, so I'd be paid under the table. I follow enough news to know Japan has cracked down on illegal work in recent months. There's no way I can accept.

Panzer rests his chin on my knee, and I scratch behind his ears, grateful to have him out of quarantine. "Might have to start buying the off-brand kibble, bud," I tell him.

At this, he flops down on the floor, belly exposed in sincere defeat. "Or I can eat out less," I amend, shamed.

It's still light enough that he and I could get a run in. I pull out my port and use the fitness app to chart a route, just a few kilometers to distract myself for a while. It doesn't seem particularly picturesque from the map, typical Tokyo concrete jungle, but when I get going, it's not bad—about half of it is along the Sumida River.

I'm up to what feels like a good speed when my port chimes, interrupting the music.

Incoming video call from Fujiwara Eika.

Breathing hard, I drop to a nearby bench. Panzer, hardly winded, gives me an impatient nudge with his nose.

"Hi, Cameron-san! Is this a bad time?"

"No, no, it's fine. I'm out for a run." In the corner of the screen, I can see my pace: over seven minutes per mile. I let myself get out of shape over the holidays.

"I wanted to let you know that Mi-chan looked at your résumé, and she'd like to talk to you."

"Okay, great. When?"

* * *

Eika tells me to meet her at Banana Garden Seven, a Shibuya nightclub that seems unfazed by city noise ordinances. It feels like my rib cage is rattling along with the chugging bass. I can't imagine how I'll have any kind of job interview here.

A hand on my arm. "Cameron-san!" Eika shouts in my ear.

She's wearing a short, frothy confection of a dress, her body swathed in marshmallowy layers. Hand on my elbow, she deftly weaves us through the scrum of sweaty dancers to a steel staircase on the edge of the dance floor. The steps lead to a balcony overlooking the main level, and off the balcony are doors to VIP rooms, each equipped with karaoke machines and a dedicated bartender.

The music retreats as Eika closes the door, then she collapses into the corner of the velvet sectional. "It's packed tonight!" she says, her voice a little too loud for the smaller space.

"The usual, Fujiwara-san? And your guest?" A bartender has materialized at Eika's elbow.

"Yes, thank you. A drink menu for my friend, please, and Toyama-san's usual as well. She should be here in"—Eika double-checks her port—"five minutes."

The tap list, at least here in the VIP room, is impressively deep, with everything from IPA to stout. I order an Austrian hefeweizen—like the ingredients for curry, good Euro-style beer is hard to find in Japan. "So, tell me more about your friend. She works at Helios, and...?"

Eika shakes her head. "It's best to wait until she's here. Mi-chan is—well, there is no one like her."

At exactly ten o'clock, she enters the room with far less fanfare than I was expecting. By the time I awkwardly stand to introduce myself, she's already seated at the table, a G&T before her. She is the most stunning woman I have ever seen in person. Helen of Tokyo.

"I'm Misora," she says in clipped English, extending a pale hand. Now I know what Mi-chan is short for, though it's hard to imagine anyone other than Eika daring to call her by this cutesy nickname. Her expression is neutral, verging on annoyed—is she only here tonight as a favor to Eika?

"And this is Cameron Green," Eika says as I shake Misora's hand. "I finally got the two of you in the same room! Mi-chan, your schedule is impossible."

Misora's expression thaws a little; Eika must be a soft spot for her. "Eika tells me that you're interested in joining one of our product dev teams."

I nod. "I was in biokintech R&D at a U.S. firm until the recent legislation closed my lab."

"That was unfortunate. We appreciate the decreased competition, but obviously it's a major market loss as well."

Before I can respond, she pulls a crisp sheet of blank magipaper out of her bag. "I'm willing to consider you for my team, but we require you to sign this non-disclosure agreement first. I assume your last company released you from any non-compete clauses in your contract when your lab closed?"

I nod again, wondering how she's a team manager at a major corporation when she looks like she's in her mid-twenties. "They can't sell what I was working on, anyway—I took the rights to my work as the bulk of my severance." Another reason I'm broke.

She pulls out her port, aligning it parallel to the blank sheet of paper. After a few taps on the screen, she puts it away again, and the NDA text materializes. "The terms are industry standard, but I need you to understand that your signature is binding."

I'm not new to the field, and I know how to keep things confidential. "Yeah, I understand," I say, reaching for a pen.

Eika lays her hand over the signature line. "I'm not sure you do, Cameron-san. It's magically binding. Sign this NDA, and you can't speak to unauthorized people about any of the work that we do."

"Can't?"

"Can't," Eika repeats with emphasis. "You won't be able to."

I look over at Misora, but her expression is blank again. "Entirely up to you."

The legal implications of this are troubling. What if their work isn't above board? What about subpoenas, and testifying in court? Most of all, I want to know how it works, because I've never heard of anything like this. I pick up the document and look it over, but I don't see anything that differentiates it from an ordinary sheet of magipaper. "That's impossible—how?"

"I can't tell you yet. But it should give you an idea of the kind of work we're doing." For the first time, Misora's mouth curves into the ghost of a smile, and I can't help observing, again, how beautiful she is. Damn.

And so—I sign. Bold black lines that push up into the text itself: Cameron D. Green.

"Good." Misora images the document with her port, messaging it off to some distant HR homunculus. She slides the original into a magifile and tucks it into her bag. "Tomorrow I'll have my assistant send an invitation to visit our facility, probably for sometime next week."

I decide to try one more time. "How does the signature work?"

A slight twitch of her lips suggests that she just might be amused by my persistence, but she doesn't otherwise reply. Instead, she stands up from the table, smoothing her gray pencil skirt. And though Eika protests her early departure, she's undeterred. As Misora disappears out the door, she looks over her shoulder at me. "Green-san, watch for that invitation."

I can guarantee that I will be glued to my port from now until it arrives.

After the door clicks shut, muffling the noise from the dance floor, Eika turns my way, her purple-lined eyes as wide and bright as her smile. "Isn't she brilliant?"

And then some, to a distracting degree.

ASAGAWA KENJI

You'd think a business in a sketchy neighborhood like this one would recognize the advantage of good security. Instead, I'm stuck with a low-tech lock that shouldn't have taken any time except the last pin won't drop into place.

Kumanaka rattles the change in his pocket impatiently, his wide shoulders resting against the chipped plaster next to the door. "Forget where to stick it?" he grunts.

"Not everyone finishes quick like you," I say.

It doesn't really matter either way, so I give in and open the door the old-fashioned way, with my foot. It's not a quality installation. The jamb gives way immediately into splinters of wood.

The inside of Pinking Custom Shoe and Repair is dusty and noticeably empty for a business that claims to have Saturday hours. Maybe not so surprising since the owner is someone with such poor judgment as to owe us money. After what we did to the guy who'd owed him, paying us should have been the top of his schedule.

There are only two doors in the shop, this service entrance and the one at the front. The main windows have a line of men's shoes on shelves, with a few chairs for fittings right behind. There's a large table by the back door covered with unsorted tools—awls, hammers, scissors.

Kumanaka is digging around by the cash register, his thick hands tossing items from the shelf below toward the wall.

I pick out the knife and sharp-tipped scissors from the pile on the table and move them to a bottom drawer. Things usually seem to be going smoothly until they're not. Then there's screaming and bleeding and it all goes to hell quick. I'd prefer the sharper items out of view in case it comes to that.

Kumanaka clears his throat and taps his knuckles on the register above his head. It would be easiest to just take the cash.

"I know withholding info gives you that special tingle, but tell me, how exactly did this fuckup happen?" I ask, leaning over to look at the lock. There's enough of a space between the drawer and the frame that I can pry the bolt open through the gap. "Not like we work on payment plans."

"Ask Funabashi," he says, picking up the stack of business cards from the counter. He keeps one and drops the rest on the floor.

This situation is off. Funabashi doesn't usually make these kinds of mistakes, at least not with the work he does for Asagawa-san. "She know about this?"

Kumanaka grunts noncommittally before wandering over to a cupboard on the other side of the room.

"If I'd fucked it like that, I wouldn't have wanted to tell her either," I say. The drawer pops open. "No good. Looks like he took the big stuff to the bank."

There's another grunt behind me. Not Kumanaka—it's coming from my left, near the back door.

Plan B came to us.

The guy, thin with a wisp of a mustache, defaults to lunging at me, one of the awls from the table in hand. Kumanaka looks over from the cupboard and gives the guy a dismissive sneer before going back to throwing things on the floor.

I'm ready, and turn my body sideways. The guy crashes past me and lands on his hands next to the counter. I lean forward to grab the back of his jacket and see business cards spread out under his left hand: Pinking Custom Shoe and Repair above not one, but two names.

A party, then.

The second guy is already through the door before I can say anything. Heavier-set and apparently unarmed but way more pissed, he rushes at Kumanaka with a wild haymaker.

No time to watch. Thin-stache is standing up with that lollipop he calls a weapon. He lunges again, and I move to the side again—just as something, someone, hits me from behind and pushes me forward.

I twist sideways as it happens but not far enough. When Thin-stache pulls the awl back, there's blood on the end. Not a good sign.

The point went in just inside the collar of my leather jacket, high enough to have missed most of the important things. No pain. The adrenaline kicked in.

My fingertips are covered in red. They don't seem pale. They aren't shaking.

Why was I thinking about that again?

Oh. This is shock. You'd think I'd be immune, but nope.

The world sharpens again. Thin-stache has the awl still in hand, but he looks even more shocked than me at this turn of events. I grab at his wrist as he throws his arm around wildly. He jabs it this time into the fleshy part of my palm.

Good.

Pushing my impaled hand toward him, I use the weapon as leverage to keep his arm in place. With my right, I grab the outside edge of his hand just above the little finger and pull it up and around. His wrist and elbow lock so he either has to release the weapon and lean forward into the motion or dislocate something. As the first smart thing he's done, the guy lets go and folds over.

Leveraging my weight against Thin-stache's arm, I push the guy all the way back to the floor where I can hold his shoulder with my knee.

In the light from the front windows, I take a look at the awl still stuck in the fleshy edge by my thumb. Unlike my shoulder, this hurts like a motherfucker. "Your customer service is shit."

"I...uh," Thin-stache whimpers. Panic. He attacked me, but he also didn't mean to actually hurt someone. What do you say to someone you stabbed? Sorry?

Kumanaka glares at me from where he has the other guy facedown, arm around his throat. "He knew where to stick it."

The awl comes out from my palm easy, pain running up my

forearm. I bring the kiddie weapon down by the guy's face on the floor. "You owe Asagawa-san money for services rendered."

"I paid, I paid."

"You know, everyone says that at first. I'm thinking most people aren't telling the truth."

"I did. I really paid it," he says, fighting against the weight of my knee but not making progress. This is depressing.

I flip the tool up into the air with my uninjured right hand and catch it by the point. "See this? I'm a big fan."

"Of the awl?" he can't help but ask.

"Of seeing," I correct calmly. "I imagine you are too. Where is the money?"

Honestly, I don't want to follow through, but the implication is enough to get him babbling. "The drawer, in the back, there's a cashbox—"

Kumanaka cold cocks his guy and stands up to dig around until he has a stack of 10,000-yen bills. He conspicuously counts out three of them, a tiny number for this level of hassle, and lets the rest flutter to the ground.

About time. The adrenaline is wearing off, and my shoulder has decided it is a real issue after all.

"Next time, get a receipt," I say as I stand up. Black rushes into the edges of my vision. Not a great sign.

Outside, we cross the street to Kumanaka's boxy minivan. I pull off my jacket and slide into the passenger seat, gingerly feeling my shoulder where the blood is seeping down my shirt.

"Move." A towel hits me in the face.

Right. Yeah. Mizuki wouldn't say anything, but she'd be out here scrubbing the upholstery when she thought no one was watching.

I lean forward, towel between my shoulder and hand, until my vision starts to clear again.

"S'not so bad," I say finally. "Might need a tetanus shot."

Kumanaka grunts, points out the window. We're at the clinic, and I missed the whole ride here.

I open the door and stumble out into a standing position. While this isn't the worst I've felt by far, pain has a way of making those kinds of comparisons meaningless. "This mean you care?"

"Find your own way home," Kumanaka says and drives off.

* * *

Last year one of the Walling Insurance office ladies got it in her head that because I technically get paid through the office, I needed a desk with my own stapler, memo pad, and cup filled with sharpened pencils. Ridiculous, but it is nice to have somewhere to sit and eat Cup Noodles a couple times a week.

It also serves as a central link. Paperwork and payments can go through a perfectly boring system of sorting and filing before shuffling off where they need to go. Unfortunately, it hides the purpose of our work even from me most of the time.

Today, at my desk there's a wine bottle covered in green cellophane. Chiyo must be back from her vacation to Hakone.

I catch the eye of Igarashi, the claims processor lucky enough to sit directly across from me, and point at the gift. Being married with two children it's doubtful that Igarashi would be a recipient of something like this, but it would make it simpler if this was an all-office kind of obligatory souvenir.

He holds up a clear plastic packet containing a lone steamed bun embossed with a rabbit.

There goes that hope. "Don't suppose she got one of these for Funabashi."

Before Igarashi can answer, the front door slams open.

The staff who are sitting jump to their feet and bend into a hasty, deep bow. I'm already standing, so I duck my head and shoulders only, taking my time about it. Asagawa-san is my mother, and I don't mind others seeing my casualness.

Asagawa-san ignores them, boots stalking across the carpet with silent precision toward Funabashi's office. Chiyo and the senior office lady, Tomohiko, follow with emergency tea just in time for the door with 'Manager' embossed across the pebbled window to shut in their faces.

Since Kumanaka and I made good on the outstanding money there I don't know how she'd have found out about Funabashi's mistake. All the same I don't envy him the meeting. If she came down here, something annoyed her.

I sit back down and throw my left foot up on the desk next to Chiyo's bottle of wine, my body angled so I can see the glass window where Funabashi's rough silhouette is bowing profusely. Around me everyone becomes impressively busy, papers shuffling, keyboards clacking. By the set of his jaw, Igarashi suddenly is working on the most important project of his life.

Both of the ports that I pull from my jacket pocket are almost out of power again, cheap pieces of hybrid garbage. The mass of charger cords in my bag has knotted up, so I tease out the ends to manually charge the ports from a battery pack.

As I finally get things plugged in, the door to the office opens and Funabashi leans out to pass instructions to Tomohiko, the more competent of the two office ladies. She power-shuffles in my direction and I meet her partway.

When I enter the room, Asagawa-san and Funabashi are silent. Great, another standing meeting—he won't sit while she stands, and she knows he has a bad right knee. She's not the kind of angry he needs to fear, but she's not happy with him.

I bow again, head and shoulders.

Her eyes flick over to give me a critical look. Silently, she pulls a black J-play burner port from her pocket and tosses it at me hard, off to my left. I catch the portable with my bandaged hand and wince, just barely.

"Destroy the old port. We won't be using it anymore." She pauses, focusing a look at my shoulder, and makes a business calculation. "You're down for a few weeks."

Fuck. Kumanaka told her.

I nod, my face blank. No need to get emotional over her sudden show of maternal concern for my well-being. "As you say."

Asagawa-san looks back at Funabashi—his leg is visibly trembling against his starched black pantleg. "Get out," she says to me.

Funabashi has the kind of trapped look where he clearly wishes that command were for him.

As I back out of the door, Kumanaka is there waiting. The network of scars crisscrossing his face seem especially prominent in the daylight. His suit smells like stale alcohol, but he's in better shape at noon today than usual. I wonder if he knew this meeting was going to happen.

Kumanaka shoulder checks my injured side and pushes past into the office. The door shuts behind me.

"Saturday was unacceptable," Asagawa-san says on the other side.

Kumanaka responds, "Can't help if he got himself stabbed."

Always quick to make anyone else around him look bad when he's in her line of fire.

"Not you," Asagawa-san says. "The kudzu here."

Funabashi's voice is smooth when he responds, but quiet. "I humbly apologize. The request was insignificant, and it came in from a local source..."

Interesting. He's not saying he's sorry for not getting paid. She didn't know about the job at all, and now he's making it sound like Saturday was the original request. In that case, it's possible that Thin-stache paid like he claimed, and Funabashi kept the money. But if so, why bother with such a small amount?

Unless this isn't the only time, just the one where he got caught.

There's dead silence, followed by Funabashi's voice, even smaller this time. "It will not happen again."

Kumanaka mutters, "Sounds like a case of stupid more than—"

And then Tomohiko is there, her face an Office Lady mask of smile and politeness, herding me away from the door and back to my assigned seating in the main office. Steering me to right where I can't hear a damn thing. I could make a fuss and stay, but then they'd know I'd been listening.

At my desk, I lean back to think. The last moment was Kumanaka's chance to tell Asagawa-san that this wasn't the original job, that we were making good on what they owed us for a job from weeks ago. He didn't throw trouble Funabashi's direction, which could mean Kumanaka was in on this too. Or, more likely, he's holding the cards close to his chest, and digging up something even bigger on Funabashi to make himself look good down the road.

I don't like not knowing who is screwing who.

"Hey," I say, leaning over to grab a folder off the pile on Igarashi's desk, "I'm going to borrow this for a minute."

He frowns but doesn't say anything, what with the most important project of his life to keep himself occupied.

Chiyo is still standing off to the side of the room, holding the tray of teacups. It takes a second, but I catch her attention and gesture for her to come over. She eyes Funabashi's door and Tomohiko before moving, and then shuffles over with her refreshments.

"Can I have one of those?" I ask.

The answer is technically no, these are reserved for the people above us on the chain. She sets down the tray anyway. "Of course you can, Kenji-san."

In front of me, she transfers over a coaster and a steaming cup, the pattern turned to face me. Lastly, she moves over a rolled hot hand towel.

"No sweets for me," I say before I end up with everything. "Thanks."

Chiyo is hiding a small smile as she bows and reaches for the tray. Tomohiko is still at Funabashi's door, watching us. Her face is expressionless, which probably means Chiyo is going to get it later. Asagawa-san never wants the tea, but the point is to be ready if she does.

Before Chiyo can go, I ask, "How was Hakone?"

"Oh, we had so much fun," she says, releasing the tray. "Of course, it would have been better if you had come too."

"Next time maybe." I'm wiping my unbandaged right hand in the crease of the wet towel, so I gesture at the wine bottle with my free left index finger. "What's the story on this?"

"The *onsen* where we went had a hot spring filled with Beaujolais Nouveau. It's so good for your skin," she says. "Sadly, that tub is in the family section, so you have to wear a swimming suit. Imagine how nice it'd feel without all that fabric."

I ignore the obvious invite to picture her naked. "You bring back a bottle for Funabashi too?"

"No, no, no, of course not," she flusters. Then she bites her lip and continues, "I did bring back another bottle for myself. I might put some in the water in my *ofuro* at home so I don't have to wear anything this time."

"Aren't you going to stain your tub?"

She sticks out her tongue, just enough to show the tip. "Maybe I'll have to use yours instead."

If she didn't work at Walling, I'd be happy to take her up on it. As it is, I do my share of stupid shit, but that's a cliff I'm not diving off.

"My *ofuro* is awfully small." I give her a broad smile over the edge of the steaming cup. "You know, I bet Funabashi's tub is enormous."

"Kenji-san."

I laugh, a genuine chuckle. "Sorry, that was bad."

She gives me a stern look and reaches for the tray again.

Pulling a pencil out of the cup on the desk, I continue. "Before I let you go, can you help me with something? I have this folder to take over to storage. What's the address again?"

* * *

Asagawa-san's decision to bench me wasn't entirely out of line—the magitech bandage failed to take, and the doc was reduced to using a cotton one. Since breaking and entering is about as low-key as it gets, this is a good morning to spend reading through Walling files, the ones that are stored in an apartment north of Ueno labeled under another business. No one had notified me of their existence, which I'm sure means they have no objections to my reading them, at least as long as they don't find out.

On the fifth floor, I open the lock to an apartment that is nothing more than three rooms filled with boxes: the kitchen on one side, a small 4.5 *tatami* mat room to the front, and a larger one by the back balcony.

Leaving my shoes on, I start with the big room to figure out the filing system. In the first box, the papers look like what I assume are standard insurance docs, listing coverage and if anything was paid out. Everything is neatly ordered by date, with new policies and payouts sorted by type, month, year.

The secret to keeping an underground business hidden is to conceal it in mundanity. My appreciation for Funabashi's work at the Tokyo branch of the British Walling Insurance Agency has gone up by a few notches seeing how well he's done at burying Asagawa-san, Kumanaka and me in a cloud of spreadsheets.

That also means that I have no idea what I'm looking for in this. I can cross-check the payments I find against what I've done in the last year. That won't include most of the work Asagawa-san does that I don't see and whatever percentage of the Walling income comes from legit insurance policies. If there are discrepancies somewhere, I'll only see what's in the work I know.

A click and the sound of a key in the lock. It's early morning on a Saturday, an odd time for someone to be here instead of in their bed or halfway across the city in Nishi-Shinjuku.

I'm not going to stay here and hope it's Chiyo.

There are two, maybe three ways out—the front door number 501, the balcony next to me, and the window in the unused kitchen. I flip the lid back on this box, slip out the sliding door and quietly inch it closed again.

The whole door is pebbled glass so this isn't a long-term solution. The balconies between the three apartments on this level don't connect, leaving an opening between them for the kitchen window. In this condition, I might be able to jump the span. Might. The failure state is a dead drop for four stories and a hard land in front of the FamilyMart on the bottom level.

There's a metal bar around the top of the solid balcony and metal edging solidly attached to the outside of the upper and lower section. I climb over the railing in the space between balconies. My hands around the bar above would be visible, but fingers clinging to the flat edge should be hidden enough.

This route puts me hanging from a balcony on the 5th floor, a slight breeze moving the winter air up the back of my jacket. The metal under my fingers is much colder than I had thought to expect.

A twitch. My left hand cramps inside the bandage, and I'm hanging by one.

There's a metal edge at the bottom of the balcony, which I prod with my foot. Solid but too small to support my weight with the edge of my shoe.

Here goes, then—

I pull up both legs and press my feet lengthwise against the edging, then release the railing and push. Twisting in the air, the fingers of my good hand catch the railing of the next balcony over. The momentum combined with a hard pull up is enough to swing my right leg over the top, and I'm lying on my back on the floor of the balcony staring at sky.

Hell yeah, I am that good.

Even so, the wound pulled open, and I can feel the throb where I'm bleeding into the bandage again. That arm is shaking, and my hand isn't going to hold my weight for that maneuver a second time.

Also, I lost a shoe.

Whatever I'm going to do next, this balcony will have to do. There are just two small problems. First, the door has a standard hardware lock that I pop open easily with picks from my wallet. Second, and more problematic, there's a magitech lock below it, one that forms a solid seal like a deadbolt. Because of course someone thought to install this level of security on a fifth-floor balcony.

At least it's cheap, so the components are exposed to the outside. I'm not my brother, who is his own fucking clean room, but sometimes magitech being in everything from ports to toothbrushes works out to my advantage. I press my bare wrist against the surface.

I pass the time looking for my shoe, but that entertainment only lasts a minute before I spot it on the balcony of 401. That leaves me with dead ports, the cold, and boredom for the thirty minutes that it takes for the lock to give out. Eventually, the mechanism sighs and I tug open the door.

"Excuse my rudeness," I say reflexively as I step inside, leaving my single shoe on.

The apartment is another business, some kind of translation service, so it's unoccupied except for a few chairs and a desk. No spare shoes, but I do find a bottle of ibuprofen in the back of a desk drawer and a Shin noodle bowl in the cupboard. There's some time to kill before I expect the person in 501 to finish their business. I add water to the electric kettle and charge my ports.

It's fifteen minutes before Funabashi walks past the peephole empty-handed and looking annoyed. I wait another ten minutes before heading out myself.

Walking in one shoe is annoying so I take it off to carry instead and go down a level to knock on the door of 401. If no one is home, I'll just let myself into a third apartment in this building.

My luck isn't that good today: A tall, blond *gaijin* opens the door. He's wearing workout clothes, sweaty around the edges, and looking confused. Since I only speak Japanese, I show him the shoe and turn up the palm of my other hand.

"Can I assist you?" he asks in surprisingly clear Japanese.

"There's a shoe on your balcony."

His mouth twitches, just barely. "Is there?"

* * *

Another week, and I'm still working through the 501 docs. The lack of recognizable names and details makes this nearly impossible. So far there are only two policies that I'm confident are jobs I did based on the timing and amounts. One was a little bit of vandalism against a store behind on its protection money, literally just a brick through a window. Almost embarrassingly old school. The other required more skill—last month I got someone fired from their job to make room for a rival who was pushing for a promotion. Both show payment amounts that match up with the amount I expect.

That's it. Two matches in box after box of documents, the same policy and claim forms over and over. If I find out that I've been reading through boxes of actual insurance records, I'm going to be unhappy.

Renewal. Renewal. Claim. Renewal. It's so repetitive that when I find a file filled with receipts for window cleaning, it's the highlight of the afternoon.

"Weekly? Who needs their windows washed that often?" I ask the empty room.

I'm starting to lose it. Time to do something. Anything.

What I need is a break, and luckily 501 is directly above a FamilyMart. It's also over the apartment with a fridge with cold beer and a Gamestasis. I take the stairs down and knock on 401, listen for Green to come to the door. After a long moment of only the generalized buzz of Tokyo, I conclude that the apartment is empty except for beer, not surprising in the middle of the day.

The FamilyMart has a hundred kinds of beverage but since I'm here and I've been meaning to background check this *gaijin* anyway, I eye the lock. I have opening the one on 501 down to a quickrun. This one is much higher quality and looks to have been recently installed. In fact, it's one of the new magitech ones, designed specifically to prevent using lock picks. The keys aren't special, but you can't move the tumblers in the lock itself individually, only all at once with a key. It's also made so there's no access to the magitech from the outside, meaning I can't pull the same trick as what I did on the balcony with 402.

The elevator is only a few steps away, but frankly I don't have anywhere I need to rush off to this afternoon and this is quickly becoming the most fun I've had in days.

Climbing off the balcony from 501 is much easier now that my hand has had time to heal. Ledge, drop down to ledge, and I land easily on my feet on Green's balcony. The locks on the sliding door are the same as the other balconies, so I open the top lock and wait for the magitech lock to give way. This time I have a port at half charge, so I can at least entertain myself with a go puzzle.

The door slides open a few centimeters before hitting something in the track. My respect for Green just went up a few marks.

Also, it's on now.

To access the kitchen window, I wedge my left shoe into the gap between the rail and the flat edge of the balcony. There isn't much of a ledge around the window, so I leave one shoe on his balcony again and swing a bare foot over the four stories of open air and a group of elementary school kids to put half my weight on thin metal window trim. At least if I fall to my death, I'll make the news as the barefoot mystery man.

Using my multitool, I disassemble the frame until I can access the mechanics of the lock from a gap in the outside and pry it open so the window slides freely. I grab the inside edge with one hand and pull myself inside, dodging a potted fern he has balanced on the ledge.

There's some kind of food bowl on the floor, for an animal. I freeze for a second, listening, but the apartment is as empty as I'd expected at the moment.

In the other room, it's a broom handle that's blocking the sliding door. I move it to retrieve my shoe and reassemble the window. Rule 1 of B&E: leave no hints behind of how you got in, just in case you need to do it again. Before I return the stick to the track, I preemptively crack it over my knee and fit it there with the cracks hidden in the edging.

Green left a spare set of keys in the pocket of a bag under the bed and his passport at the bottom of a plastic drawer he's started to use for socks. I flip through the pages and verify that he was telling the truth with his name. I take a photo of his key too before putting both items back. Entering by the front door would be less work than the balcony, and a key wouldn't cost much.

The battery on my port is already at 15%, so I grab a beer from the fridge to drink as I look through the rest of the apartment. The paperwork for his port is on top of the fridge, and the start date for the plan matches his story as well. There's dog food in an upper cupboard, as is a water bottle with a label that unhelpfully translates to University of Minnesota, Graduate Department of Biokinetic Technology. Sounds like some fancy breaker bullshit.

That could be useful if this guy is as clean from local alliances as he seems.

The most recent game on Green's GS is a remake of a bullet hell shooter I used to play with my brother as a kid. I haven't spent much time on games since I started working in my teens, but Space Zoom is one I used to dominate at. The top scoreboard only includes two scores—either the game is too new for many plays, or he gave up.

As I'm staring at the scores considering how long it'd take him to notice if I left a better score on his board, the port with my oldest number buzzes. A message from Mizuki.

> *Kumanaka Mizuki { Kenji-kun, if you have time, I would appreciate your help. Nothing urgent.)*

She knows I'm sidelined, and this is her way of making me feel needed. I'm not sure whether to feel thankful or irritated.

(Over later } No Name

The laminated garbage schedule in the middle top drawer of Green's kitchen says they sort glass on even Tuesdays in this neighborhood. I rinse the bottle and put it with the rest of his garbage before I head out.

* * *

The Kumanaka house is average size for a Tokyo central ward, which is to say small. The carport is empty, so Kumanaka himself is out. That's a relief.

"Excuse my rudeness."

Mizuki is waiting for me at the front entry. "You're never rude, Kenji-kun."

I laugh at that, and she smiles, the lines around her mouth disappearing.

Feet out of my shoes and into a pair of house slippers, I follow her down the hallway toward the kitchen. In their living room, Yuri is leaning on the *kotatsu* table on the floor. The TV is playing in the corner, the camera zooming out on a girl with a cup of coffee in her hands standing in the rain. Very dramatic.

Yuri is wearing the same school uniform as usual. A new one is hanging on a hook from the molding near the ceiling: Plaid skirt and a blazer with a fancy crested pocket.

"High school already?" I ask.

Mizuki turns to beam at me. "She was offered preferred acceptance to our first-choice school."

Sounds impressive, but I don't know much about the process. Takeshi and I both took entrance exams and we both went to a high school. There wasn't more thought put into it than that.

I raise my eyebrows and nod in a vaguely enthusiastic way.

The kitchen has freshly washed plates still steaming in the chilled air on the rack above the sink. Mizuki points at an outlet by the rolling cart. "This here. I plug the toaster oven into it. It's been hit or miss for a while and last night it stopped working altogether."

I resist the urge to sigh audibly. I'm fixing an outlet. "I'll look at it. If I need to open up more than the outlet, you'll have to find someone else who can patch drywall. Haven't had a need to pick up that particular skill set."

"Hopefully it's not that bad." She avoids my eyes and glances down and away, a surprisingly visible discomfort. Mizuki feels guilty about something.

The circuit box is easy to find. The only problem is that the line of 15-amp breakers isn't labeled. I try a few, with Yuri's shriek of annoyance letting me know when I've hit the living room. I flip it back, wait a few seconds and flip it off again. When I hear her growl a second time, I turn it back on and try another. After a little more trial and error I locate the right one.

The outlet in the kitchen was poorly installed, and using a utility knife to strip off more of the coating and reattach the wire fixes the problem. When I return to the box to reactivate the power, I consider flipping the living room breaker again but decide Yuri's had enough annoyance.

Who am I kidding? I flip the breaker on and off one more time.

"You're such a jerk!" I hear down the hallway.

Mizuki is hiding a smile in the kitchen when I come back. She has some cups out, and is pouring hot water into a teapot with instant powder. "Kenji-kun, please have a snack."

Yuri glares at me as I sit down in the living room.

"Sorry about that. The box wasn't labeled," I say.

She puts her elbow up on the table and turns her body away. There's a new show starting now. No wonder she's pissed—I probably just cut off the end of the previous one.

Mizuki sets the tray with tea on the table. "Don't you have homework?"

"Not much," Yuri says without looking.

"Getting into high school does not mean that you don't need to finish this year."

Mizuki says it mildly, but the effect is immediate. Yuri flips off the TV and stomps across the *tatami* floor as loudly as she can. The straw muffles the intended sound, making it more of a mime performance than she probably intended. When she steps onto the wooden floor of the hallway, she finally hits solid wood and doubles her effort. Mizuki and I trade a look as we listen to heavy footsteps up the stairs and to her room.

When the noise finally stops, I chuckle. "I would not have wanted to try that at her age."

Mizuki immediately looks down. She knows my mother. "Yes, I imagine not."

Oops.

"These cookies look special," I say. Individually wrapped in a matte paper, they have a metallic gold line printed around the middle.

"I bought them at Takashimaya the other day." She pours the tea for both of us, and then settles back into a comfortable kneeling position. "Are you doing okay?"

"Best I can." I shrug. "One-arm pushups get boring when it's only one side."

She shakes her head, black hair laced with gray slipping off the shoulder of her sweater. "I was worried when Soseki mentioned what happened."

I hear it so rarely I almost forget that Kumanaka has a given name. "It's nothing. A few meds to prevent infection, and it's healing fine." I pull the neckline of my shirt over so she can see what is just a fresh band-aid over a scab now.

She sighs, a deep exhalation of breath. "I'm sorry," she says finally. "It was my fault that he told her. Told your mother. I was worried, and I didn't want him to let you keep going if you were hurt."

There it is. A long moment passes and then finally I manage, "These cookies are pretty good. The green tea powder really adds to the flavor."

She passes me another one. "Yes, I agree."

TOYAMA MISORA

I can tell Eika wants me to stay and have another drink. When you're in her orbit, it can feel like there's nothing but time for friends and parties and fun. But I'm presenting to the board tomorrow morning, and they'll want to talk about my department budget, especially since I'm going to ask for money to make another hire. Little frissons of worry skip down my spine as I envision Rei's reaction to a poor performance. "Some of us have to get up for work tomorrow morning, Eika-chan."

Eika starts to pout. "Mi-chan—"

"Shopping this weekend in Ginza," I propose, cutting off the complaint. This will appease her and check an item off my list. "I need a gown for the KBC awards. Invite Hatsumi—it's been too long. Green-san, watch for that invitation."

I close the door to VIP 6 and take the back stairs to the first floor, letting myself into the staff area with the AppKey on my portable. That American. He's different from the usual strays Eika finds. He's certainly just as lost, and, as they always are, he's very easy on the eyes, but there's something else there as well. Choosing the rights to his work over what could have been a tidy cash severance was probably stupid, but it's what I would have done, too. I wonder if Eika's sleeping with him, then realize that of course she is.

Yoshida's office is by the back exit, not far from the performers' dressing rooms. Without knocking, I swing the door open, and he scrambles up from his desk, nearly knocking a cup of sake into a stack of papers. The room is a blue haze of smoke.

"Toyama-san, what a pleasure," he wheezes, awkwardly folding his massive body into a low bow. The high honor isn't really for me, but they all like to make nice, as if it might get them somewhere. Tattooed arms, still muscular from his early career in construction, are rigid at his sides, and his forehead nearly touches the desk.

"The usual," I say, pulling a manila envelope of cash out of my bag and tossing it below his nose. He's dying to reach for it, to count it, but he restrains himself. "There's a burnt-out lightbulb in VIP 6."

A message from my father pops up on my port as I get in the car that's waiting for me behind the club.

Toyama Razan { Delivered?)

(Yes, Papa. } Toyama Misora

He has always preferred the Westernized "Papa" to a more traditional "*otousan*." Maybe it makes him feel like we're close. For him, love and fear run along the same axis; I don't know that he's able to differentiate the two. Back in high school, Eika and I sampled some of my family's product once, when someone had left a sheet of tabs laying around where I could find it. We couldn't have had much more than a threshold dose, but it turned my father into a pillar of rage. I remember Eika being sent home, and then Papa gripping both of my arms in his hands as he screamed at me. It was May, but I wore my long-sleeved uniform blouse for the rest of that summer, even on the hottest days.

TR { Good girl.)

* * *

"They are ready for you, Toyama-bucho." Fumiko, Rei's chief of staff, manages to hold the conference room door open while offering me a deep bow. It isn't often that I'm invited to this room, with its plush chairs and expansive views of cargo ships moving through the bay. My office, several floors down, looks out at the windows of another building, and the team's cramped lab quarters are fully interior. The gleam of morning light on the polished table hurts my eyes.

Because this meeting is only with the audit and supervisory committee, Rei isn't physically present, but that doesn't mean she won't hear every word. Fumiko is the obvious spy, but Okamoto, Helios general counsel, is Rei's toady as well. Tamura and Sakurai are persuadable—in either direction.

At the end of the table, his back to the billion-yen view as if it's beneath him, is Fujiwara Isao, COO of Fujiwara Heavy Industries. I can feel my hand clench at my side, and I force it to relax. Even when we were kids, I never liked him, or the way he treated Eika. Bringing him onto our board as an outside director was part of the deal my mother struck with FHI when she contracted with them for my work on the Denali project. Both companies got an image rehab by supporting Replenish, and cross-contaminating our boards created parity.

"We've read your report, Toyama-san," says Tamura in her nasal voice. An *amakudari* who spent her career in the Ministry of Finance, she'll play nice as long as I can demonstrate I've gone by the book. "I'd like to start with the section on worksite innovation at the Ninh Binh factory."

A softball, fed to her by Rei or Okamoto. "Of course. The new magitech ergonomic grips designed by my team, which were installed on all production lines at Ninh Binh six months ago, feed latent energy from the laborers' palms into the machines as they work. This has reduced overall energy consumption by a monthly average of 1.8% at no cost. And this was without hiring for high MAR scores. With additional—"

"No cost?" Isao interrupts, pushing up his tortoise-rimmed glasses.

The nostrils on Tamura's thin nose flare. Product of the rarefied government air in Kasumigaseki, her sensibilities are ruffled by this breach of protocol. "Fujiwara-san—" she begins.

Isao corrects course. "Forgive me, dear colleagues. From time to time, my zeal for our fiduciary responsibilities overcomes me. But surely it is a falsehood to suggest that these modest savings came at no cost. Indeed, I look at the balance sheets and see millions of yen in salaries and R&D budget, with little to justify such an excessive outlay of funds. And yet, at the end of the report, a still more outrageous demand for additional personnel, requested because, and I quote, 'the time is opportune, in light of recent political developments in the United States, to pursue top talent from outside Japan?'"

I start to open my mouth, but he continues. "I believe I speak for all present when I express my concerns via the following questions: first, should additional funds be committed to a unit that has yet to achieve solvency? And second, this company's own shareholder report describes a robust recruitment program from elite programs at Keio and Tokyo Tech. Why not devote more effort to getting the very best Japanese engineers?"

I can feel a flush creep up my neck at the insults embedded in his inquiry. No mention of my undergraduate alma mater, Waseda, nor my graduate school, the University of Tokyo, as top institutions, layered on top of the implication that I am not among the very best. But he's not done.

"Are mere Japanese not good enough?"

Sakurai, silent up to this point, lets out a low hiss of air. "Careful—"

"Sakurai-san, I am delighted to answer Fujiwara-san's inquiries. I will address the final concern first." I find my best bland, close-lipped smile. "I think we can all agree that no one is 'mere' Japanese."

Okamoto, Sakurai, and Tamura all titter nervously. Each has more to lose in this conversation than Isao.

"And we can further agree, can we not, that this company has benefited significantly from a mixing of Japanese and non-Japanese talent?" I am walking right on the edge of appropriateness now, forcing them to think about me, about my mother and who we are. I would love to twist an answer from each of them about whether we can be considered Japanese.

Another awkward giggle from Okamoto. "She means that Chinese engineer she hired last spring. The one she's collaborating with on miniaturization."

"As for the first concern about costs"—I fold my hands in front of me on the table and pause for another beat, long enough that even Isao fidgets in his chair—"there is a cumulative value to the work being done by the industrial design team. Their efficiencies will continue to generate savings over time, but these developments necessitate an initial expenditure."

"Spend money to make money," says Sakurai, looking pleased, like he is the first to ever utter this thought. That's one vote.

"Indeed," I say, modulating my tone to avoid sounding patronizing. The man is old enough to be my grandfather. "Further, with a percentage of my time set aside for collaboration with Replenish Initiative, we have a duty to devote effort to that work regardless of whether it will ultimately result in any profits."

"As a project of your sister's, surely this is near to your heart, Fujiwara-san," Okamoto says to Isao. Well, well, so he is awake and kicking. Rei must have given him very precise instructions. That's two.

Isao grimaces. "Fine. We have agreed to a certain degree of loss as a corporate donation to this charitable development project. That still doesn't justify an additional infusion of cash—from either FHI or Helios—to pay another engineer. Aren't you supposed to be enough?"

"My expertise is magical thermodynamics, not biokintech. Perhaps I've misunderstood how things operate at FHI. Would you have a petroleum engineer run a nuclear plant?"

"Ah, I see," Tamura says, nodding. "This makes sense to me."

That's three.

* * *

Toyama Rei { Well done.)

> *(I am sincerely grateful for your support,*
> *mother. } Toyama Misora*

* * *

(Your oniisan *needs to get laid more often }* TM

Fujiwara Eika { Oh no Mi-chan :(what did he do now?)

(I'll fill you in on Saturday. } TM

* * *

"Mi-chan, you met him, isn't he do-able?"

Hatsumi mouths "save me" in my direction.

I drop my handbag on the vacant chair next to Eika's and unbutton my coat. "Who?"

"Some *gaijin* she collected at the Todai ceremony," Hatsumi says.

"Ah, yes, the wayward American. Tall"—I hold my hand up above my head to indicate a guess at his height—"and obviously works out. I assumed you were, mm... doing... him, Eika-chan."

"No, no, not my type."

"No more talking about men," Hatsumi interjects.

I raise an eyebrow at her, wondering what that's about. "I'm interviewing Green-san next week—please don't scare him off beforehand."

"There, you see, Eika-chan? Mi-chan is hiring the *gaijin*. I can't sleep with a member of her staff."

"I might be hiring the *gaikokujin*," I say, correcting Hatsumi's term from the slangy "outsider" to a more polite "foreigner." "And now you're the one who's brought the conversation back to men. Why the moratorium?"

Hatsumi is saved, however, by the arrival of our food. The girls ordered for me: a *wagashi* confection and green tea. They know me too well. We push our food together at the center of the table, and Eika adds a bottle of strawberry DBW. Once she's uploaded a few photos to her MinoSo feed, we can eat.

"I saw your NHK segment," I say to Eika, grasping for a topic that is neither work nor Hatsumi's love life.

This subject gets Hatsumi more animated. As a print journalist, she tends to look down on the news shows, especially ones like *NHK Discuss!* And for good reason. She leans in. "Ei-chan, why did you go on that show? Ito's a gross old man. Every time he spoke to you, I wanted to dive through the screen and punch him in the face."

"He might enjoy that," Eika says, expression wry. "But at least he let me talk. Mostly."

"Is that where we're setting our standards?"

"And that Koike," I add. "Who's writing his nonsense for him? It might be technically accurate, but it's a willful misinterpretation."

Hatsumi makes a "hmph" sound around a bite of her coffee jelly. "Convenient how people like him are always saying there's no evidence of a link between the environment and magic when they want to dig a big hole, but when they want to push some other agenda there's just the right amount to justify it."

"With an emerging field like magitech, people make things up to rationalize whatever they want to do. Look at the Americans. Or your *oniisan*," I add to Eika.

"Oh, that jackass, what did he do?" Hatsumi asks.

"Tried to sabotage me in the board meeting. It was straight out of his usual playbook: faux fiscal propriety with just a dash of putting me in my place."

"I'm sorry, Mi-chan." The look of pity Eika's giving me is almost as bad as Isao's disdain.

"Nothing I haven't heard before," I say, brushing off her concern even as the memory of it knots my stomach with cold anger. Hatsumi doesn't seem quite as ready to drop it, though.

"Sounds like some of the same bullshit I haven't been able to write about lately because the press club has it blackboarded."

"Oh? What's happening?" I ask.

Using her spoon, Hatsumi swirls the dregs of her coffee jelly around the bottom of the parfait glass. "Most notably, the JRP is getting momentum on the 'no buying property for *gaijin*'—sorry, *gaikokujin*—bill again."

The Japanese Reform Party has been at the center of every ruling coalition longer than we've been alive, an unbroken chain of conservative prime ministers going back more than 30 years. Papa cooperates with them when it's expedient, though the tiny pro-imperial All Nippon Party is more to his taste.

"The Natural Resource Protection Ordinance?" I clarify. I don't know why Hatsumi thinks this is related to what Isao implied about me. Though ethnically Korean, my mother and I are Japanese citizens, and we deserve to have rights that are distinct from foreigners. "I've heard some passing support."

Hatsumi's eyes narrow. She knows I mean my father; wisely, though, she doesn't bring him up. "The Kubo-gumi made a mint renting land to *gaijin* with the first bill when it passed. That'd be a good reason for the all-hands-in push to expand it so everyone can get in on the money."

"There are significant investment opportunities," I say flatly, irked to hear her say "*gaijin*" again. So concerned for their rights, and yet she can't stop using that pejorative term. "Which should go first to citizens."

Before Hatsumi can respond, Eika jumps in. "Didn't the Wa Party block it the last time they tried?"

"This time the JRP has the Civics on their side to tip the balance. For a small party, they get around. Xenophobia plus a pretext of environmentalism, and they are ready to go."

I can't let that one slide. "It isn't xenophobia to withhold some rights from non-citizens. What's next, letting them vote?"

"How can you say that?" Hatsumi's staring at me like I've grown a second head. "Doesn't Taehyun own your condo? I hope you like it, because if you don't, you're going to get stuck buying the next one."

"I'll take that under advisement," I reply tightly.

"Maybe we could go back to talking about men," Eika says, tone wistful. I feel a flicker of shame—these are my best friends, I haven't seen them in over a month, and I'm sparring with Hatsumi about politics. Besides, it's time to go to my dress appointment.

"Deal," I say, slipping cash into the tray with our bill. It's the least I can do.

* * *

Magic is found within all living organisms, from plants and viruses to primates and megafauna. The ideal environment for the generation of magic is a balanced and harmonious ecosystem. Areas of severe environmental devastation or depletion have been found to have less ambient magic extant, though the current evidence is more anecdotal than empirical. The influence of birthplace is still an area of relatively recent academic exploration, and there is significant debate. Some charitable organizations already work under the supposition that environmental depletion contributes to chromosomal atrophy or deletion, which can drastically affect magical potency. Deletion of certain genetic sequences seems to disrupt electro-magical function within the brain, damaging the individual's ability to use Syphon-based technology. It is important to note that magical ability arises de novo during early embryonic development and is not tied to genetics.

As for where magic resides, there is no precise known location, such as an organ, for example, but human beings are theorized to have an internal reservoir of magic which can vary in size from individual to individual. Researchers hope this is an energy resource that can be actively tapped in the eventual development of Syphon 2.0. The reservoir emits a certain degree of excess, which is semi-passively accessed by Syphon 1.0, though there is an element of consensual interaction between individual and device.

-*Judith Kalejaiye*, Magical Dynamics: A Modern Approach to the First Principles of Magical Science, *Introduction, p. xiv.*

* * *

I take a bite of rice, grimacing when I realize it's cold; according to the time on my port, I've wasted twenty minutes re-reading this basic passage. I also have 437 notifications. A few are work messages, but forty-five minutes ago, Eika posted a photo of me trying on my new gown, and it's been picked up by Tokyo Celeb Daily. There's already a link to a knockoff: Get Taehyun's girlfriend's dress for less!

Ignoring the comments, I unlink myself from the post and turn off notifications. Eika forgets that not everyone enjoys living in the tabloid fishbowl.

The three of us parted on good terms this evening, but I can't get that disagreement with Hatsumi off my mind. Why does she even care about the NRPO? I'm fairly certain Hatsumi's Canadian cousin Noah is the sum total of her foreign acquaintances. Sometimes it feels like she and Eika are both more interested in abstract injustices than ones right under their noses.

The front door buzzes—it must be the white glove delivery of my dress. I sign for it and take it to the closet.

So many dresses, each enrobed in the chrysalis of a filmy garment bag, each representing an event I've attended as Taehyun's accessory. Tux, tie, pocket square, cufflinks, me. Is it any wonder the Helios board doesn't take my work seriously?

With more force than I'd intended, I push the dresses aside, bags rustling against one another, to reveal a hidden access panel at the back of the closet. When we moved here, it was two apartments that we combined into one larger dwelling, and since I was the one in Tokyo full-time, I was in charge of overseeing the construction. This area used to be a linen closet in the second apartment, but now it's the perfect place for a safe.

I shimmy into the small space and hold my port to the access panel, then enter my code, and with a click, the door swings open. Setting aside velvet boxes of fine jewelry, the deed to this apartment, and an envelope of cash, I pull out my dock full of project notes. I could keep the notes on my port or my laptop, but there's something about magipaper, kept in a magically powered dock in my private home safe, that feels more secure.

I carry my papers into the office, setting everything on the desk next to the Kalejaiye book and my abandoned dinner.

Everyone uses magitech, but no one understands it. In her foundational book on magical science, Judith Kalejaiye proposed that all humans have some kind of theoretical reservoir of power they access for using Syphon-based technology. For the vast majority of people, this passive engagement uses less power than they generate themselves, so they're able to keep Syphon objects powered almost indefinitely, unless the device is particularly hungry or they're using multiple devices at once. The existence of this reservoir hasn't been definitively proven, but experts all agree that it is an accurate description of how human-derived magic appears to function.

Syphon tech requires a point of connection of some kind between the user and the object. You've probably never thought about it before, but if you've ever used a magitech bandage, for example, that silvery tab on one side is a disposable Syphon panel, and it's drawing from your reservoir to do three things: accelerate healing, prevent infection, and keep the adhesive stuck to your skin. Or when your multitool gets low on power and you tuck it into your elbow to boost the charge—you're connecting with the Syphon panel. We all do these things unconsciously because it happens every day, but each use establishes consent between the device and the user's reservoir. It's why nothing happened when your drunk downslope friend tried to hold her dead port to the bartender's bicep: he didn't consent. You might not always notice the Syphon panel, but it's there, and if it's damaged or blocked, the object will eventually drain.

As I look over my design, at the progress Eika and I made last year, I still feel like it's conceptually sound, that we've developed something that will make Syphon products more accessible for the downslope minority. With the device catalyzing an adjustment to the flow of power drawn from the user, it should all work—but this is where I need a biokintech expert. If I can finish this project, it could raise my professional profile, and prove that my position isn't pure nepotism.

That American just needs to be half as good as his résumé implies.

* * *

The door to my office opens enough for Nozomi to peek around it. "Toyama-bucho, your 4:30 appointment is here."

I follow her to the outer area of our suite, where he's waiting with a cup of tea and a magazine. It's in *kanji*. Can he read it, or is he a determined pretender? "Good afternoon," I say in Japanese, testing him. "Please, come in."

"Good afternoon," the American replies. "Thank you for inviting me here today." His grammar is crisp, he's chosen the appropriate degree of deference, and the accent is Kanto standard. A TV show would still give him subtitles, but it would be because he has blond hair and blue eyes, not because he's unintelligible.

When did I notice his eye color? That's irritating.

I gesture for him to take a seat across from my desk. "Your Japanese isn't bad," I say bluntly. "How did you learn it?"

"I lived at Chiba for six years as a child."

Hmm. A beginner mistake when he had otherwise been so fluent. "Am I making you nervous?"

His gaze meets mine, steady. "It's a job interview."

"I can switch to English."

He seems to sense this is another test. "Either is fine, although if the subject is technical, I would prefer English." A half grin. "For playground insults, though, I'll do better in Japanese."

I feel a laugh bubbling up, and quickly suppress it. He's amusing, something I didn't expect. That's irritating, too.

As the kid who went to school with crimson kimchi and *tteokbokki* in my bento, I can relate to bearing the brunt of Japanese children's cruelty. His strange name and round eyes probably attracted quite a bit of negative attention, too. I was lucky to have Hatsumi and Eika as my champions. "We'll try to keep things professional."

I give his résumé, which I have open on my screen, one more scan. On paper, he's a near-perfect fit for my team: bioengineering major, product design minor, product dev work at a U.S. firm, his name on a not-insignificant number of patents.

"Graduate credits in biokintech, but no completed master's degree?" I ask, picking at the most obvious flaw.

He shrugs. "I got a good job offer that didn't require it."

So, does he have no follow-through, or is he highly attuned to opportunity? It does say something that a firm was interested enough to recruit him while still a grad student, though. And he's here, which took its own initiative. I've been hoping to snag some top American engineers—especially a ground, if I can find one—ever since the U.S. legislation passed, but most of them seem to be staying home and retraining. Recruiting here in Asia, we have stiff competition from the South Koreans, especially Apogee Digital and SK Plastech.

"Let's do a brief tour. I'll introduce you to the team and give you an idea of what each of them is working on, and where you might fit. Our division is small, just four engineers, their support teams, and me," I say, leading him to the elevator bank. As we ride down, I send Nozomi a list of tasks:

Draw up an offer: base + 9%
Contact immigration
Schedule flight to Seoul and visa appointment at embassy
Make AppKey and map for Myeongdong
Reservation at Redology

She did all of this for Li, so none of it should be new or difficult.

"Matsuda is on vacation," I continue, "but you can meet the others. We've only existed for about two and a half years, and we answer directly to the CEO and the board. Our charge is experimental magitech, so we have more room for creativity. Though all units are responsible for revenue generation, we're not expected to produce at, say, the level of the Gamestasis team. Instead, a lot of our work is focused on enhancement of the existing Helios product line." Though I'm starting to shift us away from that, which is why he's here.

I lead him down the hall to the workspace shared by Matsuda and Li. "Li Xiaohui, this is Cameron Green. He's interviewing for a position on our team."

Xiao pops up from her bench, where she was hunched over a magnifier. "Nice to meet you," she says in hesitant English.

"Li-san works on microdevices," I explain, continuing in Japanese so that she knows he understands. "Tell him a bit about your project."

"Sure! Well, I used to be in the audio tech industry, so Toyama-bucho has asked me to develop a Syphon-based product that will improve headphones."

Li tilts the magnifier for us to see the earbuds, which have miniaturized Syphon panels embedded in their silver plastic. Green-san leans down for a closer look. "Is the Syphon improving sound quality, or—?"

"That, plus noise dampening, and keeping the earbuds in the ears until the wearer wants to remove them. Ideally, it will support the earbuds' power as well, so that they don't have to be recharged."

"With the much smaller panel, how are you drawing enough power from the user?"

He's asking all the right questions. I definitely want this guy.

Want to hire him, of course.

"Her situation isn't too different from yours," I say in English as we walk away. "She left China for political reasons." Since Tibetan independence, the entire system there has been unstable. Xiao's family is Han, but prior to the revolution, they lived in Lhasa. She and her wife decided to leave China rather than be expelled to the overpopulated east coast.

Sugihara and Araki's space is conspicuously vacant—I look up at the wall clock and see it's 5:32. One of the drawbacks of spending most of my day upstairs is that they think they can leave at five p.m. "Their primary focus is industrial design: adapting magitech to advance production processes, mostly at our factories in China and Vietnam."

"So, not a direct revenue stream, but a company-wide benefit," he observes.

"Exactly." He gets it; I wish my critics on the board did. "And this is where you would be located," I add, gesturing at the workbenches in the area beyond Sugihara and Araki's empty desks. "I also work from here when I'm not in my office, and Eika does, too, when she's around. In the back we have an advanced equipment space and a damper chamber for testing, and we work closely with the prototype lab as well." I know it's not very impressive. We're an afterthought division, jammed into the space vacated by the now-defunct portable music team.

We take the elevator back up to my office. Nozomi has handled everything I asked for, and each item is neatly opened in windows across my screen.

"So," I say once we're resettled at my desk, "if you're still interested after what you've heard this afternoon, I would like to make you an offer." I pause. "Are you still interested?"

He nods. "Yes."

I transfer the offer letter, and he pulls it up on his port, reads through it, and nods again.

"Any particular terms you'd like to negotiate?" I wait for him to ask for a bigger salary, which I can't do without compressing the rest of my team, or a nicer workspace, which I also can't get. The fact that we're housed in Tokyo HQ at all, instead of some dismal branch in Saitama, is entirely due to my relationship to the CEO.

A moment of hesitation. "I'm currently in Japan on a tourist visa. And it expires soon."

"How soon?"

"A couple weeks."

I smile a little as I transfer the rest of Nozomi's documents. "In that file, you'll find a copy of our application for your work visa, a plane ticket to Seoul in your name, and information about what you'll need to take to the Japanese embassy there. Nozomi got you an appointment for Friday. We have an apartment you can stay in, and there's a driver available, too. It will take two business days, so you'll come back to Tokyo next Monday night."

He reads everything over, then looks up, eyebrows raised. "Pretty confident I would take the job, huh?"

"I always plan to get what I want," I reply. We hold eye contact, and I feel a rush of sheer desire. For a man I've just hired to work for me. Fucking unprofessional.

"Any other questions?" I ask.

He looks at me for another long moment. I haven't imagined the heat between us—it's radiating from him in waves. The half-smile is back. "One. I think you know what it is."

The NDA. I glance at my port and realize I only have half an hour to get myself across Tokyo during rush hour. "I will tell you that," I say, standing, "at dinner next Wednesday evening."

There's a Helios tradition of supervisors taking new staff members out for dinner, although what was socially natural with the rest of my team now feels more like a date. "Meet me in the lobby downstairs at 7:00."

He looks a bit taken aback, but pleased as well. "Dinner?"

"Welcome to Helios."

* * *

The driver wedges the car right up to the glass door of Toyama headquarters, delivering me, in spite of traffic, from my mother's fortress to my father's in a perfectly punctual 23 minutes. In the quiet entryway, two young flunkies are lounging under the large *daimon* that represents our family name: a stylized rising sun casting its rays from behind an outline of Mt. Fuji. The same "To" as in "Tokyo," meaning east, and "yama," meaning mountain.

I recognize one of them: Daichi, youngest son of Watanabe Yusuke, my father's right-hand man. I exchange nods with him, expecting to walk past without incident, but the other pup is eager, it seems, to be found taking his job duties seriously.

"Well, what do we have here?" he asks, slithering out of his chair to stand between me and the corridor that leads to my father's office. He gives me a full head-to-toe, eyes lingering where you'd expect. A hand on my arm. "I didn't know they were bringing any girls in tonight."

I stare at him, torn between anger and disbelief. How can anyone who works at HQ be this stupid? Swallowing my fury, I slide my arm through his and start to walk him with me down the corridor. He shoots a look back over his shoulder, but Daichi just shrugs, smirking—he knows as well as I do what's going to happen next.

"Tanaka," I say, picking a random family name and deliberately omitting an honorific. "Can I call you Tanaka?"

He starts to interrupt me, to tell me his real name, I'm sure, but I press a finger to his lips, flirtatious. "Shh."

We keep walking, all the way to the end of the corridor; I would bet my life that he's never set foot this far down the hall. "I'm here tonight for your *kumicho*," I say conversationally, as if we're enjoying a stroll together, and his eyes widen.

As I push through the double doors into the antechamber, he can tell something's up, but he still hasn't figured it out. Four of Papa's lieutenants are seated around a small table, playing a low-stakes game of *hanafuda*. The cards are immediately dropped when they see me, and they all scramble into bows. When they straighten, I realize one of them is my old friend Hideki. He must have ridden his father's coattails into this card game.

"Good evening, gentlemen," I say. At this point, Tanaka's probably pissing himself, but I keep my elbow locked tight, holding him hard to my side.

Watanabe Yusuke, Hideki and Daichi's father, narrows his eyes at Tanaka. "What are you doing back here?"

"I—she wanted me to walk with her—" he attempts. At least he's figured out that "bringing the *kumicho* his whore" is the wrong response.

"There was some trash in the lobby, uncle," I say. "And I don't think that presents the best image of this family to the public. Is my father ready to see me?"

Yusuke nods, eyes still like slits. I release Tanaka's arm so I can return Yusuke's deep bow. This is the man my father loves most in the world—Papa has the missing fingertip to prove it. I trust him to handle things.

My father is at his huge mahogany desk, shirtsleeves rolled up to reveal the intricately inked phoenixes on his forearms. When I was a little girl, I would sometimes wait here for my mother after school. I'd do homework while he quietly gave orders over the phone, only to be startled out of my concentration by the sound of his diamond and onyx pinky ring hitting the desk when he slapped it for emphasis. The ring clacks against the desk again now as he pushes himself out of his chair and strides over to me, arms open.

"Mi-chan, my beauty, what a sight for sore eyes," he says, folding me into an embrace. His skin is warm, and he smells like pine needles—he's just come from the bathhouse. There's a comfort to being here, even as it's intimidating: when you're with Toyama Razan, you're safe from everything. Everything but him.

"Hello, Papa," I reply, following him over to the familiar brown leather sofa. He sits across from me, elbows resting on his knees. "How are you?"

The corners of his eyes crinkle as he smiles, but the black depths glitter more with malice than warmth. "We won the lawsuit today," he tells me, pleased.

I know this had been weighing on his mind. With the power of being *kumicho* comes the responsibility for the family, for the actions of all his men. Though it's very hard for ordinary citizens to pursue justice against the major families in criminal court, they can attempt civil cases; just last year the Maeda-gumi, our rivals, had to make a multimillion-yen payout to some widow in Kyushu. It was all over the news.

"Congratulations," I say, uncertain if this is the appropriate response. I wait a beat, then ask, "What was it you wanted to see me about?"

He presses a hand to his heart, as if I've wounded him deeply. "Surely you won't begrudge an old man some time with his lovely girl. Maybe I want to hear about your life."

My father doesn't truly want to hear about my life. The fact that he can't control more of it is a source of frustration and anguish for him.

"Not very different from when you saw me at the new year," I say. "Mostly work."

"Speaking of your work," he begins, and I brace myself. "Your mother tells me she hardly sees you, either. You spend all day in the same building and can't spare a moment for the woman who gave you life?"

"I try to make her proud through my dedication to my job," I parry. This week, at least, I thought I had lived up to her expectations.

He pours himself a small cup of sake and slides one across the table to me as well. If I were one of his men, this would have deep meaning; as it is, I simply wait for him to drink first, then sip. He lets the silence curdle between us, heavy and dense, before he finally says, "I have an item for you to make."

And there it is. Of course he does. I just consulted on the design of those rigged shipping labels—I wonder what he wants now.

"Oh?" I keep my voice as neutral as I can, praying my irritation doesn't leak out around the edges. There are consequences to showing Toyama Razan that your opinions differ from his. Papa never fails to remind me that everything I have, everything my mother has, is only by the grace of god. I'm not naive enough to think he means the little *kami-sama* that live in rocks and trees. That god is him.

I look at his hands: the zigzag of scars, the magitech pinky ring that holds his prosthetic finger in place. I recall again the one time he hurt me with those hands, the bruises bright purple, then yellow-tinged green, for weeks after. I force an eagerness I don't feel: "How can I help you, Papa?"

* * *

Back in the car, I close the privacy glass between myself and the driver, then tip my head forward and rub my neck. Tension has knotted up my shoulders, and I desperately want to lean back and close my eyes.

But Papa emphasized that this project is urgent; he thinks that one of his men is skimming. It's hard to believe anyone would be foolish enough to steal from my father, but his *kaikei*, the senior accountants who track all of the family's income and expenditures, have narrowed the possibilities down to three: the boss of a Kabuki-cho strip club, the manager of a pachinko parlor out in Narita, and Yoshida at Banana Garden Seven. I hope it's not Yoshida. I've always liked him—he keeps the club in good repair, and he knows where my eyes are.

By deliberate design, I'm not intimately familiar with my father's business, but the basic shape of operations is clear enough. The largest percentage of income is sourced from processing and moving product, with some smaller boosts coming from construction, real estate investment, and protection schemes. To my knowledge, the real estate itself is legit, although many of the properties house cash-based businesses used to launder the dirty income. Like the money I dropped off at BG7: it's Yoshida's job to deposit it in the club's business accounts as clean cash paid for food, drinks, entrance fees, etc. Simple but efficient.

As the go-between, I'm implicated, too—my father's way of exerting his control, even as I've tried to shift my life away from him.

So, Papa wants the next cash payments to all three suspected businesses invisibly tracked using magitech, and because he knows nothing about how Syphon works, he thinks this should be no problem at all for his "brilliant girl." I don't know which might be worse: failure, which risks his angry disappointment, or success, which will only encourage him to ask for still-more-impossible things in the future.

"Toyama-san?" The driver's voice crackles through the speaker connecting the front and back halves of the car. "We've arrived."

The apartment is dark and chilly—the thermostat has dropped the temperature into eco-mode. I turn up the heat and go into the bath to fill the tub.

The puzzle of Papa's request continues to bounce around my mind as I toss my dress in the dry cleaning and lower myself into the steaming water. How can I embed trackers into hundreds of 10,000-yen notes without having either an obvious Syphon panel or any kind of consent between the paper and the user?

My port chimes. Wiping my hand with a towel, I pick it up to peer at the message.

Watanabe Hideki { They're pulling Shibata.)

Scowling, I send back a terse "Who?"

WH { Your new friend from tonight. He's getting demoted. He'd just worked his way up to HQ)

Oh. I see.

(What you did was somewhat worse than implying the kumicho's daughter looks like a high-end prostitute, and you came back. He'll be fine. } Toyama Misora

(Besides, Osaka was good for you, in the end. } TM

WH { What's the punishment for telling the kumicho's daughter to go to hell?)

I reply with a winking kiss emoji and set down my port. I understand why this ruffled Hideki's feathers, but Tanaka is lucky he's only being reassigned.

How am I going to track this cash?

DATE HATSUMI

"Goto-san, you're fucking me here." I've got my elbows balanced on a stack of papers that are spilling out across my desk. One hand is holding my port against my ear, and the other is over my eyes. I rub my forehead through my bangs. It doesn't help. "Absolutely fucking me."

He hesitates, and then ventures, "It was only online for 30 minutes."

"It was printed on the train flyers." Last night, I was out too late, and the lead didn't even work out. Then to see the misprint on my way in this morning, complete with QR code.

"The mayor doesn't take the train. I doubt she'll see it."

"Both of her assistants take the train. They will see it. They know how to write her child's name. They know the kid's birthday." I take a deep breath. The apology on Monday is going to be hell. "I know you're new to this, but please only correct things if you know for sure what it's supposed to be."

I disconnect and look over at Okada. He always looks like a snake caught mid-molt, but he's holding his expression and tongue remarkably even.

"I know, this was the easy story," I say, hiding my expression behind a sip of tea. The bottle has been sitting on this desk since Tuesday, next to a sandwich wrapper and a crumpled stack of notes. Is this even mine, or did someone leave it here when we were talking?

"Perhaps it's good that we covered trade this week, so the *Nihon Times* didn't cause an international incident," Okada says, gesturing at the whiteboard behind him with a wrinkled hand. A few days ago, when our press club planned how we'd split the story assignments between our mastheads this month, it was clear he thought I should roll over in deference to his age. "The property bill isn't a walk in the park either..."

Local journalist Date Hatsumi recently negotiated a deal with a very tedious member of her press club. She was patient, even when he tried to wiggle out of their agreement, and she successfully resisted the urge to bop him over the head with a PET bottle. More details as the situation develops.

"The *Sekai Shimbun* can rest assured that the *Nihon Times* has this in hand."

He raises a shoulder, all casual. "What I don't understand, Date-san, is how you can talk to your editor like that."

"Goto? We were classmates." I don't add that he was at the bottom of our class from kindergarten through college, and that our bosses offered me his job first last month. I didn't take it. I like the latitude that the position I have already allows.

My glasses flash up the "message received" icon:

Fujiwara Eika { We're still on for this weekend, right?)

The story assignment list follows and is enforced by press club rules. All the same, I have a short window to get mine out before he has a chance to work people over and get support for switching ours up.

"I'm headed out. Don't steal my story, Okada-san," I say with a modicum of diplomacy.

He waves his hand at me, promising nothing.

* * *

I'm still reeling from Misora's comments on the NRPO as we cross the street to the department store. Being on the receiving end of one set of cruelties doesn't give you a universal pass on your treatment of others.

Argh, there's something I wish I'd been quick-witted enough to say when we were on the topic. Now I'd just start a real fight to bring it up again.

We duck into the ornate stone storefront before their perennial flash mob can form. The shops inside are the kind that stock ten items under individual spotlights. I'm glad it's February so I have an excuse to wear my Burberry trench and a scarf over decidedly pedestrian jeans and sweater in the land of glass and marble.

On the second floor we stroll through topical sections of designer clothing, and I go so far as to pick up a tennis shoe before seeing that it's priced at twice my monthly rent. I set it down and hope I didn't somehow leave a fingerprint on the cream suede.

In the couture dress area, a small army of salesclerks descends on us so I hang back from the commotion as Misora is swept away. Across the room, I watch a fresh-faced girl help her out of a coat that costs more than the clerk probably spends on food in a year. Misora lives in this world so effortlessly.

My fingers are halfway through buttoning my own coat back up when I realize I'm doing it.

"Ha-chan, what have you been up to lately? Tell me everything," Eika-chan demands.

"If I tell you everything-everything, I think you'll get bored about ten minutes into my morning commute from two Tuesdays ago."

She gives me a loving eye roll, and then speaks with exaggerated care. "Fine. Tell me everything interesting that you've been up to then."

"Well, there was a lady wearing mismatched earrings."

"Ha-chan."

"Hoop versus stud. I almost wrote an exposé, but my press club assigned the story to the *Edo Star* instead. Goto was despondent that we missed out on the scoop."

"You know what I mean. Are things going okay at work? How is your mom doing? Seeing anyone?"

I thought we left this behind at the café. After the mess with Taro last year, I am not keen to start anything up again. "Sure, as well as can be expected, and absolute pass."

Shaking her head, Eika makes a noise of disappointment. "Don't you think it's time to stop moping? It doesn't have to be a forever thing." She gets an impish look and adds, "You should at least get laid."

"Sounds lovely, but my schedule is very busy. You know, work, research, earring exposés." I give her a look. "How's your work going? Anything I should be keeping an eye out for?"

"Have you been hearing anything more about hiring protections?"

Oh, yeah, she'd mentioned something about that before. "For downslopers, you mean?"

Misora emerges from the dressing room in her first option. Even on her figure the dress looks severe—the kind made for a boardroom, not an award show.

The clerk is adjusting the shoulders and cooing over the plain black tube of fabric. It's false flattery, words meant to stroke an ego and make a sale.

That's why we're here. "Boring," I say.

The clerk has another option close at hand, so Misora disappears back into the changing room.

Eika turns back to me. "Did you hear that Tokyo Utility started asking about m-potential in their interviews since so many of their monitoring devices require Syphon?"

TU is in Suginami ward, my home base, but I hadn't. "Oh?"

"Isn't that horrible?"

We're interrupted again as Misora emerges from behind the curtain. She must have been able to hear us talking as she jumps in to ask, "Is it? We ask for MAR scores for our engineers." She pauses for a second, turning to show us where the beading on the dress extends all the way around. "Although asking for that for, say, someone like a technician seems a bit far. We have a new Syphon system we've implemented in Vietnam that has created efficiencies without doing a special screening of personnel."

This dress is an appropriately over-the-top gown with a black skirt and silver embroidered bodice. We both give approving nods, then Eika snaps a few photos, then turns and takes a photo of me for good measure. I'm glad about having buttoned my coat up again earlier.

"Okay, okay, I'll let you know what I hear," I say as Misora changes back into her street clothes. "Oh, and Ei-chan, thanks again for helping out Noah-kun."

Outside, they depart in separate black cars, Eika's a short-term hire and Misora's a family car from one side or the other. My moped is waiting for a replacement part, so I pull up my headphones and walk over and catch the Marunouchi line. The song streaming is that goddamn derivative pop song by the Friday Boys, "Monster Party," which seems to be on permanent loop these days.

> ... *To kill us, to save us*
> *You're nuclear, baby*
> *La la la*
> *The house is wrong, the house is wrong*
> *But inside we're so right...*

* * *

On the other side of the city the afternoon stays chilly, around 5°C, making me wish I had brought gloves for carrying groceries.

Through the aged glass at Used Books I can see that the lights are on, but she's not at the counter. Just inside the sliding door there's a table stacked with sets of *manga*, each tied up with blue plastic twine, the paper yellowed from the sun. One block of books is starting to lean off the edge, so I use my elbow to push it back more fully onto the table as I step inside.

The small space is engulfed by shelves reaching the ceiling, air dry and quiet, and books are crammed into every corner. There's a steaming cup of tea sitting on the counter.

"I'm here," I say.

"Hello, sweetie," my mom says from somewhere.

"It's *Setsubun*, so I thought I'd come celebrate the start of spring with you."

She peeks around what someone might charitably call an endcap display. There's a hole along the shoulder seam of the faded blue sweater she's wearing over dusty gray chinos. Her hands are stretched thin around a stack of books, knuckles pink with chill. "You wouldn't know it from the weather."

"I think it's an aspirational spring," I say. "Do you have a window open somewhere?"

"No, just an old building, leaky everywhere."

I keep from making an audible sigh. "I'm taking these up. You finish what you're doing."

The main room upstairs is mostly clean, though there are several bags of burnable garbage that need to go. I open the fridge, and see it's stocked more than I would have expected from what I'd brought over last weekend. I pull out the old to rotate in the new, separating out what I've brought to eat today.

When I finish, I take a minute to give thanks at the *butsudan* just inside the other room. In an ideal world, there'd be enough space for a room reserved for quiet contemplation, but the living area on her second floor is barely large enough for the two separate rooms and the bathroom it has. This cabinet takes up a significant side of the second room, her clutter covering part of her futon on the floor to make the space for kneeling.

Inside the *butsudan*, between the gold and lacquer doors and just below paintings of the Buddha and founders, is my dad's memorial tablet. My mom's name is there too, inscribed in red to show that it's a placeholder for the future. The water offering looks fresh, and there are flowers in the vase that I didn't bring.

My mom certainly didn't go out and get those on her own.

Lighting some incense, I ask his tablet, "Are you doing your share of the shopping now?"

There are footsteps up the stairs, so I finish and meet her in the kitchen. She's peeking in the plastic bag I left on the table. "This looks delicious."

"Count them out," I say, taking a seat. We're not throwing soybeans at someone in a demon mask like I did as a kid, but at least we can do the eating part of the holiday.

She opens the roasted soybeans and sorts us two piles, enough so we each have one per year of our lives. Then she sets aside the rest together with the lucky uncut sushi rolls for later.

I scoop up my pile and lift my fist in a salute like it's a cup of beer. "Evil out, and good in."

We both chew for a minute, one bean at a time. My hands are getting cold enough that I should make myself some tea, if I can find an extra cup in the cupboard.

"I hope your week was good," she says eventually.

"Worse than average. I've hit a wall on NRPO details. Everyone I talk to is happy to pretend it sprang up like bamboo, all on its own."

"Plausible deniability is the most important feature of all well-intentioned leadership."

"True enough," I say, popping another soybean in my mouth. "This is just so tiring."

She gives me an earnest look. "You're not going to let this go, are you? I know it's inconvenient, but..."

"Why would you ask me that, after everything?"

Her expression drops, and I immediately feel bad. This is as important to her as it is to me, but at least I have the ability to do something. Sometimes. The frustration I'm feeling isn't her fault.

"Sorry," I say.

No response. Instead, she's staring at the floor, still chewing. One of her arms is crossed over her body, finger running over the hole in the seam.

"Hey, Mom."

She eats another two soybeans, individually, one slow bite at a time. This again.

I let amusement seep into my tone and try once more. "Mom, do you see the window over there?"

She glances over at me, the edge of her mouth moving up a hair. "The open one, you mean?"

"Yeah, that one." I give her a real smile. "That's deliberate, right? You're just letting in the good?"

"No," she says, softly. "There's plenty of good in here. That's to let the evil out."

* * *

The front room of Mayor Mori's house has been turned into a waiting space just large enough for the five reporters who are assigned to follow her on Mondays and Thursdays. Most of the members of our Civic Action Party-focused press club are part-timers since there aren't many papers that can afford to keep a reporter on the relatively tiny political group full time. Only my paper the *Nihon Times*, Okada's *Sekai Shimbun*, the *Tokyo Daily*, the *Chiyoda Post*, and the *Edo Star* have the resources to devote someone to regularly covering the single Tokyo mayor backed by this party.

We're all there waiting at her front gate by six a.m. when her junior assistant lets us in out of the cold. Inside, Sadame brings us cups of tea, and we all settle in to wait for Mori-shicho to come downstairs for the day.

"Date, did you see that you made the *Sekai* yesterday?" Okada asks.

Just what I love first thing in the morning. "Oh?"

"Below the fold on entertainment." He holds up the article on his port. Sure enough, under the headline "Toyama Misora Models KBC Gown" is Misora looking perfectly coiffed and luminous. Then, to the side, there's my trench coat-encased elbow. "Did Diet Breakfast Water take the photo? She doesn't usually miss a chance to be the center of the shot."

Sure enough, the Mino app in my glasses is volunteering two hotlinks from the photo: one for Eika's MinoSocial page from the image watermark and one for more information on the dress from the InfraThread embed. At least Eika is getting some ad revenue off this.

"She has a name—"

I don't get to say more, as we are interrupted by Mori-shicho stopping by the doorway, teacup in one hand and port in the other. "Morning, all."

We jump to our feet and give her a proper greeting. "Good morning."

"Since we're having the press conference later, I'll keep it brief. There'll be more on the internal investigation and the progress on the homelessness issue. If you'd like to add any additional questions to the docket, please feel free to submit them before eleven a.m. to Juro." She turns away, and then looks back over her shoulder. "Hatsumi, are you hungry?"

"Yes, thank you, Mori-shicho." I follow her, feeling the heat of Okada's annoyance behind me. Yeah, that never gets old.

The living room is set up for breakfast and her husband, Mikio, is holding their dimple-cheeked daughter Natsuki on his lap to help with the learner chopsticks.

"Good morning, Mori-san. Good morning, Natsuki-chan," I say to them as I kneel into a sitting position in front of a steaming bowl of chicken and egg on rice. There's a deep emptiness in my stomach, but it's not hunger. I set my glasses on the corner of the table and lean forward into an apologetic bow. "Mori-shicho, I sincerely apologize for our mistakes on Friday."

"Oh, that? We had a chuckle. Luckily, Na-chan is not quite yet legal to drink."

At least she's taking it well. "Thank you for your understanding."

"I'm sure there were worse mistakes printed about your dad when he was mayor," she says dismissively. "And with this police situation blowing up, frankly I don't have time to worry about it."

Talk about the worst kind of headline news from Suginami ward. Guns are so rare that the police keep theirs locked up where they belong in carefully managed storage spaces. One of the local officers, a new recruit, followed the proper procedures to check the gun and ten bullets out for their monthly target practice but returned the weapon with a discrepancy—one bullet missing. One deadly weapon that might now be in the hands of the *yakuza* somewhere.

How does someone lose a fucking bullet? Aren't the police here to make things safer?

The officer's employment is under review, but that hasn't slowed the outrage. Even worse, being tough on crime is another important leg of the Civics' platform, so the mayor is probably hearing about it from all sides.

"If I may, you've had remarkable poise in all of this." I take my first bite of chicken. Hopefully this will help calm my stomach.

She reaches over to wipe some rice from where it's stuck to Natsuki-chan's cheek. The little one pinches her face up and fidgets at the attention. "Please feel free to put that in your article. You can buck the trend a little for me."

"I'm certainly happy to pass my feelings along to the *Tokyo Daily* and *Edo Star* who have the story today, but I'm sorry to say that I'm writing about the property bill this week. Speaking of which—"

Mori-shicho pointedly doesn't look my way. "I don't have any input from the ward over what they are doing on the metropolitan level."

I'm not letting this drop quite that easily. "Have you heard anything you'd want to share off the record?"

"I trust that there isn't anything you'd be writing about that topic that needs additional sources." She pulls a small slice of pickled *daikon* off her plate and slips it into Natsuki's bowl. "Honey, try this."

Clear enough. She's taking the party position, and I better fall in line. The media functions on give and take, with press club access requiring a certain amount of discretion. Is this particular article the hill to die on?

"Of course. I apologize for asking."

She gives me a fond look. "Hatsumi, your father would have been so proud of you."

I return her smile. He would have hated her politics. "Thank you."

Natsuki takes this moment to flip her rice bowl upside down on the floor, and Mikio narrowly avoids getting it on his workman pants. He stands to hand the squirming child off to Sadame, who has been lurking in the corner. Not exactly her job description as an assistant, but her face brightens immediately. I wonder if she's in the wrong line of work.

Mori-san returns with a rag and the mayor is starting to get up, too. I only have a few seconds before the day sweeps us away into a minute-by-minute schedule.

"Mori-shicho, one last thing if I may. Have you heard anything about Tokyo Utility screening for m-potential in their interview process?"

Her eyebrows pull together into a thoughtful expression. "No, I hadn't. Are there people talking about it?"

"I've been hearing some concerns about discrimination."

"Hm," she says, deliberating. "I'll have Juro look into it more and get back to you."

"Thank you," I say. "And as always, thank you for breakfast."

* * *

THE NIHON TIMES
>Politics & Governance

JRP-Civic Coalition Calls for Stronger Protection of Magical Resources
By Date Hatsumi

The ruling Japanese Reform Party, with the support of the Civic Action Party and the All Nippon Party, announced Tuesday their intent to advocate for an update to the Natural Resource Protection Ordinance that would increase defense of the nation's natural magical resources in the Tokyo metropolitan area.

Current regulations allow foreign agents to purchase space within an existing building, but they are prohibited from purchasing land. The original NRPO was passed after evidence of gestational tourism intended to improve a newborn's magical potentiality was brought forth by the JRP. The proposed ordinance update would reserve both land and property purchasing rights for Japanese citizens. This would not impact any current holdings, only prohibit future title transfers.

"As we continue to learn more about the bounty of magic that our nation is graced with, it becomes more important for our capital city to safeguard these critical resources for our own citizens and thus ensure our continued prosperity within the *region," said Hayashi Tomokazu, Vice President of the Tokyo Metropolitan Assembly and head of the Civic Action Party parliamentary group.*

The ordinance update is expected to be introduced to the legislature and referred to a subcommittee at the plenary session scheduled for June. If approved by the subcommittee, a vote would be held by the full Metropolitan Assembly later this year.

TOYAMA MISORA

It must be emphasized that a key feature of magic is that it does not, in fact, require Syphon to operate. Rather, Syphon-based technology serves as the facilitator, bridging the "wild" magic harvested from the user and the desired magical outcome. As yet, modern human beings cannot wield their own raw magical power to, for example, accelerate healing or power a small electronic device. However, the Syphon technology harnesses that raw power in service of the purpose for which a Syphon item was designed. Thus, for example, while a Syphon bandage cannot by itself heal the wearer, it can, with the user's consent, draw upon their magic to boost the delivery of white blood cells to a wounded area of the body. (For more on consent and Syphon, see chapter two.)

-*Judith Kalejaiye,* Magical Dynamics: A Modern Approach to the First Principles of Magical Science, *pg. 72.*

* * *

Hideki is the sole customer at our usual spot, a cheap *ramen-ya* near Daikan-Yama station. This area isn't technically Toyama-gumi turf, but the food is bad enough to keep away any regulars, and the owner is on our payroll.

"You didn't have to dress up for me, Misora," he says, eyeing my clingy blue dress.

"Good, I didn't," I reply. "I have an hour before I need to get back to my office."

He looks at his watch. "Kinda late for a work meeting."

It isn't exactly a meeting, my dinner with the American—but it's also not a date, something I would do well to remember. "That's my world."

"Are you going to eat?" Hideki asks.

I flick my gaze down at the bowl of *shio* ramen already steaming in front of him. "You didn't wait for me."

A long slurp of noodles slithers up through his chopsticks before he replies. "You were late. Whatcha got for me?"

"Leadership has concerns about some inefficiencies in the distribution line," I say, snapping apart a pair of my own wooden chopsticks so I can swipe a piece of corn from his bowl. "Obviously, this can't continue, so our job is to track down any leaks." Enough broth has clung to the corn that I can taste how oversalted it is. Making a face, I re-sheath the chopsticks in their paper wrapper.

"It's an acquired taste," Hideki says. "Do you have a mock-up of what you need?"

I have nothing yet beyond an idea, because Papa's expectations far exceed his patience. "No. My hope was that you and I could discuss what's possible."

"Uh-huh." Now he looks wary, and rightly so, as I am about to transfer some of the weight of this to his shoulders. "Straight talk, Misora. What do you need?"

"I have a semi-finished concept, and I'm in the process of onboarding some new R&D support. But I can't use the usual production methods." It occurred to me a few days ago that there's no need for the cash to link to the bearer's magic; it needs to connect, instead, to whomever Papa assigns this task to. That makes consent easy, as they'll do what they're told. "Oversight of my division has increased, and something of this scale will get noticed. So, I need to know what your capacity is like in, say, three weeks?"

"Three weeks?"

"At most."

He mock-glowers at me over another bite of ramen. "I don't sit around waiting for you to assign me tasks."

We both know that's only half-true. "Be grateful that I simplified my design. I had been trying to figure out how to track individual bills—and how to link each one to the Syphon consent of whoever handles them—"

"That's too resource heavy. And no way I could do it in three weeks, not even in a best-case scenario."

"I am aware," I snap, tone harsher than I'd intended. My relationship with Hideki is usually an easy one, equal parts history and affinity, and as the son of my father's trusted *wakagashira*, he occupies a privileged position in our organizational hierarchy. But he is not my peer. "Your team can, however, make Syphon-powered tracking devices."

"Something that already exists? Yeah, of course. Why, though? Just buy some."

Papa could have come up with that on his own. "Don't be obtuse." Regular market Syphon trackers are sold by private companies that share their data with the police. They're ideal for finding lost ports, less so for dirty money that's slipping through a crack in the laundromat floor.

"How are you going to boost the signal on an illegit tracker enough that it will be traceable?"

Yes, this is the whole issue. Legal Syphon trackers piggyback off the existing grid to transmit their location. I won't be able to do that with mine, meaning the signal will need to be particularly strong. But I have some ideas for that.

"Like I said. I hired a new engineer."

* * *

When the sliding doors of the Helios lobby glide open, I see he's already there waiting, hands in his pockets as he fills time reading the directory posted on the wall.

"Practicing your *kanji*?" I ask.

He smiles as he turns toward me, and I feel a fluttering, light and warm, under my sternum. Gray wool flannel trousers, matching suit coat and a button-up, no tie—he's hit the correct note of easy formality, and he looks... what was Eika's word? Do-able. Yes. Very do-able.

"Yeah, I need to learn most of the high school ones." He points to my name and title. "Toyama-bucho?" he guesses. "Is that how you prefer to be addressed?"

"At work, yes," I reply, leading him out to the waiting car, "but outside the office, Misora is fine." Why did I say that? I have never told any of my staff to call me Misora. "And you?"

"Cameron," he replies. "Cam to my family and close friends."

We settle into the back of the company car—no Toyama driver tonight. I sit a work-appropriate distance away from him on the seat, but rotate my body so I'm half-facing him, ostensibly to talk; my knee rests against his. I'm testing the waters, and he doesn't seem to mind. He doesn't move away, and when he glances over at me, the heat is back in his gaze.

He clears his throat. "So, uh, where are you taking me?"

"Redology at the Park Hyatt. They just received a Michelin star." Nozomi arranged for us to have the chef's tasting menu in a private room. She deserves a raise.

The restaurant is on the 40th floor, and the reserved room has a stunning view of Nishi-Shinjuku. The walls are painted a deep, rich red, and dotted with modernized renderings of scenes from the Chinese epic *The Dream of the Red Chamber*.

I scan the list of courses. Each has a wine pairing, which Nozomi also requested. I can barely behave myself with this man dead sober, but I take a sip of the Chardonnay. "How was your trip to Seoul?"

The edges of his mouth tease upwards, as if he's suppressing laughter at a joke known only to him. "Visa acquired," he replies. "I hadn't been there since I was a kid, so it was interesting to see what's changed."

"Tokyo, too, I imagine."

He nods. "Definitely. My sister lives here, too, and we've enjoyed visiting our old haunts to see if they match what we remember."

"What brought her back?"

"She works in the political affairs unit at the US embassy. Riveting stuff."

Given my father's ties to the All Nippon Party, that's not ideal. Yet another reason to keep my personal and Helios lives separate. "Not everyone can be a magitech engineer," I reply with a smile. "What do you think for the main course—Sichuan grilled fish or the dry chili shrimp?"

"Shrimp," he says, not even looking down at the menu. "With a side of answers about that NDA."

I did promise him. To draw things out a little, I take a bite of the appetizer, a delicate dish of seared Hokkaido scallops, before responding. "Tell me what you want to know."

"From what I could tell, it was a standard sheet of m-paper, right? The usual Syphon panel, dock-compatible?"

"It is."

He nods. "Yeah, I thought so, so I tested it."

I took the only original and had Nozomi send him a PDF. He can't have tested the document itself. "You broke the contract?"

"I can't share your trade secrets when I don't know any," he says. "But I did show the PDF to someone, and you haven't terminated me—unless this is the world's nicest firing—nor have I heard from your lawyer. So, that leads me to the only possible conclusion."

Our eyes meet, and I can tell he's enjoying this. I won't give him the satisfaction of the query; instead, I hold his gaze, waiting for him to look away.

He does blink first, but it's accompanied by a grin so disarming that I'm left feeling like the one who lost.

"It's a bluff."

The painting behind him is a rendering of Xue Baochai, *The Dream of the Red Chamber*'s heroine. In the original piece, she stands under a leafy tree, sheaf of papers in hand; for this modern version, the artist has swapped the papers for a smartport. I study the angular lines of her face for a moment before responding. He's the first member of my team to even question the NDA, much less figure it out. He's earned the truth.

I incline my head in the barest of nods. "Who did you show it to?" I ask.

"Uh, well... no one, actually."

This clever bastard. As irritating as his confidence is, I'm again pleased to have made the hire. I can't help myself—I laugh.

"Is it something you've tried to actually create?" he asks.

"Yes. I figured out a while ago that a signature is an effective substitute for in-person consent."

"That is fucking brilliant," he says. "I mean—sorry. But it's genius."

I don't need his approval, but I'm enjoying how he's looking at me, his expression complex in a way that makes my pulse throb.

"So, it would be the text of the agreement itself, which ties it to the reservoir of the signer, combined with the signature as consent," he muses aloud. "And then you'd be maintaining power to the Syphon panel wherever the document is stored, probably a dock."

"Right," I say. "But once you've connected the document to someone, then what? As you figured out, I can't actually monitor what someone is saying or doing through the document. There's nothing to flag a violation when it happens."

"Hmm." He squints into the middle distance for a moment, his fingertips drumming on the tabletop as he ponders. There's a sudden twitchy energy about him, like his thoughts are moving too fast for him to contain them all inside his body. "What about heart rate? Similar to a lie detector test?"

It's an interesting idea. "Maybe. But a lie detector test is a moment in time, and this would need to be ongoing. In any case, you don't need to think about it right now, when we're not at work."

He glances down, and I see that I've rested my hand across his fingers, which are now still. "Clearly," he replies, a low catch in his voice.

I withdraw my hand, but the air between us is supercharged, and I have to seek temporary refuge in my wine. Cameron changes the subject with a polite inquiry about my hobbies, and I spend a few minutes babbling at him about augmented reality tennis before I'm mercifully interrupted by the arrival of the entree.

After dessert, I summon the company car to fetch us, and soon we're brushing knees in the back seat again. I'm like a bottle of champagne that's been shaken up, cork straining against the wire cage. If this were a date...

But it isn't. I'm his new boss, I'm his boss, I am his boss. I recite it over and over in my mind, and still, it doesn't override the fizzy desire bubbling inside. We sit silently in the cool darkness as the car glides through traffic—silent because none of the things I want to say can be said.

The car turns onto a side street and slows. Through the dark-tinted glass, I can just make out the lighted windows of a low building, maybe five or six floors high. He turns toward me, hand on the door, and I sense he's going to thank me, the last thing I want.

And so, I lean forward, and I kiss him. It starts slowly, a whisper-soft exploration, but soon it flares into something electric. I feel his hand slip under my unbuttoned coat and slide along my waist, palm warm through the thin silk of my dress. We kiss for a blissful moment of suspended time—

Then the driver coughs, once, into his hand, and it all dissolves around me. I'm in a Helios company sedan with a driver who reports to my mother. It's no better than being in a Toyama car.

I pull away and rub the lipstick smear from the edge of my mouth. "I will see you at the lab tomorrow, Green-san."

Cameron exits the car, his expression opaque. "Good night, Toyama-bucho."

* * *

Predictably, ignoring my port for a three-hour meal has left me with a home screen full of numbers in red badges.

Toyama Razan { Project status?)

* * *

Group Chat: Fujiwara Eika, Date Hatsumi +11 messages

* * *

*Watanabe Hideki { Possible supply snag. Oniisan is
already being a shit) +4 messages*

* * *

*Akanishi Nozomi { Toyama-bucho, a package arrived
after you left the office this evening. If you would like, I
would be delighted to arrange for a courier delivery to
your home.)*

I skim them all, then prioritize my replies. First, to Papa:

(Hideki is getting started } Toyama Misora

This will give him the impression that things are further along than
they are, but it buys me some time. Next, the girls:

*(Haha. If it came down to a fight, my money is
on you, Ha-chan. } TM*

To Nozomi:

*(No need; it's lab lenses for the new hire. Please unwrap
and leave on his desk tomorrow morning. } TM*

Hideki's messages are the biggest problem. His older brother Kaihei
is my alternate timeline, the what-could-have-been of my father's
family engineering. I can't blame Papa for hoping. *Kumicho*'s daughter
and *wakagashira*'s eldest son: an easy succession plan. I'm sure Kaihei
thought so, too, could probably feel his fingertips brushing the brass
ring. He has spent the last decade finding ways to remind me that I
ruined it for him.

I will call you tomorrow, I write to Hideki. I don't have the bandwidth for Kaihei tonight.

* * *

Park Taehyun { I'm back. Where are you?)

Well. This is by far the best message I've gotten this evening.

(Five minutes away. } TM

* * *

"Hello?" I call in Korean as I enter the small *genkan* of the apartment. "I'm home."

Taehyun glides out of the office next to the entry. "Korean, that's a nice change," he says, looking genuinely pleased.

I know Rei wishes I spoke Korean more often, too, but it infuriates my father. One of my earliest memories is the crash of a dish of *japchae* shattering against the wall, followed by his angry hiss: "My daughter is Japanese. She will eat Japanese food." Then my mother, voice low but sharp with a shaky, self-deprecating anger: "If you wanted Japanese children, why fuck the Korean slut?"

Blood still hot from my brief tryst with the American, I lean into the familiar way Taehyun's lips press against mine, the way his hands grip my hips. I slide one hand up under his shirt, and not for the first time, I admire the planes of muscle on his stomach—honed during mandatory military service, maintained for his television career.

In a deft movement, he pulls the shirt off. His skin is luminous in the muted light of the entry, and almost satin-smooth—he must have gone to the *jimjilbang* while he was in Seoul. "Very spicy, Mr. Park," I murmur, and he chuckles. I've said something wrong. I really only spoke Korean as a child, I don't have the vocabulary for what we're doing now.

"Likewise. You are very hot, Ms. Toyama," he says, modeling the correct phrasing as he unzips my dress.

Though he can sometimes be difficult, I'm grateful for Taehyun. And for this apartment, legally titled to him, in a building constructed by an Osaka-based contractor—not a whiff of my father here. A little space in my life where I can be part Korean and not at all Toyama.

My port, clutched in my left hand, burbles the three-tone chime indicating a message from my mother. Taehyun pries it from my fingers and makes an exaggerated show of turning it fully off before setting it aside. My parents, the Watanabe brothers, whatever is happening between me and the American—it will all still be there in the morning.

PARK TAEHYUN

Archival footage: Perfume advertisement (15-second clip)

The camera pans across a monochrome rain-soaked street in central Seoul. A woman appears in the bottom of the frame, running to escape the downpour; the vivid red of her opera gown is the sole splash of color amongst the gray. She ducks under an awning, and the shot shifts to show her face: it is drama actress Oh Soojin of Flower Boy Ramyeon Chef *fame. Her eyes light up, and the camera follows her gaze, panning in the opposite direction.*

A man, tuxedo-clad, is running toward her, his jacket held over his head as a makeshift umbrella. As he nears, the viewer can see that he is Park Taehyun, Soojin's FBRC *co-star. He carries a single rose, the same crimson as her dress, and beckons her to join him under the jacket. Once she does, the camera goes into soft focus on their embrace, then shifts away to show the rose splashing into a puddle. In Korean, a male narrator murmurs, "Fleur de Lis, the new fragrance by Song Joohyuk."*

* * *

Not bothering to knock, I let myself into my mother's apartment, kicking off my shoes and dropping my bags by the front door. "Hello?" I call.

The sound of stockinged feet skittering down the hall from the bedrooms, some giggling, then silence. "Hello?" I try again. Nothing.

"Hmm, too bad," I say, as if to myself. "I brought presents from Jeju, and there's no one here to accept them. Guess I'm eating this big box of delicious tangerines all by myself."

Aejung caves first, launching herself around the corner, down the hall, and into my arms. "Uncle! Did you bring any presents just for me?" She peppers my face with kisses, her breath warm and childishly sweet. Only a baby when my brother Taeyong passed away, I'm as close to a father as she's had.

"I did, and one for Kijung, too, if he's around?"

My nephew peers around the corner. Seven to Aejung's five, he's more cautious. I don't come home often enough. "I'm here, Uncle."

Setting Aejung down again, I squeeze Kijung's shoulder and distribute my gifts. "Where are your mother and grandmother?"

Mouth already full with half an orange as she tears into her package, Aejung points toward the kitchen. "Making dinner," Kijung adds.

Not entirely accurate, I see when I enter the kitchen: Hyori is preparing dinner, and my mother is hovering behind her, criticizing every step. "More *gochujang*," she directs, pointing to the pork and onions sizzling on the stovetop, and Hyori dutifully adds another dollop.

"Taehyun!" my mother cries when she sees me, bustling over and giving Hyori a moment's reprieve. "We didn't even hear you come in!"

"Don't worry, mother, I had greeters," I say. She fusses over me a little, although it feels forced. I'm her second-born and was never the favorite.

Aejung and Kijung tumble in after me, dragging the giant box of oranges. "Look!" Aejung exclaims. "All the way from Jeju-do!"

"I bet it's beautiful, even in winter," Hyori interjects softly. "I'd love to go someday."

All of us were shocked when Taeyong brought home mousy little Hyori as his bride. But as the years have passed, the wisdom of my brother's choice is easier to understand. Hyori has weathered the devastation of his death with a quiet and admirable grace. She ministered to my father in the final days of his life, too, and she bears my mother's sharp tongue far better than I've ever learned to do.

"Where's the *gongjunim*?" my mother asks. She never uses Misora's name, just calls her the princess. And she asks this same question every time I come home, even though Misora will certainly never visit again. In the entire time we've been together, Misora has set foot in this apartment precisely once. It did not go well.

"*Gongjunim*?" Aejung asks eagerly. She's old enough to know she should obsess over everything pink and princessy.

"Grandmother likes to call my girlfriend that because she's so beautiful," I explain, showing Aejung a recent picture of Misora on my port. She's too little to remember meeting Misora during our sole visit here.

My mother snorts derisively but manages to hold her tongue in front of the children. "Her dress looks like a princess, too," Aejung breathes. "She's so pretty!"

Yes, she is, and that's precisely the point.

When we met, my career was just starting to take off. I'd finished a successful run on the reality TV show *We Live... with a K-Pop Star!* and had been recently cast in *Flower Boy Ramyeon Chef*, a remake-slash-spinoff of a popular show from a few decades ago. But at the time, I was only known in South Korea, and still more for the Hwacheon Incident than any TV work. After a year and a half in the military, time on the talk show circuit, and then making *We Live*, I was eager for some time away. Hong Minho, one of my *We Live* co-stars, suggested Tokyo as a great place to party and meet girls, so a group of us booked a suite at the Ritz-Carlton and flew out for a long weekend of debauchery.

The first night, we're at one of those Roppongi clubs with a pretty low cover, the kind you know is *yakuza*-owned: there are thugs at the door, and the overhead and then some is built into the cost of the watery drinks. I'm into my third and starting to get on the right side of buzzed when I see her. Tall for a Japanese woman, and the kind of hot you have to look at twice to believe she's real. She glides across the periphery of the dance floor and steps behind the bar.

I elbow Ryuya, Minho's Japanese friend and our guide for the evening. "She's leaving with me."

He follows my gaze across the club, and his eyebrows lift. "Good luck with that. You know she probably doesn't even speak English, right? And definitely not Korean."

"Never said I was interested in talking."

Shaking his head, Ryuya pulls a black marker out of his pocket and pushes up my sleeve. "Here," he says, scrawling something in Japanese on my forearm. "It's the hotel address. In case you need to catch a cab back from her place." His tone says he doubts this will be an issue.

By the time I arrive at the bar, Ms. Gorgeous is almost done mixing her drink. The seats near her are all occupied, so I squeeze in between patrons to occupy a sliver of the rail. She catches me staring—I'm not being subtle. After a quick, narrow-eyed assessment of me, she asks, in crisp English, "Do you need something?"

I lift my near-empty whisky soda and rattle the ice. "I'd take another." Instead of replying, she snaps her fingers at a nearby bartender. Once she has his attention, she makes a "one" with her finger, then points at me.

"You're not dressed like the club staff," I observe. "You sleeping with the owner or something?"

She takes a moment to skim something on her port, then pours the drink from the mixing glass into a martini glass. "No." Two olives, and the liquid a bit cloudy from their brine; she likes it dirty. "My mother did, and I am the charming result."

Though she's beautiful, I would never have thought to call her charming. Charm takes warmth, and she's frosty as a December morning. "Surely you don't want to spend tonight in your father's club," I start to suggest. What a garbage line. I'm not used to doing this in English.

Her expression a blend of pity and disdain, she turns back to whatever she was reading on her port. The bartender drops my new drink near her elbow, and as I lean forward to reach for it, she looks up again. I catch a whiff of something light and herbal—her perfume, maybe.

"How long are you in Tokyo?" she asks in Korean.

"You speak Korean," I say, startled into blurting the obvious instead of answering her question. Her phrasing isn't formal enough for someone she's just met, but given that I would like to get very, very casual with her...

She arches an eyebrow and waits.

"I leave Sunday."

Picking up her drink and walking past me around the bar, she makes eye contact over her shoulder. "Hmm. Nice to meet you, Park Taehyun."

As she walks away, leaving me wondering how she could possibly know my name, my port vibrates in my pocket.

> *Minotaur Social Invitation: Would you like to receive direct messages from Misora T.?*

I nearly break my thumb tapping "accept."

> *Minotaur DM: Come back tomorrow night. -Misora*

Ryuya smirks at me when I return to our table alone, but I cut him off. "She could speak English and Korean," I say.

"And suggested you fuck off in both," Minho guesses.

"Nope." I show them Misora's profile page. It's spare on details, but it's definitely her.

"I told you to sign up for NearMi," Minho crows, smug. He had suggested it so casting directors could ping my port at parties, and until now, it had resulted in exactly one audition for a paper towel commercial.

"Toyama Misora," Ryuya reads aloud, letting out a low whistle. "Taehyun, the Toyamas are *yakuza*. Big deal *yakuza*."

"Yeah, she said her father owned the club."

"Big. Deal. *Yakuza*," Ryuya repeats. "No girl is hot enough to merit that kind of trouble. Find someone else."

Minho nods agreement. "There are plenty of girls here. Even you're not that stupid."

But I am. Like hope, lust can twist stupidity into the shadow of a good idea. On night two, she takes me to one of the club's back rooms, though she won't quite let me seal the deal. And on night three, my last night in Tokyo, she finally comes back to my hotel.

We're in the shower together afterward when she looks down and chuckles at what she sees. "What?" I demand. She hadn't found anything to laugh about earlier.

She rotates my forearm to read the hotel's address, which, though faded to gray, still hasn't washed off. "You could have carried their business card."

Now I grin down at her. "I had big plans for this weekend, I wanted the address on something I couldn't lose."

"As if your arm is something you can't lose."

That should have told me everything I needed to know about Toyama Misora, but I couldn't get enough of her. So, I squeezed as much time in Tokyo as I could around my busy new shooting schedule. Misora quickly became an established part of my life, already familiar to the Korean celebrity press by the time *FBRC* premiered. I was advised more than once to drop her in case the show went big. It's not unusual for Korean actors to pretend to be single, so they seem attainable to their fans. My gamble was that a Japanese girlfriend would help launch me in Japan, and it paid off. For every Yuna or Minyoung sulking that I'm taken, there's a Yumi and a Minako living vicariously through Misora. I've tripled my fan base.

When the show's success exploded like a supernova, Misora was the brightest star in the firmament that coalesced around me—a sudden and tidal shift. Overnight, I had an entourage: not just my girlfriend, my friends, and my agent, but photographers, fans, assistants and hangers-on. And the money. I had never seen so much money in my life. In Korea, with the exception of upper-echelon *chaebol* and political families, everyone is ostensibly middle class. But we spent my childhood hanging on to even that much with our fingernails; what my father didn't drink away, my mother earmarked for Taeyong's education. All our sacrifice reduced to a framed business degree from Seoul National, its recipient long dead.

"Does the princess live in Seoul, Uncle?" Aejung asks, still transfixed by Misora and her pretty dress.

"She comes here sometimes, but she lives in Tokyo," I reply. Aejung crinkles her nose in distaste—my mother's anti-Japan comments have trickled into little ears. No one in today's Korea was alive for the Japanese annexation, but the old anger still smolders, and my mother can tend a grudge.

A message written in *hangeul* pops up on my port, and I tilt the screen away from Aejung's eyes. I don't know if a kid her age can read, but no sense risking it.

> Soojin { *The tabloids say you're in Korea, but that can't be right. You would have told me.*)

"I'll be a moment," I say to my family, ducking into the bathroom and tugging the door shut behind me. The thin wood veneer has chipped away at the bottom, and splinters snap off as they catch on the carpet in the hall. I twist the cheap lock, not that it would keep out even Aejung if she was feeling determined.

I've been in Jeju, just got to Suwon today. Family, I message back. I could use exactly the diversion Soojin can provide. *I can be in Seoul tonight, though.*

My port vibrates with a call, and I open the video to see Soojin smiling back at me. "Welcome home, *oppa*," she says, voice silky.

"Yes to Seoul tonight?" I ask. God, I hope so. Filming of *FBRC* series three wrapped for editing a few months ago, and I haven't seen her since. Her husband isn't as understanding as Misora.

"Maybe," she teases, dragging it out. "What's in it for me?"

The sound of a small hand smacking against the bathroom door. "Uncle! Uncle, are you pooping?"

Damn kids. Half an hour home and I've hit my wall; Aejung is lucky she's adorable.

Soojin giggles behind her hand. "Your niece?"

"For the moment," I reply blackly. To Aejung: "Yes, Aejung. Go away." Her little feet patter back down the hall.

Soojin and I agree to meet at the apartment in Myeongdong. When Misora bought it, we'd intended to spend more time together in Seoul than we actually do; instead, she's slowly appropriated it for Helios use, letting board members or even her mother stay there when we're not around. But she hasn't mentioned any need for it recently, and she knew I was going to be in Korea, so I assume it's vacant tonight.

Hyori looks relieved when I say I'm going into the city—I'm a bad influence on her children, no doubt—but my mother is unhappy. "I suppose the *gongjunim* wants you with her," she complains.

"Sorry, Mother," I say. "You know how she can be."

"Hmmph," is the only reply.

I leave Suwon behind, taking a car service into the pulsing neon of Seoul. Being back in the Myeongdong apartment is soothing—Misora's fingerprints are all over the choice of sleek wood and subtly soft lighting, everything understated and luxe. I've grown very accustomed to the lifestyle she dictates for us, and why not? There's no need to stay at the drafty old apartment that has become a dingy shrine to the family dead.

I go into the kitchen and uncork a bottle of Pinot Gris, noticing with some annoyance that there's an empty bowl of instant noodles in the trash can. The least the cleaning staff could do is handle their own messes.

Soojin arrives under cover of cashmere wrap, huge sunglasses, and a cloying cloud of floral perfume, casually dumping her crocodile bag on the floor. "It took me forever to escape," she says petulantly, voice pitched high with drama.

I slide a glass of wine to her, then pour myself two fingers from a nearby bottle of Macallan—this bit of leftovers, at least, can be traced back to the Helios board, maybe even Rei herself. How had I forgotten that Soojin is a high maintenance prima donna?

One of my many crap jobs between high school and military service was at a bougie little candy company not far from this apartment. To properly temper chocolate, you have to move cautiously, increasing the temperature in increments, and check it constantly; you can't be impatient. So too with Soojin. There's no easy tumbling into bed with her—she has to be heated up slowly.

"I'm sorry to hear that," I say in a neutral tone, sipping my scotch as she unbundles from her layers.

"We just met with my agent," she complains, sitting down at the kitchen island. "Hyungwon thinks he takes too big of a cut. Do you like yours?"

My interest in hearing about percentage negotiations between her pretty-boy husband and her dirtbag agent: zero. "He'll do," I say shortly, sidling up behind her. "Is complaining really what you came here for?"

"No," she admits with a sigh, leaning into me as I work her shoulders.

"You're stressed," I say, faking concern.

"Mm," she replies, her head dropping forward. This is almost too easy, once I get back in the rhythm of it again. She's like putty.

My port rings, and when I see the name, I know I can't not answer. Damn it.

"I have to take this," I tell Soojin. "Why don't you start a bath, get warmed up. I'll join you in a minute."

She pouts a little but flounces off to the primary suite. I slide the door closed behind her and pick up my port. "*Yeoboseyo*," I answer, seething on the inside.

He cuts straight to the demand. "I need something soon, Park."

"I can't make it appear," I snap back, letting my own veneer crumble. "I don't even know what I'm looking for."

"Bullshit," he snarls.

A few years ago, I got as far as screen testing for a part in a low-budget film noir. The script was about this bad, and I was relieved to not be cast in the role; now I'm living it. I sigh. "Whatever I get for you, I'll be blowing my cover. Do you want that to happen now, or do you want to hold out for something big?" I've read these lines for him before, so I'm expecting his response. He caves.

"Fine." And then, right before he hangs up, the reminder. I can almost mouth it along with him: "Remember Hwacheon."

"Asshole," I reply once he's disconnected. I roll my shoulders, and I can feel the tightness that has sprung up in my muscles. Soojin is going to have to share that hot bath.

* * *

I wake up alone, sprawled diagonally across the bed in a tangle of sheets. Too lazy to look for my clothes, I wrap the towel from last night's bath around my waist and go out to the kitchen to find Soojin.

She's sitting on the countertop, picking listlessly at a bowl of sliced strawberries.

"That's all you're eating?" I ask.

"Yeah," she replies. "I need to lose at least a kilo before we start shooting again." She pulls the collar of her bathrobe tighter around her neck, and I realize—it's Misora's robe.

Last night, I slept with another woman in an apartment my girlfriend owns. Yet I can guarantee that if she found out, the most Misora might say is "Change the sheets." Soojin can use me all she wants, but not some cream silk bathrobe, because the robe was imported from Italy. I sure as hell wasn't.

I walk over to Soojin, taking the bowl out of her hands and setting it on the granite counter. "Strawberries are full of sugar, you can't eat these if you're going to lose any weight," I say, pointedly cruel. I start to kiss her neck, working my way up to her ear as I undo the knot on the robe. It has to go to the dry cleaners immediately. "Wouldn't you rather, ah, exercise than diet, anyway?" I suggest.

"Mmm," is the only response. Taking that little purr as permission, I slide the sleeve of the robe off her left shoulder and kiss the exposed skin, then move back up to her lips. It's such a pleasure to kiss Soojin the way I want to—hard, mouth open, inhaling her—when we've spent years acting out unrelenting sexual tension, with no indication the writers have any plans for release.

A sound. Not from Soojin. Footsteps?

Her reaction comes faster—she jerks away from me, frantically pulling the robe around herself again. As she catapults off the countertop, she unhooks her leg from around me, taking my towel with her.

So that's how I'm starting my day: bare-assed in front of some white guy. Whatever—I have nothing to hide. I look fucking fantastic naked.

He's determinedly not making eye contact, which gives me time to scoop up the towel. "Who the hell are you?" I demand in English as I re-wrap it around my middle. He might not be looking at me, but I give him the once-over: tall, blond, decidedly Americanish in the cut of his hair and clothes. I've spent enough time in Itaewon to recognize an American, even if he doesn't have the bearing of a G.I.

"I'm new at Helios. They had me stay here while I get my work visa." His tone is flat, and it amuses me to realize that, fully clothed in a suit, he's way more uncomfortable than I am. I'm tempted to drop the towel again and really ruin his morning.

When he says "they" had him stay here, he means Misora. She's understanding, but I can only push her so far—she won't tolerate loss of face. "Shit," I mutter under my breath in Korean. "They don't need to know I was here," I add in English.

The foreigner finally looks over at me. "Who would I tell?" Then he stalks past me to the foyer, suitcase in hand.

Once the door has clicked shut behind him, I slide the bolt and return to the bedroom. Soojin is in bed again, hands pressed to her face—when she sees me, she explodes into giggles. "Who was that?"

"A problem."

CAMERON GREEN

"You may be wondering what the special occasion is," I say to Panzer as I crack open a can of premium dog food. "Well, I am officially employed."

As he inhales his dinner, I sit down to mine, a nicer-than-usual *bento* from the Family Mart downstairs. I thumb open Minotaur Social and scroll, checking in on updates from people back home. One of my frat brothers from the U had baby number two. A few of my old colleagues have found jobs in other industries. Ingrid is seeing someone new. It surprises me how little I care.

I can't stop thinking about today, the most unorthodox interview I've ever experienced. My field tends to move fast on hires, but I've never gotten a same day offer before. I've also never felt like the prospective boss was flirting with me.

I read Misora Toyama's biography on the Helios website before the interview, which clued me in to the fact that she's such a young unit manager because she's the CEO's daughter. But I didn't think to look at her MinoSo profile until now. Compared to Eika, whose page is filled with photos, links to her sponsored products, and media blurbs, Misora's profile is Spartan. I can't read all the kanji, so I tap to translate it into English. It looks like the same biography from her Helios page; her photo is even the same solemn corporate headshot. Until I get to the end.

Toyama Misora
Mino Mutuals: Fujiwara Eika

Director, Experimental Magitech, Helios KK
MS, Magical Engineering: Thermodynamics, University of
Tokyo
BS, Physics | BA, English, Waseda University
In a relationship with Park Taehyun

The disappointment cuts sharp, though it shouldn't. So why do I tap the link to his page?

Taehyun Park isn't merely Misora's boyfriend—he seems to be an up-and-coming Korean celebrity, and as such, his profile is fully public. No corporate portraits to be found on his page; rather, much like Eika's, it is full of brand endorsements and clips from TV appearances. Here, Misora is tagged in image upon image from the red carpet, always in an elegant dress, always on the arm of this tall Korean man whose face looks like it was carved from the gods' own marble.

I hate social media.

I switch over to NearMi, wondering if Asagawa is home. But no matter when I check, he never seems to be around.

Group Chat: Vanessa Green, Drew Mukherjee

(*Eika Fujiwara came through. I got
a job at Helios }* Cameron Green

VG { Cam! You didn't even tell us you had an interview)

DM { Congrats, I believe, is what she meant to say.)

(*Didn't want to jinx it }* CG

VG { When do you start? What about your visa?)

(*Next Weds night. Visa trip to Seoul this weekend }* CG

DM { Do you need any help with Panzer?)

VG { Weds. night is weird)

(Thanks, but no. I found a dog walker on Chore-Cho, she'll handle him } CG

(And it's just dinner with my new boss. Thurs is first full day } CG

VG { OK. Safe travels. After you return, let us know what you want to do for your birthday.)

* * *

When I get back home to Tokyo, Panzer is thrilled to see me, but I realize I haven't had a real conversation with another human in days—the last one was my interview with Misora. I try NearMi again, but still no Asagawa. His Minotaur profile is also pretty perfunctory. From time to time, he reposts the same photo of a takeout container of white rice.

Well, I have a copy of *The Depths IV: Subterranean* in my Gamestasis queue, and it's a two-player. I will do this the old-fashioned way. I put Panzer on his leash, and we bound up the stairs to the fifth floor.

The door to 501 has a simple sign that says "Ascent Services." Does Asagawa run a business out of his apartment? I rap on the door, but no one answers. I try again. Nothing.

Panzer whines and tugs on his leash—he wants to go for a run. "Fine, fine," I grumble. I take him on a quick 5K along one of our usual paths, feeling irrationally annoyed at everyone in Tokyo: Asagawa for being busy, Misora for having a boyfriend, the boyfriend for cheating on her.

Back in the apartment lobby, I check the mailbox for 501. It, too, is labeled "Ascent Services."

Panzer flops, cooling himself on the hard lobby tile. What the hell. I dial.

"Asagawa."

"Yes, hello, I am calling about having my ascent serviced."

"Green?" There's a long pause. "It's 'Ascent Services,' not 'Ascent Soapland.' But I could get a number for someone if you need it that bad."

Good god. Even in the nadir of this post-Ingrid dry spell, I'm not paying a hooker for a shower massage with a happy ending.

"Pass," I reply, walking Panzer over to the elevator. "I was looking for someone to play *The Depths IV* with me."

"How are you going to play a video game when you're not home?"

"I—what?"

"I said, 'how are you going to play a video game when you're not home?'" As the elevator doors open to the fourth floor, I can hear his voice through my port speaker and directly from his mouth.

Asagawa is sitting outside my door, perched on what looks like a battered computer tower. He's wearing a collared shirt that's at least two sizes too large, and he appears to have gone through the same wringer as the computer. Panzer lets out a low growl at the sight of him.

"Easy, boy," I say, holding Panzer by his collar. To Asagawa: "When did you get here?"

"When I got here." He stands up and dusts off his pants, eyeing Panzer warily.

"This is Panzer. He was in quarantine before." I walk Panzer past Asagawa to my apartment door, careful to keep myself between them. Once the door is open, I grab a bag of dog treats off the shelf by the entry and toss them to Asagawa. "Here. Make a friend."

Asagawa feeds Panzer about twice as many milkbones as he needs or deserves, but at least they're getting off on the right foot. I hold the door for Asagawa as he lunks the computer inside.

"*Ojama shimasu,*" he says politely, the standard Japanese phrase for acknowledging the inconvenience you cause by entering someone else's home. That has to be reflexive, because I know he doesn't care about putting me out.

He comes into the kitchen behind me and deposits the charred computer tower in the middle of my tiny, cluttered table. I frown. "Asagawa, why does this look like it was in a fire?"

His expression is deadpan. "It's been a long 12 hours."

"Did you start the fire? Or just take the computer out of an existing fire?"

Now he breaks into a broad smile. "I think you might be confusing 'questions you think you should ask' with 'questions you want to know the answer to.'"

Correct. "So, this thing you've brought into my home is the product of arson and theft. Great. Perhaps a better question would be: why is it now on my kitchen table?"

"You work in tech, right?"

Not with computers, but I doubt that distinction matters to him. "Sure."

"The... previous owners... were doing something magitech, but I don't know what. Anything you can find helps."

"If anything is even salvageable when you've set it on fire and used it as a chair," I comment, brushing some soot off the top of the tower. Panzer curls a lip at the mess before relocating to the living room sofa.

"It's only mild smoke damage."

"I'd prefer no smoke damage." I lift the tower and turn it so I can eye the back. "It has a proprietary power port. I don't suppose you thought to grab the cord for this thing."

"I didn't." He nudges Panzer a little, trying to scoot him over to make room on the couch.

"Wait," I say, eyeing a spatter of red-brown on the leg of his pants. "No blood on the couch." I push one of the kitchen chairs at him, then pause, feeling a flicker of alarm. "Tell me that's your own blood."

Asagawa stares at me for a moment, then sighs. "Most of it. I guarantee that all people who contributed are currently still alive and in reasonably good health."

Do I believe him? What kind of "services" is Ascent providing? I realize that, although we've hung out a few times, I hardly know this guy. I'm not even certain he's my actual neighbor.

Before I can comment, Asagawa continues, "I don't know what you think we do in Tokyo, but this isn't America. We don't kill people. If we want to bully someone, we pop them in the nose or break their store window. Statistically, you're the dangerous one here."

Alright, he's not wrong. Given Japan's über-tight gun control laws, I'm the half of the room that has ever handled a rifle. "Statistics don't apply when it's only me and some shady *yakuza* guy."

I don't actually think Asagawa is *yakuza*, but this touches a nerve—he scowls. "I'm not *yakuza*. We work for money, not whatever messed up loyalties motivate them. Speaking of—what's your fee?"

"Friends and family rate," I say, bemused by the question. "Six-pack of Super Dry and a sushi plate for our next game night. The good stuff, no imitation crab. Plus, reimbursement for the cord."

He pulls out a 10,000-yen note and hands it to me—it's a ridiculous amount of money for a simple cord, but I guess he's also covering my time. "This is nothing but curiosity. If you do find anything, I'll need it explained clearly."

"Yeah, I can use small words." Rich of me, when we're speaking his native language.

"You do that," he says, yawning. "The game will have to wait. I think it's time for me to head home."

"Oh, yeah? And where is that, exactly? Upstairs at the shoe laundry?"

"Funny. Let me know what you find."

* * *

I'm on the Yamanote loop line, headed to my first day at Helios, when a message from my sister pops up on my port.

Vanessa Green { How was dinner with the new boss?)

I tighten my grip on the grab bar as the train curves around a bend. How do I even answer that? It was the best first date I've ever had, except for the irksome detail that it wasn't a date at all.

(She's an excellent kisser } Cameron Green

VG { Hilarious. Try not to get fired.)

Yeah, no joke. I crossed an ocean to get this job, I cannot literally screw it up.

When I walk through the doors and into the Helios lobby, I'm relieved to see Xiaohui Li waiting for me instead of Misora. She patiently guides me through all the new employee basics: AppKeys for the elevator, the lab, and our office suite, and introductions to the rest of the team.

"Toyama-bucho left some HR forms on your desk. One for release of your MAR scores to Helios, and one confirming you're not taking any medications known to interact with Syphon. Also, there's tea in the kitchenette if you want some," Li-san says. "And coffee. Americans like coffee, right? Toyama-bucho isn't available this morning, but she said she'll come down in the afternoon."

The coffee is instant crystals with pre-mixed milk powder and sugar; no one who actually likes coffee drinks this swill. I resolve to bring in my own supplies tomorrow. And a mug, too—all the drinking vessels in the cupboard are no-handle teacups or small plastic tumblers. I take a tiny cup of the too-sweet coffee to my desk and log in, for the first time, to my Helios inbox. There are two messages: one about setting up direct deposit, and one from Misora.

To: Green, Cameron<green.cameron@helios.co.jp>
From: 東山美空<toyama.misora@helios.co.jp>

RE: First day

Green-san,

Welcome to Helios. I trust Li-san has helped you settle in and meet the team. I have shared several things I want you to read. Be prepared to discuss the Denali files when we meet.

Toyama

I look at the time stamp on the message: 10:17 p.m. yesterday. She had to have written it in the car on her way home from dropping me at my apartment. Guess she cooled down from that kiss faster than I did. I click open the Denali1ProjMgmt file.

"Good morning, Cameron-san," a voice calls. I look up to see Eika, dressed in her usual filmy pastels. I was feeling conspicuous this morning in my light blue striped button down, but Eika makes me look conservative by comparison. She drops a giant handbag on the desk next to mine, then unearths a bottle of water from its depths.

"I'm glad you're going to be working with us," she says around a sip. "We have a lot to get done."

It's hard to imagine she has much time for it, given what I saw of her whirlwind life on MinoSo. "Toyama-bucho asked me to read the files for a project called Denali. Is that yours?"

"'Toyama-bucho,'" Eika echoes with a chuckle, lightly mocking my lower register. "And, yeah. For this product dev cycle she's been naming all the projects after mountains."

"So, what will Denali do for downslopers?" I ask. "I haven't gotten far yet."

"Well, I can't speak to the actual science of it—you'd have to ask Mi-chan—but my central concern is people who aren't able to power up their devices or use the new magitech. People who are being left out of the future." Eika's arm nearly disappears as she excavates her port from her purse. "Here, look. I've been using this almost constantly, even video, and it's at 81%." She brushes her index finger over the Syphon panel, and the charge suddenly reads 100%.

Damn, she's powerful. I'm pretty far to the right in the distribution, which is part of why I've done well in this career, but she has to be some kind of megawatt outlier. A 19-point bump from me would take a little concentration and a few seconds; for Eika, it was like exhaling.

"It should be that way for everyone," she continues. "But you can't change where you're born or how much power you have. So, Mi-chan had this idea where an improved kind of Syphon, instead of capturing people's magical spillover, would juice the reserves and produce power in a small burst. So, you, me, a downslope person, almost anyone could use the same magitech."

She's using all the wrong terminology, but what Eika has just described would open magitech up to anyone except a complete ground. "And have you done this?" I ask. Because if they have, they are quietly sitting on something that will revolutionize Syphon. I have my name on some patents, but this...

"Eika-chan, I thought we were going to meet up in my office."

Last night in the restaurant candlelight, Misora seemed delicate and inviting, from the silky dress to the waves of hair brushing the sides of her face. Today, that snowy softness has melted away, leaving only the glacial ice beneath. She's still beautiful, but not in a way that encourages approach.

"Sorry," Eika says. "I wanted to come see Cameron-san on his first day. I was telling him about Denali."

Misora's eyes flick over to me, her expression guarded. "And? What do you think?"

I think you're the sexiest and most brilliant woman I've ever met. Too strong?

"I'm curious to see how you're making it work," I say instead.

Her mouth tightens. "Trying to make it work," she replies. "It's all in the notes. I know we're close, but it's not there yet. With your help, though, I think we'll have it ready for market testing by Q4."

At this, Eika makes a little "hmm" noise, but instead of commenting, she toys with the *omamori* charm dangling from the strap of her bag.

"Fourth quarter this year?" I clarify. Silicon Valley-style rapid disruption was the last thing I expected at a major Japanese company, where 100-year strategic plans are the norm. I'm used to big projects, but they come with equally big teams and multi-year timelines. The three of us can't put out something industry-bending in a measly eight months.

My face must convey my thoughts, because Eika chuckles. "Buckle up."

Yeah, no kidding.

"Eika-chan, we should get to work," Misora says. She turns back to me. "We'll talk at 1:00."

Eika gives me a little wave, then the two of them disappear behind

the thick door of the carbon-reinforced damper room. I return to
the Denali file, seeing that the design is as Eika described: instead
of absorbing the magical excess produced by the user like a typical
Syphon device, the battery engages directly with the individual,
effectively forcing a surge of power—enough to recharge a port or top
up other small devices. From Misora's detailed project notes, which go
back about a year, I see she's figured out the direct connection, a slickly
designed piece of magical engineering. More recently, she also roughed
out the concept for how to generate the power surge, but that's been
less successful—it seems to be where things have stalled. In the margins
on page 12, there's a note, date-stamped yesterday afternoon: *Biological
trigger function of L? Ask CG.*

Oh. I see. Eika's willingness to help me out—and Misora's speedy
job offer—both suddenly make a lot more sense. They need someone
with a background in biokintech and m-pharmaceuticals, because
Misora is thinking about basing her battery design concept on the
high-inducing mechanism of the street drug L.

I let out a long exhale. Holy shit.

Anyone who's taken a high school science class in the last twenty
years knows the basics of magical biology, but not necessarily how it
relates to L. When the Singapore Group discovered hidden genes in a
supposed gene desert, they realized those hidden genes could grant the
ability to use various kinds of ambient energy. This got called "magic,"
with Syphon tech designed to make use of it. A lot of people think the
magic comes from Syphon tech itself, but that's wrong—Syphon is the
vehicle. Just like electricity isn't generated by an overhead wire.

What L does, when you slap a patch of it on your neck or inner
thigh—any thin skin near major surface veins will do—is temporarily
goose the body's reservoir into pumping out more energy. There's no
better way to keep your port charged up than to make nice with an L
addict: you'll keep taking selfies and playing TripliCat, and they'll get
the smoothest, silkiest, highest high of their life. At least, until they
eventually burn out their reservoir. The FDA listed L as a Schedule 1
drug when a couple teenagers died from mixing it with... Adderall, I
think it was. With half the kids in the US on ADHD meds, it's a pretty

significant public health risk.

Patches vary in quality, too, both how safe they are and how high they'll get you. The premium-grade stuff sells for its weight in platinum, while the cheapest street tabs make black tar heroin look like gummy vitamins.

Bottom line: it's not the safest template to work from, although it's diabolically clever. I wonder what gave Misora the idea. She doesn't strike me as the type to have sampled L herself.

I look up and realize the others are all leaving their desks: it's noon. Eika emerges from the damper room. "Lunch?" she asks. "I'm starving!"

When I hesitate, she adds, "Don't worry, I'll have you back by one o'clock. Wouldn't want you to get kneecapped on your first day!"

I laugh, and then her eyes get big, and she grasps my arm. "Do not tell Mi-chan I said that."

I can actually spend some money again, now that I have this job. I look back at the damper room. "What about—"

"She'll have a *bento* delivered so she can work through lunch." Eika executes what could best be described as an affectionate grimace. "There's a little place a few blocks from here that's good."

As we walk to the café, I realize I'm rushing her with my longer stride. I slow down, and she gives me a grateful look. "Sorry, I'm kind of dragging today."

I can't think of a polite way to tell a pretty, image-conscious woman that she looks worn out, but Eika seems like she wants to talk. "Tough morning in the lab?"

"Yeah. Sometimes it's hard to keep up with Mi-chan."

A thought crosses my mind. "Eika-san, what are your MAR scores?"

"Never got them," she says with a shrug.

About 15 years ago, the International Association of Magitech Engineers released a white paper on ethics in magical engineering, and one of their proposals was that all engineers should be required to have validated MAR scores at a certain threshold on all three parts. A lot of people think MAR stands for Magical Aptitude Rating, but it's actually three things: Measure of Adequate Rate, Measure of Adequate Reservoir, and Measure of Adequate Renew. It's a static assessment, so you only need to take it once, but it's a standard pre-req for most magitech degree programs. If you're inadequate in any of the three areas, you really shouldn't be working in this field, because it isn't safe for you or your colleagues. In simplest terms, reservoir is your raw stash of power, rate is how quickly you can use that power, and renew is how quickly you re-charge.

"But you work in magitech R&D." I had to sign a release just this morning for Helios HR to collect my scores from the IAME.

"I run a non-profit that supports magitech R&D," Eika corrects. "I don't work for Helios, and I'm not an engineer."

"That's a bogus loophole, if you ask me." Eika has a rate that's off the charts, but her fatigue makes me wonder about her rez and renew.

"I didn't ask you, though, Cameron-san." Her tone is gentle, but it's clear that she's done with this topic. I shift gears.

"Where did you get the idea to start Replenish?"

"You know what my family's company, Fujiwara Heavy Industries, does, right?"

I nod.

"Well, when my parents turned the company over to their children, my older brother and sister were a lot more interested in running it all. But with my career in marketing, I was so much more visible than either of them."

Marketing is what she's calling it, huh? I read up a bit on Eika after I met her at Todai. Her life pre-Replenish seemed to involve things like endorsing an artisanal toothpaste brand and cutting ribbons at new nightclubs.

"After the leadership change was publicized, some of the victims of the Ashio disaster wrote to me. I guess they thought I had my *oneesan*'s ear and could influence her thinking." She sighs. "You have an older sister, right?"

"I do."

"Do you get along?"

"Most of the time."

She gives me a wry smile as I open the door to the cafe for her. "If you have any tips, I'm all ears.

"Anyway," Eika resumes once we've ordered and are settled at a small bistro table, "I didn't make much headway through direct channels. But these stories, Cameron-san—I couldn't believe some of the suffering we had caused. One letter—" her voice catches, and she looks down at her hands.

I'm missing a key thread here—it's clear she thinks I should know what the Ashio disaster is, and how it affected people. Did it happen when I was living here as a child? I'll have to look it up. "I'm sorry," I say, at a loss for anything better.

She looks up, face now stretched into a forced smile. "It's fine! I mean, it's not, but we're working on it, and that's what matters."

"Exactly." I unwrap a small *oshibori* towel and wipe my hands. "You have a few projects, right?"

"Yes. There are so many avenues to attack the problem, and I want to be certain we're not missing anything. So, there's environmental restoration, to help mitigate future issues, and the Denali project, to help people who are dealing with this now." As she talks, Eika uses her napkin to carefully clean a smear of mayonnaise off her plate, then futzes with the lettuce on her sandwich until it's just so. She hands me her port. "Do you mind?"

"Oh, uh, sure."

Eika pulls out a bottle of peach-flavored water and uncaps it, setting it on the table next to her sandwich. Then she poses, gazing dreamily into the distance... at the nearby recycling bins. I snap a few photos of her, careful to center the water while keeping the garbage out of the shot. She flips through her options for a moment, types something, and then I feel my own port buzz; she must have tagged me with a photo credit in her post.

After Eika and I part ways, I head back to the office for my meeting with Misora. She's still in the damper room, and her lunch, barely touched, has been pushed aside in favor of a laptop. "You wanted to see me?"

She glances up from her typing. "Yes. Please sit."

I sit down at the table and wait. The air is humid, heavy with that organic smell you usually find in greenhouses, and the light is sallow with fake UV glow. The many plants hanging from the ceiling provide natural energy absorption for any experiments gone awry. I don't know how Misora can work in here for hours. Her suit jacket is off, hanging from the back of her chair—it's the sole hint that she might find the climate unpleasant.

"You finished reading the Denali file?" she finally asks, looking up from her screen. "What did you think?"

"It's ambitious," I say cautiously.

"And?"

"I saw your note about L. I have some ideas."

"Do you? Good. I'll have Nozomi add some bench time to our calendars so we can work on that together. In addition, I want your help with this." She rotates her screen so I can see it.

I scan the details. A rough design for what looks like a tracking device is sketched out on the screen. I can't help myself. "Are you planning on stalking someone?"

Her dark eyes shimmer with amusement, offering a glimpse of the Misora from last night. "Some assets have disappeared from one of our factories, and I want to track any subsequent losses. The challenge is that the trackers need to provide a signal even if they're off-grid. The facility is in a remote area, and we can't expect a reliable connection. I don't need any answers now, but I'd like you to think about it."

"I will." Project work in this field isn't your usual bench-sharing with lab mates. Aside from the long hours, it involves pooling magic, which can be incredibly intimate. Collaborating on any project takes a lot of closeness and trust, and Misora is starting me off on two of hers.

"About last night," she says, eyes back on her computer.

"Yes?"

"It was unprofessional."

Is she fucking kidding? She kissed me. "I—I apologize," I force out.

She looks up from her screen. "I meant me."

Oh. I wrack my brain for an appropriate response.

"Professionalism is overrated," I finally reply.

A tiny smile plays at the edge of her lips. "Perhaps it is."

ASAGAWA KENJI

I've just sunk into chest-deep steaming water when the black port buzzes. Setting my barely opened Asahi Super Dry on the edge of the sink, I pull myself out so I can reach where my port is plugged in on the floor outside the door.

The time is 11:33 p.m. The message is an address, nothing more.

After almost a month of waiting, finally.

The message from Asagawa-san is immediately followed by one from Kumanaka. His is garbled, but I get the general idea. By the time I've dried off and pulled on clothes, Kumanaka is waiting in front of Shinjuku Gyoenmae station in his Toyota minivan. His bloodshot eyes are unfocused and the small of his tie is too long. I'm not the only one who was interrupted from something more enjoyable.

We grunt at each other as I climb into the passenger seat and buckle my seatbelt. Hopefully, he won't kill us both in a fiery crash on the way.

On the other hand, this gives me an opening to do some digging that's not in a cardboard box. "How's that thing for Funabashi going?"

"Yeah. Yeah. We're meeting it. The schedule." His speech is fast, almost too staccato to understand, and he's rubbing his neck where the patch of L was as he talks. "We got a space. Like we need. No problems."

I look out the window so his mannerisms don't make me twitchy too. Koto ward is a 40-minute drive down Shinjuku-dori and curving through Chiyoda, office buildings around us dark. "Which option did you pick?"

"Not that shitty place. That one nearby. Better. Make it easy to move 'em."

So, something's going to be transported in, and they're going to stash it for a while. But if Funabashi is involved, the plans could be legit or off-book. "What does Asagawa-san think of it?"

He has both hands on the wheel now and is rubbing the steering wheel with his thumb over and over. It's a gesture that manages to be lewd, even on a car part. "She don't care. She's bringing them in, dropping 'em. Until they're due."

So, Asagawa-san is transporting something to a place Kumanaka found. The job is big enough to require advance planning. But what is it? And who is it going to?

"Getting 'them'?" I drop the question down lightly.

"You know." He turns his head to give me a bleary frown. "Oh—"

Before his brain can get too far, I throw my weight against my hands on the dash in a sudden and solid impact. "Watch it!"

Kumanaka twists his head forward, swerves around the nothing that's on the street, and tries to focus his eyes. There are a few cars far ahead of us, streetlights overhead, and small buildings shuttered up for the night to the sides. "What the—?"

"That was close," I lie. "So, tonight are we picking up the things?"

"No, no, this is sideways. Gotta make sure these people ain't got the details, make it so they can't sell it if they do. But gonna find out what they got. Might be useful. Maybe we want it."

Obviously, Asagawa-san knows what's being moved. She also knows that we're going to this address since she sent it to us. But does she want this info that Kumanaka thinks they have too?

He keeps going. "Gonna keep it. That way we have the details."

"Details about Funabashi?"

Kumanaka frowns and moves his head back and forth. It's a nod or a head shake or a seizure or something in that range. There's no time to push further since he's turning onto a side street that the GPS says is our destination.

The address is a little two-story building that, even in the dim light, I can see needs some paint. The shutters are closed up, and light is streaming out the transom above the door.

Conveniently, there is a strip of likely reserved parking spaces across the narrow street for him to park. Getting out of the van on the far side puts me a step behind, and Kumanaka crowds me out to pound his fist on the door and yell obscenities. It's a great use of the element of surprise.

A long moment passes, and then I'm the one who's taken off-guard when the door actually opens. The guy who answers is short, sheepish and wearing a Uniqlo-brand combination of green scarf over gray checked button-down over faded T-shirt over ankle-length chinos.

"I'm sorry, but you have the wrong—"

That's as far as he gets before Kumanaka has shoved him down onto the floor of the *genkan* and stormed inside. The guy scrambles and scoots himself backward on his butt into the main room. I follow inside, keeping my shoes on as I step up onto the *tatami*.

The space inside is small for a free-standing building, just 8-mats big for the main room. It's divided into two halves by a bamboo curtain hanging down the center. On our side, I'm standing on top of cards from a game of *koi-koi*, with the Uniqlo kid to my left and a skinny guy with a squint who looks like he's going to be a problem to my right next to a tall filing cabinet. Liquid-based air-fresheners are putting out a thick scent of something floral and something that smells green. There's something happening with computers on the other side of the curtain, something's not right about the curtain itself, but I don't have a chance to figure out what right now—

There's a letter opener on top of the filing cabinet, in reach of the skinny guy, and I don't feel like getting stabbed a second time this winter.

I step forward and slap my palm down flat on the blade of the opener, trapping his fist against the metal surface. With my free left hand, I push his chest hard, so his back slams up against the cabinet drawers.

"We're here to talk." I let the front of his shirt go but keep my hand on the letter opener. "This is your notice that this project is canceled."

"By who?" he asks. His voice sounds tough but his breathing quick under my hand.

A noise behind me and I realize that Kumanaka is reaching at the curtain that divides the room. Something is not right about—wait, there are paper strips with writing taped to the bamboo, the kind of thing you see at a shrine.

Shit.

Small amounts of L in someone's system can react even with basic magitech. I don't know what the levels Kumanaka is likely on will do with who knows what this is.

There's a feeling of wind without any air movement and the scent of ozone, and he goes stiff. A small groan, and he starts to collapse.

"Ah, hell." I pull the letter opener out by the blade and throw it behind me, and then turn to grab at Kumanaka.

As I do so, the angry guy's arm slides in around my neck and he pushes me sideways, intent on pinning me against the wall by the entry.

"Tell your boss that we're under contract, and to leave us the fuck alone." He emphasizes the words boss and contract enough that I realize that he thinks we're sake-sipping, finger-cutting *yakuza* goons.

"Got the wrong idea," I grunt around his arm. The wall is coming up fast, so I drop my weight down and apply my elbow up and to his side, pushing his head over my free shoulder. His face hits the drywall along the cheekbone, a mixture of blood and spit following as he bites his tongue in the process.

Still, he keeps a good grip on my neck. I push off the wall clumsily with my own shoulder, scraping the back of my hand on the indent in the plaster that I've caused. When enough space clears, I pull up my foot and push off awkwardly, tumbling us both backwards onto the floor.

A dull cracking noise as his head hits, and his arm loosens enough for me to roll off and onto my knees. He's blinking and feebly curling into a ball, trying to remember why he thought this was a good idea. Uniqlo kid has sunk into a ball in the corner, blood on his cheek welling up from an early collision with Kumanaka's ring.

"We're not *yakuza* and we don't care who you're under." I wipe the splattering of blood off my right cheek with my undamaged hand and onto the sleeve of his shirt. "You're going to shut this shit down before we do something violent."

Kumanaka is lying in a pile next to the curtain. I grab his ankle with both hands and pull. Immediately, there is a sharp pain that runs up my arms. Barely managing to keep my grip, I lean back and slide him away by momentum alone.

Dropping his foot, my arms cool immediately. His skin is bright red, like a blush that can't decide if it's a bruise. My palms are pink and tingling.

In the other half of the room there are two women who look like breakers by all the technical shit around them. They're wearing some kind of goggles, not looking in my direction. Maybe it's really that urgent, maybe they feel confident in their barrier to keep me out. Or, more likely, they called in backup, and we're on borrowed time.

I'm not going back to Asagawa-san with this job unfinished.

The floor over there is a rat's nest of cords: power strips plugged into each other skirting a circle around the breakers, their computer, and what looks like a bonsai tree. Now that I'm looking more carefully, I can also see where a thin wire is connected into the bamboo curtain and weaving up and down through the surface.

Everything is plugged into the wall on the far side of the barrier.

The wall. Uniqlo kid is leaning against where I think it would be—

I grab his shirt and pull him toward the center of the room. Sure enough, another outlet is hiding behind where he was, down the wall from the one powering the computer. The plaster is light. Poor construction. A tap with my knuckle. There are wooden studs in this wall, not a concrete base.

The kid whimpers when I tug his scarf loose and backs up until he's huddled against the opposite side of the room. The fabric wrapped around my right fist, I punch the wall a bit above and to the right of the outlet, between the two studs. A second hit, a third, and the plaster cracks enough that I can start pulling pieces away to reveal the space between. The wiring is running out between holes in the studs. It's old, not up to modern code, so I take a tight hold, brace with my foot, and pull away from the direction of the computer.

A long second passes and finally the wire gives from where it is screwed into the outlet on the other side of the room. The pressure in the room drops immediately like a breeze going out the window. As it passes through me there is an immediate warmth, uncomfortable and non-specific. Then it's gone.

The room is still lit by the overhead fixture, but the computers are out. There's a smell—acrid—shit, that's coming from inside the wall, not far from the extremely flammable *tatami* floor.

I climb through the curtain and over the mass of wires toward an extinguisher peeking out from under some papers. Hitting the corner of the Hello Kitty-branded canister opens a hole in the plaster by the outlet, letting a tendril of smoke sneak out. Pull the pin, point the nozzle, and then spray. The fire gives in quickly and I sink back on the floor next to the slumped body of the breaker.

Leaning back on my sore hands, I breathe for a moment.

On the wall by the front entry there's an electrical box.

Yeah, that would have been easier.

I'm the only one still up after the surge. Turning onto my knees, I check the pulse point on the breaker's neck. She's still alive and breathing peacefully, so that's a good sign for the rest of the room. Asagawa-san would be fucking pissed if I lost Kumanaka on something small like this.

The goggles she's wearing come off easily but they're dead from either the energy overload or my handling them. Slowly, I crawl over to the computer, move the bonsai tree to the floor, and pull all of the cords out of the connections on the back. I could just smash the hard drive, but Kumanaka was interested in what they were doing, which makes me curious too.

First though, I need to drop off the trash.

* * *

Kumanaka is starting to come to by the time I pull into the carport at his house. He's disoriented, but able to stumble forward, leaning on my shoulder—much easier than it had been to drag him from the building into the van.

I unlock the door with his key, whisper through the open crack, "We're home." I don't want to wake up Mizuki if she's sleeping.

From down the hallway, the flip-flop of her slippers on wood. Of course she's not asleep. I think the woman gave up sleeping when she first had Rina.

"Welcome, Kenji-kun." She slips down and under Kumanaka's other arm. Together we pull off his shoes and propel him sideways down the hall to their bedroom at the end. Rina and Yuri's room up the stairs remains quiet as we stumble past. He's fading out again by the time we reach the destination, and we both slide out from under his arms and let him fall forward onto the futon.

Their living room is stuffy when I slump down to the floor. Mizuki takes a minute to pull out a teapot and plastic-wrapped cakes from somewhere in the kitchen. The teapot is the same worn one they've had for two decades. "Kenji-kun, your face—Are you okay?"

I tap my cheek, lips, nose tentatively. Huh, there's some dried blood under my nose, dripped down my shirt. There's some smeared on my right thigh too. I'm not bleeding now. A series of scrapes across my knuckles are the worst of it, which isn't much. "Doesn't hurt."

She stands up and looks down at me. There are lines shaded on her face that I haven't noticed before. "Will you accept one of his shirts?"

"Yeah, thanks." The trains are done for the night so I'm going to end up sleeping on their floor for a few hours, followed by a detour before I head home. It's probably a good idea to not look like someone who took a partial wall to the face on the train in the morning.

The warm wet towel on my face soaks away some of the ache I hadn't noticed was there. Kumanaka's shirt on the other hand... I gesture at the fabric pooling on the floor. "One of your shirts would be a better fit."

"I don't think I can trust you to take care of one of my shirts."

I laugh and pick up the cup. "Thank you for the food." The green tea is instant—calming cheap caffeine just how I like at two a.m. We both sit for a minute in silence, the faint hum of their fridge the only noise.

"Is he treating you well?" I ask, wondering if Mizuki would answer truthfully if the answer were no. She knows me, knows what would happen.

She smiles brightly. "Of course." Another cup poured, then, "Takeshi-kun stopped over last week. He said work is going well, but he broke up with his boyfriend."

"My brother still knows we exist?"

"You know he has his reasons." She looks up at me. "You don't make things easy either."

"Relationships are reciprocal."

She nods silently, and we both sit for a long moment again. I'm down to the bitter swirl at the bottom of the cup. My legs and arms are getting heavy.

"It's good that we all watch out for each other," she says finally.

"I know you paid for Takeshi's school." The paper records at Todai were a mess to read, but nothing as annoying as the records in 501. It wasn't a surprise she'd done it, knowing Mizuki's feelings on education— the world nearly ended when Rina refused to take university entrance exams. Still, this is potentially dangerous information. "I didn't tell her." My mother would not be happy.

Mizuki is smiling as she looks at her lap. "Of course not." She looks up. "She won't be around forever. And I understand why you don't like him, but Soseki protects us."

This took a turn. I grunt noncommittally. Kumanaka Soseki, protector of the innocent. I can just see him in a mecha. Or a short skirt and tiara, leg hair flapping in the shining breeze of justice.

She continues, "Sometimes he doesn't make the best decisions, but also, I know that you will help him if he needs it. Help us."

I let out a low moan. "Really? Secret promises in the dark of night? The tea was good, but not that good."

She laughs and then stacks my cup on top of hers. "You aren't half as bad as you like to pretend to be, Kenji-kun. You'll do the right thing."

I slump forward and put my head on the *kotatsu*. "If you say so."

* * *

On the top floor landing, Kumanaka is standing by the entry, a cigarette in one hand. He's also rubbing his neck where he obviously wishes he were wearing a patch of L. Trying to quit or out of money for the month already?

At one p.m., this evening-only restaurant isn't scheduled to open for another three hours but the door is cracked and there's a smell of copper in the air. I give Kumanaka a glance before reaching for the handle, and he gives me a single shake of his head. "She's busy."

Yeah, I can hear that. Apparently, the guy doesn't know anything, just started this job, only preps the vegetables, and in general isn't having a good afternoon.

The landing is open to the street, so I lean on my arms up against the railing. "What's the issue?"

"Someone's been running a game in the back room," Kumanaka says, but doesn't volunteer more. His usual level of vague.

Maeda-gumi tends to take poorly to unauthorized gambling in the city, so I can guess that we are here to send a message on their behalf. Asagawa-san usually starts with the low-level people and works her way up through the org chart and then friends and family until the decision-maker realizes their error.

"MosBurger's hiring," Kumanaka says idly between drags.

Sure enough, there's a help wanted sign decorated with a big smiling head of cabbage in the window across the street. Maybe I'll stop in after this and get a rice burger. "For you or for me?"

"Parking is shit on this street. Gotta be a better one closer to home."

"You have to at least pretend to enjoy your job if you work somewhere like that." I know why I'm in this business—I was born into it. There wasn't ever a question of where I was going. How did Kumanaka end up here?

Not that it matters for either of us. We're both in this now.

I continue, "She'd probably burn it down."

He grunts as he flicks the cigarette butt over my shoulder, toward the street. "Free food."

"True. There are a lot of them, so it'd take a while for her to take them all out."

"Aprons," he adds, though doesn't specify whether he is putting the uniform in the pro or con column. Sometimes an apron would be useful in this job too.

The sound inside has stopped, which we take as our cue. The lights are still off, giving everything inside a gray cast. Door behind me. Windows on the front of the building, but not the kind that open. There's a hallway leading to the back, where I'd expect emergency stairs.

I step carefully to avoid leaving a shoe imprint. The guy is tied to a chair, blindfolded. She likes to do that, not because she's afraid someone might see her face, but because then they don't know what's coming.

Asagawa-san is leaning against the register podium and looking at the broom handle critically. "I barely touched him," she says, curling her lip at the tears on his face. Her eyes flick over to me. "I see you decided to show up."

The message came in less than fifteen minutes before I got here. Or maybe that's a slight about what happened with my shoulder.

"He was dicking around outside," Kumanaka says, all traces of solidarity gone. He doesn't have the taste for cruelty that she does. He'll just do what he can to keep his place in the pecking order.

Green needs to get that hard drive figured out, so I can figure out what Kumanaka and Funabashi might be up to now.

"What do you want done?" I ask, letting the comments go.

She leans the broom against the register, leaving her hand on it. "Make a mess of it."

If we destroy the restaurant, it'll be cheaper to sell to someone else than fix it up. A less fun method for her, though more efficient. Usually, this means pulling apart the space piece by piece. You can also make a spectacular mess with water, but only if you don't care that it ruins the ceiling of the place below. "Are we keeping it to this floor?"

"You hear me say anything about other floors?" She doesn't ask if my ears are broken now too, but it's implied.

"My mistake," I say.

Asagawa-san doesn't respond, just turns away to do something by the register. This leaves her back open—whether it's arrogance or if she wants me to try something so she could make me regret it I can't tell.

I cross the room past the guy in the chair. He's going to need that compound fracture set. There should be more staff arriving eventually to see to that.

For all the work it takes to decorate a nice restaurant like this, it doesn't take much to slash the upholstery, pry the wooden benches apart, and generally turn everything into a pile of component parts.

Once we're done, she doesn't have any more use for me, so I head out.

Since a few weeks have passed without an update on the computer, I stop by the Ueno area to hassle Green. I didn't give him a deadline, but something is going on and this hard drive is my only lead.

When Green answers the door, he has his port sandwiched between his ear and shoulder. There's a line between his eyebrows. "Yes, I did that already," he says. "I'm calling to confirm that it was received."

I slip out of my shoes and follow him and his stream of increasingly measured comments to his living room. Panzer is lying on the floor behind the couch, looking bored.

"You didn't? This is the fourth time—no, I don't need your fax number again. Okay, yes, I'll check. Yes, that is the number I used. In person? You're an internet provider and you don't have an online... Yes, I understand." He hangs up and stares at his port for a long moment.

"So—"

"Don't start unless you can fix my internet."

Sounds like a challenge. "How long has it been down?"

"Almost a week," he says tightly. "I need that connection. Some of the software I use doesn't run on a port, and I need to download the updates to use it for your—" He gestures at the computer tower in the corner of his room and uses a word I don't recognize.

"What?"

"Oh, um," he fishes around for the word, "you know, the black rock you start a fire with."

He speaks well enough that I mostly forget this isn't his first language. "Charcoal?"

"Yeah, that thing a computer shouldn't be."

I chuckle. "So, you already had your internet set up and it stopped working? Did they disconnect it by mistake?"

He nods. "Seems that way. But why is turning it back on even more complicated than it was to get it set up in the first place?"

"Bureaucracy," I say with a shrug. I haven't bothered to have internet set up at any of my last three apartments—it's just not worth messing with the paperwork. "Be right back."

When I return after a few minutes, he raises his eyebrows. I gesture toward the apartment on the other side of his kitchen wall. "402 moved out. They must have had the same ISP."

"Remind me what Ascent Services does again," Green says, still giving me a look.

I flop down on his couch. It had seemed like a good idea to keep this hard drive that might have sensitive information out of the hands of someone who might turn around and resell it, but I guess I'm getting exactly the amateur expertise I paid for here.

There's the obvious solution. "We could just plug your modem into their connection."

Green takes a long sip of whatever beverage he has in a mug before responding. I'm trying his patience almost as much as whoever he was talking to on the phone. "And next month, when no one pays? Or next week, when someone moves in?"

The job he owes me would be done by then, and that could be a problem for next-month or next-week Green. He's sporting a pretty aggrieved look though, so I bite back a more sarcastic response and go with, "If you want to do it the hard way, sure, I can help. We can go down in person."

"Asagawa, offense intended, I don't think I trust you in public."

"I'm sure you meant 'no offense,'" I say, even though I know he didn't. "And I am in fact very good with people. I am a people person."

He makes a noise that is somewhere between a laugh and a sarcastic snort and runs his fingers through his hair. "Okay, fine. It's not like my internet is going to get more canceled."

The NH Connect office he's been referred to is halfway across the city, and somehow consists of only a single person in a tiny storefront sitting at a computer that has seen better days. Even better, it's a kid wearing your standard bargain-bin recruit suit, the tie and the jacket identical shades of cheap black.

Green jumps in to talk since it's his internet and he clearly doesn't trust what I might say. "I was referred to you by your phone help desk. My internet has stopped working."

The kid, Nishimura by his nametag, gives us a few apologetic bows and breaks out the formal language. "Honored customer, I humbly ask forgiveness for the aggravation that has been caused by this egregious bother. I will do everything that is within my power to accommodate your needs and correct the disruption for you."

Green is frowning as he parses the complicated vocabulary, but soldiers on. "I was asked to submit this form by fax, but I sent it four times and they haven't received it. Can I submit it here?"

A few more bows and yet more stilted apologies. "Again, I humbly ask pardon for your aggravation. I will assist you if you would be so kind as to complete the appropriate request." Nishimura digs through a drawer full of folders, and finally finds a blank form. "You are welcomed to complete the form over there." He gestures to the counter by the front door.

Green takes the sheet of paper and holds it up next to the one that he's already completed. They are nearly identical, except for a few fields and the label at the top. He sounds out the formal writing of the header but clearly has no idea what the combination of characters means together.

I choke back laughter into just an exhalation of breath, and finally manage to explain, "This is the in-person version of the form. The one you have there is only to be used for their phone center processing."

Green gives me a dirty look and carries both sheets over to the counter. I start to look at the form with him, but he shoots me another glare as he takes the pen from its appointed storage on the counter.

I lean backwards against the counter and stare out the window instead. Apparently, I'm a representative of everything wrong with my country at the moment. "I'm here for moral support, so don't blame me." I glance over. "That's 'start date of service.' You hungry? I think there's a ramen place near the train station."

"Okay. I spent all that time on the phone and missed lunch. What's this?"

"Speed of connection."

It takes a few minutes for him to painstakingly copy over his answers, including a paragraph explaining the issue, but finally he makes it to the end. At the bottom of the form, there is a box for his name stamp, and he signs something in it, presumably his name in English.

I frown, and Green catches my expression. "What now?"

"Don't you have a stamp? I don't think this guy is going to like that."

Green shakes his head. "This is what they always ask me to do instead."

The kid is young enough that I don't think he's going to be able to deal with anything on the form being out of the norm, but I don't press the issue. Green walks the form back up and hands it to the again-bowing Nishimura.

A quick glance through the form and, as I expected, he gets to the bottom and stares at it. "Honored customer, this field is for you to complete using your name stamp."

"I don't have one, because I am not Japanese," Cameron explains with more patience than he seems to feel. "This is my signature instead."

Nishimura exhales heavily and looks at the form for a longer time than he needs to decide before saying, "Hmmm, this is a problem."

"Excuse me," I say, and pull the form back out of his hand. I have one of my own in my jacket pocket, so I take it out and stamp the box while giving the kid a direct look. "There you go."

There's a pause as Nishimura clearly weighs whether to argue with me, finally settling on not. "Thank you, honored customers. I apologize but please wait here."

As he vanishes down the hallway, I turn to Green. "Well, that was only a little completely ridiculous."

He rolls his eyes. "I just...I can't put it in words."

"Didn't this company get bought out recently?"

"I think by JapanPhone. I guess customer service was not high on their list of improvements."

"They already have the customers, so they don't need to worry about the little stuff."

"Yeah. What is taking so long?" Green walks along the desk to look through the doorway where Nishimura vanished. Suddenly his eyes get big. "He. Is. Faxing. That. Form."

I laugh, a short bark of a noise. "Of course he is."

It takes another minute for Nishimura to return, but when he does, he gives us a satisfied smile. "Honored customer, thank you for your patience in waiting for the resolution. It will only be five to six weeks until your service is returned to operation."

"What?" Green is clearly not sure that he heard correctly.

"Five to six weeks?" I say for both our benefits. When Nishimura nods, I continue, "I can see you have some kind of customer accounting system on your screen right there. Can't you turn it back on from here?"

He looks down at the machine and shakes his head a few times. "I apologize but I do not have the authorization to reinitiate services."

"You can't or you won't?" I ask. When he doesn't answer, I continue. "How long would it take to sign up for a new account instead?"

"A new account is established in approximately two weeks."

At that Green turns away from the counter entirely. He is done with this country.

Game on. "Can we sign him up for a new account instead?"

"I deeply apologize but that is not possible. He is an existing customer."

"Then sign me up. I would like to order new service."

"I deeply apologize but it is not possible to set two services to the same address."

That's just fine. I give Nishimura a wide smile. "I would like to order service at a different address. May I have the form?"

Nishimura can tell that something is off, but there isn't any reason not to give me the paperwork. I grab the pen that he has on his desk and remain standing in front of him as I fill it out. The name and address I put in are entirely fake, but they match an ID that I have in my wallet. My name stamp doesn't match, but I've already established that I can push him to ignore that little detail.

To my right, Green is shooting me a look. I don't acknowledge it. After a minute, I turn the form around and give it to Nishimura, together with my fake ID and the deposit for service.

"Thank you, honored customer. I apologize but please wait here."

As Nishimura again vanishes down through the doorway to fax in the form, I reach over the desk and turn the monitor and keyboard around to face our side. "Green."

He shoots me an incredulous look, but scoots over to scope the customer look-up screen. There's a search field for the account, so he punches in his name. "Huh, okay, this is pretty straightforward. I think if I just remove the end of service date—" He points at a field, and I verify that he's reading the label correctly. He deletes the date, clicks save, and the label at the top switches from inactive to active. Green closes out of the window and pushes the monitor and keyboard back.

It takes another long minute before Nishimura emerges from the doorway. "Honored customer, thank you for your patience. Your service will be established in approximately two weeks."

"Thank you, Nishimura-san, you've been a peach," I say to him.

Outside the store, I give Green a smug smile. "Now, admit it—I'm a people person," I say. "And since Nishimura is probably getting fired for reconnecting your internet, I'm even helpful to both the company and future customers."

He raises his eyebrows. "If I remember right, I did the actual work there."

"Because I gave you the opportunity. Also, I paid that guy ten thousand yen for internet service I'm not going to use. You can at least buy the ramen."

Green looks down at me with an amused expression. "I don't recall asking you to do any of that."

"Huh," I say. "Good to know you are planning on paying me back the ten thousand yen for the power cord you haven't purchased yet. Yeah, I could see the machine sitting in the corner of your living room."

"Fine," he says, "I'll get the ramen if you get the beers."

Not the best of deals, but I'll take it if it gets me my answers. "Agreed."

DATE HATSUMI

THE NIHON TIMES
>*Politics & Governance*

Collection of Politically Themed Hina Dolls Unveiled at Tokyo Hotel
By Date Hatsumi

A weeklong Hina Matsuri celebration began with master artisan Komatsu Hachirou, 74, unveiling dolls in the likeness of two leading politicians. At the top of the traditional Girls' Day display, Hayashi Tomokazu from the conservative Civic Action Party is depicted as Emperor and Otsuka Kazuko from the progressive Wa Party as Empress.

These two politicians have recently made headlines for their ongoing conflict over the proposed Natural Resource Protection Ordinance and related environmental issues. "For the display, I wanted to create dolls that express my sincere hope for politicians across the political spectrum to work together for a better future," Komatsu said.

Otsuka and other leading members of the Wa Party attended the opening ceremony. "I hope that visitors to the display will be inspired to contribute to the health of our nation," Otsuka said. "May the steps of this display serve as a staircase for future female political leaders."

*When asked for comment, Hayashi said, "Hina Matsuri
is an annual reminder of the value of women as the caretakers
of future generations. I am honored to be included in a display
that represents our wish for health and happiness for girls and
their families across the nation."*

*The Hina dolls are on display at the Shinjuku Imperial
Hotel through March 3, together with a historical collection
on loan from the Johjima family, including over 600 dolls
dating from as early as the late Edo Period (1603-1867).*

* * *

"Well. This seemed like a good idea when we planned it," I
say, eyeing my moped with concern.

Next to me, Noah-kun is barely visible behind a
stack of translucent plastic drawers tied together with plastic twine. "I
think we can do it," the pile says.

"Thank you for your optimism, drawer-kun. As misplaced as it
may be."

He leans forward and sets the stack on the seat, where it all promptly
tips toward me. I catch the corner with one hand, almost knocking
over my bike in the process. Another catch, and it's all almost balanced,
if balanced is defined as a fall that hasn't decided on the direction yet.

Noah goes at it with more plastic twine. A few quick movements
and most of the roll later, the stack is attached to the bike via the back
springs in a way that's probably not a good idea.

"Looks good," I say, grimacing.

He makes a sound like a falling note. "I hope it moves better than
it looks."

With the drawers taking up the entire seat, there's definitely no way
I can sit to drive. "Let's see if we can walk it. I'll push, and you hold
the back."

With some force, it does start rolling, a contraption that's somehow
more work for two people than if we were each to carry two plastic
drawers in each hand.

A thought occurs to me. "You know, if you had gone with the dresser instead, it would have been free delivery. They'd probably even have come inside to assemble it for you."

"Now you tell me," he groans, with mock seriousness.

"I was planning on waiting until you were back in Vancouver, but I was afraid I'd forget."

A laugh behind me, and the back half momentarily veers away from me before firming back in line. "Sorry! Too funny."

There's a retiree in a navy jacket and cream scarf walking a small dog across the street. He glances over at us, then down.

"Speaking of Vancouver, how are your parents?" I ask.

"They are the same: They are happy I get to be here now. But also, when will I have a permanent job as an accountant? And am I married, and do I have grandchildren for them yet?"

Ah, the universal experience of family pressure. "Tell them that not even my esteemed cousin can do all of that at the same time."

"At least they have confidence in me." The back of the bike wobbles again. "What is that?"

It takes me a moment to realize he's pointing past my shoulders at a restaurant with a green roof that's steep at the top and then flares out halfway down. The sign isn't visible from here but as I stare at the building, a label for the business helpfully pops up in the corner of my glasses. "I think that's an Appeteriya."

"That's too bad. I don't usually come this way, and I thought it might be pizza nearby that I hadn't met."

"Oh, like Pizza Hat?" I ask, using the English pronunciation.

"S- Sorry, what? Can you say that again?"

"Like Pizza Hat?"

He breaks into laughter, enough that I have to stop to turn and look.

"Pi-za-ha-tto," I say slowly and phonetically. "Pizza Hat."

He stops, bites his lip, and then shakes his head. "Pizza Hut."

"But their logo has a hat," I say.

"Oh, that would make sense, wouldn't it?" Bookending a smile, his cheeks are pink, either from the chill air or amusement. "But no, the restaurants back home, they used to have a roof with that shape, but red. A 'hut' is like a little building, you know."

"Hut," I repeat. "That's funny."

"Your name would have been more clever, if I think about it," he says. "I could use some Hat. Just a big slice of cheese pizza. I miss it."

We start moving again, turning past a small pine tree and down the side street toward his apartment.

"There are some of those in Tokyo. I could see if you're in their delivery range."

"I'd probably have to call and order, wouldn't I?" Noah-kun sighs. "And my mom thinks I should try to get a permanent position with a company here. I don't even want to call for delivery."

I remember how awful it was trying to switch to speaking English all the time, back when I stayed with his family for those few months.

At the time, my mom was worried about what I'd been getting up to, so in the space between high school and college she sent me over there. Noah-kun was maybe fourteen, old enough that others in his place might have ignored the angry girl stumbling over her words. Instead, he told me he'd always wanted an older sibling, and we spent the two months watching hockey and playing whist with his parents.

When I left, I gave him the music player I'd brought with me. A few months ago, he said he still had that outdated thing at home. Probably a polite fiction, but I appreciate that he cared enough to pretend.

"Do you know the story about the koi?" I ask.

"The one where they're swimming up the river so they can become a dragon?"

"Up a waterfall," I say. "All these koi pushing themselves toward this nearly impossible goal, where it's the climb that makes the transformation at the top mean something."

"Makes sense. Work hard. Persevere," he says. "That is my building up there on the right."

His building is a squat wooden thing, with six apartments stretched across two floors.

"Yeah, kind of a nice sentiment, inspiring. But also, you know, follow this one path in the same direction as everyone else. Give your whole life to a company. All that. A nice metaphor—popular—but maybe not for everyone."

The entry is a bare metal set of stairs on the far end. We coax my moped into the space under the steps to get it out of the street. I keep a hold on the handlebars and kick down the centerstand.

Noah squats to untie the pile. He pulls at the knot with fingers stiff, teasing one end of the plastic twine loose. "Oh, so, Hatsumi-san. Can I ask you about something? I have a friend who teaches English. He's been here for a year and a half. Now there's a problem. His school has an apartment he is renting from them. But they are going to sell it."

I hope he isn't wanting me to act as a guarantor for his friend's new place. I put enough on the line being Noah's, and I know him well enough to trust that he's not planning on skipping out on his rent.

"Does he need help finding a rental agency?"

"Well, Corbin would like to stay in his current apartment, if he can. But he's having a hard time talking to the new property company. They have been going around and around, and he can't tell if he's just not understanding what they want him to do." Noah lifts the stack off the seat, and narrowly misses hitting the step above him.

I follow him around and up the steps. "Do you want me to talk to them? Help translate?"

"Could you? I can send you the contact person for their office. It's called Haven-something."

My stomach drops out. "Tophaven Management?"

"Yeah, that sounds right. You know them?"

He's looking back at me now, so I wave my hand in front of my face. "Your friend should move somewhere else. They're bad news."

"Bad managers?"

"No, like," I search for the word in English, "mafia."

He drops his voice to a whisper. "*Yakuza?*"

More like owned by, but not officially a part of, a Kubo-gumi subgroup based in Meguro-ku. Nothing big, but still enough potential trouble that his friend shouldn't be entering into any contracts with them. And close enough to the groups in Roppongi that I need to steer clear of drawing too much attention myself.

But none of that information is helpful for Noah, so I just respond with a nod.

"Okay. I will let him know." He sets the stack down by his door and reaches in his pocket for keys.

"Noah-kun." I hesitate before continuing. "Um, please don't bring this up with Eika-chan. She'd want to help, but she shouldn't really be talking to people like that either, you know?" Especially after she's already doing me a favor helping Noah-kun with the internship, we can't ask for more.

He lifts the stack back up so I can't see his face anymore. "I understand," he says.

"But you know what I can help with?" I take out my port and do a quick Mino search. Once the results pop up, I copy the phone number into a text to him, tacking on a hat emoji. "Time for some pizza. And later if you want some again, message me any time of day. I'll be happy to give them a call for you."

* * *

*(Hi, mom. I'll be over a bit later on
Saturday. The press conference got pushed
back to the afternoon } Date Hatsumi*

Mom { You're welcome to come over on Friday instead)

*(Sorry, you know I have a standing
commitment } DH*

(I'll be over tonight like usual } DH

*Mom { It's alright. The grocer from Inland offered to drop
a few things off on Wednesdays)*

(Oh. Are you sure? } DH

*Mom { No need to come all the way across town
twice a week)*

(OK, but only if you're sure } DH

* * *

The bartender looks up at the opening door and by the time I've made it to him at the bar he has set out my usual barley-distilled *shochu* on the rocks. I pick it up, and as I do, I'm flagged over by an arm at the back of the bar.

Yamada and Himura are real-deal *yakuza*—suits, tattoos, business cards with their group name and pins on their lapels that cause my glasses to suggest their website. As members of a mid-level Kubo-gumi organization, they're pretty laid back, coasting on rental income from the original property bill in the suit-clad part of Roppongi. This is the section of the ward that contains the Tower Ridge skyscraper and a few multinational corporations like Profuse. Everyone likes to keep the arrangement as professional as possible, making their jobs some of the lowest stress in the city.

Most Friday nights these two, and sometimes a few others from their immediate group, take to drinking at Bar Blue to celebrate another successful week complete. They started early tonight—it's only eight and their table is covered in discarded bottles of beer and a few feebly half-eaten dishes of fried chicken and *edamame*. Glad I had dinner before heading out tonight.

"Date," Yamada says, using my last name. "S'good you're here. Sit down, sit down."

Himura puts his arm around a third guy, one whom I've only met in passing once before. "Remember Eguchi, our little kitten?"

Their group's father-figure, Inoe Nozomu, is known for the eye-catching tiger and maple leaf tattoo that runs all the way down his back, tail curving around his left side. As a unique tribute to their boss, all of his men have included tigers in their own designs, mostly on their arms or upper shoulders. Funny how a group of xenophobes is so keen on a quintessentially Chinese symbol, though I would never say that out loud.

I set my glass down on the table and slide into the side of the curved booth next to Yamada. I've found that work clothes are the most effective at projecting 'one of the guys' as opposed to 'piece of ass,' but Himura gets handsy even with his buddies after a few.

"So, you're finally letting the little Lucky Cat out on the town?" I ask, tucking my glasses away into a case.

Yamada finds my comment hilarious and slaps the table a few times. The oldest of the three at the table by a good fifteen years, he likes to maintain a facade of solemnity during the day and quickly becomes a giggly drunk at night.

"Who's this?" Eguchi asks, sounding sleepy. In his early twenties, this kid is a pledge to their organization, and still in the period of initiation where they make him do things like clean the floors and stand outside the front door in the cold. Eguchi almost certainly doesn't have any tattoos yet since he hasn't formally sworn in. Once he does and builds up a good enough reputation for someone to connect him with a tattoo artisan, he'll follow suit to prove his manliness in the face of traditional bamboo needles. Until then, they'll make jokes at his expense. Getting to go out with the big boys drinking is quite the reward.

Himura pats him on the cheek with his free hand. "Dah-tay," he says, drawing out both syllables of my family name. "Big report with the *Nihon Times*."

"Report-er," Yamada corrects, with a slightly crisper slur. "She's good people. Makes the Civics happy, and that's good for everyone." He raises up on his hands and waves a hand at the bartender. "One more glass!"

"How many am I behind?" I ask.

Himura still has his arm around Eguchi, who is looking ready to slide under the table. "For the kitten, six. Us, eight. I think."

Shochu isn't meant to be knocked back, but I do it anyway. It's clear booze made for old men and trendsters, people who like to claim the traditional beverage has a subtlety of flavor that puts the base ingredient on display. I stumbled on it as a dumb teenager with not much money—a winner with moderate buzz for my limited pocket change. But these days I have more to do with my time, so this glass is an 8:2 ratio, heavy on the water. "That puts me at two," I say.

"Ha! One glass, one drink," Yamada declares.

I wave my hand in front of my face and let that go. "Celebrating something?"

Yamada raises his glass. "Yes! Tiger-father says we're getting a new contract!"

Fresh bottles of beer arrive at the table, along with a glass for me. Once mine is filled, I raise it in a salute to their boss and then chug it and slam the glass down on the table definitively. "Four," I say.

Yamada tries to focus his eyes and count, but eventually just nods. That's what I thought.

Himura starts pouring for the other three of us again. "To success!"

I take the bottle and fill his glass. There are two big construction projects in the pipeline for Roppongi this year, one American and one Asian company. "Are we toasting Profuse?"

"Naw, not those narrow-minded opportunists." A hand wave, and Yamada dismisses the entire North American continent. "The Mining Bank!"

I raise my glass, and we all salute the Chinese company's expansion with another deep drink. "To new opportunities!"

Hard to say without more information which of the groups is going to really benefit from the Mining Bank project, and thus which hands were most greased in the making of the deal. There are two major Kubo-gumi groups in the Roppongi area, the tiger cubs here and another working class group that focuses primarily on construction. If this bill passes, I doubt that the other group wants to be nothing more than craftsmen to build and hand off the buildings so these lords in the making can rake in the long-term profits.

And that's not counting the group that backs the Bayside Company, which is also in the Minato ward, just closer to the water. They might be tempted to move in here once they finish making their existing tenants miserable enough to move so they can buy it all out.

I wonder if the *kumicho* of the Kubo-gumi cares about the jockeying that will come from the property bill or if it's all just more money for them at the top.

Yamada proposes one more toast, this time chanting, "To tiger father!"

"Tiger father..." Eguchi leans forward and puts his cheek on the table. Since he's been kept busy with proving himself as a pledge, he probably hasn't had much of a chance to drink in the last year.

"Good night, kitten," Himura says, almost protectively, patting him on the head.

Wordlessly, I fish out a marker from my bag and slide it across the table. Himura uncaps it and writes something on Eguchi's cheek with a flourish.

Yamada can see better from his seat and flips his head back into a roaring laugh. Eventually he manages to choke out the words, "I love tiger papa."

"Nicely done," I say. "You are all going to regret this tomorrow!"

This hilarious comment sends Yamada off on another round of laughter. It goes on so long that Himura joins in by the end, more at his friend than with him.

I take another sip, smiling to myself behind the glass.

CAMERON GREEN

Misora is sitting across from me at one of the benches in the Helios damper room, prepping her workspace. A tiny frown of concentration creases her brow as she arranges tools and checks gauges. Everything set, she looks up at me, and I realize I'm staring. This is the first time in a long time that I've been genuinely nervous about making a link.

I've worked in this field for five years, more if you include the time in school, and I've pooled magic with lab-mates more times than I can count. At my old job, I almost always worked with Chuck. He's fifteen years older than me, and we never would've been friends if we'd met outside of work. But he came to my grandfather's funeral, and I know all about his divorce. Sharing magic forges a closeness that's hard to shake even after you disconnect.

"Ready?" To my surprise, Misora reaches for my hand from across the table. I haven't bothered with physical contact with a lab-mate since grad school. There's no real evidence that it boosts a magical connection, but if Misora Toyama offers you her hand, you fucking take it.

Her palm is warm against mine, her skin smooth, and I can feel the barest edge of short nails. And then I sense something else, something that isn't being picked up by any of my nerves: her magic. If Chuck was a head-on collision, Misora is...

Foreplay.

It's the first word that crosses my mind, but it fits. Is this what I feel like to her, too?

One look at her face tells me yes. Her cheeks are tinged pink in a way they weren't before, and a slow smile lifts the edges of her mouth. Damn.

Misora moves on before I do, deftly shifting some of her magic into the powerbank humming between us. As we begin to work, I realize that Misora's power isn't particularly strong, and when we run out of the first pool, she doesn't have much left to help me refill it. Is this why she prefers to collaborate with Eika? It makes sense, even as it's borderline unethical, since Eika isn't a certified engineer. But while her reservoir appears shallow, Misora can do things I've never seen before.

As I hold Misora's hand in my right, my left is touching the Syphon panel on the powerbank, because when it comes to objects, you do need physical contact. Or, at least, that's been true for everyone I've ever known. But not Misora—I can hear her free hand moving as she adjusts the powerbank or jots down a note, yet her progress on the work is never paused.

There's so much I want to ask her, but I don't dare disturb her concentration. Finally, she disengages, looking remarkably fresh. "How did you do that?" I ask.

"Do what?"

"All of that. Without touching the Syphon."

"It isn't difficult."

When she sees this doesn't satisfy me, she tilts her head. "Think about it for a moment. Magic—it's a genetic ability. Why would we need Syphon to use something that exists inside ourselves?"

"Because we do. We all need Syphon to be able to do anything with it."

"Do we?"

I can tell I'm not going to get further, so I change tacks. "But you think handholding helps for pooling power?"

She laughs. "Certainly not. That's a superstition."

* * *

It's 7:30, and I have to be in Nihombashi by eight. I keep checking the door to the damper room, hoping Misora will emerge soon. No leaving before the boss does in Japan. Sugihara and Matsuda are fidgeting, too.

"Cameron-san, how was your day?" I look up to see Misora and Eika finally leaving the lab. Eika wends her way over to my desk, but Misora offers only a nod before heading to the elevators. That stings. It's been a few weeks since we first shared magic, and every time we do, there's that same electricity between us, yet nothing's happened. I should probably give up and try to meet someone on Ignight, but—

"Fine," I say as I pack up my stuff. "You?"

"I stopped in this afternoon to do a little work and see if Misora wanted to go to karaoke with me and our friend Hatsumi. She has plans with Taehyun, though."

My least favorite topic. "Karaoke sounds fun," I lie. We're at the elevators now, but Misora has already disappeared.

"You're welcome to come along."

"Wish I could," I say—another lie—"but I'm having dinner with my sister and her husband."

"It's augmented reality karaoke, way more fun than dinner. And," Eika adds with a sly smile, "Hatsumi is single right now..."

"I really can't. They're taking me out for my birthday," I share reluctantly.

"I didn't know it was your birthday! It wasn't on MinoSo," she accuses, mouth screwing into a little moue.

My Minotaur Social profile has my name, job title, and a photo. Calling it minimalist would ascribe more intent than was ever there. I shrug.

"We'll have to have a party," she decides. The doors to the elevator open to the main lobby. A black car is waiting under the granite portico outside. As Eika and I leave our elevator, the one next to us glides open, and Misora steps out. She has changed into fitted pants and a black trench, her height jacked up about four inches by wicked-looking heels. She starts to stride toward the exit, but Eika waves her over. "Mi-chan!"

Not hiding her impatience, Misora gestures at the car outside.

"He's waiting for me."

Eika ignores this. "Today is Cameron-san's birthday!"

"Is that so?"

"So, we're throwing him a party next week. Right?"

Misora looks over at me again, amusement surfacing in shimmering eyes and a tiny twitch at the edge of her mouth. "Absolutely," she replies, speaking to Eika but gaze still on me. My chest feels tight yet light, like she's breathed helium into my lungs with a mere look. Even supervised by Eika and god knows who else, the prospect of spending non-work time with Misora is immensely appealing.

"Good," Eika says. "Can we use the room at One Eleven? I'll do the rest."

"Probably." Before she turns to leave, Misora gives me a curt nod. "Happy birthday." As she exits the lobby, the back door of the waiting car swings open, and a black-haired man hops out to hold it for her. When he looks up, though, I see he's not Taehyun after all. This man is also about my age, but Japanese, and wearing a leather moto jacket. The bottom edge of a sleeve tattoo is just visible on the arm that's holding the door.

"Watanabe Hideki," Eika mutters under her breath, her expression clouding over.

"Who?" I ask. It's surprising to see ink on any friend of Misora's. Tattoos are historically reserved for the *yakuza*, although I've read that younger Japanese are more open-minded.

"Just an old friend," Eika replies smoothly, her face neutral again. "Let me know if there's anyone you want to invite to the party, okay?"

Eika and Misora comprise nearly half the people I know in Tokyo. No way am I dragging Vanessa and Drew to whatever this is going to be, but—wait, I do have someone. I suppress a chuckle.

"Sure," I say. "My neighbor. I'll text you his info."

FUJIWARA EIKA

Archival footage: DBW advertisement 4 (15-second clip)

Fujiwara Eika splashes water on her face and then stares into the camera's close-up for a moment, patting her own cheek.

Cut to a shot of her bare feet as she sets a scale down on the floor in front of her. The focus remains on her bare legs as she steps onto the scale. Suddenly, two yellow fabric-clad feet step into the frame, and she is lifted up into the air so only her toes are touching the scale.

Smash cut to Eika, wearing a purple silk robe, being held up in the air by a round person-sized lemon. She is smiling as she looks down at the scale.

Yellow title card that reads "Kinoshita Diet Breakfast Water."

* * *

"We've got to stop for today, Eika-chan. Taehyun will be here soon, and there are probably several people out there"—Misora gestures toward the workspace outside the damper room—"burning holes through the wall with their eyes."

I check my watch, horrified when I see that it's after seven. Time seems like it moves faster in this room than anywhere else. "Your poor team, I—"

"They're paid well," Misora cuts me off. "If they don't like it here, they can find something else."

At minimum, I know that's not true for one member of her staff, but I nod. The truth is, I'm glad Misora and I were able to get so much done today. Now that we have Cameron laying the groundwork for the power structure thing, Misora and I have been able to get a lot accomplished. Which reminds me—"Mi-chan, I'd like us to have this ready in time for Syphon Expo XIV."

"What?" Misora's head snaps up now, attention diverted from the tools she was putting away.

"I think we can do it. I had Noah register us for a booth."

Misora doesn't say anything at first, her face neutral, but I know her compressed lips mean she's thinking at a furious pace. When she finally speaks, her voice has an arctic tinge. "On behalf of Helios or Replenish?"

"Replenish! I would never assume Helios—"

"But you did." She removes her lab lenses and rubs her index fingers along the bridge of her nose as if to erase the headache I've generated. "Our agreement is clear. Helios is giving you my time, and this space, and allowing you to dictate the broad mission of our project, but the rights are ours. And that includes all decisions to announce or market any products."

"I'm sorry, I am," I say. And I mean it. I hate putting her in this position, and I hate that she looks, in this moment, not just angry but exhausted. "The vultures are circling, Mi-chan. I thought that if I gave the FHI board a concrete date, like Syphon Expo, then it keeps us alive a little longer."

"Yes, they'll want to see a return on their investment," Misora says with a sigh. "How much was the entry fee?"

More than my little non-profit could afford, but the vintage ostrich Birkin I listed for resale yesterday should just cover it. "It's handled. Let's free your team before they starve."

* * *

The karaoke room is small, mostly just a booth with bright green walls and table.

"So, these are the goggles?" Ha-chan asks, swapping out the glasses she normally wears for a pair from the table. It's good she wears contacts too or she wouldn't be able to focus with the non-prescription lenses provided by the karaoke place. Yet another example of inaccessibility these days.

"It looks like it," I say, passing pairs off to the other two.

Noah-kun puts them on and drops his hands to the table. "Whoa. This is cool."

I don my pair, and immediately the walls and table appear to fall away in favor of a field of stars on a background of black and blue, flowing like water past us. Because this is augmented reality, I can see the others through the clear plastic of the lenses while everything else is masked by new components that are brighter and sharper than the reality they cover. A comet comes flying in next to us, sparks flying off, before veering away into the cobalt distance.

Haru looks around once and then focuses on the table that now looks like an asteroid, brushing his hand over the surface. He's not in a suit today, and the lack of a jacket or tie over his unbuttoned shirt collar only adds to his rakish look. "Is this where they're keeping the drink menu?"

The table looks like it's become stone carved into a menu. Opening the drinks list causes three-dimensional beverages with animated bubbles and foam running down the sides of the glass to unfold from the surface. Text descriptions float above each like balloons linked by strings.

"What refreshments should we order?" I ask.

Ha-chan barely looks at the list before asking for barley *shochu* on the rocks. I would love to order *umeshu*, but since I have so many shoots scheduled in the next few weeks, I pick a lemon and *shochu* instead. Scrolling through the menu on his side, Noah asks for a mug of beer.

Waving his hand in the air dismissively at that request, Haru says, "Shots and a pitcher."

We also select some *edamame* and *galbi*—it's too bad Taehyun couldn't join us tonight.

As my assistant, Noah starts to get up to call in our order, but Hatsumi stops him. "Noah-kun, you're not on the clock."

"It's not a problem," he insists politely.

I scoot out of the booth to make the call myself, and Hatsumi says, "Right now, you're our guest. And even at the office, if someone works you too hard, remember that I have some pull with the boss."

Noah is smiling but shakes his head, dark curls bobbing.

"Any time you can, take the win," Haru suggests.

When I sit again, I see Hatsumi has already started tossing songs into the queue. Classic and modern, the songs are all fast-paced, and half require screaming. I insert a song at the start of the list, and she immediately groans. Haru makes a noise in his throat that indicates he agrees, but as a more general statement.

"It's something we can all sing," I say cheerfully. "Noah-kun, do you have any songs you'd like to add?"

He brightens. "English okay?"

We all speak at least some, so I give him a nod, just as a *kaiju* rides in on a meteor to start the song I added.

Our order arrives mid-song, and Noah sets down his microphone to answer the door, then passes the drinks around. Haru downs his shot immediately, followed by a long drink of his beer, while Ha-chan takes a sip from her glass between singing the lyrics of "Monster Party" like it's her power ballad.

As we reach the last chorus, Haru pulls the glasses off and ducks out for the bathroom. I know he has a hard time with small spaces like this, both the room and the glasses, but I don't want to embarrass him by asking if he's okay.

A few more songs, and Haru hasn't returned. Noah excuses himself, leaving me and Hatsumi alone.

Hatsumi pauses the song queue. "What's with Johjima-san? He's been gone for a while."

"Sometimes he needs to take a break. It's hard for him, being with too many people in a small room like this."

"As opposed to what he's used to, swanning around the halls of the imperial palace?" Hatsumi asks with a snort.

"Ha-chan," I scold. "He's never been to the imperial palace."

"Could've fooled me," she replies. "I think he's mentioned that he's a distant relative of the emperor every single time I've seen him."

I fidget with my glass, eager to change the subject before Haru and Noah return. "Do you have plans next Thursday?"

Hatsumi narrows her eyes at me. "Depends on why."

"A birthday party," I say around a sip of *shochu*.

She makes a face. "Don't tell me this is for that American guy you met?"

"Please come!" I set my glass down and clap my hands together in a prayer gesture.

"I don't know what kind of present to get for a stranger," she says as the door opens to reveal both of the men. "Noah-kun, what birthday gift should I get for an American?"

He steps back into the room, grinning. "You could always get him a cowboy hat."

Something about that suggestion makes Ha-chan smile. "You and hats."

"Maybe it's because you are my favorite cousin, HATS-umi-san," he says, deliberately mispronouncing her name to make the English pun.

Haru is a few seconds behind but catches the door before it swings all the way shut. Rather than entering, he leans against the doorway, the reflected light from the room tinting the color of his face green. From here, I can smell the smoke on his clothes.

"Haru, you'll come to the party, right? Thursday night."

He shrugs in a way that shows he doesn't care either way. "Sure."

Right then, I realize I've invited everyone here except one. "You can come too, Noah-kun, if you want."

Noah is taking a drink of beer and sets it down to wave two hands in front of his face. "Sorry, I already have plans."

Hatsumi-chan leans forward and puts her forehead on the table for a moment. "Lucky you, Noah-kun."

"What are you dragging me to?" Haru asks, suddenly suspicious.

I smile at him. "Trust me! You'll have fun."

"Speaking of which, let's get out of here," Haru says. "There's a party at Marquis."

I know what he's really asking, and I wouldn't mind on any other day, but... "Sorry, I have to get up early tomorrow."

He scoffs at this, then looks over at Hatsumi. "Remember when Eika-chan used to be fun?" he asks.

"She still is," Hatsumi snaps, and I feel a flush of gratitude.

"Am I invited?" Noah interjects, inviting himself.

Haru looks taken aback for a second, and then shrugs. "Sure, why not."

Hatsumi and I glance at each other, managing to keep straight faces. Haru pats Noah on the shoulder and leads him down the hallway. "So, tell me, have you tried raw horse?"

"Johjima-san, you better bring my cousin back in one piece," Hatsumi calls after them. "No dents. No dings."

We make our own way out to pay. As we do, I have one more question for her. "Ha-chan, I've been trying to email people at the Fujiwara Center for Applied Magic to see if anyone is looking into links between the environment and magic potential, but they aren't answering. Any ideas of something I could say that would help?"

"Easy," she says, pressing the button for the elevator. "Go down in person. Then they have to talk to you, right?"

* * *

It's not until Tuesday that Noah is scheduled to work again, so he comes in looking as bright and energetic as usual.

Once he's situated at his desk, I turn my chair and ask through the open doorway, "How was the evening out with Haru?"

"Um," Noah says, his face turning bright red, "so, 'raw horse' wasn't a food."

The implication comes through immediately, and I realize I'm moving my lips, but no words are coming out. Finally, I say, "Maybe don't tell Hatsumi-chan." After a second more, I add, "Did you have fun?"

He nods once, chuckling nervously. "It's a story I can tell for years to come, right? That I partied in Japan with a relative of the Emperor."

I smother a grin behind my hand. Hatsumi was right: Haru does always work that into a conversation.

I get Noah started on updating our quarterly marketing budget, which leaves me with a short time to finalize some arrangements for Cameron-san's party. The menu is set, but I look over the list again and cross-check that there are enough servings for the guest count. There's nothing like running out of refreshments to ruin a celebration.

Oh, right—I've been meaning to call and invite his friend. Where was the message with his number?

I find it in my notes file, right under the reminder to pay the Replenish stationery invoice. I forward that on to Noah, and tap connect on the number. As the call rings through, a response message notification pops up: "Already done!" and a thumbs up emoji.

Before I can do more, the call connects to show a man with *kabocha*-colored hair and a flat expression. "Yeah."

"Good afternoon!" I say. "I'm—"

"—Fujiwara Eika." His expression turns skeptical. "Or at least you look like her."

I'm not surprised to be recognized, but usually people still let me say it. "Yes, both of those things are true," I respond lightly. "Am I speaking with Asagawa Kenji?"

"Did I win a contest or something?"

I'm not really sure why someone like Cameron-san would want to spend time with someone like this. But I guess that's not my decision, is it?

"Well, if you are Asagawa Kenji," I let it shade my tone that I'm only giving that a fifty-fifty chance of being true, "I'm calling to invite you to a birthday party for Green-san."

"Did he win a contest?" He seems very pleased with himself for being so difficult.

For my part, I notice that I'm fidgeting with my earring, the sapphire ones shaped like a teardrop, when my manager has been pestering me to stop.

I put my free hand in my lap and continue. "The party will be on Thursday evening. It's just a small group of friends. We hope that you can join us to celebrate."

"Sure."

On my port, I select the invitation image that I made earlier and send it to him. It's a cartoon penguin, which seems almost maliciously cheery in this context. "If you give me your address, I'll send you a paper—"

"No," he says.

Okay, then. I flash him my brightest smile and add, "Please don't forget to bring a present!"

"Yeah, I got it." This time his expression seems to be one of genuine amusement, just before he disconnects.

The screen transitions back to the notes app, and I stare at the list for a second. The theme I set is a faded cream, but it's getting a little boring to use all the time. Maybe I should switch it.

Oh, right, the stationery invoice. I turn in my chair again and ask, "Noah-kun, how many times have I sent that reminder to you?"

There's a chuckle from the other room. "Three, I think?"

"Okay, I better delete this note before I send it again," I say, and do it. "We haven't gotten an email back from Yokoyama-sensei?"

"Not yet."

My schedule is a mess right now between the Denali project, TV and advertising, and now this party. But it looks like Hatsumi might be right: If I want more on the science, I am going to need to find time to visit the Fujiwara Center in person.

MEME EXPLAINER DATABASE ENTRY:
FRUIT MAN

About

Fruit Man is a Pixelpush meme using a series of three interlinked images featuring an anonymous costumed actor in an apple costume (Fruit Man) and Japanese celebrity Eika Fujiwara shopping for Fuji apples. The first image shows Fujiwara holding up an apple and smiling, the second image shows the apple being added to an overflowing basket of other apples in the hands of Fruit Man, the third image shows a grocery store employee looking on in surprise. The meme is often used with text overlays to communicate self-satisfaction.

Origin

Mino user [rabbitmauve_42] first posted screenshots from a series of Japanese commercials for the product Diet Breakfast Water with the comment, "I wanna be a fruitman." Mino user [walkingalong] reposted this image with the words "me with candy" added to the second image. This was further edited by [burgersburgersburglers] to add the text "my mom" over the first image, and "my older sister" over the third image. This version of the meme was reposted over 700,000 times in two weeks.

Spread

After the initial popularity, the Fruit Man meme was reduced to a version with only the first and second images, most often with text added to a version of the first image to indicate a helpful person and the second image to indicate either pleasure with the gifts or gluttony. A top ten list of Fruit Man memes included egg rolls at a buffet, songs by artist Tallahassee Jones, and flowers in the month of April.

Alternatives

In some cases, the apples and Fruit Man are covered with images instead of text, such as basketballs or pizza. Versions of the meme are also used to indicate a negative reaction to the gift, such as a teacher giving homework with the basket being filled with books and Fruit Man remaining unchanged as a reference to the practice of giving apples to teachers.

CAMERON GREEN

The first floor of One Eleven Park is almost entirely a large lobby. A velvet-roped switchback leads to a podium with a cheery hostess who, based on reservation type, directs people to the correct elevator. Each glass-backed elevator is operated by yet another uniformed young woman, because Japan is aiming, apparently, for full adult employment. I'm almost to the front of the queue when I feel a hand on my arm.

Misora.

"No need to wait in line, birthday boy." She's wearing a black dress, long-sleeved yet very short, and her normally straight hair is in loose waves, her eyes dark-lined. It's only Thursday, but Misora is a Saturday night.

She's also alone. Belated happy birthday to me.

I tilt the end post to lower the velvet rope and step over to the other side. We've attracted attention, and I hear someone whisper Misora's name. A teen girl pulls out her port for a not-so-stealthy snap.

"Follow me." Misora is carrying a large Takashimaya shopping bag over one wrist, but she tucks her free hand in my elbow, steering me to the lone unmanned elevator and opening the doors with an app on her port. She chooses the 57th floor. As the elevator whirrs gently into motion, we gaze out over the Milky Way of Tokyo's twinkling lights, Misora's hand still nestled in the crook of my arm.

"Cameron." There's no work-appropriate "-san" at the end, only my first name, as if we're something more.

I look down, meeting her gaze, and the temperature of her expression drops the bottom out of my stomach. The elevator settles, indicating we've reached our destination. But before the doors can open more than an inch, Misora taps something on her port, and they wobble shut again.

She doesn't say anything else, just keeps looking up at me, hollowing me out with her eyes. This is such an obvious invitation. Praying I'm not reading her wrong, I answer it, lowering my lips to find hers.

The kiss is tense and hungry, an uncoiling of something we've each held tight for weeks. A small voice in the back of my mind has questions: why here? Why tonight? Then Misora drops the shopping bag and curves her body fully into mine, and rational thought stops.

"Can we skip the party?" I whisper in her ear as I move my mouth to her neck.

"Mmm," she breathes, sounding tempted. "You'd break Eika's heart." A long pause, then: "How about an after party?"

God, yes. I return to her mouth, knowing we should stop before this goes too far, yet sincerely uninterested in doing so. The tease of Misora's tongue against mine suggests she's similarly disinclined.

With a mechanical thunk, the elevator doors open. I back away from Misora, and she pretends to brush some lint off my shirt, but we're comically late. A short-haired woman is standing in the doorway. She grins at Misora. "Eika sent me to find Green-san, but based on the description, it looks like you found him first."

"This is Date Hatsumi," Misora says as we exit the elevator. Her hair is no longer perfectly in place, and the hem of her skirt has ridden up on one side. I've never seen her disheveled like this before, and knowing that I'm the cause is hot as hell. Disappointed as I am to have been interrupted, I'm also feeling pretty pleased with myself.

"Happy birthday." Hatsumi squints up at my face. "Nice lipstick."

I run the back of my hand across my mouth, and sure enough, it comes away with a dark red smear. "Uh, thanks."

"Eika and Johjima Haru are already here," Hatsumi says, leading us across a smaller version of the downstairs lobby. "Have you been here before, Green-san?"

"No, but I read online it's a rotating restaurant." She has my eternal gratitude for this diversion.

"Yeah, the top two floors revolve—downstairs on the 56th there's a restaurant, Ultraviolet 111. Up here they have a bunch of private banquet rooms."

Misora's port buzzes, and she hands the Takashimaya bag to Hatsumi. "I have to answer this."

"She always does," Hatsumi says, more to herself than to me.

The Founder's Room is small but opulent in a minimalist way, black granite and glass. Eika has done her best, though, to obscure the high end finishes with streamers, giant balloons, and a penguin ice sculpture that's melting onto the bar next to an overwrought cake.

"Oh, good, you found him," Eika says as we enter. She's behind the bar, lining up shot glasses. A skinny man—her date? Hatsumi's?—is slouched on one of the stools. He's wearing some kind of fancy tracksuit, but his expression is sour, like he just smelled something rancid.

"Misora found him," Hatsumi corrects, pulling an orange gift-wrapped box out of the Takashimaya bag.

"Gifts over there. What do you mean? Where is Mi-chan?"

"Phone call," Eika and Hatsumi both say, laughing as Eika answers her own question. Hatsumi leans over the bar, murmuring for a moment in Eika's ear.

"Oooh," Eika breathes. She gives me an amused little smile. "I'll want to know more about how that happened."

My skin still tingles from Misora's touch, and I can't get her suggestion off my mind. But she hasn't so much as glanced at me since we were interrupted, and it's already starting to feel like I imagined the whole thing. I look out at the corridor, where Misora is taking her call. Slowly, she rotates out of sight. "You and me both."

Eika's about to follow up when Asagawa walks in. She greets him and introduces us to her maybe-date, but he's more interested in his drink.

"Didn't think you'd actually come," I say to Asagawa. I'm glad to see him—he's the only person here not from Misora's orbit.

He gives me a sharp look. "After you gave out my phone number, be glad I only brought you this cord instead of the whole computer," he says, gesturing with the small brown paper bag in his hand.

"Where I'm from, gifts are usually a surprise to the recipient."

Asagawa shrugs and takes a sip of his drink. Looking confused, Eika relieves him of his "gift" and takes it over to the table with the others.

Asagawa's gaze follows her as she goes. "How do you know all these people, anyway?"

"Through Eika."

He narrows his eyes at me over the rim of his beer. "Didn't know you were collecting Kinoshita Points, let alone enough to win a party."

"What can I say, this is the body Diet Breakfast Water built," I reply, deadpan, with a gesture down at myself.

"From now on, I'll bring my empty bottles to your pl—" He's cut short by a yelp of laughter from the other end of the bar, where Eika and Hatsumi are attempting to pour vodka through a chute in the ice sculpture. Liquid splashes off the granite and onto the lap of Eika's date, who manages to look even more sullen.

Asagawa raises an eyebrow at me, and I shrug, feeling a little defensive on Eika's behalf. It's nice of her to want to do this for me, even if it is a bit awkward, and she's the reason I have my job, too.

"What?" I say, responding to the clear disdain in the arch of his brow. "She's a good person, and she's doing a lot to help people like—" I stop myself before I blurt "people like you," but Asagawa's downslope situation has been pretty hard to miss. I have never seen someone with so many back-up ports and chargers.

"People like?"

I indicate him with a vague hand, dropping my voice. "You know. The, er... less magical."

"If you're going to limit 'magical' to what you can do with a port."

I'm not touching that one. "Whatever you say."

My port vibrates in my pocket.

Misora Toyama { I didn't know. It's not what it will look like.)

What does that mean?

PARK TAEHYUN

Archival footage: Take Good Care of the Fridge
(1-minute clip)

A panel of minor celebrities is clustered around a large U-shaped table in a television studio. On a giant screen in front of them, overenthusiastic host Kim Changwook is in an elegantly appointed kitchen. Next to him stands Park Taehyun, titular star of the brand-new breakaway hit Flower Boy Ramyeon Chef.

Taehyun is dressed simply but stylishly, hands in his pockets. He flashes the camera a high-beam smile, and little animated stars appear on the screen, twinkling around his angular face. One of the actresses on the panel makes an elaborate show of fanning herself with a manicured hand.

"We're broadcasting today from Tokyo, where Park Taehyun resides part-time. Park Taehyun! Are you ready for us to take! Good! Care! Of your fridge?"

"Yes, please, go ahead." Taehyun gestures toward a large Subzero refrigerator, inviting Changwook to open it.

Changwook starts rifling through the vegetable drawer. As he holds up items, he shouts their names, and the words pop up on the screen in neon hangeul *text: "Broccoli! Cabbage! Eggplaaaaaaant!"*

"Oh, dear," Changwook says, looking at the disarray he's

made of the vegetables. "I can't seem to get it all back in there!"

Taehyun turns to assist with repacking the drawer, bending to tuck carrots into the back, and the camera zooms in none-too-subtly on his ringspun denim-clad backside. The women on the panel shriek and giggle, clapping their hands in delight, while the men unleash exaggerated groans. One reaches over to shield the eyes of the woman next to him.

"Oh, now what's this?" Changwook asks, grabbing a sealed container from one of the top shelves. He gives Taehyun a sly look as he opens it just a hair, then coughs at the odor coming out from under the lid. A clown-like sound effect. "Is this natto?*"*

"Yes, fermented soybeans. Not that different from cheonggukjang, *except that it's not eaten as a stew."*

Changwook looks directly into the camera, one eyebrow raised. "Your Japanese girlfriend is making you so exotic!"

Taehyun chuckles, but his smile doesn't reach his eyes.

* * *

"Take fifteen," the director tells me. "We'll reset and go again."

Shivering, I shrug into the robe offered by Mayumi, my Japanese assistant. This ad is for the newest Hitachi Bigflow air conditioner, and they're taking their AC very seriously on set. "You missed a call," she says, removing an errant feather from my hair.

I pull my port from the pocket of the robe. *Missed call, Fujiwara Eika.*

I'm on set right now, I write as I devour a ham and egg salad sandwich. This is day two of a shoot that was supposed to take 1.5 days, but we've stretched well past lunch. I miss the straightforwardness of the ads I do for JeJuice at home. Show up, take my shirt off, drink orange juice, smile at the camera.

Nothing is ever that easy in Japan.

Fujiwara Eika { Wanna come to a party on Thursday?)

That depends. Eika doesn't exactly party the way she did back when I first met Misora. She better not be angling for an endorsement or a donation. If I'm going to a party, I want to enjoy it as myself, not perform as Park Taehyun.

> *(An actual party, or a gala for some foundation? } Park Taehyun*

FE { A birthday party!)

> *(For...? } PT*

FE { A new friend who just moved here and doesn't know anyone [pleading kitty cat animation])

FE { Mi-chan already said yes)

> *(So this was decided before you even called me, then } PT*

She replies with a V-for-victory emoji, then a Minotaur Digivite arrives on my screen with the details. The Founder's Room at One Eleven—that's all Misora. She hasn't hosted a private party there in ages. Maybe this won't be half bad.

"Hey, Mayumi," I gesture her over. "Think you can get me some maddy before Thursday night?"

* * *

Wherever Mayu got this, it's good stuff. I down one minitab before leaving her apartment, and another in the car on my way to Shinjuku. Molly's sweet baby sister, with her easy high and gentle comedown, is just what I needed.

Misora wasn't home when I stopped by to change. I've barely seen her the last few days, which can only mean one thing: new project. I'm surprised she has time for some rando's birthday party. I tap her name and wait as the call rings through.

"Yeah?" She sounds distracted—she must still be at work.

"I'm about five minutes out. Where are you, the lab?"

"Five minutes—what?" Misora stumbles over the words, almost as if she doesn't understand me. She gets this way sometimes when you interrupt her concentration, like she's emerging from a fog. "No, I'm at One Eleven. Eika's having a party."

"I know," I say. "I'm five minutes away. Where do you want to meet me?"

A puff of exasperated air against the microphone. "Back door. Wild Honey is playing at the Ultraviolet tonight, do not come in the front."

As promised, Misora is waiting in the back doorway, a silhouette backlit by the fluorescent glow spilling out into the alley. She has her port held up near her face like a compact, using the front camera for guidance as she adds a swipe of fresh lipstick. While Misora is always impeccably pulled together, visible makeup is a rare detail. I can't help but be pleased that she made the effort.

The feeling doesn't last. Once we're in the elevator, she ignores me in favor of tapping a message into her port. "Who is this party for, again?" I ask. "All Eika told me was that you agreed we'd come."

"Did she?" This revelation creases Misora's brow into a scowl. "An American. He's a new hire in my lab. Eika found him at some gala thing at Todai—you know, for the center her family funded. He was pushed out of his company by that magic ban."

"Their loss, your gain," I say. Shit. This has to be the guy who saw me with Soojin. Well, better to know in advance. I've done a bit of improv, but I'd much rather have the script first.

I pull out the maddy tabs that I've slipped into a silver cigarette case. It's a sweet little high, but it spikes and ebbs like sugar, too. I already feel the bump from the car fading away, and I can tell I'm going to need it. More out of polite habit than anything, I offer it to Misora first.

She recoils, declining with an imperious shake of the head. Of course. Her highness could get daddy's pure stuff if she wanted, she won't sully herself with what I have. Fortunately, I've got Miss Maddy. Any irritation I'd feel slides off the fresh hit like a rivulet of rain.

Misora has reserved the Founder's Room tonight, a space that holds just a single round booth and, in spite of its small size, a black granite bar topped off with row upon row of glossy top-shelf liquor. I can't help myself; I will always do the math on these kinds of things. It has to be worth at least a quarter million Korean *won*. All drinkable, and for a table that can't seat more than eight.

Eika is behind the bar, pouring clear liquor of some kind through a chute carved into a ridiculous penguin ice sculpture, and Hatsumi is holding glasses under the penguin's spout-slash-beak. Given that they're both on the discernible side of sloshed, it's an impressive display of coordination. A bony twerp I vaguely recognize is sulking next to Hatsumi on a bar stool, and a tall white guy—sure enough, the one from Seoul—is on the other side of the room talking to some crimson-haired street punk.

Arm slung around Misora's waist, I instinctively pull her a little closer, as if she can ward off the bullshit to come. "Tae-kun, I was worried you weren't going to make it!" Eika chirps. "This is Haru. No last names tonight, we're going American style for our guest of honor."

Skinny offers a seated half-bow, causing Misora to dig her fingertips into my leg. She's not a fan of Eika's date. As he pushes his hair out of his eyes, I add the name to the face and realize where I know him from: an illegal mahjong game Ryuya took me to a few months ago. Johjima Haru is kind of a nothing person—and absolute trash at mahjong—but his father's a pharma bigshot and his mother claims to be a distant cousin of the emperor. The Johjima family might be from Eika's social tier, but they're not her caliber. I'm willing to cut him some slack on the attitude, though. Foreigner birthday party is not how I want to spend my evening, either.

"Where's your plus one?" I ask Hatsumi.

She cocks her head in the direction of the redheaded punk.

"Seriously?"

Hatsumi laughs. "No, he's here with the *gaijin*."

"As his date?"

A long pause as Hatsumi looks over at Misora and smirks. "If that was the intention, one of them is going to be disappointed." Misora's mouth tightens into a thin line, but she doesn't comment. There's some subtext here that's obviously not meant for me.

The American and his non-date make their way over to us, and I turn on my best feral smile. "I don't think we've met," I say, daring him to disagree. "I'm Taehyun."

"Haven't we?" he says. "It seems like it. Must be all the billboards I saw for your show when I was in Korea last month."

Misora's been distant lately, and I assumed it was work, but maybe he said something to her. She doesn't get jealous, but she also doesn't like having her rules broken.

"Must be," I reply. Game on, asshole.

Eika raises one of the filled glasses, slopping vodka onto the bar. "Thanks for coming out tonight, everyone. Happy birthday, Cameron-san!" We all clink our glasses in a celebratory *kanpai*, some more enthusiastically than others, then make our way over to the sole table, which Eika has piled high with food.

"I thought Cameron was a girl's name," I pretend to idly muse as I slide into the booth next to Misora. "There was that one model."

Irritatingly, he manages to keep cool. "It can be, but it's also a family name. My father's side is part Scottish, and my grandmother's maiden name was Cameron. I'm named for that."

"What I'm hearing, then, is that it's a girl's name."

I feel the pressing bite of Misora's fingertips on my thigh again, this time under the table. Eika tilts her head at me, expression sad, and I feel a pang of shame. I'm dumping on her party.

"Gender neutral, just like Haru," Eika observes lightly, always the one to repair the mood. She switches gears. "Let's play a drinking game! Cameron-san, can you teach us any American ones?"

He thinks for a moment, then explains, in Japanese that I have to admit is better than mine, a game that involves making a factual statement about something you've never done. If others have done it, they have to drink. Clearly the Americans have not perfected the art of the drinking game; I would much rather play a Korean one like

Nunchi or 31.

I don't catch his first example, but whatever it was, Eika and Hatsumi both drink.

"Okay, got it," Eika says. "I'll go next." She thinks for a moment, then fixes on Misora. "Never have I ever brought two boys to the same party."

I look from Misora to the American. He seems darkly amused, but her nostrils have flared in barely suppressed anger.

Is my girlfriend screwing this guy? A hot flush climbs up my neck. Misora and I don't always play well together, but having me come to her side piece's birthday party is too far.

Without breaking eye contact with Eika, Misora reaches for her glass. Instead of picking it up, though, she slides it over to Hatsumi, who drinks. Huh.

"It only happened the once," Hatsumi says, mock-defensive. "Let's see. Never have I ever... kissed someone in the One Eleven elevator."

Japanese salarymen use drunkenness as a way to criticize their bosses and have all be forgiven the next day. It's clear Eika and Hatsumi are using the same cultural loophole to double-team Misora, and they're too intoxicated to notice the signs of her genuine anger.

The American, for his part, has picked up his glass. Looking straight at Misora, he downs the whole thing.

This party is turning into a cluster. I pull out the silver case and pop a tab. Instant glow.

"Ooh, share," Eika says, holding out a greedy hand. Reluctantly, I hand it over, and Haru takes a dose, too. It pisses me off to give my stash to these two who could so easily get their own. Money practically oozes out their pores.

Haru offers the case to Hatsumi, but she declines, as do the foreigner and his friend—as if they're even welcome to it. The mood is weird now, with Misora fuming, Eika, Haru and I freshly buzzed, and the others awkward. Not that Maddy and I have any fucks to give.

"Cameron-san, open some presents," Eika demands. "That's what you do in America, right?"

Hatsumi grabs some boxes off the bar and drops them on the table.

My "gift," a download code for the first season of *FBRC* that I hastily jammed into one of Misora's monogrammed envelopes, is on top, and he reaches for it first. I suppress a wild urge to burst out laughing.

As a group, we've assembled such a bizarre collection of gifts that I start to wonder if I've taken something much stronger than maddy. Hatsumi bought him a cowboy hat, explaining that she thought he might not have had room in his luggage to pack his, and his friend—I catch Eika calling him Kenji—gives him some kind of electronics cord. They're both more amused by that than seems reasonable.

There's one gift left, and it can only be from Misora. As soon as I see the signature orange box and brown ribbon, whatever tension that wasn't already smoothed over by the maddy ebbs away. Instead of buying him something personal, Misora sent Nozomi to Hermès. The wild laughter bubbles up again.

"Thank you," he says to her dully as he looks at the crisp shirt and coordinating tie and pocket square. Misora spent a small fortune to telegraph that he doesn't matter. I wonder if she tried too hard and succeeded too well.

There's a lull as the American gets up to set his gift haul on the bar. Eika, rather giddy now, sits herself up on the back of the booth to whisper to Misora over the top of Haru's head, and Hatsumi slides into the foreigner's vacant spot to talk up his friend. Anything to avoid me, I guess—she has always seemed immune to my many considerable charms.

Left to myself, I drape my arm behind Misora's shoulders, casually letting my hand dangle the barest millimeter above the curve of her breast. She ignores me as I eavesdrop on Eika's attempts to grill her about the foreigner. Misora, unfortunately, is far too sober to give up anything illuminating, so I shift my attention to Hatsumi and Kenji. He might not be her date, but their vibe is flirtatious. It sounds like they're setting up a time to meet. Now a chuckle does burst forth—it's the American's party, and he's the only one here alone.

At the sound, Misora turns to look at me, making eye contact for the first time since the elevator. Before she can say anything, though, the world shudders, and a cacophony rises around us as hundred-thousand-*won* bottles of gin, whisky, tequila, and rum plummet from their shelves, shattering on the granite bar top. Misora ducks down under the table, partially pulling me with her, and Eika tumbles off the back of the booth, spilling into Kenji's lap.

"Oh, an earthquake," Haru says dopily. The maddy seems to have hit him hard. I would've expected a higher tolerance.

"Sorry," Eika says to Kenji with a giggle. "Anything broken?"

"No critical hit," he mutters. Eika is just righting herself when the shaking begins again, hard and irregular.

This one feels like it lasts forever. Then, with a violent crackle, the lights go out, and the slow rotation of the building shudders to a halt.

"Is it over?" I ask. Korea doesn't get nearly as many earthquakes, so even after a few years of living in Japan part-time, they're still a novelty.

Turning on her portlight, Hatsumi gets up from the booth and starts walking over to the windows, glass squeaking as it grinds between her shoes and the liquor-soaked carpet.

"Ouch! Goddamn it."

"Ha-chan?" Eika calls. "Are you alright?"

"Yeah. Just stubbed my toe on... the ice penguin, I think." She reaches the window, and I realize her outline is visible only because of tonight's full moon. Tokyo, or at least the part we were facing when the rotation stopped, has gone black.

We all slide out of the booth and flutter, moth-like, toward the minimal light. "Shit," I hear someone—Kenji?—say as he gets his first look. It's eerie: the traffic on the streets far below has mostly stopped, and the headlights of the cars fifty-seven floors below us are the only things visible. Everything else is dark and still.

I check my port: *NO SIGNAL*. "Towers are down, too." As soon as I say this, though, Hatsumi's port crackles to life:

"...magnitude earthquake has struck the greater Kanto region. Power outages have been reported in all 23 Tokyo wards and in parts of Yokohama, Saitama, and Chiba. Residents should shelter in place and brace for aftershocks," a staccato male voice intones. He starts listing earthquake safety measures, and then the message repeats.

Hatsumi shuts it off. "Radio receiver, perk of the job," she explains.

Right, journalist, of course.

"So, now what?"

"Well, like the radio said, there might be aftershocks," Hatsumi says. "Even if power comes back, the elevators won't be safe."

"We'll have to take the stairs," Misora says, "and it's fifty-seven floors. We should start now." Shining her port in front of her, she picks her way across the room to the corridor, stepping gingerly around the glass in her open-toed heels.

Hatsumi looks down at her own feet, which are encased in white sneakers. "At least I wore the right shoes for this."

It was an infusion of shady cash from Razan that kept this building's financing from crumbling when the economy dipped two years ago, so Misora knows her way around. She heads straight for a stairwell exit that's tucked off behind the elevator lobby and reaches for the door, jiggling the handle.

It's locked.

ASAGAWA KENJI

I'm stuck in the switchback for an elevator with a crowd of people large enough to give me a twitch between my shoulders, but there isn't an obvious alternative route up with this many eyes around.

As I wait, a whisper runs through the crowd and then there's Green being pulled out from the front of the line and hand-walked off to another entrance. I'm far enough back that crowd surfing would be the only way to follow, so instead I get to watch an excited group of girls snap photos of the two as they move.

There's a name being repeated in the whispers: Toyama Misora. I mino it. Her profile says she's a magitech engineer, not the type of person who typically commands a fan club. I keep scrolling and see she's also dating a Korean actor famous enough I've seen his face on the pillars in the walk-through under Shinjuku station. That explains the excitement.

When I finally make it up to the floor on the invite, I've left behind the crowd and entered a space that's the kind of quiet and empty that costs a lot of money. Green is just inside the doorway to the overnamed Founder's Room, near a woman with short hair I haven't seen before. Toyama is nowhere around now.

And somehow there, behind the bar appears to be Fujiwara Eika, The Fujika, laughing and looking as airbrushed in real life as she does on a billboard. She sees me looking and winks. This must be a common occurrence, seeing people notice you when you're walking around, casually being a celebrity.

This is the kind of night that needs alcohol, so I grab something that's sitting on the bar. It's a craft beer out of Nagano that the label crows in calligraphy is made from glacier water. It doesn't taste any better than a Kirin from the *conbini*.

From the other side of the granite, Fujiwara Eika looks me over more, covering her thoughts with the bright smile that makes her so much money. She's not telling me not to steal the good stuff yet, but there's still time. "Thank you for joining us for the party," she says.

There's a wet tissue of a man slumped on a stool, clothed in the kind of sportswear you don't sweat on. He's staring at his port and doesn't bother to look up.

"Yeah, thanks for the invite," I say to the celebrity judge from *Slipper*, the contest in which five people attempt to climb up a hill covered in oil for cash and prizes. Green is just standing there, pretending this isn't weird.

"This is Haru," Fujika says, generously introducing her maybe date to Green and me. "No family names tonight, in honor of our guest."

Haru grunts, glancing up at us and concluding we're not worth his time.

"Nice to meet you. It's Kenji," I say instead of pointing out that his expensive shoe is untied, and I could use the lace to pull his foot up and break his nose with his own knee.

Look at me minding my manners.

Niceties finished, Green says, "Didn't think you'd actually come."

I wave the computer cord I've brought at him, and Fujika swoops in, keeping that glossy smile on her face and managing to not give the Yodobashi Camera bag too much attitude as she carries it off by two fingers to add to the stack of elaborately wrapped boxes next to a penguin carved in ice.

"Was I supposed to bring something for this guy?" Haru asks when she returns to the bar.

Green doesn't hear the question since he's busy telling me about how Fujika has appointed herself to be a charity worker. As someone who doesn't look like she's ever lacked for anything, magic included, she must feel real good showing she's better by helping people she thinks are lesser.

Then I almost spit out my beer as Toyama enters the room with the actual Flower Boy Ramen Chef on her arm.

What the hell is happening here.

Seriously, did Green win some kind of contest? Stumble into some sort of useful blackmail? Have some particularly helpful *kami* grant him a New Year's wish?

We're herded over to the booth, where even with such a bizarre group of people, the party proves to be a mixed lucky bag: The food is good, and the drama is tedious. Fujika sends the help away as soon as they fulfill their functions of providing food and drink because, to a group like this, people should only exist as long as they're useful. Green kissed Toyama in the elevator and the Flower Boy Ramen Chef is feeling possessive, so everyone spends most of the time poking each other by not saying it directly. Most strangely of all, this conflict between Green and the famous Korean actor seems to not be their first.

It's not all terrible. I do pick up a business card from Date Hatsumi, the poor childhood friend in the group, activity TBD but likely fun. But mostly, I use the time to catch up on messages for an upcoming job.

When an earthquake hits, my gut reaction is *finally, something to do.*

And then something even more surprising than the guest list happens: most of the city loses power. Staring out the window, there's the reflection of moonlight across rooftops far below, stretching off into the distance. Fifty-seven floors up, most of the buildings look like piles of dirt.

Toyama Misora is the first one to get sick of staring at the dark. "They're not getting the power up any time soon, and even if they do, the elevators won't be safe. We should leave."

She leads the group to the central lobby, the fixed center that the rest of the floor had been rotating around. I hang back, count the doors: public and private elevators, bathrooms, a small kitchen, and emergency stairs. Toyama grabs the handle to the last of those and pulls, but nothing happens.

It's locked.

Fujika gasps, and Green says what I assume is a swear word in English under his breath. How the hell is the door to an emergency exit locked?

Haru tries the handle, and I push ahead of him to kick the door a few times, but it doesn't budge. It's steel, and it's definitely locked.

"Are you going to be okay, Johjima-san?" Hatsumi asks from behind me.

Her tone of concern draws everyone's attention to the fact that he is definitely not fine: his pasty face is growing paler as he drops onto a nearby bench made out of some kind of pricey wood and leather.

Johjima Haru, huh? With the scope of this group, that probably means this sea cucumber in a tracksuit is from the pharmaceutical company with that name.

Fujika sits down next to him, pushing his head toward his knees. "Steady and shallow breaths," she tells him, rubbing his back.

"What's wrong with him?" I ask. Besides being a mannequin of a person with too much money, I don't say out loud.

She shakes her head. "It's a small space, that's all."

"Alright, I'll check the stairs by the service elevator," Date says. "Not all the doors can be locked."

While she takes a loop around the floor, I eye the door again in the dim reflected light of someone's port. There's no locking mechanism on the inside to pick, and the metal jamb is installed on this side so I can't slip the latch with a card.

She's back in a few moments. Haru looks up hopefully, face sweaty and flushed. "Turns out all the doors can be locked," Date announces. Haru moans and puts his head back down.

"This is ridiculous," I say. "The lock has to be electronic or M, we can work with that." My port is at 13% power, but it's enough for a flashlight to look more closely at the door, left and then right along the wall, and eventually reflect off a painted metal panel in the ceiling. "There. Green, get me a chair."

I don't actually expect him to get me one after watching him bypass the line for the elevator a few hours ago, but he does it. With only a small amount of grumbling, he carries in a dining chair. It's still too short, so Date and the Flower Boy Ramen Chef pull one of the heavy benches across the marble floor. As a stack, the combination is high enough that I can reach the over three and a half meter-high ceiling.

Balanced on my toes and multitool in hand, I look closely at where the panel is secured. "Shit," I say. "Anyone got a six-lobe hex screwdriver?" Mine is at home, since I didn't expect the party to be this interesting.

Toyama nods and produces a multitool that's somehow larger than the shiny black purse where she was keeping it. Huh.

I loosen the four corners, and hand the metal panel and multitool off to Green. Then I step onto the back of the chair, grab the inside edge of the frame and pull myself up to look around. This isn't a standard drop ceiling, but something with larger paneling tied into supports for the rotation mechanism, so there are metal frame structures that can support my weight. I lift myself into the ceiling.

There's HVAC and wiring running through a small space, but once I figure out a way through it doesn't take much to find the controls for the box, just next to the cement structure around the fire stairs. The wires are long enough to pull back to the panel opening. "Control mechanism," I say, holding down the two components. "Suppose you could do something with these if there was power, Green?"

He takes one and looks it over. "That's a basic lock manager. It was probably on a timer to auto-lock the doors to the stairwells when the building closes and malfed due to the power shutdown. This magitech backup generator was probably the solution, but it needs to be topped up manually via Syphon. Looking at the sticker, no one's done that in months," he says. "This needs a Syphon charge. Then yeah, I can probably force an override."

Holding the m-generator between his hands, Green stares at the box extra hard but nothing happens. It'd be humorous if this port weren't dying in the ceiling of a fifty-seven story deadzone.

He disconnects the wires and tosses the box to Fujika on the bench. For all that she was giggling like an idiot a few minutes ago, she catches it out of the air cleanly between sparkling nails. Next to her, Haru is breathing into the space between his knees, the back of his neck looking sweaty.

She tries too and then shakes her head. "I think it's fried."

"Let me look at it," Toyama commands. Fujika starts to hand off the m-generator, but she shakes her head. "No, the lock box."

I disconnect the wires, and hand that part down too. Date holds Toyama's port, directing the light so she can see better. She turns it over in her hands, checking the inputs, then closes her eyes for a moment as she holds it. "Fixable," she declares.

"Eika," she says, ordering her friend off the bench. "Hatsumi-chan, look after Haru."

With an exaggerated sigh, Date complies, gingerly sitting on the bench next to Haru. Toyama comes over to where I'm still hanging out of the access panel.

"Give him your port," Toyama tells Green, pointing at me. "You, aim the lights so we can see what we're doing."

"How'd you know I've always dreamed of being a light fixture?" I ask, in my best mocking tone.

Toyama ignores me. "Eika-chan, you hold the box. Cameron, re-attach it to the cords, then be ready to do the override as soon as we have the power up."

"How are you doing this?" Green asks, taking casual first-name closeness from Toyama like it's his birthright.

"Eika is going to stand in for the backup m-generator. I will move the power from her to the device, and you'll use my port for the hack."

"Why can't I just use my own port?" Green asks.

"Because he'll have it," she says, looking up at me. "And I'm certainly not letting him anywhere near mine."

At least she's not stupid.

Green seems weirdly caught on this small detail of the plan. "But you'll trust me?"

"She's saying that what's on her port is more valuable than what's on yours," the Flower Boy Ramen Chef snipes from where he's sitting next to Haru.

"You agreed to my NDA," Toyama says, exchanging a loaded look with Green.

Date clears her throat. Haru is using her thigh as his pillow, hand clutched around under her knee. "Could you guys hurry it up?"

"Seriously, Green," I say. He hands me his port, so I now have one in each hand to hang down and point as tasklights.

Toyama looks at Fujika. "Ready?" she asks. Fujiwara nods, and Toyama closes her eyes.

I don't know what they do, but the panel on the box burps to life. Green is staring at the two, his eyebrows pushed together.

Toyama's eyes open, and they're a little bloodshot. "Hurry," she says. "Raw Eika is a lot for anyone."

Fujika giggles, and the screen flickers. "Got it," Green says, pushing through some kind of code in a command line interface on Toyama's port.

Click. Date dives for the door, letting Haru's shoulder hit the bench. "Not taking any chances," she mutters, holding it open.

I drop Green's port down to him and tuck my own away in a pocket before lowering myself out of the ceiling. Rather than touching barely charged magitech, I leave the box hanging by the wires. This earns me a side look from Green.

"They need to know about their poor state of repairs," I say, glancing at the maintenance sticker. Performance Earth, a Toyama-gumi front.

Shit, there it is. The name, the money, the connections to hold a birthday party in an empty rotating restaurant, the imperial way of talking. You don't get this kind of money through normal business dealings. Toyama Misora isn't just an engineer mysteriously dating a famous actor, she's the princess of the city's biggest underground empire.

I guess I knew that name, but in the way you might know of a baseball player someone mentioned once, not in the way you think that person really exists.

Haru coughs, shuffling to the door. "Let's get out of here."

Fifty-seven floors is a lot no matter how much exercise you do, so it takes time and a few stops to get down to ground level. There, the alleyway is empty except for used beer bottles that were tipped over from their holders by the earthquake.

"Well," Date says, "I came on my moped, so I better go check on people. Again, er, happy birthday, Green-san. Your next one has to be better, right?"

I could say pleasant things to the group, pretend it was nice to meet them, but after all those steps I don't feel like putting the effort in to lie, even for Green's birthday. Instead, a two-fingered wave is all I give, walking away. As I do, the power around me comes back on.

Behind me I hear the actor's voice, saying something decidedly not ramen-related. "Towers are back too. Call a car."

After the elevator stunt, I wonder if Green is going to end up walking, time in the money bubble over, just like me.

DATE HATSUMI

Where I'm sitting, Taehyun on my left is the most obvious person to chat with in this dead space between festivities. This week has been long enough that I wouldn't mind actually being the kind of drunk I'm putting on. But I'm definitely not gone enough to willingly hang out with Taehyun while he's high.

Instead, I scoot around to Green-san's currently empty spot on the opposite side of the table. His friend with the red hair is sitting toward the corner, port in hand, looking hot and bored. As I lean in, he glances up and flashes a crooked smile my way. Confirmation: This guy is trouble.

"Hey," he says. He pulls a different port out from somewhere and glances at it. The light from the screen brightens his face for a moment before disappearing.

I sneak a glance at Eika. She's focused on gossiping with Misora, and not likely to notice that I'm breaking her party rules. I dig out a business card and hand it over. "My name is Date Hatsumi, in case you didn't catch it."

He takes the card and looks it over. His eyebrows come together for a second. "Journalist?"

"Less interesting than it sounds," I say. Never a use in trying to hide it since my name is tied to my full news history. "How about you?"

He cocks his head to the side in a not-inaccurate impression of Eika and says, "'American style'? It's Kenji."

That's not useful. "Pretty sure 'American style' isn't a real family name."

"Tanaka," he says finally, the edge of his mouth quirking up. "Do you need my ID too?"

There's a family name so generic as to tell me functionally nothing. If I were to poll the people at Ultraviolet below, probably a third of the bar would raise their hands. "I'll take your business card."

He gives me an amused look and pulls out a case from his back pocket. I take the card with both hands and look it over. Plain paper with black writing: Tanaka Kenji. Horizon Group. Also so generic as to be meaningless.

His face hasn't been prompting a MinoSo profile icon in my glasses, but his card does, so I focus on the arrow for the second it takes to trigger the popup. All of the details match perfectly, with not one more bit of information added.

"I didn't expect we'd get so personal," he says. "At least not so quickly."

I raise my shoulders. "And I didn't expect you to be so aggressively... beige. What does an employee of"—I brandish the business card between my index and middle fingers—"Horizon do?"

"Private contractor."

"Do I want to know what kind of services you're selling?" I say, emphasizing the word services and gesturing toward his hair. He doesn't seem the kind of friendly to be a by-the-hour boyfriend, but his hair is just some gel and a blow-dryer away from the look.

"Got money you're looking to spend?"

I can't help it; I laugh. "How did you meet the *gaijin*? That must be a story."

"Yeah, it is hilarious," Kenji says evenly.

"Oh, that's how it is?"

"Sounded like we'd already established I don't impress you." He pulls out a third port from his pocket and glances at the screen.

I wouldn't say that exactly. "You're not trying very hard."

"Do you want me to?" He shifts his head to look up at me, hair falling over the edge of his eye. The strands are copper, root to tip. I wonder what the upkeep is on that.

"Okay," I say, casting around for another thread. "Tell me why you came to this party. It doesn't seem like this is your kind of event."

"I thought it'd annoy Green if I showed," he says. "My turn. You said your title, but what do you do?"

"I follow a politician around and write whatever makes her look good. Basically glorified PR." His attention is focused on me now. Suddenly, I feel self-conscious, like the words say too much and nothing at the same time. "But you don't really care about my job, do you?"

Kenji tucks the port he's been holding away into his coat pocket, and I notice the knuckles on the hand closest to me have old scabs. "I can do an amazing impression of caring, if that's what you want."

Misora and Eika are still talking quietly, and Taehyun has gone so far as to lean his head back. I put my elbow on the table and rest my cheek on my hand. "Are you trying to come off as rude? Or is it accidental?"

"Rude can be enjoyable," Kenji says, giving me a direct look.

There's a fading bruise along his jaw and it looks like his nose was broken at some point. But he's wearing a Gucci belt and an expensive fitted shirt over, well...I pull my eyes up when I realize I'm starting to stare.

"You hang out with different people from me if that's what you think."

"Probably less in practice than you think," he says, dodging the probe. "Why this job if you don't like it?"

"I can do a lot of good. Besides, it's easier for me since my dad used to be a politician." Technically true, if avoiding the crux of it.

"Used to?"

"My dad died. A long time ago." I change the subject. If he won't tell me anything in response to polite questioning, I can be direct too. "So, what is your deal, then? Are you *yakuza* or do you just look like one?"

For the first time Tanaka Kenji looks actively irritated. "I am not *yakuza*."

"Did I touch a nerve?" I ask, not able to suppress a smile.

"Not that easily. Some people have misplaced loyalties."

There's an old cut running up his arm and under his shirt sleeve. Impulsively, I reach out and push up the edge of the gray fabric, my fingers lightly touching the skin—warm, solid over muscle.

Okay, maybe I'm a little more sloshed than I thought. I'd never be that touchy with a stranger sober. "You seem to have a lot of injuries for a salaryman."

He looks at me for a long moment. Finally, he says, voice low and amused, "Were you checking out my bicep or looking for tattoos?"

Shit. Busted.

"Tattoos," I admit.

He smiles a long, luxurious smirk that straddles the line between obnoxious and making me shift on my seat. "I could have tattoos hidden anywhere. There's really only one way to know for sure."

My stomach drops out in that way that indicates I'm about to make a bad decision. A very good, distracting, bad decision.

"You have my card," I hear myself say.

And so local journalist Date Hatsumi met a handsome man who was probably trouble. When asked for a comment on the alleged trouble level of said person, Date responded that she didn't give a flying fuck.

Then the building starts to shake.

It stops. Then it starts again, the movement longer and stronger than I would have thought possible in a building like this. Glass is breaking on the bar, and lights go out. When it ends, I realize that I'm crouching under the table, exactly the way I learned as a kid.

Carefully, I make my way to the window, stubbing my toe on something on the way there. The entirety of the city, stretched out west from the window, is dark.

Tanaka Kenji comes up on my left. He sucks air in through his teeth and exhales. "Shit."

All that fuss about magic scores for hiring and Tokyo Utility can't even keep the lights on.

* * *

THE NIHON TIMES
>*Politics & Governance*

Mayor of Suginami Ward Reaches Out After Meguro Earthquake
By Date Hatsumi

Mori Umeko, mayor of Suginami Ward, spent the weekend overseeing a number of earthquake relief efforts. The ward was hit especially hard during Thursday's 7.1 magnitude quake when a fire consumed a series of five Grace Court apartment buildings constructed over 50 years ago, leaving 162 people without homes. A temporary shelter was established at the Suginami Cultural Center, and Mayor Mori personally attended the opening to distribute clean water and blankets to the affected.

"We are home to a strong community, and we will support these people throughout the rebuilding efforts," Mayor Mori pledged on Saturday.

The ward is also home to Tokyo Utility, which underwent an unprecedented two-hour shutdown of services during the aftermath of the quake. Backup systems are designed to come online after an interruption of the main circuits, but required a manual start Thursday after the automatic process failed to engage. Tokyo Utility administration is currently reviewing their emergency services policies and practices to determine the cause of the issue and further streamline protocols to ensure that the systems engage as planned during future emergencies.

* * *

With my article for Sunday submitted to Goto, I have just enough time to zip across town to Shimbashi to meet up for lunch. I find parking for my moped on a side street and take the steps to the third floor cafe, Fun-Due. Misora is already there, waiting for the host.

I'm only about two minutes late, but nevertheless, I hate looking scattered in front of Misora. "Sorry, sorry!"

"Eika has a commercial reshoot." Misora's face stays neutral. She's missing out on work time and then to be stood up.

"Yeah, I saw." I love her but sometimes Eika is such a flake. "After she planned this, too."

At the table, the menu is nothing but breads and diced produce with an array of heated dips. The cutesy logo causes my glasses to offer a chart of reviews for the place, all of which seem to fall into five stars or one, nothing in between.

I hold the menu up and point at the restaurant name. "Fun-due or fun-don't?"

A suppressed smile is what I expect from Misora, but she laughs instead. Maybe she's not as annoyed at being stood up as I would have expected.

We order a vegetable sampler platter to share, which comes with two kinds of cheese so specialized I've never heard of them. After the waitress leaves, Misora and I look at each other, waiting for the other to start the conversation rolling. We've been friends forever, but Eika's usually the one serving as a conversational bridge. I never think about how much I rely on her to be the social lubricant until she's missing.

"So," I say, fishing around. "If Eika's not going to show, this is our opportunity to discuss her poor life choices now, right?"

Misora groans, a hint of amusement showing in the corner of her mouth. "Agreed. Why did she bring Johjima Haru to Cameron's party? I thought we'd seen the last of him years ago."

"Yeah. Why can't she take up something like gambling or improv, instead of making a bad decision that we have to live with too?"

"Good question. I would sit through multiple improv performances to skip future evenings with the 437th person in line for the Chrysanthemum Throne."

I stifle a chuckle. "Do you think she could do the Kansai accent that she'd need to join an Osakan comedy duo?"

"Hideki picked one uuup, it can't be that ha-ard," Misora says, overpronouncing her vowels to approximate the dialect.

A giggle escapes me. There's a sound I never expected to hear mar her perfect diction. "At least Hideki was smart enough to move to Osaka, so he never had to suffer through meeting Johjima in college."

"Well, it's not like he had much choice in the matter. But, as I've told him before, it worked out for him in the end."

I haven't seen Hideki much since high school myself. Truthfully, I never really understood why he and Misora had hooked up in the first place, beyond mutual assuaging of teenage hormones. He went to a different school, and they only knew each other through her family, but she'd always wanted to get away from that life. And yet he'd show up on the weekends with a sheepish smile and an encyclopedic knowledge of the underground Tokyo club scene. He also gave me some of my first research introductions, so I'm indebted to him in my own way even if he probably doesn't remember doing it.

Whatever happened to their relationship at the end, I missed it since I was in Vancouver at the time. But that's a story I'm not going to push for details on at this point.

"Yeah," I say.

Our order comes, a giant platter with two steaming bowls of cheese balanced over flame. We both take up the comically long forks. Fresh carrot dipped in molten cheddar tastes just as I would have guessed— like salty oily crunch.

"Okay, Ei-chan does not get to pick where we eat anymore."

Misora mirrors my expression. "Agreed. After the pickled fruit restaurant—

"And the place where everything was foam—"

"She's done." We both laugh.

There's another pause as we both stare down at the food we're clearly not going to be polishing off. I cast about for another topic, finally venturing, "So, I'm starting to wonder if turning down that promotion was the best idea. Goto is just...the worst editor. It's embarrassing."

"You did what?"

Shit, I forgot I hadn't told her yet. I had it penciled in to tell her roughly the same week as my funeral. "It wasn't a very good offer."

Oops. In the moment before she-who-is-married-to-her-work

responds, I wonder if the *Nihon Times* has any need for international correspondents. Perhaps immediately.

When she speaks, her voice is surprisingly neutral. "I would have been happy to help you negotiate."

"Well, you know me. I like the flexibility of not being stuck behind a desk." I clear my throat. "Not that I'm all that good with using my time. You know, Noah asked me to help his American friend with some issue with a housing problem. But it's with Tophaven Management, and that'd be awkward for me to get involved."

Her expression stays even, but I get the sense that I've ventured into topics I would have done better to avoid. Misora prefers to pretend she knows nothing about the underside of Tokyo. However, there is a related topic that I've been meaning to bring up with her.

"Is Taehyun's building still owned by the Bayside Company?" I ask. BC is a front for one of the Minato ward Kubo-gumi groups that specializes in making money off foreigners who can't buy their own land.

"Yes. Have you heard anything more?"

I inhale slowly and think about how to phrase what I want to say. "Well, I think that if the property bill passes, Bayside is going to start putting some weight on buying out the condos and converting them to permanent rentals. You might want to discuss with Taehyun whose name to have on the title."

I doubt her family would actually go to bat for her since living there gives her autonomy they'd prefer she not have, but her name alone might prevent a dust-up with the larger Kubo-gumi establishment.

"I will take that under advisement."

On that somber note, we both stand to collect our things. As I reach for my bill, I notice that by her hip there's a ghost of something on her otherwise immaculate black dress. "You have some lint or fur or something there..."

She looks down and picks the offending material off between two expertly manicured nails, giving the fuzz a fierce look. "Nozomi has a dog. I think she takes it with her when she picks up my dry cleaning."

Oops, I didn't mean to get her assistant in trouble. "Okay, well, next time you or I will pick where we eat. And whatever you do, don't remind Eika-chan that my birthday is coming up now too—we've had enough partying for a lifetime."

* * *

It's finally starting to feel like spring, so the door to Used Books is cracked open when we arrive. I set the bag of groceries down next to her calculator and money box. "Hey, Mom. I brought someone to see you."

They're not related since Noah is a cousin on my dad's side, but she still likes to catch up from time to time.

My mom walks around the counter to give a welcome. Her pants are wrinkled, but her eyes are clear, and her hands look firm today. "It's so good to see you both."

His body is straight and tense, and he gives a couple more half bows than necessary. "Thank you, Date-san. I hope I'm not intruding."

"Please come in," my mom says. "Have you been enjoying the city?"

"Tokyo is good. I have been meeting up with friends and it's fun."

She nods absently and turns to me. "I'll just close up for a few, so we can go upstairs."

"No rush," I say. "I can put things away first and then we can sit down." That'll give me time to clean up whatever mess she might have upstairs.

I carry the bag past them and up to the kitchen. The air on the second floor is heavy today, but that's easily remedied. I slide the window frame open as far as it will go with the potted plants in the track. The good news is that I can see the kitchen floor this time, and the garbage is neatly sorted in the appropriate colored bags.

The back room is only fighting with the pile of newspapers, my masthead. I lost that fight a few years ago. In the *butsudan*, there's a stick of incense long burned out in front of the memorial tablet—no flowers today. I take a side trip to grab a cup of water for an offering and add it to the shelf. It's not much, but at least now it's not bare.

Back in the kitchen, I open the fridge to swap out food. There's a half-eaten bag of bean sprouts nestled in the corner of the shelf and not much else.

I clomp halfway back down the stairs and duck my head into the shop. "Mom, tell me you just finished eating all your food this morning."

"Just recently. You don't need to worry." She turns to give me that faint, breezy smile that is her default cover.

Noah towers over my mom but looks like he'd like to disappear right now. Still, I can't not ask my mom about this. "I thought your grocer friend was bringing over fresh groceries on Wednesdays now."

"Oh, he was sick this week, and I didn't want to bother any of his workers."

I resist the urge to hit my hand against the wall. "Mom, if you need something, let me know. Go ahead and lock up for a bit. I'll make lunch for the three of us."

The rice is cooking and most of the veggies are chopped for curry when they make their way up the stairs and take the chairs around the table.

"Noah-kun, do you eat curry?" my mom asks, looking pale above her navy sweater.

He's sitting straight in his chair, trying to keep his elbows from bumping into the counter covered in piles of bowls next to his shoulder.

"Of course he eats curry," I say, and then think better of answering for him. The winter I was in Vancouver we didn't have any, but that might have been because his family was trying to show me local food instead of things I already knew. "You eat curry, right, Noah?"

He smiles at that exchange and nods. "I love curry."

"Good to hear," I say. I shake my head and give my mom a stern look. "You drive me batty sometimes."

"Says the girl who used to keep her whole class waiting for forty minutes because she didn't like eating the omelet in her lunchbox."

"Noah-kun," I say, "I need to clarify that she could have stopped putting the omelet in there for me at any time."

"And miss out on a chance to talk with your terrible teacher?" She sighs. "I refused to give in—that woman would have noticed if I'd stopped sending the food you needed to learn to eat. I'm sure I would have heard about that too."

"Misora was the only one in our class who didn't push one of her buttons. Talk about impossible standards." The veggies are simmering in the dented pan with about ten minutes before I can add the seasoning. I tuck my glasses in the neck of my shirt and lean against the counter. My mom only has two chairs, so when we eat I'm going to either have to stand or sit on the floor. "You might be glad to know Eika-chan used to frustrate the teacher something crazy by wearing a different colored bow in her hair every day. I don't even know how many times I heard the phrase 'Not uniform approved.'"

My mom smiles at that. "How are your friends doing these days?"

"Misora keeps herself busy with inventing the future." And only partially dodging the past, I add mentally. "Noah-kun, how has Eika been doing? You probably know better than I do at this point."

He bobs his head, curly hair falling over his forehead. His eyelids are hooded, but his nose and chin are prominent, an inheritance from his Canadian father's side. "Good, I think. Eika-san is very busy. Because she is so kind."

"Thank you for taking care of her," I say. "I know she's a bit much sometimes."

Waving one hand in front of his face, palm out, Noah looks like he'd like to say something, but he doesn't have the words.

"Try in English," I say. "I'll see if I can translate."

Words come out, paragraphs of something that sounds rich and heartfelt. I only catch about half of it, which I repeat in Japanese for my mom. "She's kind and thoughtful. And should take care of herself more...?"

Noah wiggles his hand, this time palm down, to indicate it's mostly an okay translation, or at least close enough he isn't going to try more.

"You all keep yourself so busy," my mom says wistfully. "But, Ha-chan, I was surprised by your article on the property bill."

Can't this wait for a less embarrassing time? "I'm still working on more."

"I read on MinoSocial that there's a protest group forming, but there aren't many city locals."

There's not much that would sink my research faster. "Hmm, Noah-kun probably doesn't have time for that," I say, giving him a smile.

He looks a little caught out, maybe having lost the thread of conversation, so I shake my head and continue into a pivot. "Did either of you see I was in the *Sekai Shimbun* a few weeks ago?"

"I hadn't," my mom says. "Did that slimy man write about you?"

"Thankfully no. I'd probably never recover if Okada did that." I stand up to add the roux, and hand off my port to my mom with a photo of the entertainment page. "I think they really caught my good elbow."

"Every part of you is lovely," she says, giving the picture more loving attention than it deserves. "I wonder if I can find a paper copy."

The curry mix looks like a chocolate bar as it dissolves into the remains of the water. "You don't need a physical version of a photo of my jacket sleeve. You can see it any time you want in person."

"I know, but I just enjoy seeing you there." She hands my port off to Noah, who I'm sure is delighted to pretend to care about a photo of Misora.

"If you insist, I have a copy in my bag there." I set the two plates down on the table and take back my port from Noah. "I didn't think to get more pickled ginger, but this should be okay otherwise."

I can tell she's starving because she eats before claiming the paper. Maybe I'll be able to get it back out after all.

"This is delicious," Noah says.

My mom doesn't say anything, and instead is taking bite after bite. After who knows how many days without much to eat, I bet it tastes like a fucking banquet.

"Mom, next time if you need something, let me know."

She reaches up and takes my right hand. "Only if you promise to take care of yourself too."

I squeeze her hand back and give her a smile that encapsulates my confidence on a good day. "Please trust me that I know what I'm doing."

"As your mom, I'm supposed to worry about you."

I don't disagree with the statement, but Noah is here, and I have to take my hand back before I react with a little light screaming.

Afterwards, Noah and I walk back to the train station past store after store that's closed for the day. There's only one other person on a bicycle, speeding ahead of us. Between the rolled down security grates, the street is quiet.

I sigh audibly and ruffle the back of my hair. "How is your friend Corbin-san doing? Did he get his apartment worked out?"

"No, now he is looking for a new place."

My stomach turns. Shit, of course. Another ball I'm dropping.

He continues, "They wanted to charge too much–three months of key money and two months of deposit."

Key money isn't refundable, just a gift to the landlord to thank them for the opportunity to live in their building. The deposit could be refunded, but with a *yakuza*-tied organization the prognosis on getting that back would be poor.

I still can't offer to be a guarantor, which is probably what Corbin-san really needs in order to move. "Would you like me to get him in touch with a housing assistance organization? They might be able to help."

I glance over. Noah nods, his expression unreadable.

"Okay, I'll get in touch and let you know what I hear," I say. "And sorry for everything back there, that you had to sit through it. I promise you don't have to visit again."

Noah-kun shakes his head and puts a smile on. "It can't be helped. Thank you for trying. And thank you for the curry."

* * *

To my left is the freestanding sign for Bar Blue. It's a small enough hole that it doesn't even have a website to prompt a pop-up.

"Ha-chan, that sucks." Eika's voice through my port sounds as weary as I feel.

I'm just standing by the entrance, but I need to get this out first. "If the mayor thinks she can drop support for all those homeless people once the news moves on, she's going to be surprised by how much the press loves her work in this area. She's going to get years of good coverage on this if I have to. She is going to be known as the patron of the poor and destitute before I'm done."

"What was she thinking? That somehow you wouldn't care?"

"I doubt she realized I was listening since she was talking to Juro. I'm sure she wouldn't have said anything if she'd known."

"I'm sorry. That's hard." Eika lets out a small noise, like she's remembering something. "Come out with us tonight! We'll be at BG7."

I just want to rest, maybe for a year or ten. "I would, but I already have something scheduled."

"At eight p.m. on a Friday?" Eika asks. "Okay, then have fun with your *something*." She draws out the last word enough to make it clear what she means.

"It's work," I add sternly. I'm lying, but only a little.

Inside, I grab my barley-distilled *shochu* on the rocks from the bartender and trail my way back to where it's just Yamada and Himura today.

"Date, you're here," Yamada says, his words slurred. "Sit down, sit down."

Himura raises his glass. "Happy Friday!"

It takes a few rounds before the tension in my body slowly starts to bleed away. There are times when my imprudent high school years following Eika and Hideki around come in handy. Mostly for drinking, because we didn't do much else.

Yeah, I know I don't have the healthiest coping mechanisms.

The Kubo-gumi duo are in good spirits again this week at least.

"They declared reach," Yamada crows, referencing the mahjong move where a player makes a thousand-point bet on being only one tile away from the win. "But then they went to draw, and you know what they got?"

"Nothing?" I ask.

The flat of his hand hits the table hard enough to make the glasses clink. "An earthquake!"

I smile halfheartedly, not really getting what he's saying about this apparently hilarious bit of Kubo-gumi group infighting.

Luckily, Himura catches my expression and jumps in to explain. "They wanted to build the Mining Bank themselves. But as the decision was being made, their current project, the one they're working on now, went woo-woo-woo-bah." He makes a wobbling gesture with his arm, shifting his arm from vertical to a 45-degree angle.

"You won't believe it," Yamada shakes his beer at me, the liquid sloshing, "they– they were– Himura, you tell her–"

"They lost the Mining Bank because they were building a," Himura has to stop to look at the ceiling before forcing the words out, "a Karaoke-mi."

The humor of the situation snaps into place: Karaoke-mi is cheap entertainment, a chain one step above sitting in the street and singing along to music played off the speakers on a 20-year-old port. That means that the construction Kubo group was working on a building probably three stories, maybe four. The earthquake hit it before they finished, embarrassing them in front of the higher ups, and apparently preventing them from getting the go-ahead on what they really wanted.

In short, building a cheap shoebox at the wrong time cost that other group the chance to build a cornerstone Roppongi skyscraper.

Laughter bubbles up from my gut hard enough that I eventually have to put my forehead on the table. "People could just as well sit outside of a Kinoshita Technic"—an entertainment store known for particularly loud in-store music—"as renting a booth at a Karaoke-mi! They could have just built a bench and been better off."

Yamada still can't form sentences. "A bench, a bench!"

We all take long sips, trying to slow our breathing.

"There are some discussions of updating the earthquake codes again," I say eventually.

Himura nods at his cup of beer. "We'll do it right."

Yamada grunts and shifts into some semblance of his middle-aged workday self. "Yes, we will bring in our own people, not outsiders."

A chill hits the middle of my back. That other Roppongi

construction group is known for using local builders, people who aren't necessarily pledged to the organization themselves but who have skills and need jobs. The tiger family, notably, is not.

"This will be very good for our father," Himura adds with a beer salute. He's talking about a relationship not linked by blood, but by *sake*, specifically Inoe Nozomu. Instead of creating local jobs, they'll be strengthening his authority over the ward.

The whole thing is suddenly much less funny.

Yamada raises his glass as well. "To the earthquake!"

We all give what looks like a cheery *kanpai*.

After a long sip, I sit back, feeling the whole day's tension again. My port buzzes, so I dig it out and click the screen on.

Tanaka Kenji { Hey)

What do you know, I'm just in the right state of mind that I could make that mistake.

I put my hands out over the table to get their attention. "I'm about to make a terrible decision. Yay or nay?"

Yamada slams his hand down on the table. "Go forth and do!"

"No time like now," Himura agrees.

It's unanimous and, well, I can't disagree with advice like that.

* * *

After paying, Kenji and I take the elevator up two floors and find the room. He goes in first, casually alert, like he's casing the place but doesn't want me to notice.

I follow, dropping my bag inside, and turn to ease the door closed.

The alcohol has mostly worn off, leaving me this opening to ask myself why I'm doing this. The want is there, but this is stupid even in comparison to some of the decisions I made in my younger days.

This won't fix what the Civics are doing, or the Kubo-gumi, or any of the evils that money can buy. It won't help Noah's friend, or right what I or my mother have been through. It won't fix any of the places where years have gone by when I've failed to help at all.

And staying up tonight means I'll be tired tomorrow at the press conference and after. It'll just make the bags of groceries heavier when I carry them over to my mom.

"Leaving?" The question is neutral, no push either way.

More than anything, the openness of his tone makes my decision. I let the door make a noise as I push it closed.

"Good." This time the tone of his voice isn't neutral. The warmth of his body comes up behind me, still not touching.

I lean backwards, and it doesn't take much until my shoulders meet his chest. With my free left hand, I run my fingers along the fabric of his pant leg, past the pocket, to where I can feel his eagerness.

His hands twist my body, and suddenly we're facing each other, mouths touching then parting, thick with need. The door handle hits the small of my back as I'm lost.

After a long moment, we break off, breathing hard. I lean back to rest my head on the door, enjoying the feeling of him pressed against me. Slowly, I trail my right hand from behind his neck to the zipper on his leather coat and draw it down. He watches with intensity and amusement, and halfway he leans back just enough that I can tug the pull free at the bottom.

I rest my other palm on his shirt underneath and feel the warmth, then use my thumb to tease up the hem. His abdomen is unadorned under my fingers.

"You're going to need to look harder than that." Kenji chuckles, sliding his own hands toward somewhere that suddenly seems interesting.

What am I doing?

Forgetting everything, if only for now.

TOYAMA MISORA

After fifty-seven flights of stairs in high heels, my legs ache, and blisters have bubbled into painful existence on my heels and toes. The moment the electricity crackles back to life, I summon a Toyama car, eager to rest my weary feet. I try to catch Cameron's eye, but he's deep in his port, probably looking for transportation of his own.

The car doesn't take long, a perk of the party being in Shinjuku tonight. Taehyun gets in immediately, taking the front. Eika and Haru scoot into the back.

"You have a way home?" I ask Cameron.

"Hurry up, Misora," Taehyun growls. Either he's coming down badly from his high, or the whole evening has put him in a foul mood. Likely both.

Cameron nods. "I'll see you at work tomorrow."

Not knowing what else to say, I get in the car.

Haru buzzes down the window on his side, letting the cool evening air whip into the car, and Eika rests her head against his shoulder, dozing off almost immediately. In front, Taehyun is chatting with the driver, and weary as I am, it takes a moment for my brain to register that they're speaking Korean. I eavesdrop a little, but it's just small talk about the quake, so I open the Hail app instead, hoping I didn't leave Cameron at the mercy of a post-disaster price gouge.

All rides in your area are canceled due to unsafe conditions.

I open my text thread with Cameron.

(Drop a pin on your location.) Toyama Misora

"Hey, is anyone else like you driving tonight?" I ask the driver in Korean.

"Like me?"

"Like us."

He brightens with comprehension. "My cousin Dongwoo."

"Tell him there's another pick-up near One Eleven. Cash for both of you to keep the ride off-grid."

"Deal," the driver says, eyes widening at the stack of bills I slide through the gap between his seat and Taehyun's. Taehyun lowers the passenger's sun visor, using the mirror to make eye contact with me.

"What?" I ask. His mouth tightens, and he snaps the mirror shut.

Car should be there in 5, I send to Cameron. *Tonight was a disaster.*

The blinking dots that indicate he's typing hover on my screen. Finally:

Cameron Green (Yeah)

(Let me make it up to you tomorrow.) TM

A second eternity, then:

CG (i'm not not intrigued)

The double negative takes me back to high school English class for a moment. I smile when I realize the meaning—good thing Taehyun isn't eyeballing me in the rearview anymore.

One more message to send, to accompany an AppKey for a room at the Park Hyatt:

(Time tbd.) TM

* * *

I'm already finishing my breakfast when Taehyun shuffles into the kitchen, sleep still scrawled across his features. His back to me, posture rigid, he fixes himself a cup of steaming tea. I should have resolved this last night, but my body was aching for a bath.

"Aren't you cold?" I ask. At the first whisper of spring each year, he turns off the heat, no matter what it says on any thermometer. Designer clothes and luxe furnishings can't hide the childhood scars that surface when he reads our energy bill.

"Hence the tea," he replies, tone chilly as the air.

He was humiliated last night, I know, but I'm not offering a *mea culpa* for something that wasn't my fault. "Eika didn't know."

"Are you fucking him?"

"Without the earthquake, I would have a clearer answer for you."

"Meaning?"

"Not yet."

The teacup hits the counter, porcelain ringing against black granite. "Goddamn it, Misora. One Eleven was swarming with paparazzi last night. You trust Hatsumi and Eika, but what about Johjima Haru? Or that random *yakuza* dude?"

"I will get everyone in line."

He sighs. "I think we work well together. As a couple. Do you agree?"

"Of course." If the definition of "working well" is a recurring itch always thoroughly scratched. "You won't see him again."

"Good." Taehyun turns to poke through the fridge. As he opens and closes containers of pre-made *banchan*, I can see his shoulders are still tense with anger. He emerges with a plastic-wrapped plate of *gyeran-mari*, the rolled omelet's yellow yolkiness offset by a spiral of dark green seaweed.

"Are we done with this topic?"

"Probably."

The panther-like energy dissipates into a rakish looseness as he leans against the sink, and it's hard not to appreciate the view. My staring elicits an insouciant grin. "If you miss this while I'm gone, contact Mayumi, she'll send you a signed photo."

"Will she include a side of B-grade maddy? For the full Park Taehyun experience."

His Japanese agency has ties to Maeda-gumi, and only their cheap crap would fade as fast as what he, Eika, and Haru were taking last night. Your product is your reputation, and your reputation is all you are. This is true regardless of what the product is. Both of my parents built their worlds on this maxim.

"Not everyone has your kind of access. Or budget."

Also, not everyone is stupid, I want to reply. But maddy, molly, and their patch, pill, and powder sisters paid for this apartment. I don't need to be reminded of it. "When do you leave for Seoul?"

"This afternoon. First interview is with *Movies Time!* tomorrow morning."

The premiere, his first feature film. I'd forgotten all about it. That's why he was so angry—there couldn't be a worse time for bad press.

"The publicity tour will take a couple weeks," he adds. It's a benediction, permission to do what I will in his absence.

"I'll make the most of it."

He emits a scoffing noise around a mouthful of egg. "I bet."

* * *

Hideki's latest report on the tracker progress claims he'll have a prototype for me to work with in the lab by next Wednesday. He's already a week behind, thanks to Kaihei's meddling, and now there's been a delay on parts. I push aside my half-eaten bento and pick up my port.

(That's another month of skimmed
profits. } Toyama Misora

Watanabe Hideki { He's your father)

I'm mid-draft on a mildly threatening reply when another notification pops up on my screen:

AppKey activated.

Cameron made me wait for it, but he's in. I smile, anticipation rippling through me.

"You look happy, Mi-chan," a cool voice observes from the doorway.

I rush to my feet and bend into a bow. Addressing me as "Mi-chan" indicates this visit is from my mother, not the company CEO, but I'd rather keep things formal. I respect all that Toyama Rei has done to build this company, launching herself from my father's underworld platform into a legitimate and successful career. The rest comes harder.

"Toyama-shacho, may I get you some tea?"

Rei shoos Nozomi away with a languid wave, then glides past me to seat herself in my desk chair. Reluctantly, I close the office door and sit across from her. I've seen my mother at the negotiating table before—she always finds a way to subtly diminish her opponents.

"How was your party last night?" Rei asks.

Of course she knows we had the room at One Eleven. I suppress the urge to release an audible sigh. "It was a friend's birthday."

"Hmm," she says, laying a folded printout on my desk. It's from a website: *Asia Star Scene*, a salacious online tabloid.

I give it a quick once-over. Today's homepage features a Taiwanese pop star who trashed his hotel room in Phuket. Why is she showing this to me? I shrug.

"Was it this friend?" She unfolds the paper, revealing the second-tier story.

From last night, a remarkably sharp port photo of me, arm linked through Cameron's as we walk to the elevator. I'm looking up at him, and the expression on my face—you'd have to really know me to see it, but Rei is my mother.

"Impressive what someone can create in Pixelpush when they're both bored and malicious," I say, trying to keep my tone level. If she lets this get back to Papa, Cameron and I are done before we begin.

Rei frowns, then re-folds the paper and slips it back into the pocket of her suit jacket. "Your father and I would like to invite you and Taehyun to the house this weekend."

My parents never have us over, not with how Papa feels about

Taehyun. Rei adores him, though. Or, at least, she adores what he represents: the gauzy possibility of grandchildren named Park who are more Korean than Japanese.

"We can't," I say, too bluntly, and her eyes narrow. "My apologies, *okaasan*, but Taehyun is in Korea for the next few weeks."

"Then we will see you as soon as he's back. Fumiko will work with Nozomi to find a time." I've lost. "How are your projects?"

"Eika and I are nearing the prototype phase on a new battery," I say, sending a mental apology to Cameron. The longer it takes Rei to realize that the man from the photo is also on her payroll, the better.

"And of course I have Papa's project, too," I add. It's a trial balloon—does she know about that?

"Indeed." Her expression betrays nothing. She stands, striding to the door, then pauses with her hand on the knob to give me a hard stare. "Have your fun, Mi-chan; I won't tell your father. But then grow the hell up."

After she leaves, I take a moment to catch my breath, forehead against the cool surface of the window, before going down to the lab. Rei can get in my head like no one else.

Cameron isn't at his desk, but I find him in the damper room doing damage scans on all the components from the Denali battery project. "Need help?"

The look on his face when he sees me causes a thrill to shoot across my skin and settle low in my abdomen. I can feel my port buzzing in my pocket, but I ignore it.

"I think most of our stuff is fine," Cameron says, surprising me with the neutral topic—it's only when I come around to his side of the table that I realize Sugihara is in the near corner of the room, face inches from the screen on the ThermoCalc. She's nearsighted and too vain for reading glasses. "But you might want to look at this one."

I step close to him, certain I can feel the heat radiating from his body, though it's probably coming from the machine. As I lean forward to look through the scope, he casually sets his port on the table next to me with the Scrawl app open. He's written a single word:

When?

The component in the scanner is as pristine as it was before the earthquake. "I see what you mean," I say. "Let me make some notes."

I pull out my own port—the missed call was from Eika. I'll get back to her tomorrow. I scribble *6PM?* with my fingertip and angle the screen so he can see. We could have had the entire exchange via text, or even out loud in English—Sugihara is woefully monolingual—but there is something deliciously teenage and mischievous about this.

New Voicemail from Fujiwara Eika. I mute the notification and flip my port screen side down. "Any other damage from last night?"

"I don't think so," he says. On his port, he writes *Maybe my ego.*

We're interrupted by the *bzzt, bzzt* of a new message—my port again, not his. Reluctantly, I turn it back over.

Fujiwara Eika: { Mi-chan PLEASE call me back }

My stomach flips, a lurch of genuine nausea. My first thought is Hatsumi. For years now, we've been in a holding pattern of agree-to-disagree over her pastime of digging into the yakuza families, including my own—my firsthand knowledge of their capacity for cruelty has never deterred her. For my own sanity, I've tried to ignore her whole project. I remember too well my final words to her on the subject, the moment the wall dropped between us: *Be a groupie if you want to, but don't come to me for help when you get in over your head.*

Please don't let this be about Hatsumi. And if it is, oh, please, anyone but Toyama-gumi.

Out in the corridor, I tap *Return Call,* and Eika answers immediately. "Mi-chan, thank goodness," she says, voice thick and teary. "I really need your help."

Weak-kneed, I brace myself against the concrete wall. "Eika-chan, what is it, what's the matter?"

The story tumbles out in fits and starts as she struggles to get her composure back, but the short version is that she's getting screwed over by her siblings again: they've asked her to present a formal update on Replenish at the FHI board meeting with virtually no notice, and she needs help preparing.

"Mi-chan, how could they only tell me now? I can't do this," Eika says. I've never heard her sound so defeated.

My sick feeling has been replaced with an incandescent fury. "Yes, you can. Is Noah able to help you out?"

"He has plans after work, but yes, he's coming back in tonight. Can you come, too? Can you come now?"

"Of course." I can't leave Eika alone when she sounds like this, so tiny and forlorn. "Nozomi will help, too, I'll pay her overtime myself. We'll be right over."

I'm halfway to the elevator, message asking Nozomi to call a car and meet me in the lobby already sent, when I realize I left Cameron without saying goodbye.

(Can we push back to 7:00? } Toyama Misora

Cameron Green { Sure. Everything OK?)

I don't know what Eika has said to him about her family, and that story isn't mine to tell.

(Nothing that can't be handled. I'll see you soon. } TM

From the car, I send a message to Eika: *We're on our way.*

* * *

6:54 p.m.

(Running late. 8:30? } Toyama Misora

Cameron Green { OK. I'm here.)

9:22 p.m.

CG { ?)

9:48 p.m.

AppKey deactivated.

FUJIWARA EIKA

Archival footage: DBW advertisement 5 (15-second clip)

    Fujiwara Eika is wearing a black suit with a fitted skirt as she scampers into a messy living room. She looks around, frazzled, first peeking into a closet, then moving pillows piled on the floor. Still not finding what she's looking for, she pushes her hair back out of her face before noticing something off camera.
    Smash cut to her stepping into a pair of heeled dress shoes. A giant pink lychee is standing behind her, holding a fabric briefcase out by the door. Eika reaches for her bag with a smile.
    Pink title card reads "Kinoshita Diet Breakfast Water."

* * *

I wake to the sensation of the car coming to a stop. We're already outside Taehyun and Misora's building, so I must have done more than lightly doze off. Taehyun climbs out and, not bothering to say good night or open Misora's door, walks ahead of her toward the lobby. I feel awful about the strain between the two of them. I never would have invited Taehyun if I'd known Misora might reciprocate Cameron's interest. That whole situation is opaque to me—what is she doing?

"Well? Where next?" the driver growls, polite pretense gone now that Misora has left.

I open my mouth to give my address, but before I get a word out, Haru shares his own. His place is farther from Misora and Taehyun's than mine, up closer to Akasaka. It's not worth arguing about, though. He must be tired, too, and with the claustrophobia, I know the night took an extra toll. I twist myself sideways and lean my cheek against the back of the seat. The leather is cool and pillowy, and still gives off that new car aroma; it's no bed, but it will do for now.

Haru turns on his portlight. "Where's the stupid—aha." Finding the button that controls the divider between the front and back seats, he raises it. "That's better."

"Were you not enjoying his sparkling personality?" I ask. He laughs.

My leg bumps against Haru's as the car pulls out onto the main thoroughfare, and he drops a hand to my knee, rubbing his thumb in slow circles. It's not enough to work out the ache of trekking down the One Eleven stairs, but it's soothing. I sigh in appreciation.

Haru seems to take this as encouragement, though, because he leans forward to kiss me, hand sliding higher until it's just under the hem of my skirt. I kiss him back for a bit—he's a good kisser, I'd honestly forgotten how good—before pulling gently away.

"We don't have to do anything," I say, pretending I'm the one who wants to go further, and I'm reluctantly respecting his needs. Earlier today, I'd have said I planned to go home with Haru tonight. Now, though, all I want to do is rest my cheek against the seat again and close my eyes. "You've had such a long night."

Even in the dim light filtering in through the tinted windows, I can see him scowl, and I realize my mistake. His mouth is on mine again, his tongue insistent—this is not such a good kiss. He shifts his hand from my thigh to my breast, thumb moving in that same circular motion, and when my body responds—of course it does—he chuckles.

"That's what I thought," he murmurs in my ear, moving down my neck. Over his shoulder, I can see our reflection in the window, and I meet my own gaze. It's intoxicating, seeing this attractive couple kiss in front of me, and for a moment I'm almost outside my own body, a voyeur peeping in. Then Haru slips a hand back up under my skirt, further this time, and I snap back to what's happening.

I giggle, sounding shrill to my own ears, and wriggle my hips away from his fingers. Lowering my own hand to the front of his athletic pants—expensive or not, insultingly casual attire to wear to my friend's party—I decide I'll give him a handjob. I could almost do this in my sleep, something that sounds immensely appealing. A wild part of me wonders if I actually could.

But now he's the one who demurs. "We're only a block away, babe. I can wait until we're inside—then you can use something more fun than your hand."

The car slows, turning into the curved drive in front of Haru's apartment tower, and he exits, holding the door open. He clearly expects me to follow.

Ha-chan would tell him that all he'll be fucking tonight is himself, though wordsmith that she is, she'd find a cleverer way to phrase it. Misora wouldn't say anything. It would just be a look, that fierce look that can peel a man's skin from his bones.

Legs feeling like lead, I get out of the car.

We stumble through the lobby to the elevator. Even though I wore flats, there's a fat blister on my left heel, and it throbs with every step.

Mindful of the omnipresent security cameras, Haru keeps his hands to himself in the elevator, but all bets are off once we're inside his apartment. The door has barely clicked shut behind us and he's handsy again, his lips on my neck and his body pressing me up against the wall. His fingers fumble with the zipper on the back of my skirt.

Was he always kind of bad at this, and I was too tipsy to notice? My mind wanders to the past, trying to pick through the fog of memories. I associate Haru with carefree fun, but he couldn't even meet that expectation tonight. I feel a flush of shame as I think of how shabbily he treated Cameron-san and his friend.

"Eika, hello? I told you to help me with that zipper." Haru has pulled away, but with palms resting on the wall on either side of me, trapping me in place. His hot breath, vodka-sour, is in my face, and I can't help wrinkling my nose. His annoyed expression turns to a sneer. "Spacing out again, huh? Why can't you just take a damn pill like a normal person?"

It's like he punched me in the stomach—all the oxygen whooshes out of my body. I took pills during university, and they left me agitated and unable to sleep well, a history he knows. "I tried that," I whisper, hating myself for how weak my voice sounds, how thick with emotion.

"'I tried that,'" he mocks, pitching his voice high and whiny. "There are other medical options now, you know. Things that make a lot more sense than Pilates or whatever you're doing."

"Yoga and meditation," I correct. It feels important to win at least one point, pinned as I am against this wall with him glowering down at me.

"Whatever it is, it's not working," he sneers, pushing back on his hands and backing away from me. "I don't know why I bothered rekindling this. You haven't changed. You flit from project to project—what does your organization even do?—and you hang out with the same loser friends. Half-Korean *yakuza* trash and a hanger-on in off-brand shoes."

The dig at Replenish cuts deep because it feels true, but I won't listen to him insult Misora and Hatsumi. I take a deep breath. "Toyama Misora and Date Hatsumi are worth a thousand of you, and they don't need to pretend to be related to the imperial family, either."

His face reddens, and his mouth opens and closes a few times, working on a response. Finally, he says, "I think you should leave."

"I think so, too."

Because of the earthquake, there are still no car services operating, and the street outside Haru's building, normally busy, is devoid of taxis. Walking home from here is too far, especially with my left foot's battered condition. I open up Minotaur Maps and realize that the Intercontinental Hotel isn't far, so I book a room from my port and then start my slow, aching walk.

By the time I arrive in the lobby, the blister has burst, and I can feel the wetness seeping into the footbed of my shoe. It's a relief to bypass the front desk and head straight to the elevator with my AppKey. The room is spacious and beautiful, and the first thing I do is draw a bath. Before it's even full, I lower my feet into the steaming water, biting my lip as the heat sears the now-open blister on my heel.

I let myself cry, tears that are part pain, part anger spilling into the bathwater. When I'm done, I feel much better. I can prove Haru wrong, if only to myself. In the reminders app on my port, I set two tasks for tomorrow:

Appointment with Dr. Honma
Visit the Center

* * *

The words "Fujiwara Center for Applied Magic" are barely visible through the glint of sun reflecting off the windows when I arrive. Moving closer, the angle changes and suddenly the eye-squinting brightness has gone in favor of a gradient from light blue into cerulean, blending into the sky.

Inside, there's the entry area that extends up three floors, including simple chairs of wood and indigo serving as a lounge to the side. With classes not yet to start for another week, even the nearly silent close of the front doors in their track is a noticeable noise.

Before the reception, we were all given a tour of the completed facility, so I know to walk past the classrooms, the auditorium, and to take the staircase to the second floor to find the administrative offices just beyond the sign for the lab spaces. Since my feet are still protesting even in a kitten heel after all the stairs yesterday, I take the elevator nearby.

The woman sitting at the front desk is focused on her computer until I step up to the high counter that circles her workspace. She looks up and startles to recognize me, then springs to stand and bow deeply, hands clasped at her waist. "Ah, Fuji—Fujiwara-san. Welcome."

She's older, wearing eyeliner that frames her eyes beautifully. Her nametag says "Miyazaki."

I bow back in a quick, short movement, and make a show of looking around. "Miyazaki-san, it's so wonderful to see this space being used after the opening. It seems like it will be so lively when the students are here too."

That seems to break the ice, and her smile moves from an edge of fear to more genuine. "Yes, it will be such a transition to see them join us for the new school year."

Miyazaki-san continues nodding in a slighter bow but also glancing over at her desk. On a hunch, I lean forward over the counter—she has a bottle of strawberry Breakfast Water sitting there.

It takes a second of digging through my bag to find it, then I flourish my sparkly gold marker to ask, "Would you like me to sign...?"

Her eyes brighten, but she waves her hand in front of her face. "Oh, I couldn't ask you to do that."

"It wouldn't be any problem," I insist.

Niceties aside, she's almost vibrating with excitement as she brings the bottle around the desk to hand it to me with both hands. "Thank you so much, Fujiwara-san."

"Don't tell anyone, but this is my favorite flavor," I say conspiratorially. I sign and then before handing the bottle back ask, "Would you like to take a photo together?"

She very much would, so we take a few double selfies, both with V-signs and quiet pose, one finger quirked in front of our mouths.

"That one is my favorite," I say at the end.

"My granddaughter is going to be so excited," Miyazaki-san says, cupping her port with both hands and looking blissful. She's wearing a soft cream sweater, with a neckline outlined in a simple coral pattern that brings out the coloring in her cheeks.

"And you have such a beautiful top on today."

"You are much too kind," she says, patting her face before setting down her port to give me a few more appreciative bows. "Sorry for all that. Is there something I can do to help you today?"

This time I bring out a business card to pass to her with both hands over the counter. "Maybe you know, but I also work for the organization Replenish Initiative."

She takes the card and the angular logo entwined with vines unfolds above her hands to reveal my title as director. Working in this field, she's surely seen so many of these animated cards, but she still watches it unfurl raptly. "Thank you for this."

"I've been hoping to meet with Professor Yokoyama. I have tried to contact him by email, but maybe he has been out of the office."

"Ah, I see," she says. "Yokoyama-sensei is a very important person."

"Yes, our organization has been hoping to further explore questions of how environmental degradation may be impacting magical potential in newborns."

Miyazaki-san winces visibly. "That makes sense."

"So, I was wondering if I might be able to schedule a meeting."

"I see." She nods, clearly thinking through how to respond. "Hm. You know that the university is so appreciative of your family's role in creating the center."

I wave a hand in front of my face politely to stave off the gratitude for the billions of yen that went into this building. "Oh, it was nothing significant."

"We have all been so humbled by the generosity. It has also been so kind for your esteemed brother, Fujiwara Isao-san, to be offering so much time in serving on the advisory board for our department."

"Ah, I see." Growing up, the envelopes for our new year's money always looked equally shiny. Then eventually I realized that as the eldest son he was always receiving much more than me, even controlling for age. Isao-*oniisan* saved it all and finally spent his nearly two decades of savings on a trip to an expensive resort abroad. He returned with a prestigious internship.

I let the tiniest bit of frustration show through in the tension around my mouth. "Do you think that between all of his important work, Yokoyama-sensei might be able to see me just for a few minutes?"

She exhales through her teeth. "Unfortunately, that's difficult. He is not in the office today, and as the Johjima Endowed Chair in Applied Magical Sciences, his calendar is very busy."

My family name is on the outside, yet they won't even take a few minutes to say no to my face.

"But," she says, glancing around and dropping her voice to a whisper, "I think that another of our faculty might be in the office today, if you have time to talk with her."

"If it's not too much of an inconvenience."

I follow her down a hallway, past office after office, including one labeled Yokoyama that has the door shut and the light most definitely on, until we get to the far end. Because of the way the space is organized, we're now in the middle of the building far away from the sunlight-filled windows.

She taps her knuckles on the partially open door softly. "Shimizu-sensei, are you available? I have a guest here."

There's an affirmative noise, so Miyazaki-san pushes the door open. The space is tiny, barely wider than the door itself, and just deep enough to contain a desk. It's lit by a fluorescent panel that almost fills the ceiling, lending the room a sterile feel. The woman inside stands. She looks even younger than me, but she's wearing a somber grey suit.

"Shimizu-sensei, this is Fujiwara Eika. Her family..."

The woman nods, and gestures to the sole chair in front of her desk. Miyazaki-san backs away, and from one side of the doorway gives a quick hand wave that's part goodbye and part motion that I should enter.

I give her a short bow and enter to give Shimzu-sensei a deeper one. She returns it and we exchange cards. Her title is "Assistant Professor, Magical Analysis."

"Thank you for your time," I say. "To explain, based on the current data, our organization believes that environmentally depleted areas are more likely to produce downslope children."

She nods. "The Santos and Monteiro project. Innovative work, but it's too bad the sample size was so small."

"As I've heard," I say, giving her a smile. The expression is not returned, so I keep going. "Our organization has been hoping for further exploration of how environmental degradation is impacting magical potential in newborns."

"Weather."

"Weather?" I ask, confused.

"You mean whether environmental degradation may be impacting potential. The work so far isn't much more than a hypothesis."

I rub my hand down my leg, suddenly seeing how much the

pale blue of this suit is out of place. "Yes, whether. While we've been watching closely, there hasn't been any follow-up on the study."

"Yes, that would be interesting for the field," she says, not giving me anything.

"Is there maybe even a graduate student who is in need of a project? Replenish Initiative may be able to provide some funding for their time."

Anxiety shoots down my back at making this open-ended promise. Noah's going to be busy looking for any margins to move around, and I'll have to see if I can find any projects to take on to make this work. But without more research on this topic, it's clear we're never going to be able to get people to listen.

Shimizu-sensei gives me a long look, then nods. "I can think of one or two that could use a nudge. Please send me your formal call for proposals and I'll get the word out."

"Thank you so much for your assistance," I say, bowing in my seat.

She stands to bow, indicating that we're done. "Thank you for your support for the field."

A glimmer of hope. Now, I just need to make the financial parts work.

Outside in the hallway, I realize I have only a faint idea of how to find the exit. I dig in my purse to find my port to mino for a building map. There's a message indicator, so I open it to see what's come up now.

Fujiwara Isao { We are looking forward to your presentation at the Tuesday morning board meeting. A thorough accounting of Replenish Initiative's activities and expenditures over the last 18 months will be extraordinarily helpful as we determine FHI's charitable giving capacity for the upcoming fiscal year. We've reserved thirty minutes. An accompanying fifty-page written report is standard.)

* * *

As I drive back to Azabu-Juban, my throat is tightening, and my hands start shaking around the steering wheel. I thought we had more time. Repeatedly, I use the Ocelot voice assistant to try to contact Misora, the car erroring on my thick and hiccupping voice before finally going through.

At the Replenish office, Noah's packing up for the day when I arrive, but he sets it all back down when he sees my face. "Are you okay?"

I shake my head, throat thick again. "It's my family—" I choke out. "They just let me know that I need to do a presentation for the board on Tuesday. About funding for Replenish."

"Today is Friday." He raises his eyebrows in concern. "This is the first time?"

He asks it gently and it's a fair question, but also, I have to make sure he knows this wasn't me. "I checked my messages and my emails—I didn't miss anything. They didn't let me know until now."

"What do we do?"

It warms my heart to hear that he's invested enough to want to help even though he's scheduled to go home in a few months, and we're already past his workday. "Can you please, please help with the financials? They need a report, and I don't even know where to start."

Noah unlocks his port with his thumb and nods as he looks at the screen. "I have to meet a couple of friends. But I will be back. Is seven okay?"

I nod, not trusting my voice.

"By eight for sure."

My port buzzes, and it's the call back: Misora knows me and my family, and the confidence in her voice as she says she can help is so strong that I can't help but feel better.

Not long after that there's a crisp knock as Misora arrives with her assistant.

"Everything is going to be fine," Misora says firmly. "Tell us what you need."

They follow me inside, and I sink down into one of the faux leather chairs around the glass-topped table I'd bought, envisioning meetings where I could convince people who could do something to help, to make the world a better place. Instead, I'm fighting for every yen as my own family tries to stop us from doing anything.

"I don't even know," I say, picking up some of the pieces of paper and moving them around. "Where do we begin?"

Misora's assistant, Nozomi, clears her throat. "I brought some templates of annual reports. We need a financial section and a narrative, correct?"

"Yes. And then I have to give a 30-minute presentation." Speaking isn't a worry for me, but I have no idea what a board looks for, and what if I don't talk about the right things? Or even worse, give them a reason to cut us off?

"Okay, here's what we're going to do," Misora says. "I'll outline your presentation and create a deck. You work with Nozomi on framing the narrative report, and then you can fill in the details on the slides. As for the financial piece—when is Noah getting here?"

"He promised he'd be here by seven. Eight at the very latest."

Nozomi gives Misora a look, but she doesn't seem to notice. I pretend I don't see it either, because I need their help and I'm afraid to ask.

We split up as ordered, with Misora using my desk in the other room while we work at the main table. Nozomi is clearly nervous at first talking with me, but after I make a few half-hearted jokes and compliment her manicure she switches to a serious face and focuses on pulling a narrative from my scattered thoughts.

Noah comes back at 7:02, right at the same time as the boxes of fried food arrive from Ding-Dong Chicken. I break out some simple dishes from the cupboard and pass out food to everyone except Misora, who says she's not hungry. We've all been working hard, and we need a good pick-me-up to keep going.

Taking this break as a cue, Misora says, "Alright, Eika-chan, you and Noah can manage from here. When you have everything ready, let me know, and I'll share it with Okamoto. He'll prep some easy questions for you."

My stomach drops, and I reflexively grab at her hand. "No, not yet!

I need to practice the presentation. You do these kinds of meetings all the time, but I don't know what to say, or what the others might ask me. Please, Mi-chan."

She and Nozomi exchange another significant look, but she relents. "One hour."

There's a burst of lightness through my body. Just having her here to take charge, I can tell things will be okay.

Misora sends a message on her port, then sets it aside again. We go back and forth, with her asking questions and then correcting my answers where they're inaccurate or incomplete.

At 9:48, Misora and Nozomi's ports both ping at the same time. At the other end of the table, they talk quietly for a moment, and then Misora excuses herself to the bathroom.

As soon as she's left, I slide into the seat next to Nozomi. "Is everything okay?"

She nods, looking shy again. There's a lock of hair that's come loose from her hair clip, forming a flyaway in her otherwise smooth coiffure.

I put my hand on the back of hers where it rests on the table and lean in. "You can tell me. Is something going on with Misora?"

A swallow and Nozomi breaks eye contact to say, "She had a date scheduled for tonight."

"Thank you so much. For everything," I say, then sit back, biting my lip. I need to find my lip conditioner.

For her part, Nozomi rubs her hand as she takes it off the table and puts it in her lap.

When Misora returns from the bathroom, she beelines over to the kitchen counter. She has fresh makeup on now. "I'll take some of that chicken after all. Do you have a container?"

"I thought you weren't hungry," I say, starting to pack fried potatoes into the bottom half of a lavender rabbit-shaped bento box. There was a time in elementary school when I'd wanted nothing more than a lunchbox with cute characters like my friends, anything other than the lacquerware formality that our family's chef preferred. As an adult, I can buy whatever style I want, so I have enough to share.

Once I have the base layer in, I reach for her favorite spicy chicken, but she stops me. "Plain, please."

So, this food isn't for Misora. It's not for Taehyun either. Whatever is happening, at least I haven't ruined her entire evening. "You'll come back tomorrow?"

"Yes. Fill Noah's data into the slides, practice, and I'll grill you. No mercy, I promise."

"What a friend," I deadpan. "Thank you, Mi-chan. I owe you."

She waves that away. "Never."

INTERSTITIAL

WASHINGTON TRIBUNE
> *Opinions*

How Do You Like Them Apples?
By *Matthew M. Williams*

These days there is one bright spot on everyone's social media feed: Fruit Man. Played by an anonymous apple costume-clad actor, Fruit Man is the photo incarnation of the American dream, a recipient of endless bounty.

Yet, in the midst of abstracted gauzy happiness, we ignore the source of such largesse.

The photographs featured in the Fruit Man internet meme were taken from a series of Japanese commercials for the product Diet Breakfast Water. The woman serving as the source of the generosity is an actress named Eika Fujiwara, who, on the other side of the Pacific, is more well known for being the head of an NGO focused on addressing inequality in access to magical resources.

Here in America, we have chosen to outlaw private work in magic, arguing that the people of our country cannot be trusted to use this technology responsibly. While the Redwood Incident was evidence that some people might misuse these resources, there was little discussion of intermediate steps such *as regulation before the rush to pass an outright ban.*

It should be no surprise, then, that one largely overlooked provision of SB-114 is an exemption for military research. As a nation, we have blocked individuals from using magitech devices and banned corporations from developing, importing, or selling them, while placing no limit on government access. Indeed, if the Pentagon wanted to develop a magical nuclear bomb, there would be no public oversight and no limits on the amount of taxpayer dollars that could go to fund this endeavor.

Our supposed safety comes at the cost of private innovation, even as the deficit continues to balloon in the name of national security. We have created a time of magical plenty for the military, a present from the American people.

TOYAMA MISORA

The door to 401 swings open. It's one of those apartments where the hallway floor is a high step up from the door level, creating a natural bench for putting on shoes. Cameron is on the hallway level, holding the collar of an enthusiastic German Shepherd. "He's excited to meet you."

I hold my hand out for the dog to sniff. "What's his name?"

"Panzer." When I laugh, Cameron gives me an appreciative smile, and a warm glow washes over me. I am not here for the dog.

After I slip off my shoes, Cameron offers me a hand up out of the entry. Fresh from the shower, his hair is damp, and he's changed into casual clothes, just athletic pants and a thin T-shirt. I know he's a dedicated runner, but this simple attire highlights the leanly muscled outcome in a way his work clothes can't. I wonder if he can feel the thrum of my pulse in his hand.

Before either of us can say or do anything more, Panzer pushes between us, burrowing his head into my bag. Right—my transparent excuse for being here. I pull out the lavender bento. "I brought him some chicken and potatoes."

Cameron takes the container, looking amused. "You don't seem like the purple bunny type."

"Eika."

"That makes more sense. Is she alright?"

"I think she will be."

He opens the lid and sets the bento on the floor. Panzer immediately hoovers up the food, then carries the container over to the corner, where he starts to chew on it lovingly.

"I hope she didn't want that back."

I shrug. I will buy Eika a thousand replacements.

"And what did you bring for me?" Cameron asks as he draws me against him. The teasing lilt is cut through with desire, and the sudden dark intensity in his eyes leaves me lightheaded.

"Me."

We pick things up where we left them in the One Eleven elevator, now unbound by the rules of a semi-public space. I slide my hands downward to grasp the hem of his T-shirt, breaking our kiss just long enough to tug it up over his head. The skin of his chest is warm, still radiating the heat from the shower, and he recoils with an involuntary shiver at the touch of my hands.

"Sorry," I say. I can't tell him they're cold because I walked several blocks on this chilly spring evening to reach him. Not wanting anyone in Toyama-gumi to get suspicious about why I'm at this particular address, I had the driver drop me at a nearby *izakaya*.

"You know, I don't mind," he replies with a soft chuckle, pressing one hand on top of mine. The other tangles in my hair as he tips my head back to deepen our kiss. It feels so good to have him kiss me like this, as if it's worth doing for its own sake, instead of a mere signpost along the road to something more.

And yet—I'm impatient. Redology was over a month ago, and I have been carrying this bundled-up lust for him ever since. Withdrawing my hands from his, I trace my fingertips down his abdomen, reaching for the drawstring on his pants. Before I can untie it, he stops me.

"Hey. You have catching up to do."

Fair enough. Not only am I still fully clothed, I haven't even removed my jacket. I shrug out of it, and he turns to hang it on a hook near the door. I remove my sweater, tossing it aside, and unhook the eyelet fastener on my pencil skirt, too. He helps with the zipper, and the skirt drops to the floor.

"Better?" I ask.

"Better," he replies, giving me a once-over. His voice is caught somewhere between whisper and growl, and the sound sends arcs of desire skittering across my nerves. When I reach for the drawstring a second time, he doesn't stop me.

"This is happening," he murmurs, a note of disbelief in his voice. He traces his lips down my neck and along my collarbone.

"Finally," I reply, the word ending on a gasp as he lifts me. I wrap my legs around him, and he carries me through a doorway to the right, depositing me gently on a bed that seems to fill the entirety of the small room. I have a scant moment to wonder how he got it wedged in here before he's distracting me again, nimbly removing what's left of our clothes.

In the wan light coming in through the window, I can just make out his silhouette, the moon tracing silver along lines of muscle and bone. He starts to kiss his way down my body, setting little fires en route. And I want that from him, oh, I do—especially if his kisses are a preview—but not yet.

I draw him back up toward me, our bodies in parallel, and whisper, "We have all night."

There's a rustling sound as he produces a condom from somewhere next to the bed. He settles himself on top of me, and I wind my legs around his waist again, lifting my hips. Our eyes meet with the realization that we're crossing every possible boundary—things can't be the same after this—before sensation sweeps all thought away.

I'm awash in him, in the way his body moves against mine, in his soapy masculine scent. He eventually warns me, voice strained, that he's nearing the edge, but he holds back, waiting for me to tumble over it first. I plummet fast and hard, left shaky and gasping. After he follows, he semi-collapses onto me, most of his weight still propped up on forearms and knees. His breathing is ragged, and I can hear mine is, too. For a few moments, we hold like that, limbs tangled and skin flushed.

He kisses me again, then gently disengages. "I'll be right back."

I stretch out across his bed, willing my brain to stay in off mode, to enjoy this without anything tarnishing the sheen of my high.

Light spills in from the hallway, and Cameron pokes his head around the door. "The bathroom is across the hall."

When I emerge, I can hear him in the kitchen, talking to the dog. I follow the sound of his voice down the short corridor, disappointed to see he's pulled the athletic pants back on. It's a good look for him, but now I feel extremely exposed. Spotting a basket of fresh laundry nearby, I swipe an old T-shirt off the top.

"Do you want some water?" With his back to me as he opens the refrigerator, he hasn't noticed my borrowed attire. He turns, bottle in outstretched hand, and bursts into laughter when he sees me.

I look down to read what's printed across my chest. *Coed Naked Hockey: On the Ice, It's Twice as Nice!*

"Would you like a robe instead?" he asks, still chuckling. "There's one hanging on the bathroom door."

I toy with the hem of the shirt where it's brushing my upper thigh. "Or I could take this off again, but—"

"But—?" His tone says *I'm not not intrigued.*

"You'll have to match me." I gesture at the disappointing athletic pants.

Without a word, he agrees that this is a fair deal. We barely make it back to the bed.

* * *

I never spend the night. Not ever. There are countless reasons not to, but the main one is avoiding the look: that one men have first thing in the morning, when they think they know you just because you've let them touch you.

To my surprise, Cameron doesn't have the look. I can't read him, but I can tell he's searching my face for something, too. "Good morning," I offer. I give him a reassuring smile, hoping he understands that he was well worth the wait.

He leans over to kiss me, stubble scratching at my chin and upper lip. "Do you need to get back to Eika's?"

I peek at my port, ignoring the many notifications bleeding across the lock screen. It's after ten a.m. "Not for a few hours...."

His smile makes it clear he gets the hint. "I have to take Panzer out, won't take long," he says, rolling into a sitting position and stretching. As he does, I notice lines of black ink near his left shoulder blade: a simple compass, marked with an N for north. Here in Japan, tattoos have such a hierarchy of meaning—I'd forgotten until right now that Westerners just get them for fun.

I have no tattoos myself, but I went to all the sittings for Hideki's first one. He was eighteen, a bit young, and I probably shouldn't have been allowed to accompany him, but no one in Toyama-gumi says no to the *kumicho*'s only daughter.

We sit wordlessly, the artist working on Hideki's left arm while I hold his right hand. The rhythmic popping of the sharp bamboo needle puncturing skin makes a disconcerting white noise. For the most part, Hideki is stoic, but when the design moves into the sensitive flesh of his inner elbow, he winces, grip tightening on mine.

"Almost done, right?" I ask the artist. He doesn't look up, just grunts. He's doing this ink for Hideki because of who we are, but he's made his opinion of us clear.

The result is beautiful: a long-finned orange and black koi that starts low on his forearm and curves up onto his bicep, framed by licking fingers of waves. The traditional meaning of koi is overcoming adversity— the muscular fish are able to swim against strong currents and even up waterfalls, hence the background waves.

"What possible hardship have you ever had?" I tease.

"Kaihei as an older brother isn't enough?"

We laugh, but then Hideki adds, "Anyway, it's not a koi. It's a butterfly koi, which is actually a carp, not a true koi at all."

"What's the difference?" To my untrained eye, it looks just like the koi my father keeps in the pond in our garden. He pays someone to handle their complex maintenance, but he likes to sit by the water and feed them. I think he appreciates their silence.

"They're a crossbreed with Indonesian river carp. They have a mutation that makes their fins keep growing, and if you handle them like regular koi, you'll break their fins."

It's so perfect for him that it makes my heart ache, but I can't respond without costing him face, so I squeeze his hand again instead.

Cameron and Panzer have only been gone a few minutes when there's a knock at the front door. I grab Cameron's robe off the bathroom hook and wrap myself in it, smiling at the memory of last night.

"Forget your keys?" I ask as I open the door. "Aren't you lucky that I—"

"Oh. Hello, Toyama-san." It's Cameron's friend from the party, looking as unpleasantly surprised as I feel.

I sketch a quick bow, then realize I don't remember his name. "Hello...?"

He looks amused. "Kenji."

I am not calling this stranger by his given name as if we're intimate. Keenly aware that I'm naked under this robe, I double-knot the belt and cross my arms over my chest, covering myself as best as I can.

He clears his throat. "Green's not here, then?"

"No. He should be back soon, though." Not soon enough. Making my reluctance obvious, I add, "Would you like to come in and wait for him?"

If he's polite, he'll decline.

"You'd think Green would buy a pair of slippers," he says, looking down at the floor of the entryway, which contains a jumble of Cameron's running shoes and my dress heels, but nothing for guests.

I don't respond.

Giving me a challenging look, he starts to step out of his shoes.

"Please go ahead," I say, gesturing at the kitchen. The absurdity of this would be laughable if it weren't so awkward.

I follow Kenji-san down the hall. He deposits a six-pack of Kirin Ichiban on the kitchen table and peers into the adjoining living room. It should really be the bedroom, but Cameron has squeezed in a sofa and a *kotatsu* table, and the open futon closet is being used as a shelf for the television. He may have spent part of his childhood here, but he's so very American. In its own way, it's charming.

"He's not in there, either," I comment dryly.

"I didn't think you'd hide the body in such an obvious place." He makes himself comfortable at the table, proffering the beer. "Want one?"

"It isn't even noon yet."

"There something you want me to grab you out of his fridge instead?" he counters.

What an asshole.

It's Cameron's apartment, but as I'm as close to a host as there is, I can't let a guest, even an unwelcome one, drink alone. "Fine," I say, holding out my hand.

One eyebrow sardonically raised, he hands me a bottle. Crap—I have no idea where Cameron might have a bottle opener. I don't need this jerk knowing that. I go back to the hall to grab a multitool from my bag, and as I do, I see my card case as well.

"I don't think I ever gave you my card," I say. Pulling out the case, I flip through until I find the one I want. I have at least thirty Helios cards in here, my name and title spelled out against the backdrop of the corporate sun logo, but that doesn't send the message I'm looking to convey.

Hands outstretched in a demure two-handed grasp, I offer my personal card. When I activate it, the Toyama *daimon* on the front separates into brushstrokes of black ink that form into the four *kanji* that make up my name. I don't have a title on this card, of course. The fact that it's a Toyama-gumi card, and my name is Toyama, says it all. Kenji has the decency to accept it with both hands; as he takes it, the calligraphy flickers out, replaced by the static printing hidden underneath.

He's downslope. That's worth knowing.

He holds out a card of his own, much simpler than mine, with "Asagawa Kenji, Assistant Manager, Sales and Services" printed in ordinary ink across the front. It says he works for an insurance agency in Nishi-Shinjuku.

Yeah, right. I wonder what the "services" part of "sales and services" actually entails.

Asagawa reads my card again and gives me a measured look. "So, Toyama-san, do I need to be worried about Green? Knowing the city and the dangers of things like... traffic."

"You don't seem like the type who would worry about anyone." He either hasn't picked up on or is deliberately ignoring all my subtle cues, so I might as well be as snide as I want to be.

"I didn't think that caring about your family would require carrying a sign."

Isn't that a peculiar choice of words. "Family? Or do you mean associates?" I ask, aiming my gaze at my card.

He makes a derisive sound, something adjacent to a laugh, but less warm. "Even friendly associations can be dangerous for a naive *gaijin* in Tokyo."

I narrow my eyes at him. I don't know what Cameron and I are doing, but it's best for Asagawa to think that the expiration date is coming soon. "Some associations are brief."

"Better than short-lived," he replies with pointed emphasis.

"Indeed. I've seen what happens to those who are indiscreet." I let the edge of a threat creep into my tone.

"I keep my mouth shut." He stands up and slides the remainder of the six-pack toward me. "You have my card."

And he has mine. It's not until after he's left that I realize he called me "Toyama-san" before I ever gave it to him, though. At the party, I was never introduced as more than Misora, yet somehow, he knew who I am. I have an unusual given name, to be sure, but you'd have to already know something about my father to associate me with Toyama-gumi. This Asagawa guy does not work in the insurance industry.

I grab my port. The voice that picks up at HQ has an undertone of mirth, as if I interrupted him mid-riposte. It's a Saturday, which means the B-team is on duty.

"This is Misora," I inform him bluntly. "Who's in charge today? Put me through."

"Y-yes, Toyama-sama," he stammers. The sound of a hand covering the microphone, then a muffled, "Oi! Watanabe!" Well, that's convenient.

"This is Watanabe." It's neither Hideki's mellow tone nor Kaihei's sneering bass, but it's too young to be Uncle Yusuke, so that leaves one person.

"Daichi-kun, this is Misora. Connect me to your older brother."

All of upper-tier Toyama-gumi, including Papa, have ports that are linked together in an illegal intragrid. Connecting first with HQ and getting patched out means that, should law enforcement ever check my call log, it will look like I was chatting with my father. Toyama or no, I'm ostensibly a respectable corporate researcher; I need to limit the number of high-profile *yakuza* in my call history.

"Watanabe Kaihei."

"I need something from you."

He laughs, a low, coarse chuckle. Almost before he says it, I know how he'll respond. "And I'd be more than happy to give it to you."

"How helpful," I say, pretending I don't understand his double meaning. There are times when I don't mind going a few rounds with Kaihei, but I want to be off the phone before Cameron gets back. "I have someone I want you to check into." No one is better connected than Kaihei. It's the only reason I'm willing to deal with him.

"Why?" The need to know apparently trumps the need to needle me.

"For a friend of mine. She's, uh, seeing this guy, and he's kind of shady." I have to seem evasive enough to turn curiosity into suspicion. "His name is Asagawa Kenji."

"Never heard of him," Kaihei replies. A pause. "Wait—did you say Asagawa?"

"Yes."

"I'll get back to you."

CAMERON GREEN

The alarm on my port goes off at seven a.m. A more optimistic version of me had set it last night, thinking I'd take Panzer for an early run. Distracted by Misora, I haven't paid him much attention this weekend.

Misora. I smile to myself as I roll over to hit snooze, but the drowsy pleasure of the memory fades when I see I have a blitz of unread messages. With so many, the screen only displays a preview for the first one:

I'M PREGNANT! +23 *Messages*

Heart hammering all the way up in my throat, I open the string of texts.

It takes my stupid sleep-fogged brain a moment to realize the message is from my sister. Sending it early this morning from Tokyo, she caught our brother at night, Munich time, and our parents in the late afternoon in Minneapolis. The remaining messages are a flurry of congratulations and questions.

Well, I'm sure as hell awake now.

I shoot off a *congrats!* of my own and then open a separate conversation with Reilly, Vanessa, and Drew.

(Thrilled for you guys, I really am, but I think I speak for both myself and Reilly when I say: don't do that to your brothers.) Cameron Green

Reilly immediately replies with a laughter emoji, followed by *Yeah, true.*

Vanessa Green { Sorry!)

She's not. She is laughing herself sick, guaranteed.

Drew Mukherjee { Who did you think it was from?)

VG { [grinning devil emoji])

                    *(Poor kid doesn't stand a chance with you two
                                        for parents } CG*

Reilly Green { But lucky to have us as uncles)

VG { Nice dodge attempt, Cam.)

Then, in a message just to me:

VG { Lunch on Tuesday?)

                    (Maybe. How much crap am I in for? } CG

I look at my calendar, and the only thing listed on Tuesday is my weekly with Misora at one p.m. I might need to see a friendly face beforehand. We left things in a good place this weekend, but I don't even know what vocabulary or verb tense to apply to the situation—I slept with my boss? I'm sleeping with my boss?

Ugh. I pull a pillow over my face. It smells like her.

Panzer whines at me from the doorway, then lets out a short woof. "What is it, bud?" Setting the pillow aside, I scrounge up a pair of joggers and a T-shirt. "Gimme a minute."

He goes over by the door and barks again, louder this time. Barking on a Sunday morning; great, I'll be the toast of the building.

"He probably smells the food," a voice says from the other side of the door. I unbolt it and pull it open.

"Asagawa, what the hell? It's barely after seven."

He holds up a FamilyMart sack, and the faint odor of boiled eggs wafts my way. *Oden*, maybe. "Time for breakfast, then, Green, since you have so much work to do today."

"*Oden* is not breakfast. Not for me, anyway." Reluctantly, I back up to let him in, seeing suddenly what disarray the apartment is in. I hope there aren't any obvious clues that Misora was here. I'm not awake enough to take shit about that from my family and Asagawa, too. "Wait—what work?"

"Lost the cord already?"

The cord. Oh, damn it. Asagawa follows me down the hall to the kitchen, where a giant Kuroneko delivery box full of my birthday gifts is still on the table. Nozomi had it delivered yesterday afternoon— tactfully, she waited until after Misora left. I open the lid.

"Any interest in a cowboy hat?"

Asagawa gives me a look that I choose to interpret as mild exasperation. No sense of humor in the morning, I see. "Fine, fine." I brandish the cord. "Let's see if this thing will even turn on."

I sit cross-legged on the *tatami* floor to connect the soot-crusted tower to my TV, which can double as a monitor, while Asagawa sets himself up at the kitchen table. I plug the new cord into the back of the tower, then plug the whole thing into the wall socket and flip the switch.

Zilch. It got too fried in whatever dust-up put it in this condition in the first place. I will have to do this the hard way.

"Hey, grab my multitool from under the sink, would you?" Asagawa disappears for a moment, then returns, tossing the tool my way. I unplug the tower again and unscrew the panel on the back. A stroke of luck—it was magitech-assembled, which means I can repair some of the busted circuits myself.

"Look, this first bit is going to take a while. Would you take Panzer out? His leash—"

"In the hallway, yeah. Twenty?"

That should be enough time for me to get the hard part done. I nod.

"Ready to see if it turns on?" I call to Asagawa when I hear the front door open again. I've gotten nearly all the circuits back in place. It was easier than I expected, and I only got a slight zap when a misaligned connection snapped the magic back on me. I probably should have done this outside, but there's such a minor amount of magic in this kind of old tech that it hardly matters.

Panzer, unleashed, bounds in to give me an enthusiastic slurp on the face before settling on the sofa. Hand wrapped around the Syphon grip of the multitool so that a very low wave of power passes through, I use the pincers setting to reset the final circuit. Doing this without lab lenses is like working with my eyes shut, but the circuits are simple enough that I can manage by feel alone. To Asagawa, it must look like a tiny, awkward pantomime; honestly, that's how it feels, too.

"Is this what they were doing at One Eleven?" he asks once I've finished.

"Er, not exactly."

"You being deliberately vague, Green?"

Only to the extent that I can't explain something when I don't fully understand it myself. I meant to ask Misora more about it, and then— well, I found better ways to occupy my time with her. But it remains a worthwhile question.

Before I can reply, Asagawa continues. "How did you meet those people, anyway?"

"I already told you. Through Eika."

Asagawa lets out a derisive snort. "And how do you know the famous Fujiwara Eika, recently arrived *gaijin*?"

"This gala thing my sister got invited to."

"Your sister sounds connected."

I shrug. "Not really. But she works at the U.S. embassy."

With the tower reassembled, I'm ready to try plugging it in again. I flip the switch, and the TV brightens with a burst of static that quickly resolves into a loading screen. I connect it to my Wi-Fi network and download the freeware I'll need to decipher any scrambled files.

"I don't suppose you know what you're looking for."

Another wry grunt—I am clearly not giving him whatever he wants to know—but he lets it go for now. "These people were looking into something being moved. Can you find out what and where?"

The first few files I find are corrupted beyond recognition, and they all have anodyne names like "Aug18List" and "Attendees_0412." I click on a spreadsheet called "KeyLog_Ginzan773." Unlike the others, it opens—into a list of what looks like expired AppKey codes for an *onsen* resort up in Yamagata.

"Anything?" I ask. Asagawa shakes his head.

"What about that one?" he says, pointing to a file I haven't opened yet. The *kanji* in the file name are ones I don't know; I can, however, read that the simple *katakana* at the end says "labels."

The file opens. Most of it has broken down into garbled lines of text, but there's a stray QR code. When I scan it with my port, it dead ends into a 404 error on the Kuroneko website.

"Some kind of shipping labels, probably," I say to Asagawa, tilting my port screen his way.

He frowns. "That's it?"

"Yeah. Rest of it is shot to hell."

Asagawa mutters a curse under his breath.

"What were you hoping to find out, anyway?" I ask.

"How you know Fujiwara Eika."

I unplug the computer. "Now who's being evasive?"

* * *

Vanessa meets me outside a noodle shop near Helios. She's unbuttoned her coat to accommodate the spring warmth, and now that I know to look, I can see the faintest convex curve to her abdomen. The girl who convinced me and Reilly we had to eat the paper inside the fortune cookie in order for it to come true—she's going to be somebody's mother.

"You seem on edge," she observes after we've ordered our bowls of curry *udon*. "Is this about whoever you were panicking over this morning?"

My sister knows me too well. I nod.

She doesn't waste time looking smug. "Well, who is she? How did you meet?"

"Work."

"That seems like a bad idea."

"Says the woman having a baby with her former TA." I break apart a large chunk of tempura sweet potato with my chopsticks and dunk a piece in the thick curry broth.

"I waited to ask him out until after he posted that damn A minus," Vanessa replies with a wry smile. "Is she at least in a different department?"

My noodles are fascinating.

"Cam. Cam." A pause, and I can feel her sharp gaze on me as she pieces everything together. "It's your boss, isn't it? Oh, Cameron. Not your best call."

"We're not all perfect like you." Though I aim to keep my tone light, the irritation creeps in. We get along better than a lot of siblings, but there are still years of history—fortune cookies included—as baggage. I know sleeping with Misora was a giant fuck-up that has the potential to upend my career. I also know I'd do it again, if she's offering.

Vanessa puts up her hands, palms out, in a gesture of peace. "Is it serious?"

Not wanting to answer that question, either, I shrug.

"You should check into your company HR policies or see what's in your contract about this kind of thing."

"Thanks, will do, mom," I reply, raising a piece of onion in a mock toast.

"Figured I'd better start practicing now."

"Any ideas for a name?" I'm grateful for this opportunity to change the subject.

"A few. Drew likes his great-grandmother's name, Anjali, for a girl, but I can't decide. It's too early."

"If you want a family name, there's always Cameron," I propose. "Gender neutral, so you could use it either way. And if you guys stay in

Japan for a while, it's easy for the locals to pronounce."

She laughs, but it fades quickly. "Yeah, I don't know about Japan over the long term."

"I just got here, you can't lure me back and then ditch me. Was it the earthquake? I had forgotten about those."

A frown. "Haven't you been following the news?"

"Not really."

"You might want to get caught up. The All Nippon Party has been pushing the JRP to indulge their worst impulses, and now they're trying to ram through a bill that will prevent foreigners from owning property anywhere in Tokyo."

"That's crappy. But you and Drew are in a U.S. government apartment, you don't own any property anyway." And it's not like I have any plans involving real estate.

"Cam. Think about what it means for a bill like that to be passed. You might be fine. I might, too. But Drew? This baby?"

Growing up here in Japan, Vanessa and Reilly and I all became accustomed to the mixed fascination and revulsion our light hair and round eyes triggered in our classmates. It's not that I think the U.S. is better; in many ways it's much worse. But here as at home, there's an unspoken hierarchy to race, and if you can't be Japanese, life is easier if you're white. Whiteness in Japan is mostly a curiosity, and thanks to Hollywood, can be desirable, too. But if racist xenophobia is on the rise, then I can see why Vanessa is worried for her husband and future child.

"It won't pass. Japan would be an international joke."

"As if that's stopped legislatures before. Or did you forget that the U.S. banned magic?"

She has a point. "But JRP has been pretty neutral in the past, and I thought All Nippon was motivated more by nostalgia than anything else." This conversation is fast exhausting my knowledge of Japanese politics.

"This isn't the ANP of 20 years ago," Vanessa says. "They've gotten a lot of backing from Japan First; some of their leaders aren't even bothering to hide their ties anymore. It's becoming the political arm of a hate group. Given the potential threat to Americans residing in Japan, we're closely monitoring their activities."

"What's their rationale for this?"

"It's concern-trolling-as-legislation. They're claiming that magic might be a limited resource, so they need to preserve it for Japanese citizens."

"By keeping *gaijin* from owning property? That doesn't even make sense."

"Does it need to?" Vanessa replies. "Most people don't pay any attention to politics, and they don't understand how magic works, either. The coalition sponsoring this bill knows that, and they're capitalizing on it to achieve what they actually want—phase one of their planned immigration reform."

"And by reform, you mean limitations."

"Yes. How long is your visa good for? I expect they'll tighten that up next."

"Shit," I say. I don't know what else to offer.

"To put it mildly." Vanessa checks her watch. "On that upbeat note, I have to get back for a meeting. I love you, don't be stupid."

* * *

"Green-san?" Nozomi's voice breaks through the silence of the outer suite. "Toyama-bucho is ready for you now."

Misora's office is a small space compared to the typical American corporate office, but every surface is luxe, from the leather seating to the curved glass desk. It's like the Seoul apartment's workday sibling. Not looking up from her screen, Misora waves me toward the sofa near the windows. I sit, feeling agitated, as she finishes typing and strides over to take the chair across from me, eyes now on the second screen of her port.

"Let's start with an update on the status of your projects," she says, finally glancing up. Although she's nominally looking at me, her gaze seems fixed on a point somewhere over my shoulder. Another pang of worry ripples through my gut.

"Uh, yes, right. Denali is proceeding well, and I think we'll meet your next deadline without any problems."

"Good." She scans some notes on her port. "What are the component temperatures like during energy transfer sims?"

"Everything I've tested stayed below 35 ° C, but it's been hard to get a consistent average read on what it'll be like once they're assembled. When do you think a complete prototype is possible?"

Using a small stylus, Misora adds some comments to the project notes. A wisp of her subtle perfume reaches my nose, that same scent she left lingering on my pillow. It triggers memories I can't indulge in right now. "That depends on Eika. She's been busy, but that should wrap up today."

"Even if she's not available, I could—"

"We'll wait for Eika."

I want to press her on this—why hire me for my particular expertise and then make me check simulated heat readouts, something that could be done by anyone, instead of having me continue with the biokintech core of the project? But I can't risk irritating her, especially not after what Vanessa mentioned about immigration reform. Misora is the anchor keeping me legally moored in Japan.

"I'd like to focus our time today on the tracker project. The supply chain issue I mentioned last week has been resolved, so we can move forward."

"Yeah, of course." While I'm much more interested in the battery, I've spent some time on the tracker over the last few days, and I'm pretty pleased with what I've come up with. I share the rough schematic from my port to Misora's, and her brow furrows as she looks it over.

"I recognize this is a draft," she says, "but do you have an estimate for how long it might be able to push a signal?"

"It's going to depend, to some extent, on the potency of the user. If you look at the second tab, I've worked out a formula for calculating—"

Jump! For joy! You gotta gotta gotta... JUMP! Misora's port is ringing. I've never heard it off manner mode before, and I can't believe that this, of all songs, is her ringer. I start to stand, but she gestures for me to stay put. Instead, she goes over to the windows, turning her back to me.

"Eika-chan?" She listens for a moment, giving periodic "mmhms" in response. "Congratulations, I knew you could do it. Go celebrate with Noah-kun. We'll get drinks soon."

Misora pivots to walk back to where I'm sitting, and the transformation is visible—whatever Eika's good news was, it has lanced the tension from her. She smiles at me now, leftover glow from the weekend radiating out from her like the warm amber of a lamp.

I hear myself take an unsteady breath. Did I really think one night with her would throw ice water on this? Because it's only fuel.

"Misora—" As I say it, I realize this is the first time I've used her name outside my bedroom; I see she notices, too. I don't want to ask this, but I think I have to. I need to know what she thinks we're doing, and have her understand how precarious this is for me.

"Yes?" Sitting down on the sofa next to me, she gives my knee a squeeze, then trails her hand incrementally upward. Ascertaining the destination of that hand suddenly seems much more important than what I was going to ask.

"'Jump 4 Joy,' huh?"

A light chuckle. "It was Eika's favorite song when we were kids."

"My little brother's, too." I remember Reilly playing it on repeat.

"Sometimes I forget you spent your childhood here," she replies, still casually running her fingertips across my thigh. With her other hand, she tilts her port screen so I can see it, then uses her thumb to tap *Lock Door* and set all her contact lines to *Do Not Disturb*.

"It's going to be stuck in my head all day."

She swivels herself into my lap, knees on either side of my hips. Oh, my god. "Sorry," she murmurs against my mouth, so very obviously not.

ASAGAWA KENJI

The white stone clicks into place and I can see it finally—she's run a literal circle around me and taken a third corner of the board. I thought I had blocked her early, but my protective eye formation was false, and she's killed every piece I'd placed there. There's no coming back from this one.

"Do you just invite me to play because you enjoy the carnage?" I ask with a raised eyebrow and half a smile.

Mizuki hides her expression with a sip of tea. "You're improving every time, Kenji-kun."

"That's polite-speak for 'still an embarrassment.'"

With a quick series of motions, she picks up the last eight pieces played and places her index finger at an intersection on the second line. "If you had played here instead, and if I had tried to attack here, it would have gone like this." She puts down the stones, white and black alternating. "There wouldn't have been any way for me to take the corner then."

I frown at that. "What if—" I shift the stones around so that the attack from white starts one point closer to the corner, drop in a black response. Oh, this formation would have taken only two moves to block. "I see."

The front door slides open. "I'm home," says Rina, the older daughter and absolute charm of the Kumanaka family.

Mizuki calls out a "welcome home" as she pours the dead stones she's collected from me back in with the others in my bowl.

Rina pokes her head into the room, her eyes narrowing as she sees me. "Look who has time to play games."

As a high school graduate who doesn't currently have a job, she shouldn't give me an opening like that. I respond with a broad smile. "And what're you doing with your time lately?"

"I think," Mizuki interjects smoothly, "that there are some clothes hanging on the line that could use folding."

Rina turns on her heel and storms down the hallway.

"Nice seeing you," I call after her.

Mizuki ignores my comment, dropping a handful of stones into her bowl. "Since I'm a beginner myself, I appreciate that you're willing to practice with me, Kenji-kun."

"Yeah, yeah. You say you're terrible at this and you're still holding my feet to the fire. Twist that knife." I pick the few remaining black stones out of the one corner I'd managed to hold and sweep the remaining white stones toward her. "I'm not sorry to say you'll have to wait until next week to beat on me some more. I have a businessman who isn't going to threaten himself."

"Do you need a tie?" she asks, starting to get up. Kumanaka dresses in a full suit every day, and I doubt it's because he loves the feeling of a freshly pressed collar.

"Takamine is not under any illusions that I'm taking time out of my office job to meet up with him."

The Chiyoda line connects at Harajuku to the JR loop line, which takes me to Ikebukuro. There's a bakery in the station with tables to sit. I order two beverages and eat a curry bun while I wait. Two doors. A hallway to a small walk-in bathroom, but there's no exit from that direction. Both of my ports are dead, so I plug them in to charge, leaving me watching the one staff person cleaning behind the front counter.

The sun is dropping past mid-afternoon by the time Takamine finally shows, his own middling-quality business suit hanging poorly on a stiff posture. He's decided to back out.

"Asagawa-san." The gap in our social standing is enough that his use of the last name and title is bordering on an insult.

"It's Kenji," I say to remind him that an aged businessman owes favors to a punk he considers beneath him. "I ordered you oolong tea."

He ignores the drink and jumps right in, running straight through his list of planned excuses, his face the mask of concentration.

"That's too bad," I say when he finishes.

"There've been audits, tough audits on the paperwork in every division," Takamine says, fingers flipping his port end over end against the table. "I can't cover anything in the system right now."

"I'm sorry that things are so difficult. But I hope that you can appreciate my position too."

"Your position?" he asks, setting the port down. He knows better. It's a programmed response.

"All this work I've put into helping you, well, I have to justify my time just like you do." I raise my eyebrows, widen my eyes: innocent/tired/worried.

"I see." He looks away, deep silent breath. This is a game to see if he can get out of what he owes to take the pressure off his ulcer, off the office he feels is family. Takamine is less excited to be a partner in this exchange now that he's gotten what he wanted.

Honestly, it didn't really take any time to break into his office building and get his rival fired. Nothing more than a piece of paper left on the printer that made it look like she'd been selling industrial parts at more than the company's set price and pocketing the difference. It was just a matter of setting up the pieces to fall. That I'm asking him to do something similar in practice to what I created in fiction is the problem.

He continues, "This was supposed to be done for a fee."

This is the first I've heard of it. "I don't think your manager would be happy to know about our conversations."

His mouth tightens, enough that I have to start weighing what options I have in the here and public. If I'd known we'd changed the terms, I'd have brought more leverage to this meeting or picked a different place. In a bakery, direct violence is more likely to result in police. Someone left me out to dry, intentionally or by indifference, but if I fail that'll be all on me.

I lean in and put my hand over his port where it's resting just past his fingertips. "I understand that this situation might not be what you signed up for and I humbly apologize for not having been given the correct information."

There's an almost audible exhale from his side of the table.

Casually, I move my hand and slide his port off the table, where it hits the floor with a hollow click. He leans over to reach for it, and I take the opportunity to hook my shoe in the support bar of his chair and pull it forward until his chest is against the edge of the table. With my foot between his legs, he's trapped unless he wants to make a scene.

"But you really do need to think about my position," I say quietly. "I've been given a job here, told what you are supposed to do for me in this meeting. Now, I find it at least as annoying as you do that this isn't what you were promised before. But that doesn't change the fact that if I don't bring back what I'm supposed to, there are going to be consequences that hurt."

He glances over at the employee, who is wiping down the counter in front of the front display. I tap the table with my knuckle to bring his attention back to me and shake my head. "Don't you think that I'd be willing to give you, and her, as much of a consequence as I think I'll get to avoid that?"

Takamine pulls his arms back and braces his palms against the table, but his only options are to push hard enough to topple the chair backward or to dive to the side, either one messy. His eyes are wide, swinging side to side, searching for an escape that isn't here.

He knows that I can find him at work. At home, if need be.

Finally, after a long moment, he instead reaches behind his shoulder and awkwardly pulls the soft-sided briefcase from where it was hanging on the corner of his chair, setting it next to the still-full cup of tea on the table. With trembling fingers, he plays with the zipper, refuses to meet my eyes. He did bring it, just in case, and now he's going to go through with this.

"Like I said, I'm just trying to keep this easy. For everyone." I let his chair go free and add a clear plastic folder containing two order forms from my own black-checkered bag to the table.

Takamine pulls out a monogrammed pen with its own special case and a metal box covered in smiling radish decorations. "Only two you want to order?" he asks.

One pump is listed on each invoice, the specific make and description stretching a full line of numbers. "Yeah, I'll take two and then you'll be paid in full."

I leave it unstated that this payment is probably only good for as long as we don't want something else out of him.

He takes the order forms to his side of the table and adds a few marks with the pen. Then with a shaky hand, he opens the radish tin and removes two official-looking *hanko*, one oval and one rectangular. For each order, he makes an imprint of bright red ink running off the edge of one request and onto the corresponding payment record—matched pairs, ready to be separated.

As he fans the ink dry with his hand, I say, "I can take those. Someone over with installation will send them into purchasing for us and it'll be less suspicious than sending them in yourself."

A lie, but an easy one for him to accept. Hundreds of jobs run through the authorization department a week. This makes it harder to trace it back to him; easier to disassociate from trouble, to plead forgetfulness.

He nods and secrets his tools back away, careful to keep them safe from the unscrupulous. The papers I pull back and secure in my folder. I don't know who the pages are going to, but I do know the individual orders are meaningless. The stamp imprints are going to be made into duplicates.

"Thanks for your cooperation," I say as I pick up his port, the corner a little scuffed but the screen unbroken, and slide it across the table to him.

He bows and thanks me, the tilt of his head just enough to indicate a bare kind of respect in spite of the gap. "It's been good to work with you." "Better to be finished" is left hanging.

Papers secure, I can't help myself. "No need to be polite. We both know I'm a pain in the ass."

* * *

The smell of peaches and citrus sneaks up from behind me a second before I feel fingers poking my sides. "Chiyo," I say.

"Eeeeeh, Kenji-san," she sighs into my ear. "You have such disappointing reflexes."

Better I don't use them: my reflex would be an elbow to the temple. "It'd be different if you were more stealthy."

Igarashi leans in, his beer glass is at an angle dangerously close to pouring the contents in my lap. "Yet still she tries."

That would not be the first time when bonding with the Walling office has resulted in an alcohol splashing. Casually, I push his glass upright. "She should try another hobby. Definitely not *ninjitsu*. Maybe sumo?"

"Kenji-san!" She pushes between the two of us, her face pink. "Such a meanie."

"Both my job and my hobby."

We're at a traditional bar with the table set into the floor, my feet hanging in the indent below it. Chiyo leans forward, putting her hand high on my thigh as she reaches toward the table top. "You need more to drink!"

Subtle. My ignoring of handmade Valentine chocolates has not deterred her efforts.

She grabs the larger bottle and with a shaky hand pours enough into my glass that it overflows foam onto the table. She tries to pick up the glass for me, but I grab it before she can. Half smile, raised eyebrows, show good humor. "Thanks."

To my right, Funabashi's drink is getting low. I'm not sitting in this spot by chance—he likes to make me fill his managerial glass so I don't forget where I rank. I take a long but shallow drink of my own glass for Chiyo, and then lean forward to grab another bottle from the table. Not accidentally, I loop my shoulder in front of her arm, forcing her to either move or lock her elbow uncomfortably. She withdraws her arm and I pour for Funabashi. He ignores his glass, continues telling Hanaoka and Tomohiko on his other side about his recent trip to Okinawa.

I lean back and look over at Igarashi. "How's the progress on the house?"

He gives me a pained look. "Still on the market. There doesn't seem to be much draw for houses in our neighborhood right now."

"Best of luck." I raise my glass and we both drink.

As he sets his glass down, Igarashi starts to say something, but we're interrupted by Chiyo again pushing between us. This time she's determined, setting her own glass down on the table and climbing in. There isn't room for her to fit between our hips, so she slips her legs in between mine and sits on my left thigh.

"Did you two hear about the new pitcher for the Tigers? Seven games in and he has an ERA of 1.36," she says. Her bangs are clipped back from her face with a plain clip that's starting to tarnish around the ends. There's a distinct flush around her cheeks and down her neck, vanishing into her shirt that has mysteriously become unbuttoned at the top.

Both Igarashi and I groan dramatically. He says with disapproval, "Chiyo-chan, you live in Tokyo. How can you possibly root for them?"

"My support isn't related to prox...proxim..." She wrinkles her forehead and continues, "...nearness." Speaking of near—strands of hair are sliding out of her clip. Her body is warm and uncomfortably close and soft on my thigh.

I lean back, putting my weight on my left hand and digging out my orange J-play portable from my right pocket. These two minefields are better not engaged.

She's not happy with this decision. "Kenji-san, you can't miss discussing the best sport, can you?"

I show her the black screen. "Looks like I'm not."

"Oh, poor you. I can help!" She grabs the port out of my hand and presses it against the hollow of her cheek like she's making a dimple with her finger. A long moment and nothing happens. "Just kidding! Igarashi is much better at this."

He takes the port from her and dutifully lays it in the crook of his arm. "I guess, yeah."

"Oh!" She suddenly lunges forward toward my right, and grabs Funabashi's face-down port from the table in front of him. "Maybe you need a charge too, sir?"

Funabashi snatches the port out of her hand in the air, fast. Faster than normally necessary. "No, that's quite alright."

Between his fingers I can just see a series of messages, the glance too short to see more than one *kanji*: Snow.

There might be legitimate reasons to be talking about the weather, but the temperature hasn't been cold enough for it in Tokyo the past few years. Funabashi's recent vacation took him far south, not north. There's also the possibility of quoting a movie or song lyric, but that seems out of character for Funabashi, whose interests as far as I can tell are eating plain white rice and making sure his paperclips are alphabetized.

Snow is also the first of the two characters in Yukina, my mother's given name.

Now who would he be talking to about her by text message?

Chiyo has already popped to her feet and is navigating the awkwardness with a series of short bows bent over and around the edge of the table. I sit up and bump my knee into the back of hers, removing her support. She drops down hard onto her left elbow and right hand and the whole table jumps. My nearly full glass teeters on a corner, tips over in my direction. Liquid runs off everywhere, mostly off the edge and down my pant leg. Funabashi slips his port into his jacket pocket as he moves to the side, neatly avoiding the mess. It was worth a try.

There's a long pause around the table, and finally Tomohiko asks, "Are you okay, Chiyo-chan?"

She lets out a long dramatic wail: "I spilleeeeeeeeeeeeeeeed."

There's a collective release of tension as everyone laughs at once.

Igarashi hands me my port and his wet towel. Kneeling, both Chiyo and I try futilely to sop up the mess on the table and the wooden seat. A moment later our waitress arrives with a bucket and some larger towels. We scoot back out of her way, as I use another towel from the table to catch as much of the beer oozing from my pant leg as possible.

"Kenji-san, I'm so sorry. I don't know what happened." She's pink across her whole face, and so apologetically eager.

I smile, roll my eyes upwards wryly. "I wish I could say this was the first time I've taken a beer bath," I say. "That said, I think this is my hint to head out."

"Do you need help?" she asks.

Tempting, but while on Monday all is generally conveniently forgotten from these outings, there are some lines that once crossed are asking for trouble.

"I'll be okay." I weigh whether to say more—sometimes a hit of true information can be a helpful motivator and I'm clearly not someone she should be following around like this. No, not useful here. Too many people, and casting myself as more of a forbidden object is probably not going to motivate her in a way I'd want. "See you at work."

The air outside the *izakaya* is cool, but not cool enough to help after spending that much time with Chiyo sitting on my leg. Whatever Funabashi is up to is going to have to wait until I can focus. Leaning against the railing by the sidewalk, I pull out a different port, one that's still at 42%, and flip through a few port numbers before picking one.

(Hey, this is Kenji } No Name

Date Hatsumi { Really? Did not expect to hear from you)

DH { What's up?)

(Just got hit with a glass of beer } No Name

DH { Actually hit with the glass? Or the liquid inside the glass?)

DH { Also you were probably asking for it)

(True on both } No Name

(But mostly the liquid) No Name

(How's your night?) No Name

DH { Boring)

DH { You bored too?)

(If that's what you want to call it) No Name

(You prefer we can get a drink) No Name

DH { Don't you want to get out of those wet clothes?)

(That's a terrible line) No Name

DH { Did it work?)

(Where are you?) No Name

DH {Shibuya, you?)

I'm in Shinjuku a few stops away, but no need to share that. There are plenty of love hotels in that area, market demand from the number of bars.

(Not far. Meet at Shibuya station?) No Name

DH { Looking forward to it)

* * *

"I'm starving," Date says to the ceiling an enjoyable time later. "Want to get something to eat?"

"Haven't we both had enough to eat?"

"Ha, never heard that joke before." She elbows me. "I'm going to hit up Yoshinoya if you want to join me."

I'm tired, but the bit of bar food I had before my self-induced accident has worn off. I grunt something that approaches agreement and roll off the bed in search of my now only slightly damp pants.

Yoshinoya is a bright storefront in the middle of a now-darkening side street. There's a single salaryman at the counter, his tie loosened and coat resting across his legs. Even in an entirely empty restaurant he wasn't willing to take up the stool next to him.

We take a seat at the other end, and order basic beef bowls. I pay for both of us, and she gives me a make-up-smeared side eye around the corner of her glasses.

"You carry an awful lot of money around for being a not-*yakuza*, not-salaryman. What do you do again, Tanaka Kenji?"

She's digging at my cover story to see if I'm going to give different answers this time. That seems to be a habit of hers, not surprising from a journalist. Interesting that my actual last name hasn't made it to her from either Green or Toyama-hime. Are they hiding something or did she just not think to ask?

"Horizon Contracting. Tanaka," I say. "Private contractor. Did you lose my card?"

"Right. That is what you said before."

Her frustration at half-answers is entertaining. Leaning my elbow against the counter, I pull out a smile. "I do say a lot of things, don't I?"

"So, what kind of private repairs? Ceiling repair man?"

"Sometimes, if that's where the money is. You'd be amazed what you can find up there."

Date cracks half a smile as she pulls her port out. Her face drops as she reads. "Speaking of money, Eika forgets I can't afford this crazy club she likes." She tucks her port away again. "The only reason I could do it last time was she threw me a party there."

I'm not particularly interested, but I manage a non-committal *hm*.

"You know, for my birthday Misora bought me a pair of designer tennis shoes that are so expensive I'm afraid to take them out of the box." She sighs. "Yeah, dumb thing to complain about, right? I mean, I'm proud of having gotten myself to where I am, considering everything."

The little I caught on their backstory, she graduated from a fancy school with her friends. Can you even count someone as getting there themself if they stepped off an ivy elevator? For once I don't say it, though. My beef bowl isn't here yet, and I'd like to eat something before I pick a fight.

She continues, "It's just that with The Fujiwara Eika and The Toyama Misora around all the time, I can't not see it—you know, what I don't have."

I know the local Toyama affiliate, the Oishiro-gumi, down to their shoe sizes (24, 25.5, 26, 26, 28.5, 29). Walling is strategically located on the edge of much more prominent group territories, in the space overseen by that group of *yakuza* who lack ambition, the area serving as a buffer between the bustling hotspot of Kabukicho, the political Nishi-Shinjuku 2 area, and the Korean heritage groups of Shin-Okubo. None of the Oishiro-gumi want more than their regular L proceeds and the appreciation of the local small business owners for low protection costs. We work outside the area and stay out of their way. They don't need to acknowledge our existence, which is a win all around.

The top of their hierarchical chain is a mountain peak so far out of reach that I haven't paid them much attention. Toyama Razan is a household name in our circles, akin to the prime minister, but with a lot more direct authority. When I agreed to come to a *gaijin* birthday party, the last thing I expected was to meet his daughter, the Toyama crown princess.

It was even more surprising to find her gracing Green's 1LDK apartment with her presence not long after. When she answered the door, my first instinct was to bail, at least until she guarded the hallway like she owned it.

Our beef bowls arrive, and Date is still talking. "—last weekend," she concludes.

I take a bite of beef and savor the sweet flavor.

Date's enjoying complaining, but there's no way that Toyama-hime hasn't pulled some strings to help out her friends. Fujiwara Eika in particular seems to have done very well in all this. She'll probably regret it—*yakuza*-tied celebrities often find that what seemed like a favor is a leash in the end.

Date is also quietly taking her first bites, so I use the opening to ask, "How did your group meet Green again?"

She points her chopsticks at me. "I'll tell you, but first you have to give me a real answer: same question to you."

We're playing a game. I make a face as if I'm reluctant to divulge such important secrets, and then pretend to cave. "You know how his sister works at the US embassy?"

"Yeah," she says, not specifying if she knew or if she just wants me to continue.

"I took him hostage at an embassy function."

Date stops a bite of rice halfway to her mouth. "What? Really?"

I give her a long even look, and eventually we both smile at each other knowingly. "Truth? I broke into his apartment. He came home and then his reaction was so funny that I kept doing it."

She closes one eye in consideration. "I don't know if that story is more or less believable than the first one. Why break into a *gaijin*'s apartment in the first place?"

"Auxiliary questions weren't part of the deal. How do you know Green?"

"Oh, you know, Eika-something-something." She waves her hand in the air vaguely.

"Eika-something-something?" I repeat back to her slowly. "That is the worst story I've ever heard."

Her cheeks bunch up as she gives me an impish smile that reaches to her eyes. "I didn't say it was interesting, only that I'd tell you."

I chuckle and give her an appraising look before turning back to my rapidly cooling food. "And people say I'm shifty."

Between bites of her own bowl, she manages to reply: "I'm lucky to have a very trustworthy face."

We finish our food and walk back to Shibuya station before the trains can stop running. She heads off toward the Keio-Inokashira line, and the loop line connects me back to Shinjuku. Soon I'm finishing the short walk to my building. Stairs up to the second floor, I'm at my door. It's only been about 12 hours since I left, but it feels like days. Time to collapse.

I step inside and flip off my right shoe.

Directly ahead, Asagawa-san is sitting at my table, staring at my wall. She doesn't turn to look at me immediately.

How did my mother find my apartment? Was I followed at some point? Payment trace? Did Kumanaka break our unspoken agreement to not share each other's personal information?

"I'm home," I say. New first item of business: move. For tonight, maybe a hotel in a different ward of the city.

"Welcome," she says, clearly meaning the opposite.

Inventory: main door behind me, balcony ahead but past where she is sitting. Pocket knife in the cupboard by the TV. Chopsticks and silverware in the kitchenette around the corner. Water glasses above the sink. A few pens in a bag on the floor. Umbrella behind me. Hammer in the closet. Nothing would be visible from there.

I smell like beer, too. Positive: She probably doesn't expect much if she thinks I'm boozed. Negative: Resemblance to Kumanaka.

"There's been a break-in."

I frown. "At Walling?"

"You could call it that, but not the main office."

Hell, she's talking about the storage room where I've been spending so much time lately. Tilt my head, mimic confusion. "What are you talking about? Where?"

Her eyes are flat and black and dead. A long moment and then, "Sit down."

I look at my small table. There's a ceramic plate sitting in the middle, left from my lunch yesterday. I'd rather not.

"Fucking sit down."

I fucking sit.

She turns toward me and puts her arms on the table, her fingers closer than I'd like to the plate. The same square black ring that crosses two knuckles she's been wearing for years is on her right hand, and her shirt is the plain high-necked style she's always worn. Takeshi and I used to play hideout in her closet filled with black shirts and pants.

She wasn't pleased with that, but then she generally wasn't pleased with much that children do.

"The hard drive," she says. Abrupt turns in conversation are her favorite method for keeping people off guard.

At the end of a long day, it's working. "What?"

"From the job in February."

"I drilled it and disposed. Like we normally do," I say quickly. With a crinkle between my eyebrows, I project mild confusion. The statement is true enough—that is what I did once Green finally made good on our agreement a few days ago.

Too bad there wasn't much left on the drive to be recovered in the first place, just something about shipping labels. Since I seem to be dancing around information on contraband, discovering that it's being transported without any details on when or where gave me nothing new.

But tracking numbers for her own shipment aren't something she should need to get from a third party. After all, I thought those breakers were looking into what she was doing, not the other way around.

Asagawa-san makes a small sound, no comment. She doesn't need to say anything more.

"I apologize." I didn't know she wanted the drive. She didn't tell me. If that was what Kumanaka was trying to say, he could have been clearer before he passed the fuck out that night.

She gets up. I stand immediately out of respect. We're done.

"Useless," she says as she steps past me, boots heavy on the wooden floor.

"Kumanaka—" I stop, there's nothing I can say that won't cause splashback to him, to their family. "Before I drilled the drive, I took a look in case it might be valuable."

She turns to look at me, her eyes black and empty, somehow staring down at me from just below my height. She's waiting, listening. An opening, maybe.

"That job at Pinking, something was off—"

Within even those words, I realize my mistake: The pause was a trap. To her mind, there's no good reason to go behind her back, to look at the details she's deliberately withheld. No one would trust a hammer to make decisions.

I don't try to avoid what happens next because it would only make things worse.

A flash of black, then white sparks across my vision. My cheek burns as her hand hovers in the air for a moment before dropping. She has a sharp punch. The back of the hand here is a statement of contempt.

I resist the urge to touch my cheek where her ring bit in.

Shit. Shit.

Dropping to my knees, I put my hands out flat. The floor under my fingers is scuffed and dusty, with white crumbs from where I haven't cleaned lately. The scar on my right thumb is still there from the time with the glass, stretching across the inside in an arc to the top of the first knuckle.

Forehead to floor, I close my eyes. "Excuse me. I spoke out of turn. I won't do it again."

She rests the heavy heel of her boot on the flat fingers of my left hand, next to my cheek, just enough pressure to make it clear that she could but she isn't.

"No, you won't," Asagawa-san says, and for once we are in agreement.

* * *

There isn't much that I really need to keep in my apartment, but leaving things I just bought four months ago behind isn't my favorite thing to do either. I have a large bag for this purpose, one that I usually keep my clothes in. On top I add my towel, soap, a pair of shoes, coats, small bag of tools, and pour my silverware drawer into the bag, including the awl I accidentally kept from being stabbed a few months ago.

The two glasses and stack of plates are going to have to stay, too breakable. My futon, too big. Same for the table, the TV, the vacuum, the washing machine, the fridge, the cooktop. No reason to even buy one of those anymore when I eat out and a hot water pot would do for quick meals.

The set of free weights I just bought last month makes me pause but I want to leave now and it's literally dead weight. Replaceable online with quick delivery.

There's a set of backup ID cards in a box over my sink. She might have found them so no good for securing a new apartment, but they can still be used for work purposes. I drop the tin into my soft-sided briefcase.

I leave a short stack of ten-thousand yen bills on the table with a note that just says "sorry, had to leave." It's enough to cover cleaning the apartment out and hopefully prevent the landlord from looking too hard into where their tenant went when the rent doesn't show up next month.

There are plenty of hotels in the area, thousands in Tokyo in general, so I have options of where to go.

When it starts to hurt, I realize I'm flexing my right hand. I make myself stop. I don't want to be seen right now, don't want to talk, don't want to be on a camera somewhere.

Another plan, then. Although they don't give specific addresses, online rental listings include the room number and a photo of the building front. It doesn't take much to find a building I recognize from the area, one far enough away that it feels like a move.

Since the trains stopped running an hour ago, there aren't many people outside even in this busy area. I take a route through a backstreet of the 2-chome area and cross over into 5-chome on the other side of four-lane Yasakuni-dori. Around another alleyway, and I come up the side of the building I'd found online. There used to be some kind of music store here but it's a FamilyMart on the main floor now. At some point the city is going to be nothing but convenience stores.

The front entry has a keypad for the sliding glass door after hours, well-lit and not exactly where I want to stand until I punch through possible combinations to find the right one. The side street has a roofed area for trash, and next to that the emergency stairs with a tall metal door, locked of course. I climb over the gate and open the door from the inside, grab my two bags, and climb the nine flights of stairs to the apartment in the listing. I knock just in case, and when no one answers I pick the lock.

Inside the air is musty—this apartment has been empty for a while. The one-room space has carpet to sleep on, and the utilities are running so I can at least use the toilet and wash the cut on my cheek. On Monday I'll use one of the IDs I had in my wallet to sign a formal rental agreement. Tonight, I can finally get some sleep.

I plug in the knot of portable chargers. If she needs something done, tonight more than any other time, I need to answer. On my orange port there's a low-priority notification—Green posted on social a photo of some shirt a few hours ago, the design covered in roman letters. I respond with a picture of a Lawson pack of white rice from a few weeks ago, the same photo that I've sent to him five times already. Almost instantly the photo adds a small gray (1) after it, but he doesn't comment. No need to encourage my behavior.

All things done, I lay down on the floor, a pile of T-shirts serving as a pillow and blue-gray light diffusing through the pebbled balcony door by my feet. The walls are covered in some kind of cream wallpaper, textured, that runs up the sides and around the beams supporting the ceiling. The sound of traffic from Yasakuni-dori is an intermittent hum.

I roll over onto my hands and do one push-up and then another. It feels satisfying, so I keep going.

I was halfway through high school when Takeshi left out the window, a few belongings in a bag. I didn't know what to do, how to stop him, short of hurting him. After he was gone, I didn't know what else to do besides protect him however I could. Our mother never wanted children, but once gained she didn't want one taken away.

Somewhere around fifty I stop counting and just keep going until I'm breathing rapidly and my muscles are burning. Finally, I drop down and roll onto my back, lying there with the dampness of my shirt sandwiched between me and the carpet.

Takeshi should have known what would happen. Maybe he did, and he just didn't care. He didn't offer to take me with him, going somewhere unknown, nothing to carry with him including family ties.

"Get out of here" was all he had to say, vague about whether he meant the room or the life he was leaving behind.

I turn onto my side and stare at the long empty wall, the reflections from the street outside leaving a column of cold light smeared across the space.

"Hell," I say finally to the empty room. "I think my sweat stain of a brother was right after all."

TOYAMA MISORA

Watanabe Kaihei { BG7. Tonight.)

He must have something on Asagawa. At least we're not meeting at HQ. With no completed tracker to show, I'd rather not risk an encounter with my father. Excuses don't land well with Toyama Razan.

Taehyun is in the living room reading a script when I step out of the bedroom. "Would you?" I ask, facing away from him. The zipper on my dress has snagged on the fabric, and it's stuck partway. He worries at it for a moment, fingers warm against the skin of my back; then it loosens, and he slides it up to the top. It's oddly intimate, given our strange limbo right now.

"Nice," he says appreciatively as I turn around. "Where are you headed?"

"I have to meet Kaihei at the club."

Taehyun has never met Kaihei, but he's heard plenty. "Sorry."

"Yeah, me, too. What's that?" I ask, indicating the script.

"A commercial for Shin *ramyeon*."

"Ramen is a little too on-brand for you, isn't it?"

He gives me a pained look, nods, then goes back to skimming his lines.

"Taehyun."

"Yeah?" He doesn't look up.

"Is this working for you?"

"It's the same thing we've always done," he says slowly, turning a page. "How long are you going to let this go on?"

"You and me?"

"You and I can continue indefinitely. You and him."

I shrug. "I don't know." And that's the truth, too.

* * *

Opening the door to VIP 6, I see I'm not the first to arrive. "You're the wrong Watanabe," I say to Hideki as I seat myself across from him. He already has my G&T waiting.

A few short months ago, I sat at this exact table with Eika and her stray American. How things have changed. "Where's Kaihei?"

"They're coming," he says, and I wonder who else that includes. "But I wanted to see you first. Misora, I know I'm the last person who should give you any kind of advice. But this Asagawa guy—you've gotta drop him."

Of course Hideki knows about my inquiry. For two brothers who don't particularly like one another, he and Kaihei certainly do blab.

"Why?"

He fidgets with his glass, the ice clinking against the sides. "I don't know what Kaihei is planning to tell you, or what all he has on Asagawa-gumi—"

"Asagawa-gumi?" I interrupt. "He's part of an organization? Why haven't I heard of them?"

"It's small and independent. No official ties to us or any other family—deliberately so. Asagawa Yukina keeps herself unassociated so that she can take work from all of us."

Yukina: Asagawa's mother, I suppose, or maybe an aunt. I lift my drink, inhaling the crisp juniper aroma before I sip. "And?"

Clink, clink, clink. He keeps swirling the ice around in his whisky, until finally I reach over and still his hand.

"Look, this is secondhand, but I checked around with some of the guys, and one of them hired her in the past. She gets picked up for the kind of work no one wants to do themselves." He leans forward.

"Misora, Morimoto has hired her."

I've heard Papa refer to Morimoto Hisataka as "one sick fuck" with chuckling approval. Six years ago, a Helios board member tried to oust my mother in a nasty little coup. When that failed, he somehow managed to draw a bath and open his own wrists... with ten broken fingers. The police ruled it a suicide.

"No," I say. "Morimoto does his own wetwork."

Hideki looks unconvinced. "It's what I heard."

I take a longer swig of my drink.

The door swings open, and Kaihei pushes his way in. He's accompanied by one woman, a petite wisp who I vaguely recognize as the face of Plum-Plum skincare, and almost a dozen men, all in their late twenties and early thirties. I can match each man's face to someone in my father's inner circle—these are the sons, nephews, younger brothers and cousins of his closest advisors.

"What is this?" I ask Hideki.

"Kaihei's drinking club. I thought you knew."

Hideki and I stand, and I observe that none of them were forewarned I would be here—surprise registers across several faces.

"Good evening," I say coolly, and I make note of how each one responds.

From Kimura, Yamaguchi, Fukui, Tanimoto, Koizumi, and Hamasaki: proper bows. Fully bent at the waist like the mountain fold of an origami, as if it were my father standing in my place. Honda, Matsushita, Abe, and the woman offer lazy nods. Takahashi sneers, but he doesn't matter—his father is Papa's lawyer, he's not real Toyama-gumi. And bringing up the rear, Sanada Naoya.

Sanada Akifumi is one of my father's most trusted lieutenants: he answers directly to Uncle Yusuke. He's a good man, loyal and intelligent. Unfortunately, his nephew Naoya is a waste of the pasty skin that holds him together. Only his uncle's position and his friendship with Kaihei have allowed Naoya to claw his way up the Toyama-gumi ladder.

His gaze starts at my feet before moving oh-so-slowly up my legs. The white dress I chose for tonight is modestly cut across the neckline, but it's short, and it clings. As his eyes continue to travel upward, I notice that the others have gotten quiet, and I can see Hideki's hands clenching and unclenching in my periphery.

"Good evening, Misorrrra-san," Naoya drawls, hitting the "r" with a rolling machismo.

Hips; abdomen; breasts. Each part is being catalogued and judged, but there's no wash of discomfort like when I stood half-dressed in front of Asagawa. Only anger.

Two can play at this.

I don't bother with the slow pan up his body—I just zero in, right below the belt. And stare.

At first, he laughs. But when I don't look away, letting the time stretch out instead, he starts to fidget. I tilt my head and squint, leaning closer, and a few of the guys titter; the petite woman smothers a smile behind her hand. "I think you're unzipped," I finally say, and, dear god, if Naoya isn't stupid enough to look down and check.

"Or not," I shrug, and the quiet chuckling turns full-throated. Everyone is laughing except for Naoya; even Kaihei looks amused.

Tension broken, I can sense Hideki relaxing. He waves everyone over to the bar, and they troop past me, jockeying to be served first.

"Tell me what you found," I say to Kaihei, more than ready to leave.

He gives me a wolfish grin. "I left a file for you downstairs in Yoshida's office—told him you'd pick it up when you drop this month's cash."

The cash I don't have, because Papa's holding it at HQ until it can be tagged with the new tracker—the tracker I haven't finished yet.

"Why is it always like this with you?" He knows perfectly well the cash is still out.

He looks away from me, and I follow his line of sight toward the bar, where Hideki is setting up shots for all the other privileged sons of Toyama-gumi.

"That was nearly a decade ago."

He's still watching his brother, jaw set tight. "And the Korean actor? Or Asagawa Yukina's punk son?"

Letting him think I'm sleeping with Asagawa Kenji had seemed like a good way to hide the real reason for my inquiry. But I should have known Kaihei would take it as a personal slight.

"God, you're lazy," I say.

That pulls his attention away from Hideki. "What?" he snarls, voice low and cold.

"Lazy," I repeat. "There are a thousand paths to what you want, but since it wasn't handed to you on a silver platter, you blame me."

I lean closer to him, keeping my tone even. "You think I don't understand what's happening here tonight? You want me to see what you're creating. Fine. I have only one thing to say to you about that."

Kaihei crosses his arms over his chest, expression defiant. He's waiting for me to issue my challenge.

"You can have it. All of it." I grab my jacket off the back of the chair and don't look back.

* * *

Yoshida looks relieved to see me. "Toyama-san, what a pleasure."

"Likewise, Yoshida-san." He waits expectantly for me to hand him the usual thick envelope. If he were in touch with any of the other club managers, he'd know that he's one of three to get paid late this month... but, of course, he's only allowed to report upward. All communications are tracked in the intragrid; Papa hasn't stayed *kumicho* this long because he blindly trusts his men.

The silence grows heavy and awkward, neither of us willing to ask for what we want. Finally, he pulls a small plastic case out of a desk drawer. "Watanabe's boy dropped this off for you," he says, passing me the datacell.

I pop it out of the case and slide it over the Syphon panel on my port, then give the data a quick skim. It's the usual Watanabe work-up: Asagawa's old addresses; his known associates; a rap sheet that details a few minor scrapes with the law. With everything downloaded to my port, the datacell is blank, so I toss it in the nearby recycling bin and stand. "Thanks."

My hand is on the doorknob when Yoshida clears his throat. "Mi-chan—please—" The desperation in his voice, combined with the familiar address I haven't heard from him in years, makes me freeze.

Yoshida was barely out of his initiate phase when my father took power. I was too young at the time to fully understand everything that was happening, but I know it was ugly. Ugly enough that my father assigned loyal men to guard me and my mother, and Yoshida was one of those men.

Like my mother, Yoshida's wife is ethnic Korean, so Papa knew he could be trusted. I remember him walking with me to school, hand on my shoulder, telling me different trivia depending on what I was studying at the time. "Did you know Venus is the only planet to spin clockwise?" he'd say when I told him I was learning about the solar system. Or history: "Fukuzawa Yukichi, the man on the 10,000-yen note, founded Keio University." As I grew up, so many of the men in Toyama-gumi started looking at me differently, in a way that would have boiled Papa's blood, had he noticed. But never Yoshida.

As I sink back into the chair across from his desk, I hear him tell me about how his son needs cram school to get into a good university. About how there aren't many chances for a boy with "parents like his." How his mother wants him to have legitimate work and a bright future. Words brilliantly targeted at all my weak points, whether Yoshida realizes it or not.

I open my wallet and count 117,000 yen. Keeping enough to cover incidentals, I hand over the rest. Eleven Fukuzawa Yukichis.

"I do sincerely apologize for the delayed payment from headquarters," I force out, the words tasting like ash in my mouth. I am giving my money to a man who is stealing from my father.

He stammers out his gratitude, and I hold up one hand, palm out. "Don't."

I could let this go, let Yoshida get caught in the dragnet that's coming—because even if my cash keeps him from dipping into the till this month, he'll still eventually be discovered. But then I think of what I saw upstairs, the lion cubs eager to flex their claws over the pride. I may have told Kaihei I don't want any of this, but that doesn't mean I truly want to see him have it, either.

"I hope that will be enough to keep the lights on," I continue. We both know the club's utilities are auto-deducted from the accounts of the shell corporation that owns BG7. "I think this month's payment may be... different from what you're used to."

Yoshida's quick, thankfully—he nods nervously and squirrels the cash into a drawer.

For a surprisingly low price, I've bought myself an ally.

* * *

Meetings always crowd my mornings, so it's well into the afternoon before I make it down to the lab. Cameron is alone in the damper room, a pleasant surprise. I flip the TESTING light on and slide the safety bolts.

He's at the bench, fiddling with the thin cover for a charging panel. It isn't high-risk work, but the plants in here can soak up any power leak.

"Isn't that Matsuda's project?" I ask.

"Yeah, he's been having trouble getting the interface to link, so we swapped—he wrote my last report."

"I knew that Japanese was too good to be you."

"Thanks," he says dryly as he uses a tweezer to lift what looks like thin air. Through his lab lenses, he can see and manipulate the magical structure Matsuda has created, but I'm not wearing mine. "How has your morning been?"

Am I imagining the faint rebuke in his tone? I left his apartment after he fell asleep and haven't seen him since. Staying overnight is a relationship, and I'm already in one of those with Taehyun.

"Busy." I'm about to follow up when his port rings.

"Could you grab that?" he asks, setting down the tweezers and pushing his lenses on top of his head.

A familiar face appears on the screen with the incoming call—Hatsumi's official *Nihon Times* portrait. Frowning, I hand Cameron his port. Hatsumi has no reason to be calling him.

"This is Green."

He listens for a moment, brow furrowed. He's keeping his voice low, but I catch the name "Asagawa," and my chest tightens. I noticed her talking to him at the party, but never thought she'd follow through with someone like him. How many times do I have to tell her that if she keeps pulling at this thread, the whole thing will unravel?

"What did she want?" I ask when Cameron ends the call.

"Asagawa's family name. And his parents' names, too."

I'm fairly certain Asagawa Kenji sprang, fully formed, from the head of a malevolent Shinto god.

"Also," he continues, lowering his lenses and picking up the Syphon panel again, "she said something about keeping a wall of guys she's slept with?"

I force a laugh, even as my sick feeling intensifies. "She might."

"What does she—ouch! Crap." The interface sparks, and he drops the tweezers, bringing his right index finger to his mouth.

"Are you alright?" I hop down off the bench and get a first aid kit out of the top drawer, but he waves it away.

"Yeah, I'm fine. This thing isn't encoded quite right."

"Want me to look at it?"

"Do you have time?"

I grimace. "Not really. I came down here hoping you could help me with something, actually."

"On the tracker?"

"Yes." The battery went out for prototyping three days ago, so until it comes back, the tracker is our first priority. "I worked on it a bit this morning, and the core track function works well now, but it's pulling everything away from the adhesion mechanism."

Even with Cameron's help, there's no way I'll have it by the time I see my father tomorrow, but Papa will want a status report. He's going to have to release the April payments to the club managers and risk the lost cash. If only I could tell him that won't be a problem this month.

"Okay. I'll check it out once I'm done with this."

"Then I'll leave you to it."

"I would be distracted by you anytime."

I lift his hand, making sure the burn is minor before bringing it to my lips. What am I doing? This is the kind of thing you only do if you stay the night.

He leans down so that his face is close to mine. I tilt my head to kiss him, but his lips graze my earlobe instead, the seductive warmth of his breath rousing a shiver. "When are you going to come over again?"

I close my eyes, longing to arch myself against him even as I know that I shouldn't. "Tomorrow night."

Now his mouth finds mine, a teasing prelude. Tomorrow can't come soon enough.

Alone in the elevator, I start to write a message to Hatsumi, then delete it. Whatever she's doing—sleeping with unsavories and passing up promotions, all in the dogged pursuit of an ending to a story that will never, ever be happy—it's her problem and her choice.

The elevator stops, not yet at my floor, the doors opening to reveal Helios General Counsel Okamoto Junpei. "Good afternoon, Toyama-bucho. And congratulations on the big sale. Winning over Fujiwara-san is quite the coup."

Sale? To give myself time to think, I return a deeper bow than he deserves. Fujiwara-san—he can only mean Isao.

"What do you think changed his mind?" I ask, trying to keep my tone light while my mind races. What did we sell to FHI?

"The numbers on the energy savings were impressive. More so than he was giving you credit for in the meeting. He had the FHI finance team run the numbers, and the evidence was all there—implementing those grips at scale across Fujiwara projects worldwide will be worth millions." He gives me a weasely grin. "I wish my daughter owned more of their stock; this will land big once it gets out."

"Speaking of FHI—I meant to thank you for the help you gave Fujiwara Eika at the FHI board meeting."

"Oh?" he says, tone now wary. He shifts his briefcase in front of his body, as if worried he'll need to ward off a blow.

"She said it went well."

"It... went."

"And?" This tedious man.

Okamoto scratches at a patch of dry skin on the back of his hand. "Fujiwara-san comported herself well enough, but I don't think it will ultimately have the desired effect."

I mull this over as I return to my office, declining Nozomi's offer of tea. Eika didn't mention any new developments when she was here earlier this week. For once, it's Hatsumi's situation that's less complicated. I'll handle that first.

Seated at my desk with the tall windows framing Otani Bright Tower behind me, I initiate a video call. As I wait for it to connect, I open Kaihei's file again. Asagawa Yukina, Kenji's mother, has done a not-insignificant amount of work for Toyama-gumi over the years that Papa has been *kumicho*. Nothing too high-profile—Morimoto isn't one to share glory—but the Asagawa organization has quietly handled some issues I'd assumed were in-house jobs. Kaihei's findings indicate that her work is done cleanly and according to instructions; in the margin, he's added an editorial comment: *Useful tool. No loyalties.*

The call connects. The icon in the corner of my screen indicates he has his video turned on, but the image resolves into nothing more than a pixelated smear of black and gray.

Some rustling, and the port emerges, perhaps from a pocket, to reveal Asagawa's face. He's inverted, with what looks like a system of pipes in the background. When he sees me, he drops to his feet, a cleaner movement than I'd ever give him credit for.

"What are you doing?"

"Day job. You looking for Green?"

Years spent in proximity to my father's men have accustomed me to hearing this kind of casually rough speech, but not to having it aimed in my direction.

"I'm looking for Hatsumi."

"I'd text you her number, but I don't think you want me giving it out to Toyama-gumi."

Since he's raised the topic of family—"From what I hear, I'm not nearly as much of a threat as your mother."

"You sell yourself short."

I wonder whether that was intended as flattery or intimidation.

Either way, it's a mistake, but I fake a laugh.

"If Hatsumi wants to go again," he continues, "I'll tell her to check in with you first."

"Thank you, no. I have no interest in the details of my friends' personal lives." Offer a meager olive branch, add a gloss of humor: "You've met Johjima Haru."

"I preferred the earthquake. Well, much as I've enjoyed this exchange of vague threats—"

"I need to know that you keep your personal life separate from the family business."

"No one cares who I screw," he says, now obviously amused.

That must be nice. "I do, if it puts my friends at risk."

"Then we agree."

With nothing more I want to say, I end the call.

* * *

(*Any developments since the board
meeting?* } *Toyama Misora*

Fujiwara Eika { *Not as far as I know…. Why?*)

(*Ran into Okamoto. Picture he painted
was less than rosy.* } *TM*

(*When are you free to meet?* } *TM*

FE { *Oh, no! :(I'll check my schedule and let you know*)

FE { *Any weekend plans? A certain American???*)

(*Lunch with Taehyun and my parents.* } *TM*

FE { *Ohhhh. Better leave a generous offering
in the* kamidana. *Hahaha*)

* * *

"None of the politicians want to do what's necessary to preserve the nation, so they let in more foreign companies who abuse our land and then leech away what little magic is left when they're done. Mi-chan, your soft-hearted friend, the Fujiwara girl—even she knows we have to preserve our environment in order to protect our resources and our native-born people. The solutions are right in front of them—NRPO isn't a new idea."

Papa pauses to take a bite of rice, a welcome respite for the rest of us, then chuckles to himself. "The assembly might finally get something done. What a novelty."

I've used my chopsticks to pick up and put down this same piece of grilled *unagi* a half dozen times, seemingly unable to do anything else. I can't imagine a greater perversion of Eika's entire cause; the bitter irony is that it's FHI, not any international company, that has stripped rural Japan down to the bare earth in their hunt for minerals. I look over at Rei, pleading with my eyes for her to do or say something, but her gaze is fixed on her plate, her shoulders slumped inward.

It's Taehyun squeezing the sides of my knee, fingertips pressing hard into bone, that finally snaps me into action. He can't be the one to interrupt this, and my mother is collapsing on herself into a black hole of shame and fury.

"Papa, why don't we go out to the garden? I have a present for you."

Wanting an ace in my pocket if pressed on the tracker progress, I had concocted a story in my mind about how this is a congratulatory gift for winning his court case, but he doesn't even ask. No one is more entitled to his privileges, after all, than a rich man. I lead him outside and along the covered *engawa*, perching myself on the edge with feet dangling like a little girl as he approaches the box at the side of the pond.

"Is this what I think it is?" he inquires, dark eyes shining with genuine delight.

I nod, stretching my face into a reluctant smile. The tape sealing the box reads "Live Fish," so it's a bit of a giveaway. The wood floor of the engawa creaks underneath me as my mother and Taehyun step outside to join us.

"Husband, what did you get?" my mother calls. We're a pretty little domestic scene again, Rei's flushed cheeks and Taehyun's clenched jaw the only signs of what happened moments earlier.

Papa opens the box to reveal a platinum butterfly koi swishing inside, luxurious fins fanning in beautiful but agitated patterns.

"That will be lovely with the others," Rei says. "You have a taste for white things lately, Mi-chan."

I freeze.

"Does she?" Taehyun asks, voice tight. Papa is ignoring us, busy checking water temperatures before he puts the new fish in the tank he keeps in a small shed nearby. It will quarantine there for a few weeks before joining the other koi outside.

"Indeed," Rei continues. "For example, that stunning dress you bought for the KBC awards."

That dress is black and silver. All three of us know it. I nod, feeling my teeth grind against each other. Rei and Razan, the earthquake and the tsunami. Just when you think you've survived one and have started to survey the damage, the other hits you with breathtaking force.

Mercifully, Taehyun rises to the occasion. Sitting down on the edge of the *engawa*, he braces one arm behind me and peers up at Rei. The midday spring sun highlights the structure of his face; he's so handsome it almost hurts to look.

"Misora might follow trends, but she always comes back to the classics," he says smoothly.

Rei smiles, clearly pleased by both the answer and the delivery, and a surge of gratitude and affection for Taehyun courses through me.

Ready to transition the koi, Papa lifts the water- and oxygen-filled bag from its bubble-wrap sheath. In the dappled light under the shade of the plum tree, the fish's pale fins flash silver. Watching the koi twist in frustration at its watery prison, I lean back against Taehyun's arm; in my ear, he murmurs, "Beautiful, just like you."

I don't miss the barb wedged beneath the compliment. Just like me, indeed.

* * *

(Leaving for your place soon. <1 hour } Toyama Misora

Cameron Green { Looking forward to it. Food?)

(Yes, I'm starving. You choose. } TM

* * *

To: 東山美空 *<toyama.misora@helios.co.jp>*
From: Prototype Team 3 <prototype_3@helios.co.jp>

RE: Project Q77719

Toyama-bucho,

I am pleased to inform you that we have completed the prototype for Project Q77719 ahead of schedule. It is securely stored in your lab.

Suzuki
Team 3

* * *

(Quick detour. ~1.5 hours. } TM

CG { OK)

* * *

Headquarters is between my parents' house in Denenchofu and our apartment in Azabu-Juban, so I ask the driver to drop me off there before he takes Taehyun home.

"Haven't you worked for your mother enough today?" Taehyun asks as I leave the car. But he seems glad to be rid of me.

Helios is open for a half day on Saturdays, but by now, early evening, everything is shut down. When I step out of the elevator into the hall outside the lab, motion-sensor lights flicker on. The air is stuffy from the HVAC's midday transition to eco-mode.

Any of my staff can get to their desks in the outer lab during off hours, but the inner workspaces, with the testing machines and precious IP, are accessible only to me as unit director. I hold my AppKey under the scanner and enter my code, and the door clicks open.

As Suzuki promised, the prototype is locked in the small safe in the damper room. Lifting it out of the cardboard box, I peel away the packing material, as excited as Papa with his fish. The prototype team has fitted the battery to a dummy port, so I can test functionality with a common device.

I should wait for Eika and Cameron and share this victory with them—but I want a moment to savor it alone. Eika and I were working on this long before Cameron showed up, and while Eika was vital in development, it's my concept, my engineering, my device. I flip the "on" switches on the testing machines.

The prototype passes each test beautifully, as if it's already set for retail. Heart thudding in my throat, I force a massive battery drain, drawing the dummy port down to a 1% power reading. Here goes. Stepping out of my heels and onto the patch of soft grass at the back of the room for grounding, I press my thumb to the Syphon panel.

100%. Instantly.

I gasp, leaning against the wall of pocket plants behind me for support. The port is heating up in my hand, and I'm starting to feel a little lightheaded—I set it on the bench, breaking the connection. The 100% holds, so I touch the port tentatively, opening a power-hungry app. The battery reading flickers down to 99%, then back up again. It's hot, and a faint pulling sensation shoots up my arm, leaving my fingers tingling. I close out of the app and withdraw my hand.

It needs some work; this isn't a surprise. But it's fast, and it's powerful.

This is big. It could change my whole career.

* * *

I flip open the lid on the box of pan-fried *gyoza* first. A puddle of grease has started to congeal underneath them. "We should have gotten steamed ones instead."

"Or eaten them when they were hot. I'll nuke them," Cameron says, putting the box in the microwave.

"While that's happening—I have something to show you."

"Pretty sure I've seen it all at this point," he says as he sets the timer, "but I wouldn't mind seeing it again."

I chuckle, shaking my head as I dig the dummy port out of my bag.

"Is that what I think it is?" he asks. "And if it is, how have you been here for an hour and are only showing me now?"

I pretend to ponder. "Somehow, I ended up naked under an American. Again."

"It wasn't just under." Cameron gives me a wicked grin as he sits down at the table.

"Tell me what you think," I say, holding out the port.

"Hmm," he says as he takes it from me, faux thoughtful. "I liked both but would opt for you on top if forced to choose. Great view, five stars."

"Did you just rate my performance?" The look he's giving me is both teasing and intense, and I feel my heart rate tick up a notch.

"Yep, guess so. You could reciprocate."

I think for a moment. Punning in English isn't my strong suit. "Excellent staff. Would definitely come again."

Laughing, he powers up the dummy, and I watch him flick through a few apps, holding his hand against the battery. "It's still pretty warm," he observes, "we'll need to fix that."

He lays the port flat on the table, forcing a power drain the same way I did back in the lab. The screen flickers, then goes black—it's dead. He reaches out his hand, and the port snaps back to life with a sizzle. Hm. It didn't do that last time; something is still off with it. Disappointing.

Abruptly, Cameron jerks his hand away. "I can't—" he chokes, his voice raspy, a note of panic underneath. "Misora, I can't disconnect."

There's a staticky odor of ozone in the air. "What? But you're not touching it—"

"I can't revoke the consent."

I reach for him, and his skin, so warm just moments ago, is icy cold. Meanwhile, the port is crackling on the table, scorching the wooden surface. I slap my palm down on the port, gasping as I get hit with the firehose of power it's pulling out of him. Pain radiates through my hand from the heat of the charred port.

He slumps forward, forearms on his thighs, head in hands. I think I've managed to sever his connection. I look for something—anything—organic to dump this power into. My shallow reservoir is completely refilled, I can't hold it much longer.

The first thing I see is Panzer, but this could kill him. It feels like I'm being scorched from the inside, white heat straining the seams of what knits me together.

And then I see it. Careful not to touch Cameron again, I lean across and sink my hands deep into the soil of the fern on the windowsill. The plant ghosts into a smoking wisp, and the terra cotta pot cracks open, spilling ashy dirt down the wall. Woozy, I drop to the floor.

My hand trembling wildly, a nasty burn seared into the palm, I reach up to graze Cameron's leg with my fingertips. "Cameron? Are you alright?"

He doesn't move for a moment, and I wobble upright so that I'm kneeling in front of him. "Cameron?" I can hear my own fear. Panzer nudges at his master's arm with his nose, letting out a low whine.

Slowly, he pulls his hands away from his face and looks down at me. "I think," he says, voice still rough, "I think it might need work."

I slump against his thigh under a flood of relief, and he runs shaky fingers over my hair. "I'm okay, I'm okay," he repeats.

Waves of nausea roll through my stomach, part terror, part magical aftermath. I want to sob into his leg, but I can't put that on him, too. We sit like that for a few minutes, both taking in slow, shuddering breaths.

"You should lie down," I finally say. I'm recovering quickly, other than the rhythmic thrum of hot pain in my hand. He's going to need a lot of sleep, though, and he'll feel terrible for a day or so, too. I exhausted my reservoir once during grad school, and the punishment from my body was swift and brutal.

"Okay," he says, trying to stand. His knees buckle, and he falls back into the chair. "Nope."

There's no way I can get him back to the bedroom by myself, he's so much bigger than I am. Maybe we can make it to the couch, though. I slip one of his arms over my shoulders, pushing with my knees. He staggers against me, and I stumble under his weight, but we somehow make it into the *tatami* room. Gently as I can, I lower him to the sofa. He's shivering, and I see goosebumps dot his skin.

"I'll get you some blankets and pillows." I stop in the kitchen to wash the dirt off my hands, hissing with pain as the icy water hits the burn on my palm, then go grab everything off the bed. One limb at a time, I shift him onto his back, pillows under his head, blankets tucked tight.

"Misora—" he says weakly. "Stay with me?"

"Of course."

He turns onto his side and lifts the edge of the blankets with an unsteady hand. I flick off the lights, then slide under so I'm facing him; we both just fit if we stay on our sides, pressed close. "I was so worried."

"I'll be alright." His voice grows faint. "You'll figure it out. Probably just need to redesign the port, not the battery."

His eyelids slowly drop closed, but I'm wide awake now, energized by his words. I lay still, his chest gently rising and falling against mine, as the implications of what he said rocket around my brain. Redesign the port, not the battery. Such a simple inversion of what we're doing, and yet—

It's brilliant.

DATE HATSUMI

When I wake up, my head is pounding and my mouth is dry. The familiar weight in my chest is back. Damn it. Why now? It's not even close to the anniversary of when he died, and I have things I need to do.

Right, the text from last night. Now Noah's friend is having problems finding somewhere else to live, which shouldn't be surprising with the vote on the property bill happening next month. While the NRPO technically only blocks foreigners from buying property, not renting, the practical impact is fewer possible apartment building owners. Thinking of how much they'll be jacking up prices next month if this vote goes their way probably has landlords jacking off morning to night.

I know all this and yet I've done precisely nothing for Corbin, or anyone else for that matter. I'd hoped that a night of sleep would make me feel less like a jackass.

Breaking news headline: It didn't.

I lie there for a long moment, staring bleary-eyed at the ceiling of my perfectly serviceable apartment that no one is trying to kick me out of, at that corner where the trim was installed crooked.

Way back in high school, we used to spend our time out after dark and up to no good. On one particular day, we were in a line waiting for tickets to something we wanted to attend. Misora or Hideki, even Eika probably, could have made them happen had we planned ahead but on that day, we were in a line. Two jerks, guys in their early 20s, jumped ahead of us and at first it wasn't a big deal. Then we made it to the counter and got our tickets—the last ones available. That meant that the girl behind us would leave empty-handed.

I didn't know her really, had only seen her around here and there. I don't think I've ever even known her name, but I was mad about everything at that point and on that particular day the situation really pushed my buttons. I made a scene with the guys who were walking away.

One thing led to another, and we all ended up at a nearby dive with half-assed policies on serving minors, me and one of the guys drinking for the ticket. I won, but I made myself so, so sick. None of the four of us ended up going out that night. I don't know if the girl even got her ticket.

The thing is that I didn't do it because I wanted to help that girl. If I'd meant to help her, I could have just given her my ticket instead. I wanted the fight, I wanted to feel like I'd made those greedy assholes pay.

Am I still doing that?

I take a deep breath and look at the time on my port. It's an hour to when I need to be at the dedication, and I'm wasting the time I need to get ready. Thirty minutes on the train. That leaves half that time to get ready. My trousers need steaming. Do I care about eyeliner today? In the scheme of things, it doesn't seem like it's worth the effort.

Now I've taken ten minutes to decide. Shit. At this rate, I'm going to make myself late.

Maybe I can convince myself to get up a different way. Some coffee. If I don't want to keep going from there, at least my head will feel better. Yeah, that seems reasonable.

The floor is cold when I stand, and dizziness means I have to sit back down for a minute while the room stops spinning. Finally, I make my way into the kitchen to chug half a bottle of Pocari Sweat and follow it with a large cup of instant coffee paired with a painkiller. My stomach isn't going to be happy, but hopefully my head will lay off for now.

I lean forward to put my arms on the edge of the sink and stare over the counter into the living room. The chart on my wall is there as always, a reminder.

Better pull on something, anything approaching reasonable, and head out, even if I have to put on makeup while I'm standing on the train like a teenager hiding it from my mom.

Amazingly, Okada doesn't comment when I roll in, glasses on, at one minute to the start of the event. Mayor Mori is dedicating a medium-term relief site for the earthquake victims and we're just here to document the formalities. I know it's partially because I've been hyping her volunteer work that she's moved up in the polls for re-election and that she's not pushing these people out. Nonetheless, it feels like a lot of work for not much right now.

One ceremony is much like another, with this one if anything duller than usual since Mori-shicho doesn't even take questions at the end with the Q&A scheduled for Monday.

"Are you coming tonight, Date?" Okada asks.

Oh, right. I'd forgotten that was today. Okada is finally hitting the age for mandatory retirement, and a Press Club send-off party is its own kind of required. "Yeah, I'll be there."

His suit is clean and pressed, made from a fabric with a hint of sheen. The fake smile he gives me says he's pleased I'll be going, but he's disdainful that I am, too. A lifetime of working, and the satisfaction he gets is that people are going to his retirement party out of obligation.

I'm looking at my future there. When a company hires a cohort from the same class, there aren't many opportunities for individuals to move up outside of group promotions, and I gave my chance to Goto. Bravado to Misora aside, I've really fucked myself over.

Before the party, I need to take care of my normal weekend duties. It's almost an hour on the train, standing in a press of people, to get over to my mother's store. I wish she hadn't moved halfway across the city, even if I understand why she doesn't want the constant reminder of living in Suginami ward anymore.

"Hi, Mom."

She is sitting on her stool by the front entry, like always. "What did I do to deserve this visit, Ha-chan?"

"It's the weekend again," I say slowly, shifting the bag of groceries from one hand to the other.

"Oh, right, of course. Time goes so quickly these days."

It's so hard to tell whether a statement like that is the same kind of normal mistake that everyone makes, or if I should read more into it. I take the steps two at a time and swing the fridge door open. An assortment of food is on the shelves, and most of it even appears to be fresh. At least she's eating.

I pull a pack of chicken thighs that is about to go, and push what I've brought to the back of the shelves to keep it all on the correct rotation. Sticking my head halfway down the stairs, I ask, "Mom, want me to make anything?"

"No, I'm okay."

"I know you're okay, but is there anything you would like?"

She turns to look at me. "I can let you know what I want just fine too, Ha-chan. My voice still works."

"Oh, hell, I'm sorry. I—I'll be down in a minute or two."

The electric kettle on the counter is empty, so I fill the old metal pot and put it on the stove. While I wait, I pour a glass of water into the plants on the window ledge and check the other rooms to make sure everything is as clean as the kitchen. With the exception of the ever-growing mound of *Nihon Times*, it is.

There's what looks to be fresh water sitting on the shelf of the *butsudan*. I kneel down and light some incense, ring the bell. "Hey, Dad. Thank you for watching out for mom. I know she's a handful."

As always, her name is there in red, next to his in black on the memorial tablet. What must she think every day staring at her future? Shouldn't that be considered bad luck?

I suppose there is some comfort in knowing where you'll be when you're done, assuming anyone is around to remember you by then.

"I'm still here," I say softly.

A few minutes later, steaming cup of oolong tea in hand, I meander downstairs again. "You may be entertained—"

"Ha-chan, did you use the water from the faucet?"

This again?

"We had the water checked two months ago. It is fine to drink. There is nothing wrong with it." I know—raising my voice doesn't help. Pointing out that the water is apparently good enough for Dad wouldn't do any damn good either.

I take a long, deliberate sip of the tea, burning my tongue in the process, then try again. "Do you need me to get you some bottled water?"

"No, no need for that. Now what were you saying?"

I set my cup down on the counter next to a stack of browning, outdated travel books, and lean on my palms. "Tonight is Okada's retirement party."

"Oh, you don't say," she answers vaguely. She rolls one of the buttons on her cardigan between two fingers. "Have you given any more thought to the protest movement?"

"No, Mom, that's not a good idea. You know that."

"There are so many people who are going to be affected, and most of them can't even vote. Even Wada Isamu barely had more experience when he started running for—"

"I'm already looking into the property bill." I don't have enough hours in the day to solve every problem in the city, and bringing up that ass Wada is not going to inspire me to drop everything else and take up a political banner. 'When I have enough, I'll do something."

"I know," she says quietly. "I'm just so worried about the pregnant women."

That catches me off-guard. "What?"

"What they're going to be doing after this. With the camps."

"The camps for pregnant women," I repeat. "Who is saying this?"

"Amity Unbounded. They broke the story last night on MinoSocial."

"Mom. AmiU is a crackpot organization that makes shit up for the attention. I've told you before, and I'll say it again, do not look at the garbage they claim is news." Even talking about them near a microphone is probably going to trigger ads on my port for weeks. Her MinoSo feed must be just fringe vomit, top to bottom.

She breaks eye contact and kind of shrugs. The discussion is dead, but she's not going to stop reading them either.

I can't deal with this today on top of everything else.

A ding and the door slides open to admit an old woman, stoop-backed and pushing a square plaid bag on wheels. I take that as my cue. My mom isn't happy to see me go, but there isn't much she can say in front of a customer.

* * *

For the second morning in a row, I wake up staring at the ceiling. Today, it's strangely clear—I slept with my contacts in. My mouth tastes like death and my head is pounding. There isn't anything I need to do today, which is good because I don't think I can make myself move at the moment.

Shit, the party. I feel a sudden spike of anxiety as I prod the blur of memories buried under a haze of alcohol and loathing, but the details mercifully slip away.

On second thought, I need something to do today, a reason to get out of bed. My hand fumbles across the top of my nightstand, eventually touching the hard edge of my port sticking out from between a tube of lip balm and a week-old cup of water. I give it a minute to charge on my arm, and the device helpfully resumes an internet radio stream.

> ...*warn us*
> *You're jealousy, baby*
> *La la la*
> *The house is wrong, the house is wrong*
> *But inside we're so right*
> *Dance round and round the* sakabashira
> *Wood supported, crown inverted, roots free...*

Ugh, too fucking early, Friday Boys.

I stop the music and instead select Eika's name from my priorities contact list with my thumb. It rings and rings, rolling over to her voicemail. What's keeping her busy on a Sunday morning? I check MinoSo, but the most recent thing she posted was from a launch party for a face cream from yesterday morning. That's odd.

I can't call Noah, not when I'm feeling like this.

The other names on my priority list are Date, Goto, and Toyama. Not exactly an all-star lineup of moral support, especially after how I left things with my mom yesterday. I tap Misora's name and listen to the ring, my eyes closed.

"Hello, Hatsumi?"

Okada stands, a wide slash of a smile across his face as he raises a glass—

"And here's a toast to Date Hideaki, the only reason Hatsumi has done anything with her life. Has anyone ever done so much for a person by dying without accomplishing anything?"

Tension wells up from my shoulders and tightens my throat. Okada always hated me. He worked his way to a prestigious Todai degree, while it looked like I waltzed in with built-in connections thanks to everything I'd lost.

That Okada thinks it doesn't make it true.

It doesn't make it not true either.

"Hello?" she repeats.

Say something, anything.

"Am I nothing but the story of the girl whose dad died?" I whisper between dry lips. "No. Don't answer." That was unfair of me to ask.

Misora exhales, and then responds softly. "We become what we make ourselves."

I should have known better than to call Toyama Misora of all people.

At least the spike of anger down my spine is enough that I can pull myself into a sitting position. "You've been holding it in about the damn promotion, huh? You know, not all of us are in it for the money."

"My work can help a lot of people," she says, her tone even. "There's nothing wrong with making some money in the process."

Oh, fantastic. I can have this fight. Let's go. "You mean Eika can help people. And you can make money off her good intentions."

"Eika's good intentions would go nowhere without the backing of a company like Helios to actually get things done. Some of us use the positions we're in to enact change."

Low blow, and one that wouldn't sting if it weren't so fucking accurate. How many years and all I've accomplished is getting Morishicho on track for reelection. That doesn't mean that Misora is blameless though.

"Funny how that change only ever benefits you." I leave space for her to respond, but she doesn't. So, I add, "How's your foreign boyfriend's living situation going to look when the NRPO passes?"

Her voice is tipping into ice now. "I've told you more than once that Taehyun's building is not a problem."

How stupid does she think I am? "Come on, Misora. I saw you kiss Green-san in the elevator. You had dog fur on your dress that day at Fun-Due. Then I found out the other week that guess-who has a dog. I know what you've been doing."

"Why are you worried about something that's temporary?"

She doesn't specify if she means temporary like an apartment lease or like a short-term amusement. Not that she needs to—she can decide on that distinction anytime and what would he be able to do about it? Move back to America?

"Did you fuck him before or after he got that work visa?" I snap.

As soon as I hear the words come out of my mouth, I wish I could take them back.

Obviously, I don't really know his circumstances, but Green-san likely has options as an engineer, at least more than Corbin had as an English teacher. I'm really projecting here.

I clear my throat. "Shit, I shouldn't have said that."

She makes a noise, a breath of annoyance, before responding: "He seems to be enjoying himself. As I assume you are, although... Asagawa Kenji? Really."

Hell. Of course Misora would know. Even though it was years ago, I don't think I'll ever really forget the time she called me a groupie.

I bite back the urge to deny that he's *yakuza*—it wouldn't help my case.

How did she hear about him?

Never mind, that's obvious. Either Green-san told her I called, or she was there when it happened.

Green-san is surprised to hear from me weeks after the only time we'd met. Pleasantries accomplished, I jump right into it. "This is a bit awkward, but your friend who was at the party, do you know his family name?"

"Asagawa?" *he asks, with a grace note of pity.*

My mind starts racing. Kenji being a member of the Asagawa-gumi explains a lot. It's also not a particularly useful line of investigation, since the group is independent, just a few people, barely worth a mention as far as I've found.

And I bet that my asking about this is giving Green-san the wrong impression. "I don't think he's going to call me or anything. This is for my wall." *I look up at the collection of yakuza hierarchies and notes. No good comes of sharing my personal crazy.* "My wall of, uh, hot guys I fucked."

Okay, surely even on short notice I could have come up with a better excuse.

To his credit, Green-san manages to respond with only, "Well, it's been nice talking with you, Date-san, but I have to go walk my dog now."

After an experience that mortifying, how could he not have told her? This conversation with Misora is turning into a year in review of my most embarrassing moments.

"You got me. But it's already over," I fib.

Misora doesn't respond.

After a few seconds of dead air, I cave. "Do you think I'd get serious about someone like him? Someone who bleaches his hair like a juvenile delinquent?" I cringe hearing the words, complete classist bullshit, coming out of my mouth. I lighten my own hair a shade, and yet here I am looking down on him because somewhere deep down I think I'm better than he is.

Who am I to be judging someone? I tried to drunk-source someone at a damn birthday party, something I could tell a few sentences in wasn't going to be helpful. "Did you know he gave me not only a fake last name but also a fake business card? As far as I can tell, it was just for the fun of it, too: he's part of some small-time organization, nothing interesting at all."

Misora finally responds, "Small time doesn't mean 'not dangerous.'

Ha-chan. I worry about you."

Not words I expected to hear from Toyama Misora. What can I even say to that?

"It wasn't ever serious." I tip my head back and search for what to say. "After all, he has the emotional depth of a teacup. Not that I was looking for fulfillment," I finish, trailing off.

"Except in the crudest sense of the word."

I laugh for the first time today, a coarse sound that comes from my gut. It's a release I didn't realize I needed. "Yeah, I did find that."

It's unfair of me to put the weight of the NRPO on Misora. She's in her own liminal space, trapped between both the tensions of her own family and the racists bent on seeing her as not fully Japanese in her own right.

When I was young, I had a dexterity game that involved stacking wooden animals using chopsticks. Along those lines, Misora's life has always required a defter hand than I can imagine. It's amazing she's been able to keep some semblance of independence from her father for as long as she has. Moving in with Taehyun when she did was a clever play, the piece that's the foundation to all the others.

"I'm sorry. I know it's complicated for you."

"It is. I wish you would assume I am acting in good faith."

She's right. All I've been doing is asking her to argue with me.

"Okay, then—with the property bill looking likely to pass, I think there may be other crackdowns coming. I'm starting to look into what rental protections for *gaikokujin* there are in leases. I have Noah-kun's and a stack from an advocacy group, but it looks like most of them are through the same realty company. So, assuming things aren't too temporary, is there any chance you might be able to get me a copy of Green-san's lease?"

"Last I saw, he left it laying on top of his refrigerator. Do you want me to ask him, or just take it?"

"Well, it's for his own good, at least in a generalized way, so I guess however you might want to do it," I say. "And Misora—"

"Yes?"

"I hope that whatever happens, you're happy."

Even ending the call on a positive note, I feel washed out, empty, too much inside too little of me. I need to do something I don't have to think about, anything that will let me just be for a little bit.

(You free?) Date Hatsumi

Usually, Kenji responds immediately. This time he takes almost an hour. It's a real pick-me-up to my ego right now to be staring at my phone and waiting for a response, let me say.

Off the record, I know I'm using him as much as he's using me. It's all just so simple and easy—yes or no and nothing more. Things with Taro were always complicated. He needed me to be less than I am in order to help him be more. I couldn't do it, couldn't constantly undercut everything that's important to me because that's what he needed and needed and needed.

Finally, my port vibrates as one message pops up, followed by another.

Asagawa Kenji (Not today)

AK (Tomorrow?)

It's not what I expected, and suddenly I realize how much I did want to see him. My throat is tight as I type, just a simple and easy response—

(Yes) DH

* * *

Pants in hand, I have a sudden thought. "Crap, what time is it?"

Kenji props up on one elbow and points at the clock on the nightstand: 1:03 a.m. He stares at it for a moment before saying, "I can walk home."

I sit back down on the bed. The trains stop at one and don't start until at least five. What a night to have left my moped at home. Technically, I could walk too, but it would take hours and I'd prefer not to, having spent all day on my feet.

At nine the hotels switch to minimum overnight payments. "We have the room anyway."

"Yeah. Might as well shower." Kenji stands and stalks toward the immaculately clean bathroom.

From this angle, I can't see the purple and yellow bruise across his face, but I can see everything else. "How much time do you spend working out?"

He shrugs, a careless gesture that highlights the muscles across his shoulders and back. "Probably more than you'd think."

"On behalf of me, thanks." I close my eyes and listen to the spray of water start.

It's dark when I become aware of anything again. I'm curled with my right hand on his hip, my cheek and left shoulder pressed against his back. I'm also drooling on my own shoulder—gross. Hopefully he didn't notice.

For a long frozen moment, I stay there and enjoy the warmth. Kenji is breathing evenly, but not slowly.

"You awake?" I ask softly.

A quick movement in his muscles, and I realize I startled him. "Yeah."

He's lying on his shoulder facing the clock. There's barely any light in the room, just an edge of white around a window cling and the reflection of the blue numbers on the clock over his silhouette.

"What time is it?"

"Three thirty-five," he says quickly enough that I wonder if he's been staring at the clock.

"How long have you been awake?"

"Haven't slept." Then after another long pause, "Doubt I could like this."

Not sure what that means. "The room? Or was I making you uncomfortable?"

"Yeah," Kenji says.

I move my head and roll forward so my damp shoulder presses down into the sheets, and I'm on my stomach still leaning against his back. We're well on his side of the bed, but he doesn't move or push back against me.

Both of us are only partially dressed and the blankets are on the floor—the room is warm enough that pressed together I'm the right temperature. I slide my hand from his hip up around his waist and pull myself up close enough to him that my breath is reflecting off the back of his neck and the ends of his damp hair are against my forehead. He's solid and here and I suddenly want to know something, anything that will anchor him here with me. "Tell me something true."

There's dead air long enough that I wonder if he's going to respond at all.

Finally, he says, "You first."

I try to think of something innocuous. "When I was little, my parents and I lived in the Zenpukuji part of Suginami, and my dad was really busy but every Sunday we'd all walk up to the park. It was close but not a huge place. Mostly lake and two swings and a slide. There was a clock in the park, and he used it to show me how to tell the time."

As I'm telling the story, I can hear my voice tighten, feel the moisture building up in my eyelashes. Apparently, I can't pick an easy story to tell. Hopefully he isn't noticing this stupid display of emotion. If he is, he doesn't react.

I continue, "When I was really little, reading a clock with a face was hard, but I remember the first time I did it. The look on his face was so bright and proud. It was like there wasn't anything I couldn't do. Something so small, but I guess I remember it because of that."

Again, there's a long period of silence. I open my mouth to say something, think better of it, and then try again but can't come up with anything to say.

He starts, "When I was little."

"Yeah?" I say it so quietly the word barely comes out.

"When I was little, we all—all four of us—were up in Tochigi. Maybe she was thinking she might be happy with a normal life for a while."

I don't ask any questions about who he is talking about. I want to hold my breath until he finishes, but I'm worried that if I do anything, even that, he'll stop talking.

"Ashio is a tiny little town in the mountains. Nothing there, but it meant that we could run around like crazy, my brother and me. We used to play hide-and-seek all over. We got really good at it, to the point where it would take forever to find each other. One day, I was hiding, and I was pleased with myself because I'd wedged my body into the gap between two roofs by the Yamazaki. After a while, I started to wonder when he was going to give up and come calling my name, but he didn't. I waited a few hours even. You might not be surprised to know I was a stubborn kid."

An involuntary puff of air from deep in my chest hits the back of his neck, and I can't help but pull myself tighter against his back.

"Finally, my dad comes along calling my name instead, and I hear this note of terror in his voice. I guess we'd had some kind of confusion over whether we were playing another round, and Takeshi had been home that entire time. My dad had realized I wasn't around, and my brother didn't know where I was, so he'd gone out looking for me. When I climbed out of the spot where I was hiding, he got happy. Really happy. Even though I was a little big for it by then, he carried me home on his shoulders, humming the whole way." He clears his throat. "I don't think my mother let my brother off easy. He paid attention to where I was after that."

I kiss the back of his neck, a tentative gesture.

Kenji moves immediately, rolling onto his back and looking over at me in the dark. I can only see one side of his face illuminated by the blue light of the clock. The intent look and the half-smile are back as he runs his hand up my side in a way that gives me goosebumps. "If that's what you're thinking, we can make the time go more quickly."

He raises himself up on one arm and kisses me under the line of my chin. I run my free hand up against his shoulder, feeling the heat in my body rise. The moment is gone so quickly I wonder if it even happened. "Thank you," I manage.

He stops, his mouth over my collarbone. He's close enough that I can feel the breath of each word. "For what?"

I shake my head and sink my fingers into his damp hair. "Nothing," I say, pulling his head up toward my mouth. "Nothing important."

DATE HATSUMI

SEKAI SHIMBUN
>*National News*

Wada Elected Governor After an Electrifying Race
By Okada Arata

Exit polls indicate that independent candidate Wada Isamu has been selected by over 40% of voters as the next governor of Tokyo. This election included nine other independent candidates, as well as candidates backed by the Wa Party and the All Nippon Party. Wada is a newcomer to politics, but well-known from his 13 years as director of Enomoto Pharmaceutical and spokesperson for the Council on Medical Advancement. He ran on a platform advocating changes to regulations guiding medical research that he argued would allow for faster innovation, as well as limited privatization of the public health system to halt rising costs.

"We look forward to streamlining the bloated healthcare system, and opening up a brighter future for all citizens," Wada said at a recent rally.

The election was held following the sudden resignation of the previous governor, Ishii Bunta, amid allegations of corruption. Evidence that Ishii had personally benefited from the sale of public land in Koto ward was uncovered in June.

Subsequent investigations found that he had engaged in securities fraud in conjunction with known members of the Maeda Group.

Early polling in this gubernatorial election showed Date Hideaki, the current mayor of Suginami ward, in the lead but his support dropped dramatically after an accident at a campaign rally on July 14 left him hospitalized through the remainder of the race. His platform called for an increase in spending to combat homelessness and opposition to the Natural Resource Protection Ordinance proposed by leaders of the Japanese Reform Party for consideration during the next legislative session. Date is currently projected to finish in second as the recipient of 27% of the vote.

* * *

Wada Isamu barely lasted a year and a half before resigning in the midst of his own scandal. The affair had been an open secret for years, his mistress a regular at the Council on Medical Advancement charity events. The JRP got the first property bill passed at the metropolitan level, and their support for the person who had been a political darling melted away. Wada didn't even notice and pushed for the legalization of pseudoephedrine-based medications to benefit his pharma buddies. The Toyama-gumi, ever protective of their own illicit proceeds in a market with limited alternatives, made sure that photos of his indiscretions were plastered across the news morning to night.

There aren't many successes that Wada could point to from his short time in office: The property bill. A minor ordinance on salmon processing. A public park opened in Taito ward. The bills on healthcare introduced but never passed. Nothing that benefited him in particular.

Wada was nothing but a temporary firework from the pharma lobby. He was new money, though not as mortifyingly nouveau riche as the Johjima family, so his star landed back in the same stalwart business morass he launched from. Even his advisor, Koike Nenosuke, has had more staying power—he slid into a position in the Strategic Assets Agency, and is now that charming familiar face holding up the conservative side of televised political debates.

"Oh, come on," I mutter, looking closely at my hand. I've done a great job poking a pin right through the skin at the tip of my index finger.

I used to keep my research in a sensible, organized series of folders, but hanging it all up lets me see the overview. It's also a needle to my own eye about what I'm doing, self-recrimination that I still have neither found real justice for what happened seventeen years ago, nor have I managed to let it go.

The pin goes back into the wall through Wada's pixelated forehead this time. Aside from profiles on the election and each of the twelve candidates and their entourages, the majority of the space is dominated by an outline of the three big yakuza groups, the organizations who had the motive and means to engineer a rigging accident that left a staffer paralyzed and a gubernatorial candidate in a coma for two months.

The Toyama-gumi gained nothing from Wada's election and had no conflict with my dad's policies in particular. As best I can tell, Toyama Razan and his lackeys were focused on a competitive influx of cheap cocaine from China at the time of the election and were genuinely unconcerned until Wada started his own incursion into their main source of income.

The Maeda-gumi at the time was in the midst of a succession battle, and the factions ended up backing two different candidates. One finished at 5% and the other 12%, all consistent with the polling in the month leading up to the election. Similar to the Toyama-gumi, I haven't been able to find any indication of individual disagreement with my dad's politics.

The Kubo-gumi, on the other hand, made no secret of supporting the JRP's property bill before the election and raked it in afterwards. They'd been a distant third-rate organization, and now they've risen in the ranks enough that even the Toyama-gumi has started working on cutting into their property profits, at least here in Tokyo. A looser organization than the other two, Kubo-gumi underbosses are known for exercising significant independence. Any of them could have acted either for their own gain or to curry favor with their *kumicho*.

Which cuts down my investigation to a perfectly manageable 18,000 *yakuza* members who could have been involved.

The person in the Kubo-gumi that I keep circling to is Inoe Nozomu, the noble tiger father. Of everyone in his organization, he had the most significant benefit from the passing of the property bill. Before it passed, he had aspirations but limited success, a person notable more for his status as a prep school dropout turned *yakuza* heavy than anything. Afterward, he moved into leading his own family, one in a neglected section of Roppongi that turned into a *pachinko* machine permanently set to "win time." Today, he remains several steps below HQ, but with his territory's ongoing profits he's a force in the organization.

And yet, even though he had the results and likely the means, he couldn't have done anything at my father's rally himself—at the time it happened, he was serving a 6-month prison sentence.

I glance at the time on my port. I need to be at Mori-shicho's house by dawn. Before I leave, one last look at the announcement from *Biz Monthly* that I added just last night:

> *Investors celebrated the formal announcement that the Mining Bank of China will be expanding to Japan. The Tokyo headquarters for the bank will be located in the new Roppongi View Tower. Designed by German architect Volker Hofmann, the 47-floor skyscraper is projected to take three years to complete and will utilize new innovations in green construction. The Mining Bank of China will offer loans for small and large businesses, as well as limited consumer products.*

The morning air is chilly on my arms as my moped zips through silent streets, following a blue directional arrow in my lenses that I don't need. Around me, the entrances to buildings with the aluminum gates pulled down look like open mouths, frozen in the streetlights. I make it to the mayor's front gate with the other reporters a few minutes before

Sadame lets us in, the five of us all equally excited for complimentary tea after the morning chill.

Mori-shicho is up early today—almost as soon as Sadame has passed out the cups, she's at the doorway to greet us. "Morning, everyone."

"Good morning," we say together.

"There aren't many updates outside of the reusable bag awareness event at TESCO this morning. We're moving the Q&A to late afternoon, so we'll only have about 30 minutes. If you let Juro take down your questions, I'm confident we can get through everything." She turns away, and then looks back over her shoulder. "Hatsumi, breakfast?"

"Yes, thank you, Mori-shicho," I say politely, tucking my glasses away as I follow her down the hallway.

In the back room, Natsuki-chan is wearing a tan puppy hat with floppy white ears and a matching polka dot dress. She's hitting her hands against the tabletop in a seemingly random pattern and giggling as she watches the miso soup bounce in the bowls with each thwack.

Mori-shicho kneels by the table and leans over to smile at her. "Na-chan, let's let the soup sleep."

There's a momentary pout, but it ends when the mayor's husband, Mikio, comes into the room with a tray of rice bowls. Natsuki-chan grabs his pantleg, on the side with his prosthetic, her dimpled smile back.

"Good morning, Mori-san," I say to him, sitting at the other end of the table. "Natsuki-chan, you seem to be feeling energetic today."

The two-year old notices me for the first time and hides behind her dad just as he tries to sit. He manages to land on his hip and not drop the tray.

"Na-chan, be good," he says, and gets an unrepentant "woof woof" for his trouble. Natsuki is taking her hat seriously.

Turning away from their hijinks, Mori-shicho says to me, "I have good news for you, Hatsumi. Juro followed up on what you had heard about the interview screenings for m-potential. There were some rumblings of concern out there about the practice, so the municipal council is on board with new guidelines requiring job postings in the ward to list the m-potential requirements up front."

That doesn't solve what Eika is worried about in the slightest—all it would do is give employers a stronger tool for discrimination, while wrapping it up in the bow of government approval.

"Oh, really?" I manage.

"This should save people the effort of applying if they don't meet the standards."

I want to pound the table like Natsuki. Woof woof.

"Thank you for looking into the issue," I say with a bow, my bangs dangling over my plate of fish. "I'll bring up your diligence with the press club to see if we might be able to highlight it in an upcoming issue."

"More word of mouth about the good work in our ward is always appreciated."

"Do you think that there might be any possibility of a campaign to encourage businesses to be more inclusive about the m-potential in their hiring?"

She gives me a side glance and exhales. "I don't think that it would be possible at this time."

"I see. Thank you very much for your work on this," I say. Motherfucking hell. I may not have control over exactly what I get to write about within the confines of the press club and my home paper but I'm certainly not going to be pushing this story for coverage. "Thank you also for your work with the displaced citizens. I'm working on a feature on the supplies that the Civic Action Party sent over for their temporary housing last weekend."

Mostly cheap sheets and donated plates, but I guess the junk they gathered is better than nothing. Since most of the people living in the lost buildings are older, they've been relying on family to help them recover and some either only have family in distant parts of the country or don't have family at all.

Between bites of tofu, she nods. "I expect that this situation will be resolved with permanent housing by the end of summer."

That's surprising. "I had heard that Next Investments was having trouble with the official approvals to rebuild." They've had to resubmit the applications three times now with additional documentation.

"Is that so?" she asks, her voice so passive that I realize exactly what's happening.

It's been bothering me for weeks that the Mining Bank of China project was finalized now. With the property bill outstanding, it's not the time for a foreign company to be planning new construction. They can't own the land, but they could work out renting some, and that'd be much cheaper than renting a whole building. So, if the property bill is up in the air, then it'd make sense for them to wait and see what happens with the vote in June.

It only makes sense for the Mining Bank to move ahead if everyone already knows the NRPO is going to pass.

Next Investments is a Vietnamese development group and, post-property bill, they are going to be sitting on land that they can't use. Worthless to them because no one is going to be willing to build on land they don't own. But for a Japanese company, it'll be prime Tokyo real estate.

As devious as it is terrible. "I see. Is the new developer already in the works, then?"

Natsuki has given up on eating and is crawling around on the floor, her hat lost to the excitement of a half-assed somersault.

"Nothing specific enough to publish," Mori-shicho says, taking the conversation off the record, "but Dai Construction has expressed interest."

A Toyama-gumi front company and exactly who everyone—Civics through the JRP—is hoping can benefit from the new property bill. Worse, a big developer, which means that to make this worth their time, they're not going to put in a tiny wooden structure either. If a single one of the displaced people makes it into the new buildings, I'd give Koike a kiss on the cheek.

I chew through a mouthful of rice, the kernels tasting like paste. "Is it worth the delay, bringing in new developers?"

Mori-shicho smiles, the edges of her mouth not stretching high enough to reach her eyes. "This will be just a little longer, but it's the best in the long run. You know those weren't the kind of people that we want in this ward."

But the Toyama-gumi is?

I'm trying to think of a polite way to respond when Mikio scoops Natsuki-chan up into his arms and tries to wipe a trace of sauce from her cheeks. "No, no, no!" she fusses, shaking her head back and forth.

You and me both, I want to say. Woof woof.

* * *

It takes three glasses of Asahi Super Dry before my bullshit day starts to melt away. Himura has his arm around Eguchi, who must have entertained the two of them enough with his first outing to have warranted a second.

Yamada is regaling us with a story designed to embarrass. "The lucky kitten here, he was supposed to be cleaning the storage room, when tiger-father came in. He got so flustered that he poured the dustpan right into the filing cabinet!"

"But not into 'D' for dust, which would have been understandable," Himura says between swigs of beer. "Or even 'G' for garbage."

Eguchi's cheeks are bright pink, and not just from his low alcohol tolerance. I have to join in. "At least he didn't think 'burnable trash' and set the whole thing on fire."

A solid thump and then another as Yamada hits his hand against the table, an actual tear coming out from where he has his eyes pinched closed with laughter.

Eyes firmly fixed on the bottom of the glass, Eguchi manages a sigh and half a laugh at his own misery.

Himura notices and pats his shoulder. "It happens to everyone. When I was a pledge, they left me out to guard the front door for 28 hours straight. I woke up leaning against one of the trees there, just as tiger father was walking around the corner with a politician friend of the family."

There it is—my opening. I've been waiting for a moment as perfect as this for more than a year. I can finally ask my question.

Himura continues, "Thought I got myself upright and smoothed over fast enough that he wouldn't know. He looked right at me as he went through the door I was holding, and didn't say a thing. After he went in, I realized I had an evergreen branch sticking out of my hair!"

Barely managing to stay upright, Yamada gasps out, "We called him '*maiko*' for months."

I chuckle. The young girls training to be geisha performers are known for their elaborate hair pieces, including seasonal pine-themed ornaments. "I don't suppose that anyone tried to make you do a dance to go with it?"

Himura points at me with the lip of his glass. "I learned to play the *shamisen* just to make them shut up. Next party I challenged them all to beat me at a musical battle, one on one."

"Yeah, yeah. He was just this skinny kid and he showed us all up. We agreed that he had earned his, show them," Yamada prompts.

Pulling his arm back from Eguchi's shoulder, Himura pushes his sleeve up on his bicep to show off where his tiger is flanked by pine branches and a three-stringed *shamisen*. Eguchi looks at the ink, a little starstruck.

"Fuck," I say appreciatively.

Yamada giggles. "So, little lucky cat, play your cards right and someday you'll have a dustpan on your shoulder!"

The beer I'm pouring into Yamada's glass almost ends up on the table. "Enough, enough." Okay, here I go. "Yamada-san, you gotta have a story about trying to impress some political big shots when you were a pledge, too."

Pinned to my wall, next to my rundown on tiger father, is a screenshot from a *Daily News* broadcast showing the one lead: A young Yamada, standing right behind where the interviewer is talking to Koike about Wada's lagging poll numbers. It's dated two weeks before the accident that injured my dad.

Immediately, Yamada turns pink himself and starts chuckling. "You know, I did. Back when I was a pledge and we were in that other family, we only got one day off each month. This one particular autumn I used this day off—gotta make sure you know, this is the one day of that month I had free—I used this day to go to a political debate because of this girl. Seki Suzu, her name was then. Given name written 'bell,' and, oh, she's just a perfect clear note. A big fan of politics, since she was studying to be a civil servant. Smart as can be."

His eyes wander off into a thought for a moment before he continues. "So, then when I got to the event, I made sure to fall over a barrier and knock a giant foamcore sign right into where some suit was walking away from a press conference. She saw it happen, saw the whole thing."

Wait, what.

That can't be the whole story, right? The link, the reason why I've been drinking with these guys for over a year, is that Yamada was chasing tail?

Himura is taking his turn to hit the table with his fist with glee. "How did she take that?"

"Well, she married me," Yamada says.

"Fuck," I say again, this time for entirely different reasons.

They're all drunk enough that they take my word as encouragement to cheer and pour another round in celebration. I pound mine back and barely notice that I've stood up to let Yamada out to pee.

Can it be that simple? There's really no link between these guys and the Wada campaign after all? I mean, yeah, it was a long shot to start, but I thought that maybe finally I was onto something. Now I'm back to square one, not a single lead.

Come on. There has to be something these guys know that can help. Please.

There's a gap in the conversation, so I say to Himura and Eguchi, "Have you guys heard of the Asagawa-gumi?"

Lowering his glass slowly, Himura gives me an odd look. "Where did you hear that name?"

"Not a work thing, just in passing. Someone dropped a couple names, and I didn't recognize the organization. Do you?"

"Well..." He glances over at Eguchi, and a thoughtful grin slowly spreads across his face. "This doesn't leave this table, okay?" I nod, and he continues in a low voice. "Sometimes people want a thing done that's so bad you wouldn't want to look at yourself in the mirror anymore. That's who you'd call."

This from someone in a line of work known for violence, protection rackets, smuggling, drugs, and a cocktail of other illegal behaviors. "Uh-huh," I say, letting the skepticism swirl through my voice.

Himura pushes the glasses and bottles on the table to the sides with his hand. Pulling Eguchi in with him, he leans forward and drops his voice again. "Their head, Asagawa-san, she's crazy."

Something clicks, and Eguchi's eyes go big. "Is that the woman who—"

"Yeah, she once cut off someone's finger with a plastic train pass."

They're pulling my leg and I'm not letting that one go. I lean in as well, and ask, "Do people still use plastic train passes?"

Neither of them laughs like I expect. Instead, Himura shakes his head. "I heard she fucked up her own guy's face with her fingernails."

Eguchi is hanging on Himura's every word, and I'm not sure if this tall tale is for his benefit or mine. The story continues, "I'm not talking just little stuff either. I don't know for sure, but that explosion last year in the bay. That was product that belonged to the Maeda-gumi. I don't know anyone else who would do something like that, risk pissing off that many people no matter how much someone might offer to pay."

"Yeah, and this woman's kid can fly, right?" I say.

Himura moves his head back and forth, weighing his words. "I met her kid once and he has a mouth, yeah, but he doesn't seem batshit like her. At the same time, I don't know. Different body, same mind, in my book." He puts his hands up, the one from against the table and the other from around Eguchi's shoulder. "I'm just saying, if you see a pit of snakes don't put your foot in it, even if you think only one of them is poisonous."

I shake my head and realize that even in the midst of my skepticism I've been holding my breath. If Himura is making this up, he's doing a good job of selling it. "If this Asagawa-san is that crazy, why would anyone deal with her?"

Himura takes a deep drink before answering. "We're respectable people, and for the most part we do respectable things. But sometimes you want to pay for crazy."

Suddenly there's a hand on my arm, and I jump. It doesn't move or give. Instead, the grip tightens. When I look over, it's Yamada, his face white and angry.

"Stop. They shouldn't be talking about this. Don't go passing that name around. Don't go asking people." He leans in close enough that the smell of alcohol on his breath is overwhelming, but there isn't a hint of slur to his words anymore. "You're cute, and it's adorable to see you digging around and asking about people, but if you think you can—" He shakes his head. "You're going to get us all in it."

"Huh?" I glance over at Himura and Eguchi. Both of them are frozen, their eyes fixed on Yamada.

His grip tightens around my arm, digging in deeply enough that there's pain shooting down to my fingers. For the first time in months, I'm being reminded that for all their joking, these are very real *yakuza*, and genuinely dangerous men.

Yamada is practically hissing when he says, "These two are young and stupid, but I have a family."

He pulls me out of the booth, and I barely manage to keep my bag in hand. The bartender looks down, plausible deniability. At least Yamada is dragging me to the front—I don't know what I'd do if he was taking me to the back. Scream? I'm losing my breath, and suddenly he's pushed me to the ground outside.

"Don't talk about this. Ever. You're done."

The door slides shut as I'm there on the ground, staring up in shock. The Bar Blue sign is there next to me, a feeble light in the midst of a dark Roppongi alleyway.

Oh, fucking hell. What am I about to do?

ASAGAWA KENJI

It takes the weekend to get the new space into a kind of order: futon and washing machine set up for delivery and a few small items like a 100-yen plate, a mug, and a 4-liter water boiler on the counter. A hot soak in the *ofuro* and a cup of green tea go a long way toward making the space comfortable, even as I'm waiting for something to sleep on.

I also change the lock to the best option I can short of magitech and follow Green's method of dropping a broom handle in the track of the balcony door. There aren't any windows in the small space, and the building is made from reinforced concrete, so those small tweaks make it as secure as possible without major construction.

On Monday morning I drop into a branch of the rental company in Takadanobaba, two stops up the loop line. My hair is tucked under a grey knit cap, and my clothes are about as bland as possible—tan sweater and gray pants. The tape on my cheek and not wanting to see the apartment in person are odd, but my ID, financial documents, and stack of cash for deposit and key money are all in perfect artificial order. The agent hands over the door code, a secure 0000, and instructions on the office where I should stop to pick up the now-useless keys.

I switch into a generic blue workman's outfit for a few hours of breaking-and-tinkering. I've been working on this project for a few weeks, forcing early replacements of impeller parts along the feeder canal for the Arakawa River. The impellers have a finicky repair schedule, and adjusting the tension of the screws is all that's needed to set the part up to fail in the short term. Whoever bought the copies of Takamine's stamps is going to be making a tidy profit when they charge full price for installing replacements that they've ordered using a back-channel discount.

In the afternoon, I turn my attention back to another curiosity—Funabashi. I've been thinking about who he might have been messaging off and on since Friday. He would never use my mother's name in a message to her directly, at least not and be walking afterwards. There wouldn't be a need with Kumanaka. It's also possible that he's talking with police, but it seems surprisingly bold to use her name even in that context.

In short, there aren't a lot of options, and the reason is probably dangerous.

Getting ahold of his port might offer clues, but it's just as likely I'd give away my advantage and find any message threads neatly deleted. Instead, I have another method of investigation to try first.

When I slide into my desk at Walling, Igarashi has stepped out on an errand over lunch, but Chiyo is here, happy to be interrupted from filing. The other desks around us are mostly empty from lunch, making our conversation relatively private in the open space.

"Kenji-san! Did you have a good weekend?"

"Yeah," I say vaguely. "You?"

"Well, Mister Wiggles was molting this weekend, so he was in a mood." She holds up her hand to show me a bite mark on the outside edge.

"Uh, are you okay, Chiyo?"

She waves her hand in front of her face in embarrassment. "It's okay, it's okay. I shouldn't have touched him when he couldn't see well. He was just afraid."

"I take it that Mister Wiggles is not poisonous."

"Oh, no, not at all." She hides a smile behind her hand. "He's a sweetie, just like you."

Last year, the vet made a mistake and sent Mister Wiggles home with the wrong family. I don't understand the appeal, but tracking down the tiny black, white, and red snake seems to have made me a friend for life. "Yeah, a sweetie, that's me." I clear my throat and drop my voice. "Wanna do me a favor?"

She forces a straight face and leans in closer. "Is this a secret favor? Sounds exciting."

I take out a plastic package of tissues from my bag and hand it to her. It's the same kind of advertising packet that teenage workers spend their time handing out at train station entrances everywhere. They're useful and I don't know anyone who doesn't keep one or two around. The only modification that I've made is swapping out the marketing tracker for a stick-on tracker that's made to attach to small electronics in case you are prone to misplacing them. Stuck to the back of the advertisement card, next to the tissues, it's nearly invisible.

"Could you charge this?" I ask with a smile. Magitech is the only reason they can get the sticker so small and still able to connect to the internet.

Chiyo takes the packet and eyes it with amusement. "Why do your tissues need charging, Kenji-san?"

"In case I lose them," I say evenly.

She solemnly puts the packet between her hands and concentrates for a moment, doing that thing I can't ever quite understand. A moment passes and she pulls her hands apart with a wink. "Here are your tissues, safe and sound."

"Well, about that," I say, flashing her my most charming smile. "I was wondering if you could help me lose them too."

That really throws her off. "Eh?"

"I was thinking of buying someone a thank-you present, and I want to see where their favorite shop is."

"Oh." She cocks her head to the side. "Who?"

"Guess." I flick my eyes toward Funabashi's office.

Chiyo covers her mouth again, and she looks up at the corner of the room for a moment as she thinks through what I'm asking. Finally, she nods decisively. "Okay."

That was easier than I expected. "Really?"

"Kenji-san, I owe you," she says. "And I trust you too."

I'm not sure where people are getting this idea that I'm somehow an honorable person. It makes me uncomfortable. "Thank you. In his bag."

On the other hand, this favors thing is working out. I wonder if Igarashi has figured out his house problem yet.

She tucks the packet into the pocket of her suit and gives me another cheesy wink. "I can lose your things anytime, Kenji-san!"

It takes a few days before Funabashi goes anywhere besides his house and the office. There isn't anything stopping him from talking to someone on the train or otherwise in transit, but there isn't much I can do about that. He knows my face and I'm not going to hire someone else to get involved on such a sensitive topic. While I wait, I get through another three impellers and watch the black port for messages from Asagawa-san, but she's ignoring me for now.

I'm at a FamilyMart flipping through a monthly news magazine gushing about Toyama Razan handing out earthquake supplies for five minutes and dedicating a pre-school on one of his properties when I glance at the tracking app and see that Funabashi is in Setagaya. That's a perfectly boring residential part of the city to spend a workday afternoon in.

It takes almost thirty minutes to get across the city to Gotokuji on the Odakyu line, where the tracker takes me to a bank of lockers in the station. I walk around the area as the marker stays a fixed point, but no Funabashi. I use a burner port, one with a number I don't think he knows, to call his. When it connects, the top locker on the left end starts to buzz. Interesting.

The sun is warming up as I walk outside from the entrance nearest the lockers. There's an English language school, a dentist, and a bakery. Nothing remarkable, except—

There's Kumanaka's van parked illegally in front of a coffee shop.

A tiny two-story building, the sign outside unpronounceably labels the place "L'ange Café." Not a bad choice for a clandestine meeting— it's the kind of hole in the wall that's impossible to properly surveil because there is only the wide outside and then three tables filling a postage stamp of floor inside. To my advantage, the size of the seating means that the tables are all by the front, even if they are mostly hidden by a half-curtain covering the windows. From across the street, I can just make out a wide suit-clad shoulder facing out. Kumanaka.

Alright, so Funabashi and Kumanaka are meeting outside the office. For something small like skimming money through double payments, they could talk about it behind a closed office door, and no one would be the wiser. Whatever they are talking about, it's too dangerous to do it in the office.

The only thing that makes sense is if they are working against Asagawa-san.

If I ignore the weirdness with the payment from the Pinking job, it fits. Asagawa-san is bringing in something big enough that it needs temporary storage space. To make it worth hiring out, whatever the contraband is would need to be dangerous enough that a *yakuza* organization doesn't want to move it themselves.

She's clever, though: By putting Kumanaka in charge of the storage piece, he'll be the one with the product under his control for the time between delivery and distribution. That means that unless someone knows when the product switches from her hands to the storage, the connection between her and what's being moved is missing.

That's why Kumanaka would have wanted the data from the shipping labels to give to Funabashi. There're still the questions of why those breakers had that info in the first place and why Asagawa-san seemed to want their copy too. But whatever the story there, I ended up with the hard drive of data instead, only it was hopelessly corrupted.

I take up a spot in a small alley just across the street and dial Kumanaka's number. It rings for several long seconds. The arm inside moves to pull something out of a jacket pocket, but Kumanaka doesn't answer. I send two messages instead.

(Never figured you for French coffee } No Name

(I'm going to call you again in one minute.
Pick up. } No Name

That causes some movement in the cafe, hopefully Kumanaka

going somewhere private. I cue my port to call him again. This time he answers on the first ring.

"You alone?" I ask.

His voice is quiet, but he grunts, "I'm in the shitter. What?"

I take a breath and speak, keeping my voice even. Only someone very stupid or very stupidly overconfident would go behind her back. "I know what you're doing. I'm calling to ask if you're taking new members for this group suicide attempt."

There's a pause on the other end as his rusty brain attempts to process my words. I add, "Grunt if you want help."

There's a rumble, and then he asks, "Why?"

"You did such a great job of selling the aprons."

He actually chuckles at that, a rare gravelly sound.

Next, I have to make the big ask, the question that doesn't sound like one. "But you missed what you needed – something that connects to her."

He clears his throat but doesn't disagree.

I continue, "I have more access than you. Give me an opening, and I can get something." I exhale. "But I want to keep this between you and me. There's no need to loop Funabashi in on where you're getting the info. You know he's just going to try to backstab us anyway."

They're both going to do that, but at least handling things this way, I'm framing it as us two against Funabashi. Of the two, I think Kumanaka would prefer me on his side, if only because he thinks he can push me into following his lead.

"Okay," he says. "Get something we can use."

"Let me know when," I say and hang up.

That's it, then—three hands holding the knife by the blade, and if anyone lets go, we'll all end up cut. Yes, I could run back to Asagawa-san and spill my guts about the conversation, but the outcome would be exactly that. There is no amount of supposedly well-intentioned treason that she's going to accept.

It's chilly in this alleyway, so I head back toward the station.

When Funabashi returns to the bank of lockers to retrieve his port, I'm leaning against the end, out of sight. He startles when I step around the corner but regains his composure quickly.

"I thought you called him," Funabashi says. He's got a pair of faded pants and a long-sleeved golf shirt on. It's the first time I've seen him in anything but work attire. He looks old, and not in a respectable way.

"I wasn't going for subtlety. Did Kumanaka think he had you fooled?"

He puts the key into the locker and pulls out his bag. "Indeed. He always thinks people are as simple as himself. You're not so foolish."

He's trying to flatter me, which I make an eyebrow-raised show of believing. I'm not letting Kumanaka cut me out going forward, even if it means setting myself up as the target for Funabashi's inevitable attempt to take over control of my mother's business instead.

"That's why I thought we should have our own chat about the future. You're the one with the police connection."

He nods, correcting softly: "Prosecutor."

A bigger scope than I would have expected. Prosecutors aren't going to move without enough of a case that a conviction is guaranteed, but they have resources to make things happen. That likely means an investigation that's been in progress for months, maybe years, looking for something solid enough to hang their full case on.

"I'm the one putting myself on the line to find something we can use," I say. "And we can both agree that Kumanaka isn't leadership material."

"Yes," Funabashi says, closing the locker door with a definitive click. "However, with the right arrangement, our continued working relationship is in everyone's best interest. Don't you agree?"

"Yeah, that's my thought too. Before I do this, let's be clear about who is going to be directing things in the future."

He smiles in a vaguely pained way. "There are many things that I don't have an understanding of on your side of the business, and I doubt that my family would be happy if I decided to learn. So, you don't need to worry that I have any intentions of a career change at my age."

I return his expression, careful to keep the edge of victory that I'm feeling out of it. "Then I look forward to working with you, now and in the future."

ASAGAWA KENJI

A buzzing noise wakes me early from my first night in a proper futon again. I reach my hand out from under the comforter and dig my way through the nest of cords to find the red burner port. It's Kumanaka asking me to drop off his bag of tools.

I don't have them, and in fact haven't ever borrowed so much as a wrench from him. He wants to tell me something in person.

The sun is up and starting to heat the early morning air when I catch the Odakyu line from Shinjuku to Yoyogi Hachiman and meander through narrow roads to their house. Instead of Mizuki, Kumanaka meets me at the door looking surprisingly unwrinkled. He steps down into the *genkan* with his slippers still on and grabs my shoulder so he can grunt directly into my ear. "This morning, there's a job at 11. You'll have a window through 2 at least. I'll try to make it longer."

I nod, and he uses his grip on my shoulder to push me back and look me in the eye. No trace of bloodshot in his eyes for once, and we trade a look for a moment until I give him another nod. "Thanks."

He gestures at the door behind me with his chin and starts putting enough pressure on my shoulder to make it clear that it's time for me to go. I roll my eyes and start to comply.

"Why the hell is he here?" asks Rina from behind me, an edge to her voice.

I turn to see her halfway down the stairs. She's wearing jeans rolled up and an oversized sleeveless shirt, one of her house slippers hanging onto the edge of her toes as she slowly puts her foot down on the next step.

There's no way I can avoid answering that warm welcome. "Because I know you miss me so much."

Past the steps and down the hallway, Mizuki steps out from the kitchen, a towel in her hand. "Oh, Kenji-kun. Did you just get here?"

Kumanaka puts a shoulder in front of me. "He was dropping something off."

"Won't you stay for breakfast?" Mizuki offers.

I smile at her broadly, ignoring the look of disdain from Rina on the stairs. "I wouldn't miss it."

Dressed in her new school uniform, Yuri is already seated at the *kotatsu* in their living room, her attention focused on her port. She looks up enough to see me enter and scoots over to give me room to sit down, turning her body so that she's leaning against the tabletop with her back to me.

Rina flops down in a lazy kneeling position to my right and gives me a dirty look before turning to Kumanaka. "I thought he wasn't going to come over so much anymore."

Mizuki clears her throat as she steps into the room, carrying a tray of bowls of rice sprinkled with *nori*. Caught out, Rina looks down and flushes. "Sorry."

As Mizuki leans over the table to set down the tray, she casually puts a hand on Kumanaka's shoulder. He reaches up and covers her hand with meaty fingers, a surprisingly delicate gesture. I lean back and look away, suddenly uncomfortable to see such a private moment between them. Yuri is playing a puzzle game on her phone, a match-three of cartoon cat heads.

Two more trips with the tray and Mizuki's brought in the rest of the giant breakfast spread, including soup and eggs. There's a tiny grilled threadsail filefish for each of us at the table except her. I look down at mine but don't say anything other than joining in the communal "thank you for the food." She wouldn't want me to make things weirder by pointing it out.

There's a long silence as everyone starts to eat, until finally Yuri breaks it. "I have practice today, so I won't be home right away."

Mizuki nods like she already knew, and Kumanaka surprises me by jutting his chin out appreciatively. "You show 'em," he says.

"What club?" I ask.

Rina shoots me another look over chopsticks filled with rice. "Why do you care?"

"*Karuta*," Mizuki interjects gracefully. "The upperclassmen say she's quite good for just starting."

"Huh," I say noncommittally. I would not have expected a poem-matching game to be Yuri's club of choice. The *obake* variant, which uses monsters instead, was great for learning to write when I was six. The competitive version with *waka* poetry was more Takeshi and our dad's deal. As the youngest, I got stuck reading the clue cards and periodically getting nailed by the matching playing cards they were fighting to grab first off the floor.

Mizuki isn't finished. "Rina also just started a new job." There's less pride in her voice at this one. Rina not going to college is still a matter of profound disagreement in the Kumanaka household, one of the few decisions that Mizuki isn't willing to approve of in anyone, whether it's me or her own daughter.

"Oh?" I ask, already tired of the conversation. Rina starts from such a point of simmering disgust that she isn't even all that fun to bait, though her vocabulary of swear words can be quite impressive. Truly she takes after her father.

"Yeah, in Kabukicho," Rina says, daring me to comment on her taking up employment in the seedy heart of Toyama-owned territory. "I found the job on my own."

It's intended as a jab toward my own employment via nepotism, but it sails wide. "Yeah, well, preferential treatment sounds better than it works out to be in practice," I say mildly.

Kumanaka drops his fish on the table for the third time in a row. "She's been doing you a favor keeping you on the side. She thinks you don't have the stones to do the real work."

A snort of a laugh escapes Rina, and she catches her dad's eyes with an appreciative smile.

I set my rice bowl down. "Exactly how much do you owe to the

Toyama-gumi for your habit these days? Or have you been able to keep ahead of it this time?"

The slightest of coughs from Mizuki, and I stop short. She's looking down at her food, as are Yuri and even Rina now. Kumanaka meets my eyes evenly, daring me to add more.

My participating in this whole domestic situation was a bad idea to start. "Thank you for the meal," I say, moving my chopsticks to a neat position sitting across the rice bowl. "I need to be going."

With a few hours before my window, I use the time to collect a few tools, including a pair of gloves, from my apartment, and then idly walk around the neighborhood. I wait until just after 11 to take the train to Nakai station. Still technically in Shinjuku ward, the area is nothing but cheap apartment buildings interspersed with the occasional house. I circle the area, the neighborhood looking even more dirty and nondescript than I remember.

There's a small gap between the two cement block walls behind my mother's house, one that I'm almost too large now to navigate. I make it to the midpoint and lean forward so I can look into the back yard through what approximates a decorative filigree block. Two stories with dark gray walls and the main floor windows closed up with the hurricane shutters—it looks just like I remember.

I put my hands on top of the wall and hoist myself over into the back yard. Bare dirt, with just a few weeds daring to creep into the corners, there's no cover here. The space on the other side of this wall is her bedroom, and there's no direct entrance into the house from here either. The cement block wall circles the house, including the sides, and makes for an access point to the tiny edge of roof above the first floor and around the two rooms that form the second level. I climb up, and wedge into the space between this house and the next where I'd only be clearly visible from the street at just the right angle.

In this space, I take a few deep breaths. I've been in and out of this window plenty. Even with stiff hands, I only need a minute to pry the lock open with a screwdriver via a section of loose window frame. I always kept the window well-oiled, and although it's been years, the glass slides open silently.

Inside, our old bedroom is completely empty except for some dust in the corners. The closet is completely bare—Asagawa-san is many things, but never sentimental. I'm sure anything I left behind when I moved out didn't make it past the first garbage pickup.

The last thing I want to do is close and lock the window, but I force myself to do it in case I need to leave another way. The less evidence of a B&E, the safer I'll be. The other room upstairs has a vacuum and a rack with drying black shirts in the corner but is otherwise similarly empty.

That leaves the stairs down to the main floor.

Kumanaka knows that if I'm caught this will be on him, too, I remind myself. Asagawa-san wouldn't be inclined to believe that I'd be so stupid as to do this on my own, and I'm not so macho as to think I'd be able to keep a secret she might want to get out of me in earnest.

Deep breaths. I know this house. I know where to look.

I make my way down and, fingers light on the knob, open the door to the main floor. The hinge emits a loud creak as I do, and I freeze in place momentarily, but nothing happens. There's a smell on this floor, something vaguely like egg. Sometimes I forget that she needs to eat.

The front room is a space that she keeps as an office. There's a handful of papers, all stacked in an orderly pile. Nothing of use. The desk drawers are locked, but easy to pick after years of childhood practice. Office supplies: cords, a stapler, some tape. The closet is filled with tools and knives, all meticulously organized, but nothing so illegal that it'd be worth reporting.

The kitchen is similarly clean, even the storage area in the floor that's intended for rice but where she has in the past kept contraband temporarily. As I close the panel, there's a noise and I freeze for a moment, listening. Outside, a car is honking down the street.

A pen sitting with a list—*windows, bank, eggs, potato starch*—on the table is the only sign that someone has been here recently.

The bathroom is clean, just a few bottles of soap, a plastic holder clipped with drying socks, and a single towel hanging on a hook outside the door.

This leaves her bedroom, the space I least want to check. The largest of the rooms, she never opens the window shutters, making the space dark and empty and closed off. When we moved here, my brother and I and her—

My black port buzzes, startling the hell out of me. It's Kumanaka. "What?"

"Shit, I don't know, she left," he says, breathing heavily, sounding like he's fighting off his own panic. "Fifteen minutes ago."

Fifteen minutes ago? I want to ask what the fuck took him so long to call, then, but no time. "Got it," I say and hang up.

What the fuck? Is she coming here? How did she know?

I'm staring at the portable in my hand, and then—"Shit!" I tear off the back of the phone, the Syphon cover that's attached to the plain old manual battery on this model. I'm not stupid enough to leave GPS on as a function of the port itself, but there it is: the same brand of tracker as what I had Chiyo plant on Funabashi, only in this case incorporated into the battery itself. I've been carrying a fucking tracker around with me since January. I've been charging the tracker for her.

There's a noise outside—her car?

The front door is out. The window from her study is in the front too. The upstairs is an exit, but the door to the stairs is too loud. The window from the bathroom is too small. The windows in her bedroom are closed with metal shutters, too loud to open.

I pry out the battery and set it on the table next to her grocery list. If I had more time, I'd leave a snarky note to make it look like a deliberate statement, but I don't and can't.

The closet in her bedroom is the classic style, with sliding doors and a shelf in the middle, a large space on the bottom to fold up and store a futon. Hers is in it, but with just enough space that I can wedge myself on top and silently close the door.

Immediately the space heats up with my body between bedding and the bottom of the shelf, my shoulder pressed against the support beam and a wooden corner biting into my ankle. Regardless, my fingers and toes go cold as I will myself to breathe silently.

For a long minute I don't hear anything, and then the front door opens.

That's how she found my old apartment. It was only two floors, so easy to deduce which one was mine from a GPS dot.

Footsteps, but I can't tell where, only that there is movement and then she stops.

My new apartment building is ten floors. Should I move again? The thought is exhausting, but can I live with staying, knowing she probably knows where it is?

There's a noise, the creak of the door to the stairs, her footsteps going up.

Oh, fuck, Green's apartment. I've spent a lot of time there—

But no, wait, he's probably in the only hidden space in the entire city, living directly below the Walling storage.

Her footsteps move in a circle through the two rooms, stop where I entered. I'm not surprised she would know about that childhood trick with the window.

No wonder she was pissed to catch me in a lie that day. It looked like I'd been spending even more time with their files than I have.

She circles back around, down the stairs, and I hear the stair door shut again. A creak, and then the swish of shoes on the *tatami* outside this closet.

I close my eyes and hold my breath.

The moment stretches out, ten seconds, twenty, and before I have to take another breath, I hear her shoes move off and down the hallway. The front door opens, and there is silence.

I'm not so stupid as to take the sound of the front door as proof she left, so I wait probably fifteen minutes before moving again. The wooden beam is still digging into my ankle, and even though I can't feel my fingers and toes the heat is enough that sweat is beading up on my face, my neck, and the small of my back.

Finally, I don't dare wait longer and potentially miss my window to leave, so I reach over and wedge a finger in between the wooden frame and the door and pull it open just a crack. Silence and darkness in this room. The hallway beyond is lit from the front door, and there are no signs of movement.

I slide the door open far enough that I can climb out and roll onto my feet. Using my right wrist, I push sweaty hair out of my eyes, and with my left hand, rub at the indent on my ankle, all while keeping an eye toward the hallway. No signs of movement.

One second—my ankle was angled down and couldn't have been pressing against the shelf.

I reach back into the closet and feel around the foam and batting of the futon until my fingers touch something square and hard, a rectangular case tucked into the corner. I quietly set it on the floor and pop the latch with my gloved hands. What have we here?

"Shit!" I push myself back on my hands, and barely stop myself from kicking the case away with my foot. "What the—" I follow that with a string of swear words that would make even Rina proud.

Nestled in a pre-cut foam form is a handgun and a clip, the first one I've ever seen outside of movies. Dangerous, not just as a weapon, but illegal enough that even few *yakuza* would consider owning one lest they find themselves suddenly and definitively in jail.

This is it, what she's shipping. Here is something on her in her own house, and it's all we need.

＊ ＊ ＊

After I've returned the case to its corner in the closet and made my way far away from Nakai station, I make the dead drop of the information per Funabashi's instructions. By his description, there's a prosecutor who has been cursing the lack of direct evidence and is poised to jump given the right details for a sure conviction. It's almost a high to think of not wondering about the shadow behind me going forward.

I find myself walking back to the Kumanaka house. Truthfully, he didn't have to call—he would have been screwed either way if I had been caught, but a call on my list of recents would have only served to underline his deliberate involvement. I owe him an apology, and Mizuki, too, after my behavior this morning.

When I knock, she answers the door right away. Her eyes are red, moisture lining the corner creases. "You just missed him," she says with no preamble.

What is going on? "You okay?"

Mizuki looks down and away, her hair falling down to cover her face. "Is now the time to ask that question?"

She knows. He told her.

"This is a good thing. We'll keep working on our own." The words sounding lame even as they come out of my mouth.

Her shoulders are tensed, and she tries to speak several times before managing to make words. "She'll burn it all down."

"What?" The question comes out flat. I don't doubt that my mother would want to, but how?

Mizuki's words pour out suddenly, the heat of them burning. "Don't you know? She has a failsafe for this reason. The information she has on all of those people who hired her, it'll release if she doesn't stop it."

I put my hand on the doorframe to steady myself. "Why would you know this?"

"She told me so I'd stop Soseki from doing something stupid. But you—I didn't think—" She sits down on the step up from the entryway, hands grasping her elbows. "You complain about your brother, but did you ever once think about us in this?"

I didn't. I don't have anything to say to that except—"I'm sorry."

Mizuki takes a deep breath, and finally meets my eyes. "Relationships are reciprocal." She stands and reaches toward the handle at my elbow, prompting me to back up. "Come back later, Kenji-kun. Right now, I can't—I can't talk to you."

The door slides shut, leaving me standing there alone on the front step.

I wish she would've hit me instead. It would have hurt less.

* * *

The sound of clicking heels warns me that Tomohiko is bustling over to my desk. She dips her head and apologizes for interrupting my cup noodle, but Funabashi would like to talk to me in his office. There can only be one topic he'd want to discuss with me, and I'm surprised he wants to do it at work.

Inside his office, he barely looks up from his paperwork as I enter. I shut the door behind me and sit in one of the chairs in front of him, my feet out.

After he takes a moment to carefully shuffle some papers into different piles—must make sure I still know where he thinks I rate—he looks up at me. His mouth is pursed, and he doesn't seem to want to break the silence first.

"Are we having conversations at work now?" I ask. "That seems dangerous."

Funabashi reaches down and starts to fiddle with his port, flipping it end over end against his desk. "You may not have heard. My contact notified me about an hour ago that your mother was arrested."

No. Who would have told me?

Keeping my expression blank, I wonder where to start. Her personal accounts are likely frozen, the house under watch. I wonder if the police will contact me to try to dig out connections. Good thing most of her funds are housed in this business as far as I know.

Finally, I say, "That was quick."

Funabashi has moved on to more pressing matters than the fate of my family. "Let's talk about your future here."

"As we discussed before, I am looking forward to continuing our working partnership," I say slowly and in as polite a tone as I can manage. It's not going to be neat, but this is where the negotiations can start.

"Do you know anything about the insurance industry?"

I smile. "You know that's not the point."

"I am a manager of an insurance company. That is the only point." He shakes his head. "I will not be able to keep you employed here."

I'm not surprised that he would try something, but I am surprised that he would think he can get away with it. "This company belongs to my mother."

"Walling Insurance is a licensed local branch of an international corporation. This domestic entity is co-owned by 34 shareholders, with investments ranging from 3-5%, none of which have any controlling interest. Your mother contributed to the bottom line, but she did not in any way own this business."

I remain silent. Even as the details are exposing just how little I know, he's giving me more information about the financial structure than I've ever had access to before.

Funabashi continues, "And if you did want to push a claim on funds that she generated, you have none. She's in prison, not dead. Even in the event of her death, you would have no rights as you have an older brother who would inherit."

If he wants to play rough—"We are both criminally liable for these activities in some way. I don't think either of us wants information passed to the police."

He sets the portable down flat with a decisive click. "Interestingly, I looked through our records and there is nothing that ties me to your, or your associate's, behavior. Although you have been employed here, I think that your criminal actions have been purely on your own initiative."

Hell, even after months elbow-deep in the records, I have nothing on him. I might as well have been trying to read Korean. That doesn't mean that the evidence doesn't exist, only that I don't know what it looks like. I can't even threaten him that I know where the records are, or they will conveniently disappear into some other part of the city.

He thinks he has me, and it's his time to gloat. "I am a respectable salaried manager at this business, and you are an unemployed, well, nothing right now. Don't waste my time making me go to the police."

The door to my right slams open, and Kumanaka stomps in. In the main part of the office, the staff are staring until they see me look back out from the doorway. Then they become enthralled by something on their desks.

"Funabashi," Kumanaka grunts. "Think you're smart trying to double-cross me?"

I stand because there's no way this is going to end well. "It seems to be his specialty."

Kumanaka's thick elbow flies up and back. This isn't my first time in a room with him, so I'm ready. I duck under both the movement back and the sharp return.

"Violence doesn't fix this." If it could, I'd have tried it too. Funabashi's point about our relative status is accurate. Were the police to come, he's not the one being escorted out in handcuffs. Even if Funabashi were to disappear down the road, it's become clear that neither of us have the knowledge to step in anyway.

Funabashi is standing now, too, his port held up in the air, emergency 110 dialed in and his finger over the call button. "You need to leave."

"We're not going to make trouble," I say. At least not at this moment.

Kumanaka's scarred face churns through a few emotions—anger, hatred, disgust, and then what passes as consideration—before settling into a sneer. "Watch yourself."

Then, just out of spite, he pushes a pile of papers off the top of the file cabinet on his right and storms back out. Funabashi and I are left staring, his portable still in the air.

I put both my hands up and smile. "I don't see why you would not want to work with us when we are so charming," I say. "I'll get my things and see myself out."

Funabashi doesn't move his hand from the phone as I back out of his office. I close his door calmly, just as Kumanaka is slamming the front door hard enough that I can feel the impact in the floor. Everyone is still keeping their eyes down, but they are clearly tense as all hell.

My cup noodle has gone cold, so I drop it in the garbage can. The only other thing on the desk is my pencil cup, which technically doesn't even belong to me. I grab the bunch of pencils and shove them into my bag with my phone chargers.

It's a weird enough action that Igarashi looks up at me from the corner of his eye.

"Breakups are hard," I comment.

He tips his head to the side in question, and I shrug. I'm not going to get into specifics with him, at least not in the middle of the office. What I said is enough he can pass at least vague news on to Chiyo.

And with that, I leave Walling.

PARK TAEHYUN

Archival footage: We Live... With A K-Pop Star
Cast Interview (1-minute clip)

The six primary cast members of popular reality television show We Live... With A K-Pop Star *are seated side by side on wooden stools in front of a white background. Each holds a set of paddles with the faces of the cast members on them. Idol Lim Bora from pop group P1XY is in a plush chair across from them, reading questions off cue cards. Her jumpsuit is made of a galactic orange iridescent vinyl, and she has a manicure and lipstick to match.*

"Okay, next one," Bora says brightly. "Who can eat the spiciest food?"

Paddles go up quickly, and it's unanimous; everyone has chosen Son Jiwon. She hides behind the paddle with her photo on it, giggling. "It's because of my mother; her kimchi recipe uses extra gochugaru*!"*

Bora smiles. "That one was too easy. I think we all remember the homemade kimchi stew episode!"

"I'm still recovering," quips Hong Minho, shifting on his stool with a mock grimace.

"Oh my!" Bora exclaims. "Alright, let's make it a little harder. Most likely to get drunk in public?"

"Easy, too easy," whines Jiwon, her voice hitting a nasal

pitch as she flips over a paddle with Minho's face. All of her castmates have agreed except for Minho himself, who has selected Park Taehyun.

"Park Taehyun?" Bora asks. "Really?"

Taehyun, for his part, just laughs. "Deflection, it's all deflection."

Minho looks straight at the audience, eyebrows dancing behind the plastic frames of his glasses. "Don't believe him," he says, faux serious. "When the cameras are off, it's a different sto—oof!" Taehyun has jabbed him in the ribs with one of the paddles.

The camera pans back to Bora, who shakes her head in chuckling disapproval. "So, you're saying there's more to the Hero of Hwacheon than meets the eye?"

Minho claps a hand over his heart. "The stories I could tell you, Lim Bora. The stories I could tell!"

* * *

"**S**hin *Ramyeon* Well-Being Freshly: the same taste you love, now with organic ingredients for your family."

Trite. I toss the script onto the sofa next to me and tilt my head from side to side, stretching my neck. The silence in this room is oppressive. "Ocelot, play some background music."

On my port screen, an animated cat bows, showcasing its patterned back, then bounds offscreen as jazz filters out of the apartment's speakers. One of Misora's many touches: when she remodeled, she ensured speakers were mounted throughout every room in subtle locations. Though she rarely listens to anything herself, she knew this was a detail that would matter to me. She footed the bill for that feature, too, as she did for all the high-end extras we enjoy, from Subzero fridge to gesture-operated window shades. Even now, as my career is cresting, owning this place would be beyond my reach. My name is the one on the title held by the city government, but another document, already signed by me, cedes full ownership to Misora—all she needs to do is file it.

My stomach is rumbling, so I go into the kitchen to scrounge something up. Misora has a few pre-made meals tucked in the fridge in matching containers, each with a precise amount of rice, greens, and protein, but I dare not raid those. There are some vegetables left from this week's delivery box, so I decide to make *japchae*. We don't have any beef, but the mushrooms I find in a brown paper bag on the middle shelf will substitute nicely.

There is something soothing, almost meditative, about preparing food. I've always enjoyed the results of my labors, from working at the chocolatier in Seoul to creating big meals for my housemates when I was on *We Live... With a K-Pop Star!*. As I've gotten older, I've learned to appreciate the process more too. During the first series of *FBRC*, they had a professional chef film the close-up shots of my character doing prep work, but between seasons I took lessons in knife skills, and now it's my hands dicing onions and deboning fish in the B-roll.

I break down a red bell pepper, then peel and julienne a carrot, pleased by the even size of the resulting matchsticks. I'm just finishing the mushrooms and lowering them into their marinade when my port chimes: *Incoming video call, Fujiwara Eika.*

I answer the call on the kitchen monitor. "If this is about my behavior at that *gaijin*'s party—I was high. I'm also not sorry."

Eika laughs softly. She's seated in a fluffy white chair in front of a plate glass window, Tokyo twinkling behind her. "I understand why you were upset. What are you making?"

"*Japchae*." I realize I don't remember the word for *dangmyeon* in Japanese. "Clear starch noodles with vegetables."

"Ah. *Tomen*, it sounds like."

"Yeah, that's it. Anyway," I continue, starting a pot of water to boil, "upset is too strong—more like annoyed. Unless you know something I don't?"

"No. Mi-chan and I keep missing each other. Now she's not answering her port. Is she home?"

"She's at BG7 tonight."

"With Hideki?" Eika worries at her lower lip with her teeth.

"No, I don't think so. Why would she be with Hideki?" I'm not thrilled to hear that Misora might be at the club with her high school boyfriend, even if they have been just friends for years. That plus the American means there are two different ways she could get me bad press.

Eika frowns. "Hmm. Taehyun, do you know what Mi-chan has been working on lately?"

"That project with you, I thought." Frustratingly, Misora doesn't leave much laying around. She's careful. "Listen, I'm going to join a table at Palais tonight, play a few rounds of mahjong, want to come? Bunch of people from my agency, it will be fun."

"Mahjong gambling is illegal!" she replies with feigned shock. She rubs her forehead, closing her eyes for a moment. "Oof, sorry. I'd like to, but I shouldn't."

"Are you feeling okay?"

"I'm trying a new med; it just makes me a little dizzy. The doctor said it would take some time to adjust." Before I can respond to that, she gives me a bright smile. "You'll tell Mi-chan I called?"

I doubt I'll be seeing her again tonight. "Sure."

* * *

Palais is a new-ish club in the up-and-coming glitz core a few kilometers from our apartment. It doesn't have much of a discernible theme, but the vibe of the decor is very "Moulin Rouge on acid"—neon colors, winkingly garish art, and more satin than a whore's lingerie drawer.

Mayumi lets me in the back entrance and slips a small baggie into my hand. "We're in Room 4. There's a girl in a red fox costume outside the door, you can't miss her."

"Order me a vodka soda. I'll be right back."

There are a few other men already inside the VIP toilets, so I duck into a stall and use an old 10,000-*won* note to take the bump off the back of my hand.

I wait in the stall for a bit, flushing the toilet for show. When I exit, there's only one other man remaining—our eyes meet briefly in the mirror over the sink as we wash our hands, and a flicker of recognition crosses his face. He's probably seen *FBRC*.

But when I follow him out into the hall, he heads for the room with the crimson vixen standing outside. She swings the door open, and I go over to where Mayu is standing with two drinks.

"Here—vodka soda as requested."

The room, already hazy with smoke, is occupied by the usual suspects. I count heads. "Eleven people for mahjong?"

"Didn't think all of you would come. You're late, so you wait for a seat."

I lean closer to her, picking up a faint aroma from the sticky red gloss she's wearing. Cherry, maybe.

"Who's the guy playing West at table two?" Sugimoto Aoi, a commercial actress I know only because we're repped by the same Japanese manager, is draped across a chair next to him, legs in his lap.

Mayu's lips purse into a shiny bow, and she beckons me to lean down even further. "Watanabe Kaihei," she whispers into my ear.

I nearly have to suppress a laugh. This dude, with his expensive haircut doing some heavy lifting to compensate for a weak chin, is who Misora complains about? He looks like a well-groomed weasel. Whatever business he and Misora had to handle tonight at BG7, it must have been brief.

"But he's—"

"Yes." She knows—everyone in this room knows—my very intimate connection to Toyama-gumi. Her voice drops so low it's almost inaudible. "Palais is neutral turf, and he's been dating Aoi. She brought him along tonight."

Tokyo is huge, but these kinds of encounters are more common than you might think. There are hundreds of clubs across the city, and hundreds of people just in this one, but of those hundreds, you can count the occupants of the VIP rooms on a few sets of hands. It's not simply young elites, it's a certain type: those of us who need, on a visceral level, what this place has to offer.

A spot at table one eventually opens up for me, so I don't end up with Watanabe, though I catch him looking at me occasionally out of the corner of my eye. I play for a few hours, my skills—and my awareness of the room—progressively blunted by alcohol. By the time I stumble home, I'm a couple hundred thousand yen lighter, yet buoyed by whatever Mayu gave me. It's higher quality stuff than she usually gets. I wonder if the Maedas are making a move on the Toyama brand.

The rooms of the apartment are cool and dark. A small lamp is on, though, in our bedroom, and as my eyes adjust, I can see Misora has fallen asleep sitting up in bed, book in hand. That's a pleasant surprise. Given that she walked out of here earlier this evening dressed like sex, I wasn't expecting her to come home and chastely read about—I squint at the title—Dynamic Magic Thermosomething.

The tableau before me is a glimmer of our normal life—I can't count the number of times I've found her asleep with her work, notes in her lap, cold tea languishing nearby. I undress and slide in beside her, reaching across to turn off the lamp. She stirs.

"Hey, I'm home," I whisper.

Misora rolls toward me, blinking sleepily. I kiss her, harder than I'd intended, but she responds with equal fervor. Running a hand up the curve of her hip, I deepen the kiss, then push her gently backward so I can position myself above her. She abruptly stiffens, pulling away.

"Don't." She's wide awake now, and she sits up in the bed, duvet clutched to her chest.

"What's wrong with you?" Damn, do I ever not like having my chain yanked.

"I don't want to." She starts to get out of bed, reaching for a robe, so I flip the lamp back on.

"What do you mean—?" That wasn't an I-don't-want-to kiss.

"I'll sleep in the *tatami* room." When we remodeled these two apartments into one, Misora insisted on a formal Japanese-style room, complete with *tatami* mats on the floor and traditional furniture. If she sleeps in there tonight, it's the first time the futon will have seen any use.

"All this for an American, Misora?" The lust has ebbed; now it's anger making my blood pump faster. "Or are you moving on to a new flavor?"

She freezes in the doorway, slowly turning to face me. "Excuse me?" she says, voice hard as glass.

I get out of the bed and pull on a robe of my own. "It would seem, even to the casual observer, that you prefer foreigners. That's all."

She's just tired enough to bristle at this. "One American hardly indicates a preference."

"And me."

"You? Did you forget that I am Korean too?"

I let out a short bark of laughter. "Your mother's ancestors could have been born on the sacred slopes of Mt. Baekdu itself, it wouldn't make you Korean, Misora."

I have wanted to give her this particular piece of my mind for the longest time. I move closer, my face near hers. I have ten-plus centimeters on her, enough to be intimidating—not that Toyama Misora intimidates easily. I switch to speaking Korean. "You've spent your entire adult life resisting your Japaneseness, bitter that you don't fit whatever mold of Japanese femininity your father wanted to smash you into, and you think you can hide behind Korea as if you have any damn clue what it means to be one of us?"

There are ruddy blotches of emotion on her cheeks, and her lips are pressed into a nearly invisible line, but she doesn't take the bait. "Incisive analysis, but we're not doing this tonight, Dr. Freud. I have a busy day tomorrow."

All of her tomorrows are busy. I continue to grip her wrist. "My career is tied to this relationship, and I'm not letting you ruin it for me. We don't all have rich parents to fall back on."

Though I expect another flash of anger, I get only a weary sigh. She looks down at where I'm still holding her arm. "Can I go make myself a cup of tea, or would you like to march me to the kitchen?"

I let go.

I sit at the counter as she heats the water, realizing we've reversed positions from the last time we sparred in this room.

"I take it you didn't do well at mahjong," she says, setting out two cups.

"I did fine," I lie. "The problem is what I found waiting for me here."

"There are 40 million people in the greater Tokyo metropolitan area, Taehyun. I'm sure you can find one who wants to sleep with you."

Of course I can. That has never been the point.

She carefully pours two cups, leaving a precise aesthetic distance between the top of the liquid and the rim. Misora isn't any more upper class than I am, but she fakes it so well.

"The KBC awards are next week, and I have my premiere this summer," I say. I need her with me for those. I can't let her end this; she's the only way I'm getting out of the giant fucking mess I'm in.

"I know. They're on my calendar. Speaking of," she continues, taking a sip of her tea, "my parents would like us to come to lunch next weekend."

Aha. She needs me too. Having a meal with her parents is like performing in an elaborate *kabuki* where I'm the only one who wasn't given his lines. But I'll do it, of course I will. What choice do I have?

* * *

Compared to some of the homes I've seen in Hollywood movies, Misora's parents' house isn't particularly large or impressive. But when you remember that it's Tokyo, and you realize that in addition to the house, they have enough yard for Razan to practice his golf swing—then you get how wealthy the Toyamas are. It's not hard to imagine Misora growing up in this house. The rooms—intimidatingly formal with their garden views, delicate *tatami* mats, and priceless Japanese art—seem architecturally engineered to create a person like her.

Instead of the expected housekeeper or butler, though, we're greeted at the door by a *yakuza* thug. He looks out of place, as uncomfortable in these refined surroundings as I am. The Toyama palace is a far cry from the shabby apartment my family still occupies.

Misora gives the thug a silken smile, transmitting a graceful enthusiasm that only I can read as bullshit. With the exception of Watanabe Yusuke, she's never spoken a positive word about any of these men who occupy her father's orbit. I have a vague sense that there are several main Toyama lieutenants and sub-lieutenants, yet Watanabe is the only one she's ever mentioned by name.

We hand off our coats and are directed into a large room with a glassed-in view of the rock garden that occupies the center of the house. It's annoyingly asymmetrical in that fussy Japanese way I've never understood. *Wabi-sabi*, Misora explained once, this strange idea of finding beauty in imperfections.

I follow her to the table at the center of the room, and she kneels at one of the sides, somehow managing to look comfortable within the tight confines of her silk dress, bare feet tucked primly beneath her.

"Anything I should know?" I ask.

She's looking straight ahead, eyes following a small brown bird that's flitting around one of the rock sculptures outside. "You've done this all before," she replies, so quiet I can barely hear her. This isn't a house for raised voices. "She's in your corner; say whatever you need to say to keep her there, short of making any promises. He'll try to bait you, so don't take it. He thinks Koreans are hot-tempered."

"Like his own wife?" I growl, feeling a flush creep up my neck. When Misora frowns, I realize that was her test run, and I've already failed.

"What a pleasure to see you, my children." It's a velvety voice, so similar to her daughter's, but with a sultry warmth Misora can't manage. Rei is only speaking Korean because her husband isn't here; still, I'll take it. She must be at least fifteen or sixteen years my senior, but she is sexy as hell. Exactly the kind of Korean woman I always thought I'd end up with, even if her citizenship is now, by marriage, Japanese.

Daring to entertain filthy thoughts about Toyama Razan's wife— and in his house, no less—if he can read it on my face when he enters the room, I'm dead. "It's a pleasure to see you too," I offer, and she gives me a gracious smile.

"Mi-chan!" a second voice booms, a gregarious sound that hides the sinister nature of its owner. Misora accepts her father's embrace; I get a short nod, which is, frankly, better welcome than I expected.

With Razan here, we'll have to switch to Japanese, and both women do, chatting about the spring weather as we all stand together at the window, gazing out at the garden. I'm not able to follow the entire conversation—they're speaking too quickly—but I pick up enough to ascertain that even the subtext has subtext. The topic is ostensibly the flowering fruit trees, but I can nevertheless tell that, somehow, Misora's parents are criticizing her long absences—and am I being blamed? She takes my hand, though whether it's moral support or a request for the same, I don't know.

Rei's port pings. "Lunch is served."

She leads us to a dining room set with a chair-height, Western-style table, and I feel a flicker of relief. This context evens the playing field—at least I don't have to juggle Japanese table manners on top of the imperial *keigo* language Razan expects to hear.

We're served a first course, elaborately beautiful and nearly flavorless at the same time. Misora waits for her parents to take their first bites, then, politely, she comments, "It was so lovely of you to invite us today, *okaasan*."

More subtext, though this I can follow: Why are we here?

Rei mirrors Misora's steely smile, and in that expression more than any other, they look so alike. "We heard you have a movie coming out, Taehyun," she redirects, a move straight out of her daughter's playbook. "We would love to hear more about it."

Razan grunts into his water glass. He very clearly would not love this.

"It's a historical drama." After the words leave my mouth, they seem to hang, menacing, in the air above the table. For Koreans, the first half of the twentieth century was marred by countless Japanese war crimes, and our filmmakers have recently taken an interest in showing the period as it really was. I enjoy letting them all squirm for a moment, but Misora finally pinches my knee under the table.

"It's about the Three Kingdoms era," I say, choosing a point so far back in time that it's inoffensive. They'll figure out it was a lie when the film is released this summer.

"How fascinating," Rei says, pouring glasses of *sake* and distributing them around the table. "It must be so nice to finally have your career settled and be able to start thinking about other things."

In my periphery, I can see Misora's jaw clench. It begins. Well, I'm content to let Misora bear the brunt of her parents' dysfunction.

"Of course it's an honor to star in one movie," Misora replies, "but more films would be ideal. Maybe even expansion to outside markets. Taehyun has so much talent, it would be a shame to hold him back."

Rei sips her sake. "Moving without caution isn't advisable, though. I think it's best to stay where we belong and be satisfied with what we have."

We're not talking about my career anymore. Does Rei know about the American? If so, then she is on my side. I sense an opportunity.

"I've been fortunate to have the good advice of my family as I consider my options," I say. "The film was an interesting diversion, but as my mother reminds me, my loyalty is first and foremost to the TV series that launched me."

Rei's black eyes are boring into me over the rim of her *sake* cup. As she takes another sip, I see a tiny crinkle at their corners. I've amused her.

"Your mother and I would get along," she says, setting the cup down with a *click*. "Perhaps we can meet someday soon."

Ignoring his wife's comment, Razan turns to Misora. "And your work, Mi-chan?"

"Fine. Busy, though. Someone keeps devising extracurricular projects for me." She plies him with a gentle smile, more of her lipsticked bullshit. But Razan looks pleased, and Rei lets out a light chuckle. These two made her, yet they can't read her. It's both perplexing and sad.

Razan starts to ask a follow-up question, and for a moment I feel hope—maybe he and Misora can carry the conversation for the rest of the meal. But Rei lays a hand on her husband's arm. "No work at the table," she says. "You'll give us all indigestion."

She shifts the conversation to the Tokyo Giants, a dully neutral topic that should trouble no one, and for a few minutes all four of us actually chat about baseball. No subtext, no hidden meanings, just player trades and RBIs. Then Misora mentions a pitcher who was recruited after his retirement from the Boston Red Sox, and Razan's expression sours.

"Americans," he grumbles. "He should play for a team at home."

"I think he wasn't good enough to play in the American League anymore, dear," Rei says.

"Too many *gaijin* in this country," Razan says, glowering right at me. "Taking jobs, corrupting our way of life."

"Papa—"

As Razan continues, a bilious, hissing anger bubbles up in my chest. And then it rises, expanding to fill my entire head, blocking out his words. But I can still see the spots of pink that tinge both women's cheeks—why can't he? Somewhere under my fury, there's astonishment at how unaware he is of the two people who are supposed to matter most.

Misora's voice finally cuts through the roaring in my ears. "Papa, why don't we go out to the garden? I brought a present for you." She takes Razan by the arm, leaving me alone with her mother.

Rei folds her napkin, laying it next to her plate. "I should ask him not to bring up politics, he can get so enthusiastic," she says mildly. But her hands are trembling.

"Politics," I hear myself echo in Japanese. Is that what she tells herself it is? I switch over to our shared first language. "How—when you're Korean—"

All the color drains from her face, and the look she gives me is as dead-eyed as anything I've ever gotten from her husband or daughter. Without a trace of irony, she responds in Korean, "I am Japanese."

* * *

Misora doesn't stick around for much of a debrief after we leave her parents' house—she doesn't even make it all the way home with me. Instead, she asks the driver to drop her at Helios headquarters. I guess we're both going to pretend I don't know her actual plans, as if I haven't been able to see her texting in English while she's sitting right next to me.

(Anything happening tonight in this
sorry town? } Park Taehyun

Ryuya responds to my message almost immediately with an address in Minato. As a promoter for up-and-coming pop groups, he always knows which nightclub is going to be hot and when.

No place, however, is hot at 5:00 p.m. I find him in the alley behind the club, taking a cigarette break outside the back door.

"Where's your woman?"

I draw a cigarette from his proffered pack and light up. Misora hates when I smoke—she says it's the smell, but I think it has more to do with Razan. "This isn't a Toyama joint, is it?"

"No." He peers at me through the blue wisps of his own exhalation. "You two split up? I know some journos with questionable ethics, if you want to get your story out ahead of hers."

"I bet you do." I take a long drag and lean against the club's plaster wall. It's cool through the thin cotton of my shirt. "No, we're still together." Whatever "together" means when my girlfriend has plans to get herself dicked by an American tonight.

Why does he irk me this much? Partially it's that he saw me with Soojin, and he was so damn sanctimonious about it. As if his precious Misora isn't doing the same thing to me—and this isn't even the first time. But after the lunch today, it clicked. I'm taking all the heat from Razan—when I'm Korean just like his wife—and this fucking white guy is sailing under the radar, getting the best parts of Misora while I keep putting up with her crap.

"Who are you promoting tonight?"

Ryuya nods his head toward the club's interior. "Idol Hands, they're a girl group. I told them you might stop by, and the response was... enthusiastic."

I should ask him not to bring up politics, he can get so enthusiastic.

I crush my cigarette under my heel. I feel a need to corrupt the Japanese way of life. Starting with one of these pop stars.

Ryuya takes me inside to the stage. For the moment, the girls are hanging out in their street clothes and doing a sound check. They're not quite what I expected—more EDM than pop, and they're actually a duo instead of a group. Both decline to give their real names, introducing themselves as Hidari and Migi: Left and Right. How cute.

I'd ballpark them both at around 23. Their affect reads bored, but I can tell they're excited to meet me because they keep shooting each other wide-eyed glances. Perfect. Against my better judgment, I invite everyone back to my apartment. We have about four hours until they're due on stage.

Ryuya takes Migi into the study on the thin pretext of showing her our view of Tokyo Tower, leaving me alone in the living room with Hidari. She's petite and doe-like, hair cascading down her back in long waves, but her outfit is grungy: ripped tights and cutoff shorts. It's an odd combination to my eye, but I don't follow Japanese women's fashion.

I sit on the sofa, feet up and arms thrown over the back as she wanders around the room, eyeing Misora's carefully curated decor. She leans down to look at a framed picture, a rare vacation photo of me and Misora on a beach in Saipan. We look happy and in lust, swimsuit-clad and limbs wound around each other, but what you can't see is Misora's port on the towel just outside the frame, buzzing with an endless stream of emails and texts.

"Her bikini is cute," Hidari says, and I laugh.

"Is that what you want to talk about? Toyama Misora's bikini?" I'm projecting relaxed, eyes half lidded as I watch her, but I'm feeling impatient.

She glances over at me, shrugs, then continues to browse the shelves. "What do you want to talk about?"

I opt for direct, hoping to throw off her equilibrium. "Well, since you're going to have sex with me, we could start with your real name."

A little intake of air tells me she's shocked, but she doesn't produce the mock-indignant denial I'd expected. "Tomomi," she says, gaze molten.

It takes less time than I would have liked, and it's awkward. Tomomi seems checked out—at one point I catch her staring at the bedside table, almost as if she's memorizing what's there. She's not here to be with me, she's here for Park Taehyun. Which is different.

Tomomi gets out of the bed and walks toward the closet, running her fingertips along the surface of Misora's dressing table; she pauses to give herself a spritz of perfume. "Make yourself at home," I say wryly. Ignoring me, she flicks on the closet lights, unselfconscious about being nude in the middle of Misora's suits and dresses.

She's immediately drawn to the evening gowns, reaching for a satin-wrapped hanger draped in clear plastic. Noting the black silk and silver beading, I realize it's the one Misora will wear to the KBC awards next week. I scramble out of bed and take the dress from her. Why do I keep bringing home girls who mess with Misora's stuff? "Not that one," I say, pushing some other dresses aside so I can re-hang it without crushing the delicate fabric.

As I hook the hanger over the bar, I notice something. A small black access panel, like the kind you'd hold a port up to. Leaning further into the row of dresses, I see the faint seam of a door. My heart starts to pound. This could be something, this could finally be something.

I send Tomomi back to Minato with Ryuya and Migi, hoping that in my distraction I didn't miss her swiping something, because she seems like the type to want a souvenir. As soon as they're gone, I return to the closet. I want to tear into the dresses, but Misora is very particular about her things—I have to move them carefully, or she'll realize I've been in here.

As I carry dresses over to the bed by the armful, I think back on when we got this apartment. We'd been together about six months. I was renting a 1LDK in Shibuya, trying to get to Tokyo as often as I could to see her, and she had a studio not far from Helios in Shinagawa. Ostensibly it was only to sleep in when she stayed too late at work, because like many young Japanese professional women, her parents' house was still her official address. It quickly became clear that it would be easiest to move in together, and as my profile started to rise with *FBRC*, a luxe Tokyo apartment with my gorgeous Japanese girlfriend seemed like the right way to highlight my new status.

The hunt for the perfect place took ages, especially with Misora's precise tastes, and we ended up buying two neighboring apartments for a gut job. But since I was making constant trips to Seoul for filming and promotion, sometimes multiple flights a week, Misora volunteered to handle all the construction. I remember when she showed me the blueprints for the new design.

Misora unrolls the sheet of extra-large paper on the table. "So, the main spaces here will be a living room, dining area, and kitchen, and off to this side of the entry will be a study and a Japanese-style room."

I try to make sense of all the boxes and lines. "What's this?" I point at the southeast-facing part of the plan.

"I saved the best bay view for our bedroom. Plus a bathroom and two closets—the big one for me and the smaller one for you."

I let that go. "I like the sound of 'our bedroom,'" I say instead, draping an arm around her hips.

"Me too."

"And this?" I ask, indicating a black box between the large closet and the hall powder room.

"Stabilization mechanism," she replies without a hint of guile. "In case of earthquakes, since it's such a tall building."

Misora's evening gowns are piled high on our bed, leaving me room to maneuver. I squat down and trace the seam in the wall from the floor up to standing height. It's definitely a door.

"'Earthquake stabilization,' my ass," I mutter. I start to reach for the entry panel, then hesitate. Misora has access to technology that isn't available to the average consumer; who knows what she's rigged back here. The last thing I want to do is set off some kind of alarm. Though it amuses me to think of her rushing home from the American's place in a panic, there's no faster way to guarantee she moves whatever it is she's keeping in here to Helios or another similarly restricted place.

Fortunately, I know just who to call. He answers on the third ring, voice betraying his mild surprise. "You finally have something for me, Park?"

"I might." I describe what I discovered.

"Put everything back the way you found it. I'll send you instructions soon."

* * *

Promoting my show has taken me all over Asia, but this will always be my favorite skyline: Mount Namsan, its slopes pink with blooming cherry trees, and Seoul Tower perched on top. It's good to be home.

I poke my head out of the bedroom to see whether Misora's army of stylists has finished. The hairdresser is packing up her tools, so Misora stands up and does a spin for me.

Being annoyed with her hasn't affected my vision. And in any case, we have an audience. "Stunning," I say, stepping close and resting my hands at her waist. "Are you willing to be seen with me?"

"You're always so handsome," Misora replies, reaching up to adjust the knot on my black bow tie. With this performance, maybe she should be one of tonight's nominees too.

The red carpet drop off is a congested mess, full of reporters and photographers eager to be the first to spot the biggest stars. Which, for the last few years, has included me. It is still unreal.

I turn to Misora. "Ready?" She only shrugs—she doesn't get high off this like I do.

I exit the car first, then turn to offer her a hand. The camera flashes spot my vision with white, and the onslaught of questions is a deafening din. Seulki, my publicist, shepherds us to the press line of credible journalists and TV hosts, whose questions have all been pre-screened, but I can still hear the catcalls from the swirling scrum of paparazzi.

First up, Cha Eunbi, host of *Hello, Seoul!*. I've done her morning show before, so I know the drill: flirt with her and give short answers. Don't offer her the rope she needs to hang you.

She softballs me at first, actual questions about *FBRC*: filming for the next series, and how I feel about being nominated. "And now, what all our viewers really want to know..." She rotates herself toward Misora. "Your dress. Who are you wearing? And is the designer Japanese or Korean?"

Oh, no. Please tell me she thought about this. Please, not a Japanese designer.

"He's new, his name is Lee," Misora replies.

"Korean, then." Cha Eunbi looks satisfied.

"American, actually."

As we walk to the next interviewer, I lean close and pretend to nuzzle her cheek. Voice muffled by the clicking camera shutters, I whisper into her ear, "Go fuck yourself, Misora."

The photo that gets splashed across all the gossip magazines is taken as she pulls away and looks up at me with a silky smile. It sold because it's a real smile—she looks so incredibly goddamn happy.

I will give her this: she can sell a narrative. Even when not a shred of it is true.

The rest of the interviews pass in a blur. Together, we dodge questions about our future, our plans for marriage and children. Misora gets asked several variations of "What's it like to be with Asia's hottest bachelor?," and while that moniker is gratifying, in my current mood her pitch-perfect answers all land like jabs.

I win my category, best actor in a drama series. Backstage there are more interviews. Winning should mean better questions, and it does—a producer sits me down with Kim Jangmi, one of the anchors on *KBC Evening Edition*. Again, some easy pitches, but then she hits me with a curve: "Your character's arc has taken a darker turn this past season. I think everyone in Korea, maybe even Asia, knows about your heroism at Hwacheon. How do you use that experience when portraying Kyongwan's story on the show?"

My mouth goes dry. I've talked about Hwacheon on television a hundred times—I've even talked about it before with Kim Jangmi.

Blood on the snow, the deep red a lurid gleam against pure white. And not from the trout we'd poached and gutted, no, not only from that—

"I didn't mean to." My own voice sounds like a rasp in my ears.

"Excuse me?"

It's Misora, somehow, who rescues me. "I'm certain you're not suggesting that an actor of his caliber needs personal source material."

"No, no, of course not!"

"It's time," Misora continues, "for Taehyun to celebrate. I think he's earned it, don't you?"

Before Kim Jangmi can protest her interview getting cut short, Misora goes in for the kill. "But we would be absolutely delighted to give you an exclusive with both of us tomorrow morning at our home here in Seoul."

Once we're out of earshot, I can't help myself. "You're only rewarding her bad behavior."

"Interesting way of expressing gratitude," she replies sardonically. "Thank you, Misora."

CAMERON GREEN

"Is Toyama-bucho available?"

Nozomi pops to her feet and bends into a crisp bow. A pattern has developed over the past few weeks: as the workday wraps up, Misora leaves the lab, the rest of the team departs, and then I follow her upstairs. Nozomi's role includes efficient transportation arrangements and silent judgment—even as she looks down at her own feet, I can feel her somehow giving me side-eye.

"She is not expecting you, Green-san."

"Oh." Misora didn't come down to the lab today, but I assumed that the rest of the plan still stood.

"In fact, she is no longer here." Nozomi's neutral expression wavers—is that pity?

"I see. Thank you." I remember to add the polite end-of-the-workday acknowledgement as I turn to leave. "*Otsukaresama deshita.*"

"Green-san—"

"Yes?"

"Her work meetings are always up to date on her calendar in SunDeck."

What is Nozomi trying to tell me? I know how to access our team files. "Okay...?"

"Any non-Helios public event, however, would likely be on Minotaur Social."

I have just enough dignity left to wait until I'm in the hallway to pull out my port. While the MinoSo app loads Misora's profile, I punch the down button for the elevator.

The most recent post from Misora herself is a two-week-old Helios press release announcing a new magitech peripheral for the Gamestasis, but since then she's been feature-tagged in scores of posts by other accounts. Most of them are from Eika or something called "Ramen Girls: The Official Park Taehyun Japan Fan Page."

"TONIGHT'S THE NIGHT!" the latest Ramen Girls post crows. "We'll be livestreaming from Seoul as your favorite chef competes in the category of Best Actor in a Drama Series. Don't miss the red carpet! It all starts at six p.m.!"

The elevator in front of me dings, doors opening to reveal that the carriage is already occupied by a woman in a charcoal suit. I hear my own intake of surprised breath as I clock who she is.

The portrait in the lobby doesn't do her justice. She's younger than I expected, for one, and far more beautiful too. I wonder if the unflattering painting is a deliberate bid for gravitas.

I jam my port into my pocket, knowing she couldn't have seen me gawking at her daughter's boyfriend's fan site yet still feeling caught out. I bow as I take a step backward. "My apologies."

Eyes narrowed, she doesn't reply. Instead, she reaches for the panel of elevator buttons, and the doors glide shut again in front of me.

* * *

(So I encountered Rei Toyama today } Cameron Green

Vanessa Green { And???)

(Remember when you met Sec of State Jackson, you said how amazing it was to meet your professional idol, and how inspiring she was? } CG

VG { Best day of my career)

(Yeah, it was not like that at all } CG

(You guys have dinner plans?) CG

VG { Some friends from work are coming to check out the new Vietnamese place near us. Want to tag along? It will be pho-n!)

VG { Pho-n. Fun, get it?)

(I will ask Asagawa instead) CG

VG { Cam?)

VG { Don't banh mi!)

* * *

(Any interest in sushi and Kaiju Smashfest? I need to blow off some steam) CG

Asagawa Kenji { 8p?)

(See you then) CG

* * *

A knock at the door: Asagawa's here, a plastic bag with trays of FamilyMart *makizushi* in hand. He has a nasty cut on his cheek with a purpling bruise underneath it, but I've learned to not ask about things that might connect to his work. Panzer and I picked up some cans of Asahi on the way back from our walk, so that plus the new game I'm downloading onto the GS, and we should be set for the night.

We disappear the sushi and make quick work of the first few levels of the game. Asagawa stands up, stretching a little. "Bathroom," he says curtly, and I nod, waiting until he's out of the room to swap our controllers so I can recharge his. The display on the front of the GS reads *P1: 100% | P2: 26%*. Thinking I'd never need it, I didn't buy a connector cord.

Asagawa comes back out of the bathroom, a snarky little smirk on his face. I take the bait: "What?"

He grabs two more cans out of the fridge, handing one to me. "Awful lot of condom wrappers in the trash in there. You know you can't knock up your hand, right?"

I whip the GS controller at him, Frisbee-style, so that it hits him square in the gut. Unfortunately, he still manages to catch it one-handed.

"Why don't you die in a fire," I suggest.

Still grinning, he flops back down on the couch next to Panzer. He cracks his beer, propping his feet up amongst the empties on the *kotatsu*. "How is the *yakuza* ice princess?"

Ice princess is probably apt enough, but—"*Yakuza?*" I echo, confused.

"Well, you see, Green, when a group of tattooed men love organized crime very, very much—"

"I know what *yakuza* are, jackass," I interrupt. "What does that have to do with Misora?"

Another grin, and I realize I've confirmed what he was fishing for: he didn't mention her name first, I did. Well played, I guess, although he could have just asked.

"Seriously, though," I press. "Misora, *yakuza*, I don't get it."

"You're kidding." Then, the grin dropping away, "Goddamn, Green. Do you really not know who her parents are?"

"Her mother is the president of Helios."

"Do you know who her father is." He's exasperated, which is perversely pleasing.

Though her mother looms large in my world, I've never thought about her father before. Male and named Toyama Something, I suppose; that's all I've got. "No."

"You have to be the only guy in Tokyo who could be regularly dicking Toyama Razan's daughter and not have any idea," Asagawa says, disbelief, amusement, and concern commingling in his tone.

Feeling increasingly stupid, I shrug. Who the hell is Toyama Razan, and why does he matter? My fingers itch to grab my port and Mino the name.

"The Toyama-gumi is the biggest *yakuza* family in Tokyo, maybe even Japan. Toyama Razan is the current *kumicho*. And Misora's father." He says each sentence with slow deliberation, a *soroban* sliding beads of information on humanity's dimmest abacus.

Nothing Hollywood has taught me about the *yakuza*—tattoos, money laundering, ritual mutilation—jibes with either Misora or the elegant woman I encountered earlier. "Her mother couldn't run a legit company like Helios and be married to a known criminal."

Asagawa laughs. "Where do you suppose her mother got the money and influence for that company? Especially when she's a *zainichi kankokujin*. Doesn't matter how long they've been here, that's a small step from *gaijin* to most people."

I haven't heard this term before, but it's easy enough to translate: Japan-resident Korean. I would never admit it, but it stings that Asagawa knows all of this about Misora when I don't. So much of her is hidden from me.

"How do you know all about the *yakuza*?" I deflect.

He shrugs and reloads the game. "I hear stuff."

I'll bet. Probably in the same place where he got that shiner.

"Shit," I say as I realize something. Something not good.

"What?"

"The night of the earthquake, Misora sent a car to take me home."

At this, Asagawa lets out a little snort. "Of course she did," he mutters under his breath.

"I thought at first it was a Helios car, but the driver wasn't in uniform, and he was pretty rude."

"Rude with tattoos under a nice suit?"

"It's not like I strip-searched him. Maybe. I don't know, it was dark." But as I say it, I remember the guy who picked Misora up at Helios on my birthday, and the tattoo peeking out of his jacket. It was right in front of me, and I didn't want to see it.

Asagawa takes a long pull of his beer. "At least you had the sense not to bone the *kumicho*'s daughter until after his thugs had your address."

My address is in my personnel file at Helios anyway. If things go south with Misora, I'll be a different kind of fucked.

* * *

After Asagawa leaves, I take Panzer on a short walk, then I brush my teeth, undress, and get into bed.

I do not get on my port and go down a Wikitaur rabbit hole about Rei and Razan Toyama, giving myself a headache from trying to parse the complex *yakuza* hierarchy. Fortunately, since I don't do that, I don't learn any distressing fragments of bloody Toyama-gumi history, all of it spearheaded by Misora's own father.

And then, when Misora is back on Saturday, I don't stay silent as she leads me to the bedroom, lying awake long after her breaths have settled into the steady rhythm of satiated slumber.

I definitely don't do that.

* * *

When I wake up on Sunday, she's gone, a used glass in the sink the only sign she was here. At least she stayed the night; that alone is rare. She's left a note, too, I see as I open the fridge, her monogrammed notecard pinned in place with a magnet.

I couldn't sleep, so I went to the lab. I'll see you tomorrow. -M

She's clearly absolving me of any expectation to work today, but this could be my best chance to talk to her—it's more neutral than my apartment, yet still private.

"If I don't make it back alive, move in with Vanessa or Asagawa—your choice," I tell Panzer before I lock the door.

I expect to find Misora at her workbench, or maybe the simulator, but she's seated at the damper room conference table with a closed laptop in front of her, her port flipped screen down. Instead of her usual prim posture, her shoulders are slumped, and her fingertips are pressed against her eyelids. I hesitate in the doorway, a paper cup of espresso in each hand. The door-ajar alarm bleats in protest.

Misora's head snaps up at the sound, listless expression rearranging to one of irritation. "Didn't you see my note?"

I push the door shut behind me with my foot, silencing the alarm mid-chirp, and cross the room to hand her one of the coffees. "Here, before it gets cold."

She lifts the cup and takes a sip, waiting. I want to ask if she's okay, ask what it is that has cast a shadow under her eyes. Whatever it is, it happened this morning. I am forever grasping after Misora's moods, but like Tantalus, what I seek is just out of reach. She masks so much of her life that I can never ascertain the source of her ire—or joy, I realize, recalling that afternoon in her office when Eika called with some unknown news. I benefited from that, but the why of it remains hazy.

I should have stayed home this morning. But I'm here; what else to do but plow forward? I sit in the chair next to her, setting my own coffee and port on the table. "I did see your note, but I wanted to talk to you."

"Oh?" She shifts in her chair, expression guarded. "What about?"

"I, uh—I learned who your father is."

I expect a flinch, or a denial, or a reasonable explanation that will help me sleep at night. Instead, she lets out a long sigh. "I see."

I wait for more. After a beat, with some reluctance, she says, "Do you have a particular question about him? I prefer to keep my personal and professional lives separate."

"Oh, sure. Like when we have sex in your office," I mutter. I had planned to keep the focus on one topic—her father being a *yakuza* kingpin who could end me with a gesture—yet this is what tumbles out. If things go badly here, I'll be worse off than when I left the U.S. for Japan.

"What is it you actually want to ask me?" Her expression is unreadable, her tone flat.

Well, hell. I'm in it now, so I guess I'll plunge ahead.

"Do you care at all about what could happen to me? Or do I just fill in the spaces when Taehyun's not around? I know when you're with him, Misora, it's all over MinoSo."

There's more I could say, about the battery she brought to my apartment and what happened that night. I've tried not to think about it too much since, but when I couldn't disconnect from that prototype, it felt like I was bleeding to death through my pores. As if whatever makes up the core of me was gushing out in waves of shimmering heat. And then, once I'd crested the pain, a peculiar euphoria. The damper room is humid and warm, yet I feel a chill at the memory.

"Of course I care," she says. Our eyes meet, and in that moment, she looks so hurt I would give anything to retract what I've said. "Taehyun isn't—that is—"

My port vibrates, buzzing against the surface of the conference table. We both glance down at it.

Kenji Asagawa { I need your help with something.)

"Do you need to go?" Misora asks. Her expression has once again been schooled into illegibility.

I can't leave things like this with her.

Another buzz.

KA { And not the amusing, Green-the-slacker doesn't bother to do this for two months kind of help. Today)

Asagawa wouldn't press for my help like this unless he needed it.

And yet—— I can't walk out of here, not without answers. Yeah, I'm worried about the fallout for my career, my visa, my life in Japan. But also, because Misora... is everything.

Oh. Oh, goddamn it.

I'm falling in love with her.

KA { Oi, Green. Why is this the one time you're not surgically attached to your port?)

Of course I would realize this now.

Misora's been scanning all of Asagawa's texts as they light up my screen. She clears her throat, then hesitates; when she finally speaks, her voice is hollow. "Go. I'll come to your place tonight."

She hasn't moved from her seat, yet she's somehow so far away from me.

"Are you okay?" I finally ask.

Jaw clenched, she shakes her head.

* * *

Asagawa tells me to meet him at a Katsuya *donburi* shop in Shinjuku 3-Chome. All I've had today is the latte I drank at Helios, but it feels like acid in my stomach, so I bypass the meal ticket machines and go inside to find him. He's inhaling a breakfast set, polishing off the *natto* and raw egg as I slide into the opposite booth.

"You look like fresh garbage," he observes by way of greeting.

"Same to you," I grouse back. The slice on his cheek is thoroughly scabbed over now, and the bruise underneath has gone from deep violet to ochre and green. There are circles under his eyes, and he looks like he could use about three years of sleep. Well, so could I. "What's the emergency?"

He takes a sip of his tea before responding, and it occurs to me that I haven't seen Asagawa drink anything other than beer before. I've never really thought about him doing mundane things like eating breakfast. He's been less a person than a caricature to me: the guy with the missing shoe who became my kind-of friend, a funny Japan story for people back home.

"So," he starts. "So, to fill you in, Asagawa-san—er, my mother—went to prison recently." A pause to let that sink in, and I need it. Do I tell him I'm sorry to hear that? Ask what she did?

I settle on a half-incredulous, half-concerned expression.

"I turned her in," he continues.

Now mostly incredulous. "I—wha—"

He points at the cut below his right eye. "She's a terrible person, she deserved it."

I noticed his injury the other night and didn't say anything, thinking it was a work-related casualty. His mother? I try again: "I'm—"

"Don't. I kinda earned it."

This is such a shift on how I've thought about Asagawa up to this point. I start to say that no one deserves it, but he's not interested in letting me respond to anything.

"Don't make it awkward." He takes a bite of rice, staring me down as he chews. My eyes drift to his cheek again, the dark red gash in the middle of the technicolor bruise. His own mother.

I think of my mom, the accountant who drives a Volvo and plays in a local bocce ball league. She likes used bookstores and golden retrievers, and if you don't keep an eye on her, she'll peg herself a few extra points in cribbage. Leanna Lindholm-Green would murder someone for giving me an injury like that, much less do it herself.

I should really call her.

"So, what do you need me for?" I'm trying to do as he asked and not be awkward.

He pinches another bite of rice with a small sheet of *nori*, forming a ball. "With her in prison, there's information sitting out there that some bad people don't want released. And it's getting sent from somewhere. I need it to not do that."

That gives me an inkling of what he needs. Asagawa has apparently decided that I am the solution to his many tech-related problems. "Okay. What do you have?"

He slides a ticket for a breakfast set across the table. "You better eat, it's going to be a long day."

I've gotten used to those, thanks to Misora.

I'd managed to not think about her during Asagawa's story, but now her face materializes in my mind's eye, and my gut churns again. I don't feel like eating, but Asagawa clearly needs a mirage of normalcy, so I take the ticket and flag down the waiter. "A whole 390 yen, you shouldn't have."

Not quite his usual smirk, but it's smirk adjacent. "420 with tax."

As soon as the tray is placed in front of me, I pick up the dishes with the raw egg and *natto* and deposit them on Asagawa's side of the table. "So, how do you know all of this is happening?"

"This guy, Takamine—we worked with him on our last job. Yesterday his boss got an anonymous email spilling the whole deal, and he was fired."

I break apart a cheap pair of wooden chopsticks. "So? How do you know that has anything to do with your mother?"

"I was told she had a failsafe—pre-set revenge in case she was ever taken out." He stirs the egg into the *natto*, and the bright yolk clings slimily to the pungent fermented beans. Nauseated, I shift my gaze to my soup, seeking one of the few pieces of tofu.

"And you said Takamine was the last person you worked with? So, a last in, first screwed type of setup?"

"Yeah. I was hoping that, if you had access to it, you could trace the email that was sent to his boss, figure out where it came from."

"And how am I getting access?" I think I know and wish I didn't.

It's the first time today I've seen him look like his usual self. "Hurry up with your soup."

* * *

Takamine's office is a squat gray four-story building ten minutes from Ikebukuro station. It has a small parking lot with a gatehouse, and an iron gate has been drawn across the driveway. It's a fairly low barrier, clearly intended to keep out cars, not people. Asagawa hoists himself over, then turns to look at me.

I point to the sign on the gatehouse. "It says they're closed on Sundays."

"Of course they are." Asagawa has no patience for my concerns about breaking the law. But then, he's also a Japanese citizen. "You're two meters tall and spend all your free time running in a straight line. Jump over."

"1.9 meters," I correct under my breath. Once I'm on the other side, I glare at him. "If we get arrested, I'm saying that you kidnapped me."

"Takamine's company is on the second floor," he says. "So. How are you getting us in?"

"Hilarious. That's your problem. I'm only here for the tech part."

"Fine." He points at the front doors, which are thick plate glass and look in on a small mail area. "Wait there."

And with that, he disappears around the back of the building. I try to hide myself from view of the street traffic by slouching behind one of the portico columns. Combined with my height, my hair stands out like a beacon in this country. I'll never understand why Asagawa dyes his—shouldn't a low profile fall under his job description?

After about fifteen minutes, which I fill by probing at the company's email server from my port, I catch something out of my peripheral vision. It's Asagawa, standing on the other side of the doors. He swings one open to let me in.

"Ventilation ducts?"

He shrugs. "Can't give away my trade secrets."

It takes us a few minutes to find Takamine's boss's office. I can't help grinning once we're inside and I see the computer. It's even older than the hunk of junk Asagawa dragged to my apartment, though in significantly better condition. I could probably do this one without my lab lenses, too, if I had to, but I'm glad I thought to grab them this morning. The company must have adopted Syphon authentication standards ten or so years ago and then never bothered to upgrade their hardware. I fake the boss' access biometric on my port and push it to my multitool. Holding the adaptive tip of the multitool to the finger panel convinces the computer that it's reading its owner's Syphon signature, and it logs me in.

"Seriously?" Asagawa asks. "You got the easy part."

"Hmph." Working quickly, I pull up the email program and find the incriminating message, forward it to one of my dummy accounts, and then erase all signs of the forward. "Alright, let's go."

Back in the train station, we duck into a tiny salaryman bar called "Standing Shots Style." We have to buy something, so Asagawa orders two bourbons, and the bartender slaps bowls of peanuts and seaweed-wrapped rice crackers in front of us. Ignoring the snacks, I open the email in an app that will show me the underlying code.

"Huh."

"What?"

"Your mother go to Reykjavik often?" I turn my screen so he can see, then remember it's all in English. "IP address says it was sent from Iceland."

Asagawa frowns. "I don't think she even has a passport."

"Yeah, it was spoofed. It makes this harder, but not impossible." I squint at the rest of the code. "Also, it was sent from a dock."

"A what?"

It's weird how Asagawa being downslope makes him unaware of certain small things that are common knowledge. But that's Eika's soapbox, not mine—and I'm sure he would just love having her pity.

"A dock is a place to charge magipaper. Like—a hub, kind of, for keeping documents topped up with Syphon. It's safer than keeping something on a laptop or tablet, so for anything that contains private or proprietary information—trademarked designs, medical charts, wills and legal contracts—it's smart to keep it on magipaper."

Asagawa looks skeptical. "And a piece of paper can send an email?"

"With the right settings on the dock, yeah. She could have rigged a system where, if she doesn't check in with it in periodic intervals, it triggers."

He tips his head back, looking up at the ceiling for a moment. "I can never tell if you're bullshitting me on this magitech stuff."

I suppose if it doesn't work for you, it would seem made up. "No bullshit. Now you just have to figure out where she stored the documents."

"Just," he says, puffing up his cheeks and blowing out an exasperated breath of air.

Suddenly hungry, I take a handful of the peanuts. "Don't you have someone—anyone—you've worked with that you could trust to help you with this?" What I don't add is how strange I find it that he called me for help. I might be one of the most tech-savvy people he knows, but I'm also a *gaijin* he met a few months ago. Even I have people in Tokyo I could call on: Drew and Vanessa, Misora—

Misora. There's the gut twist again.

Asagawa takes a sip of his whisky. "I did, but he buggered off."

I don't know whether to believe this or not, but the subtext is clear: I'm all he's got right now. Great. I give up and sip my bourbon, too; its dusty burn fits my mood, even if it doesn't help with my stomach.

"So, what else can you get out of that code?" Asagawa asks.

"Not much. Since she's spoofed the location, its main use was telling us it came from a magidock. But we can assume she'd have to regularly visit the dock to top up the Syphon—she could adjust the timer on the auto-send function remotely from her port."

"Would it have to be her, or could someone else be doing it for her?"

"Depends on how she set it up, but it could be someone else. Where do you think she's storing this, her house?"

"No, definitely not her house." He chews thoughtfully on a rice cracker. "What does a dock look like?"

It feels crazy that he doesn't know this, either, like he's some kind of time traveler from fifty years ago. Eika's right. Magitech is shutting certain people out of living the way the rest of us do.

"The simplest ones look like a file folder with a Syphon panel. She has to be using a higher-end version, though, so it would look more like an aluminum briefcase with slots for the folders inside. Or a file cabinet, if she has enough documents. There would be a Syphon panel and a touchscreen of some kind. Have you seen anything like that around?"

"Yeah, the cases," he says. "Battery life on those folders is worse than your average port. Dead almost as soon as I pick them up."

This would make him very useful to his mother. She could have him courier all the documents she wanted, knowing he'd never be able to access them. Huh. I'm getting a fuller picture of Asagawa in one afternoon than I've had in all the time I've known him.

Asagawa's silent for a bit, sipping his whisky and staring at the dark blue *noren* curtain that divides the bar from the back room. "How often would you have to top up a dock like that?"

I shrug. "More often than that lock manager at One Eleven for sure, because Syphon would be the primary power source, not the backup. Weekly, maybe."

"Weekly," he echoes, still fixated on the Zen circle design on the *noren*. "Green, how often do you wash your windows?"

What? "Uh, never."

"Yeah, same. But a couple months ago, I found some receipts for a recurring window washing task set up through Chore-Cho. You know what that is, right?"

"Yeah." It's the task solicitation service I used to find Panzer's dog-walker. Post the chore, get responses, choose the best-fit bid and pay through the app. Super convenient. "And it was set for weekly visits? Pretty clean windows."

Asagawa nods. "The receipts had a billing address, but I used to be at that place all the time, and those windows got washed once every six months, tops. Do you have Chore-Cho on your port?"

"Yeah," I reply, following his train of thought. I like that this is information we can access without any B&E, too. I tap the app icon, a yellow square with the outline of a purple butterfly, and start a search as if I'm looking for work. A few window-washing chores come up, but they all seem genuine.

"These are all current jobs, right? Can you look up old ones?"

"Doesn't seem that way." I think for a moment. "But—when I set up Panzer's dog-walking task, I could look at similar completed tasks to get an idea of the market price."

"Great. Create a new window-washing task."

"Under my own account, which is tied to my Minotaur profile? Yeah, no."

"Fine, I'll make an account," Asagawa says, pulling a port out of his pocket, "but this is dead, you'll have to charge it first."

Holding my hand on the Syphon panel for a minute resurrects it back up to 54%. Asagawa fakes a profile and initiates a new chore: *Lazy gaijin needs his "windows washed."*

"I see she didn't smack your delightful sense of humor out of you," I grumble, then instantly regret it.

Asagawa doesn't seem too ruffled, though—his attention is focused on the list of comparable tasks.

"What about that one?" I say, pointing.

Primary Chore: Wash the windows at a small office in Ebisu.
Additional Chores: Top up Syphon on magidock, if needed.
Supplies: Provided
Address: Tap here for directions

"Well, that was easy," Asagawa says, tossing a 1000-yen note on the bar. "Let's go wash some windows."

* * *

There's a direct JR line from Ikebukuro to Ebisu, so it only takes us twenty minutes to get to the address, which turns out to be a small leasing agency. "Does this seem right?" I ask Asagawa.

"I don't know," he admits, peering in through the glass door. "Maybe. Hey, there's someone in there." He raps on the glass. "Oi, you! We're here to see your magidock."

A bony man with thinning hair opens the door. He reminds me of Araki from work, but older. "We're closed tod—" he starts to say, when Asagawa throws a fist back and punches him right in the face. Blood gushes from his nose, blooming into bright roses on his poly-blend button-up. "What the hell?!"

I'm thinking the same thing, though commenting, or even reacting, doesn't seem prudent right now. I'm supposed to be a good wingman in this situation, but punching bystanders wasn't part of the deal.

"Didn't you hear me? I asked where your magidock is." Asagawa looks down at his knuckles, frowning at the streak of red. "I'd hate to have to repeat myself."

The man backs up, hands raised defensively, as his nose continues to drip crimson. He points wordlessly to a desk in the corner. Asagawa pulls on a pair of gloves and looks over at me. "Don't let him leave."

Other than maybe my height, there is nothing about me that suggests "enforcer," but the man is too busy dealing with his bloody nose to try and get past me anyway. Asagawa is rooting through all the desk drawers; it feels like forever before he pulls out a steel case. "Got it, let's go."

He turns to Bloody Nose, who's now holding what looks like half a box of tissue to his face, and hands him a 10,000-yen bill. "We weren't here."

Once we're safely down the street, I turn to Asagawa. "What the hell was that back there? You didn't have to hit him."

"Efficiency, Green. I don't have all day."

"So much for the famous Asagawa people skills," I grumble as he buys a bottle of water from a nearby vending machine and uses it to rinse the traces of blood off his hand. "Don't know why you were so concerned about the Toyama family when you're the one bringing me along to fights."

Water splashes on the concrete as Asagawa snaps his head up to look at me. "Fucking shut up," he hisses. "I'm concerned because you don't know not to throw that name around."

"It's my boss's name," I say, annoyed by his chastising tone.

"It's a lot of scary people's boss's name, too. When we're carrying around something like this case, and there's blood on my shirt, there's really only one way to interpret that name."

Things I'm around thanks to him, which was my point in the first place. But it's not worth pressing the issue.

"I'll need to look at that more closely, and I'd prefer to do it sitting down." I point at the small Hawaiian-style shaved ice shop across the street.

"It isn't summer," Asagawa objects, but he follows me anyway.

"*Irasshaimase*," calls the twenty-something behind the counter when we enter, tacking on a lackluster "Aloha" when she sees me. Once we're seated at a table, pineapple-themed menus in hand, I notice that the shop is called "Pine-Pine," but they've transliterated the *katakana* into English as "Pain-Pain." This feels so apt that I start to laugh.

"He'll have the mango *kakigori*," Asagawa says, a look of—what? commiseration?—passing between him and the waitress. "Do you have *ujikintoki* this time of year?"

"We do." They both seem to silently agree this is regrettable.

I lift the case, which I've been carrying so it doesn't short out, onto the tile-topped table. I haven't used this particular brand of dock before, but they're all more or less the same. I rest my left hand on the Syphon panel and close my eyes, giving everything a quick scan.

"Can you fix it?" Asagawa asks. I open one eye to see him chewing on a wad of *mochi*. Our desserts have arrived.

"Depends on what you mean by 'fix.' Can I stop it from sending? No."

"That is literally the only definition of 'fix' in this particular situation, Green."

"The send function only has an owner override. Without your mother, there's no turning it off. This will happen unless she's around to authorize a top-up."

Asagawa's spoon clatters to the tabletop, leaving a dark green trail of melted matcha ice on the bright tile. "So, this whole day was pointless?"

"No. I can't do a digital override, but I can magically bend the Syphon circuitry back on itself."

"Try again in plain Japanese. I don't speak nerd."

I sigh. I'm so used to talking to Misora and our team about these things, I forget other people don't understand them. "I will force it to send the documents to itself, on an accelerated schedule. Plain enough for you?"

"That'll do."

I pick up my spoon to eat my *kakigori* before it melts.

"Really?" Asagawa's eyes flick to the case. "Priorities, Green."

"It's not going to send the next one for a few days. The least you can do is let me eat in peace."

The task itself doesn't take too much time, just concentration. Fortunately, this place is quiet, and we're the only customers. I imagine it's a different story on weekdays, given the high school nearby.

"Okay." I put the case back on the floor and push it toward Asagawa with my foot. "It'll finish cycling through everything in the next few hours."

My port vibrates, the special pattern that indicates a message from

Misora.

Misora Toyama { I'm wrapping up here. Should I meet you at your place?)

"Her?" Asagawa asks.

I nod. "I gave it a strong charge, so handle it with gloves and it will be fine."

"Got it. Thanks."

More gratitude than I expected, to be honest.

INTERSTITIAL

EDO STAR
> *Opinions*

Government Must Protect Our Resources
By Tachibana Tsutomu

The United States Department of Defense has started to develop magic technologies to be reserved for military use. Yet the details of this research remain secret, making it unknown whether such work is being conducted on their own shores or on other land currently controlled by the American military.

After the August 5 loss of 69 million square meters of old-growth forest, including the Redwood Shrine Tree, Americans have shrunk from conducting their poorly grounded research on their own land. Today, there are over 80 American military bases located across the nation, including in Yokosuka, Kanagawa, at the entrance to Tokyo Bay.

With unknown actions happening on our shores—dangerous experimentation allowed by the current weak leadership in the National Diet—we can only wonder how long it will be before a magical tragedy happens here.

Americans would have our nation beholden to their military, but we are strong enough to protect ourselves. Revise Article 9 of the constitution and allow our nation to proudly *remilitarize, regaining the pride in ourselves and the respect we are due in the world. In doing so, we will preserve the land and the magical resources gifted to us by our forebears for future generations.*

Only through rejecting ineffectual leadership and securing access to our nation can we finally end the theft of our land, theft of our magic, and theft of our self-determination.

TOYAMA MISORA

I'm standing outside the door of Cameron's apartment trying to summon the will to knock. Some enterprising individual, having either a rich sense of irony or zero knowledge of the occupant, has taped an ad for a nearby English cram school under the peephole.

There's a reasonably priced TOEFL class that starts in 20 minutes. I wonder, could I pass for a high schooler? An hour spent taking vocabulary practice exams couldn't be worse than having this conversation.

Panzer barks on the other side of the door, and I can hear Cameron shushing him, then the locks tumble and the door swings inward.

"Hi," I say.

"Hey," he replies, stepping back to let me in. The air in the entry feels as charged as the first time I came here, but in an infinitely less pleasant way. Panzer wedges his head under my hand, and I scratch at the base of his ears even though he's the traitor who gave me away.

"Can I get you anything to drink?" Cameron asks as we walk down the hall toward the kitchen. "Tea?"

I nod. "Thank you."

He turns to the refrigerator and pulls out a one-liter PET bottle of cold jasmine. He's not much of a fan of tea—he must have bought this for me. The tension in my shoulders eases a bit.

I step over Panzer, who has sprawled himself in front of the kitchen table, and into the living room. The *kotatsu* table is surprisingly free of its usual detritus of beer bottles, chopstick wrappers, and convenience store receipts, so instead of sitting on the couch, I kneel on the far side, hands clasped in my lap.

Cameron sets down a pair of too-full glasses of tea, then drops into a cross-legged position across from me. "How was your day?" he asks.

"Fine," I say. "Though not as productive as I would have liked."

He sighs, his dissatisfaction with my reply evident. "I never thought I'd have this version of you in my apartment."

I eye him warily, taken aback. "Version?"

"Helios Misora."

My gaze flicks over to the Gamestasis, its controllers tucked neatly in a cubby, the silver charging panels in their handles glinting in the bright overhead light. He doesn't know that was my idea: making it possible for players to charge the controllers as they gamed. Or that I leveraged that concept, and the attendant profits, into my current position. He has Helios Misora in his apartment every day.

I look back at him, spreading my hands in a semi-shrug. I don't understand what he wants from me.

He turns away for a moment, reaching up to grab something—magazines?—from the shelf by the TV. As if he read my mind, he says, "I want to understand this. These. You."

He slides the magazines across the table, and I register that the one on top is a frothy teen weekly with celebrity photos and makeup tips—not exactly his usual reading material.

Oh, damnit. Not this picture, which went tabloid-viral after the KBC ceremony, of me gazing up at Taehyun with a besotted-looking smile. It's humiliating. I hate that Cameron has seen this, but of course he has. He goes to the FamilyMart downstairs on a daily basis, walking down the row of newspapers and periodicals to get to the cooler in the back.

Eager to hide the embarrassing photo, I shift the magazine to the bottom of the stack.

The second magazine is *Metro Monthly*, which is exactly what it sounds like: a light but newsy collection of Tokyo goings-on. The cover story is an anodyne profile of the new executive director of Kato Medical Group, but there's a page marked with a FamilyMart receipt.

As I set it aside, I notice today's date and the list of purchases: magazine, magazine, one-liter bottle of jasmine tea. I don't know how to interpret the meaning of these items as a set.

The marked page is filled with another too-familiar smiling face: My father. He's been *kumicho* for so long now that magazines like *Metro Monthly* don't bother with a full work-up. This is pure propaganda, no doubt bought and paid for by a Toyama-gumi subgroup looking to curry favor. The piece highlights the donations Papa made to help people after the recent earthquake, and the prose is so fawning it verges on purple, a different kind of humiliating.

I feel my shoulders slump. Finally, I say, "There are things I don't tell you... because I don't want you to think less of me."

With my eyes, I beg him to accept that, to understand how difficult it would be to give him more. I see his expression soften, but he presses on.

"Right now, I think you lie to me. What's worse than that, Misora?"

"Plenty."

He stares at me, waiting, but I don't know what else to say. Finally, he sighs. "I think I might be falling in love with you, and it fucking sucks."

I hear my own sharp intake of breath. This was the last thing I expected. As my mind races, I say the first stupid thought that coheres into a complete sentence. "Because of Taehyun?"

"Partly," he replies, frowning. "You've got to give me something here, Misora. I can't work for you and do whatever we're doing and watch you be with him without having some idea of why."

I need to choose my next words with care. "My father—you obviously already know he's the *kumicho* of the Toyama-gumi."

"Yeah."

I close the magazine, not wanting Papa's eyes on me while I explain this. "His politics are... somewhat to the right of center."

Cameron nods for me to continue.

"He's developed relationships with politicians in the All Nippon Party. You've heard of them?"

Now he fidgets in discomfort. "My sister has told me some things. That they're anti-foreigner. But isn't your mother ethnic Korean?"

That little tidbit could have only come from Asagawa; *Metro Monthly* wouldn't be so crass. "He needs her," I say simply. There are some things I'm not ready to tell him, and some things where I don't know the full story myself. The shape of my parents' relationship is a mystery to me.

"What about Taehyun? He's definitely a foreigner."

"He is... tolerated. Not well, but he is, mostly because my mother likes him." I meet his gaze again, holding eye contact. More than anything else, this is the part I want Cameron to understand. "He's also an ideal smokescreen."

He's silent for a long moment. The air between us is so still, I realize, because I'm holding my breath. When he gets it, it's visible in his eyes—it's the same eureka expression he'll have in the lab when he's solved a tricky problem, except that this time the satisfaction is blunted by fear.

"For me."

"Yes."

We've stepped away from the precipice of whatever happened this morning, but I've injured him in a way I don't know how to fix. *I think I might be falling in love with you, and it fucking sucks.* He's hedged it with all kinds of self-protective qualifiers, but that last part lodges itself up under my ribcage, and the guilt is piercing.

"Do you want me to stay here tonight?" I ask. Tomorrow is the Emperor's birthday, and Helios will be closed. I have so little to offer him, but this much, I can give.

His hand bolts across the table, grasping for mine. Tea splashes out of my cup, staining the white coat of the doctor on the *Metro Monthly* cover. "Yes."

* * *

I awaken to my port alarm as it vibrates gently under my pillow. Cameron, sprawled behind me with one arm thrown above his head, stirs but doesn't open his eyes.

Panzer greets me in the hall, tail waving in eager anticipation of breakfast. I pat his tawny side instead, and he gives me a doleful look.

"Sorry, boy," I whisper. Gathering my clothes from where I tossed them last night, I shake them out and give them a quick scan for wrinkles. They're not great, but Eika will be the only person at Helios today. We've agreed to use the holiday as catch-up time on the battery work, and I want to loop her in on my new ideas for the port redesign too. I've gotten as far as creating a preliminary mock-up, and I think it has real potential.

Cameron's kitchen is fairly bare, but I scrounge up a protein bar and toss it in my bag for later. Taking pity on Panzer, I fill his bowl with what feels like a reasonable amount of kibble, then turn to grab the last of the jasmine tea from the refrigerator. Cameron's lease documents are still laying on top, coated with a fine layer of dust, and I remember Hatsumi's request. Surely, he won't mind if I send them to her? I shake the dust into the garbage bin, then sit down at the table to scan each page with my camera.

With my forefinger, I trace the rectangular scorch mark on the tabletop, the exact size and shape of a port. That night was terrifying, but it was thrilling, too. It got me thinking about a lot of possibilities, things I've only begun to explore. I send the scans in a message to Hatsumi, hoping it doesn't wake her. Should I add anything else? She said she hoped I'd be happy.

"Are you happy?" I ask Panzer. He cocks his head at me, then nuzzles my hand until I scratch his ears. Belly full and head patted, he is happy indeed. How effortless he makes it seem.

I start typing a follow-up, but before I press send, Hatsumi replies.

> *Date Hatsumi { Thanks. Does this mean...?)*

I delete my message and start over.

> *(For the time being. Good luck with*
> *the article. } Toyama Misora*

* * *

"Morning!" Eika calls across the lab. She plunks a tea thermos and a large takeout box on the bench next to me and starts opening containers. "Have you eaten?"

"You're late," I say. My stomach rumbles as I catch the savory aroma of miso soup. Caught up in the work, I forgot all about the protein bar in my bag.

She looks up from opening a steaming box of rice, eyes twinkling. "You're welcome for the breakfast, Mi-chan."

"Thank you. Did you have a late night?" I ask, pouring tea.

Eika nods, closing her eyes for a moment as she takes a sip. "I've been so tired recently. Like I can't stay on top of everything."

"Are you getting sick?" Eika has a deft hand with makeup, but the dark circles under her eyes still peek through the concealer. "We can do this another time."

"No, no, it's fine. The situation with the mine in Hokkaido isn't going well. I'm worried they're going to pin the blame on Replenish, Mi-chan, even after all the work we've done."

I think of what Okamoto said to me in the elevator. Why didn't I follow up on that? This could become a big problem for me too. Rei agreed to allow use of Helios workspace for this project, and to release me from a percentage of my duties as our corporate donation to Eika's work, but the part of my actual salary for time spent on this project is being covered by Replenish. If FHI kills Replenish, the Helios board won't let me keep spending 25% of my time on a project they don't believe in. Especially not with Fujiwara Isao whispering in their ears.

"When's the next FHI board meeting?"

"They've completely restructured the board, and since they've moved me off to my own subcommittee, I won't get to attend again until the full meeting in June. Kimiko's assistant won't even let me see their minutes."

The board restructuring must have been what Okamoto was hinting at. But that can't be right. Before Eika's parents left Japan, they entrusted each of their children with an equal ownership stake—Eika has as much right to participate in FHI activities as Kimiko or Isao.

"You're a shareholder. What percent of the company?"

"No idea, I'd have to check. Why?"

"Three percent or more and you have a legal right to those minutes." I pull up a contact card on my port and airshare it with Eika's. "This is my parents' lawyer, he's excellent."

Takahashi Saburo is widely known to have ties to Toyama-gumi. Most recently, he was in the news for successfully fending off that wrongful death lawsuit brought against my father; he was so effective that Papa didn't end up paying a single yen of *mimaikin* in restitution. It might be good to remind the elder Fujiwara siblings that Eika has certain connections.

"Oh, Mi-chan, a lawyer? I don't know...."

"Give him a call. And find out your percentage."

"Alright, alright, I will. Thank you." She opens a container of mini omelets and gives me a sly smile. "How's Cameron-san?"

My turn to sigh into my tea. Do I say anything? Do I tell her it was one perfect month of him being just what I needed until he upended it with his *I think I might be?*

Her expression is so eager, though. "He seemed fine when I left his apartment this morning."

Eika laughs, and in that moment, she's her usual self again. "Ooh, you're even staying the night? It must be good."

I take another sip of tea and wink at her over the edge of the cup. I'll let her imagination take things from here. It's easier than telling her the truth, even if she is one of my oldest friends.

Incoming Video Call: Watanabe Hideki

Well. Speaking of old friends... I don't want to take this in front of Eika, but with Papa breathing down my neck, I could really use some good news about the trackers. I set down my tea and press "accept."

"Hey," I say, holding my front-facing camera close to my face so Eika is out of view.

Hideki squints at the screen. "Where are you? Not the lab, I hope."

"Where else?"

"So disrespectful to the Emperor on his birthday, Misora." He waggles a wafer-thin Syphon panel in front of the screen. "Look! It's done and ready to test."

Just the news I needed. "When can you get it to me?"

"Are you free for a late lunch?"

I glance over at Eika. Her expression is unreadable, but the dark circles under her eyes are still plainly visible. I shouldn't ask her to work more than a few hours, anyway. "Yes. The usual place?"

"See you there." He ends the call.

"Are you two working on something together, Mi-chan?" Eika's mouth is pressed into a line of—what? Worry? Disapproval?

"A project for my father. Hideki's quite skilled at mechanical things, you know," I add defensively. "Especially for someone without a formal education."

"Hmmph," she says, giving me a hard look, and I feel a wisp of cool anger rise up through my core. This judgment is rich coming from Eika, given what happened between her and Kato Sayuri, and now the latest Johjima Haru debacle. It's on the tip of my tongue to ask her if there's a different set of rules for people from society families.

Instead, I simply say, "He's Toyama-gumi."

She looks skeptical, but to my relief, she relents, nodding. "Okay."

"Okay." I elbow her in the ribs, eager to lighten the mood. I don't want to fight with both Eika and Hatsumi in the same weekend, not to mention whatever it was that happened with Cameron. "Eat up, then I'm putting you to work. We're going to finish this today."

* * *

"I'm not sure any of this qualifies as lunch," I say, frowning at the menu in front of me. "'Salt-broth ramen,' indeed. How is that different from any of their other ramen? It all tastes like the sea." It's probably also about as hygienic.

"Get the fried rice, then."

"Is it good?"

Hideki chuckles. "None of it's good."

This is confirmed when our food arrives. The *yakimeshi* manages to somehow be under-seasoned, but I eat it anyway, suddenly ravenous. It's been hours since Eika brought me breakfast.

"I'm surprised you're not already testing the tracker out," Hideki says around a slurp of *tonkotsu* broth.

It's true that I'm not known for my patience. I flip my left hand, revealing the still-bright sear on my palm. Hideki lets out a long curse when he sees it.

"What the hell happened?"

"Tested something without adequate prep first. A stupid mistake, the kind a first-year student would make." I'm still annoyed with myself about it. I should have thought about the fact that all Cameron's apartment had was that measly houseplant. We're both trained, we both know better.

I do some of my best thinking with him, but also some of my worst.

"Toyama Misora admits to making a mistake." Hideki looks around the restaurant, which is empty save for us, the owner, and an aquarium of dispirited tropical fish. "Where's the *dokkiri* camera?"

"Remember when Eika used to do that show?"

"I do." He widens his eyes and forms his mouth into an "o." It's uncannily like the surprise Eika would feign as she made eye contact with the camera, and I have to laugh. Her history of hosting silly reality shows is why she can't gain traction with Replenish, though. Sometimes I wish she would have stayed in her lane.

"How is Eika?"

"Not thrilled I'm meeting with you." The instant the words are said, I want to take them back. Hideki knows why; for a beat, he doesn't respond.

"And Hatsumi?"

"You know how she can get. There's always a villain to eviscerate with the power of her mighty pen. Right now, she's shadowboxing against the new version of the NRPO."

That gets a raised eyebrow. Like me, Hideki stays out of the murkier aspects of the family business as much as he can, but as the son of the *wakagashira*, he's well aware of the politics. "But she must know that—"

"She does, which is why we don't discuss it much." I push my empty plate to the center of the table. "Surely this has earned me my tracker."

Hideki hands it over. "And you're not even dead."

"Yet."

Once we've paid and gone outside, I feel confident enough to give the tracker a test. Most of the area is concrete, but there are trees in the pavement every few meters that could serve as a basic backstop. Taking an old receipt out of my wallet and holding the tracker to it, I consent, and a low wave of power pulses into the Syphon panel. As the power engages, the panel fades, disappearing into the white of the receipt; even the printed text is visible through it. That was a Cameron innovation, and a clever one. You'd have to know it was there to spot the tracker now.

"Alright, now what?"

"It should keep drawing a small amount of power and push it out to my port." The push function here is the same concept as the battery, though I've fixed the shaping error that prevented Cameron's withdrawal of consent. I hand the paper to Hideki. "Walk a block or so away."

As he does, I follow the yellow dot on my port's mapping app that indicates the tracker. Sure enough, the dot is traveling down the sidewalk at the same pace as Hideki. A wave of sheer joy coursing through me, I gesture him to come back.

"Does it work?"

"It does. I'm going to need a lot more of these."

For once, he doesn't seem irritated to have me assign him extra work.

* * *

Bidding Hideki goodbye, I use Hail to summon a ride—by unspoken agreement, we have always kept our Daikan-yama meetings off the Toyama-gumi grid.

(I was thinking I'd come back up,
if you're free } Toyama Misora

Cameron Green { nice timing. I just got home from a run, was about to get in the shower)

(Eika and I finished the battery plan. I dropped the schematic at the prototype office } TM

CG { ... you could have mentioned that first)

CG { !!!)

My port vibrates again, but this time with a message from Hideki.

Watanabe Hideki { It was like old times just now :))

WH { I've missed you)

I stare at his words for a few moments, start to tap out a reply, then erase my message.

WH { As a friend, Misora. God, you're arrogant)

Smiling at that, I switch back to the chat with Cameron, where he has added another line of exclamation points. Hatsumi said she hoped I was happy.

I think I might be.

ASAGAWA KENJI

Kumanaka isn't at their house when I arrive, but Mizuki seems to already know about my mother's arrest. She has tea and cookies out.

I want to ask for a beer instead, but don't. "Sorry. I don't have much good news for you at the moment."

She's keeping a calm face but sitting awkwardly straight. Having both of us in this situation must be terrifying.

I didn't want to come. I didn't want her to think I was going to disappear either.

Need to break the silence. "Unless you need pencils." I pull the bunch out of my bag and drop them on the *kotatsu*. They're round pencils, so they roll across the flat surface. Three make it all the way across and fall off on the other side. "I have plenty of those."

She forces a weak smile. "I know you'll figure things out. We're in this together."

"Yeah, don't worry," I say a hair too fast to sound natural. How long do I need to stay?

A quiet moment, and then she starts, "I know this isn't important..."

"Another outlet giving you trouble?"

"Actually, Rina has been having some difficulty with her employer. They haven't been paying her full wages."

I frown. One more person who doesn't want to hear from me, probably ever. But she still lives at home, and they could use the money if things keep going like this. "Doubt she wants my help, but I'll ask.

Is she here?"

"She's out for the day." The sudden relief on Mizuki's face makes me want to hit someone, possibly Funabashi. Possibly myself.

I'm glad that Takeshi at least doesn't seem to know. Yet. She may need to ask him for some of his engineering money for their mortgage before this is all over. I may need to ask him for her.

"Thank you for being here for us," she says, bowing her head low enough she almost touches the *kotatsu* with her forehead.

I don't know how to deal with this behavior. I finish my tea quickly and make an excuse to head out. She follows me to the door and repeats the low bow, this time to the floor. She's always been painstakingly polite, but this is creepy.

Back at my apartment, I crack a beer and pace back and forth a few times across the carpet as I down half the can. The single room is longer than my old apartment. It's also mostly empty except for the futon, a new set of weights, and the bag with my clothes. I should order a *kotatsu* or something someday when I have money again.

There's a message on my silver port—Takamine, of all people. I thought I'd heard the last of him, his bad suit, and his order forms back in March.

> *Takamine { you shit)*

> *Takamine { today my manager showed me a message)*

> *Takamine { i'm done)*

> *Takamine { how could you have done this to me and my family)*

So it starts, things burning down.

I'm not too worried about Takamine himself, a middle-aged asshole who got what he deserved, but he's the least of the people ready to be pissed off while my mother is safe in police custody. This will get uglier fast, and like most of her victims I can't see where these hits are going to be coming from.

I should get this call to Rina out of the way so I can figure out what to do about this final fuck you, about the office, about everything. My port is at 12%. Should be enough for a short conversation since she won't want my help.

Rina answers, her voice sharp. "Yeah?"

This is going to go well. I keep my tone mild. "This is Kenji. Your mom said you're having some issue with your job."

"Of course she did. Of course."

"I said I'd call and offer to help. Anything I can do?"

"I don't need you to swoop in like a big brother and take care of me. Everything is fine."

I can feel the tension in my shoulders again. "I said I'd call and offer but if you don't want my help, okay." It comes out a little louder than I intended.

"I bet it makes you feel real good to jump into other people's problems, like you're some kind of costumed hero."

"Does it make you feel good to yell at someone who is just trying to help your family?"

"Where do you get off thinking that you have any right to stick your nose into our business? Do you think you're a member of our family? You're not. You're not my big brother. You're not my little brother. You're certainly not my dad."

"No," I say. "I'm not."

"Then why do you keep hanging around?" Her voice has dropped into a growl at this point. "Unless you're screwing my mom. Is that what you're doing?"

"No. Are you?" I say, and hang up before she can answer.

My hand is actually shaking. "Fuck you," I say to the port. In response, it helpfully blinks 1% and shuts off. I throw the damn thing at the floor, where it rebounds off the carpet and lands in the folds of the comforter.

Fuck it all.

* * *

I'm not in the best shape when Green joins up with me to look for the source of the data. Since I didn't sleep last night, it takes twice as long as it should to open the door at Takamine's building and I lose my temper with the old dipshit at the leasing office. Good thing there wasn't a security camera there to record that mess.

We do make short work of it all though, even if Green is the worst heavy I've ever seen. Who helps a collar find tissues? It's embarrassing enough to make me miss Kumanaka.

At least for some things.

To his credit, Green does whatever magic he needs to make the case stop making my life hell, which is valuable. I don't know if I could find someone else in this city with a skill set to do that and who wouldn't have another use for the information.

"I've got to go," he says, back on his port. "I gave it a strong charge, so handle it with gloves and it will be fine."

He hasn't asked about payment beyond eating the food I ordered for him. Is he going to ask later, or should I offer?

I wipe my hands off and go with, "Got it. Thanks."

The work he did was on a panel on the outside of the case, so it's still closed and locked. I pop open the tiny mechanism easily with picks. Inside is a stack of m-folders, manila with a patch threaded with silver. Wearing gloves, I pick up one and open it. The page inside looks like normal paper, maybe a little thicker, with regular text and a scrollbar on the edge. This one is the email I've already seen about Takamine and his work. I hit the scrollbar to see if there's more details on the job or just that ending, but the text flickers and fades out.

I set that page aside, pick up the next one. This is something about the Maeda-gumi but there's a password on it. I fan the stack and see that most of them are like that. As I pull them out, the pages dim, a few going blank almost immediately.

The glove suggestion must only work on the case itself. I'll have to come back to this at some point with some help.

The port Green charged at the bar has two messages.

Date Hatsumi { You free?)

As much as I'd like the distraction that Date Hatsumi is offering, I've gotten almost no sleep in the last two days and I doubt I'd hold up my end of the entertainment at the moment. I respond and suggest tomorrow instead.

> *Igarashi { Kenji-san, would Saturday night be*
> *acceptable?)*

He and Chiyo are being snoopy, not that I have anything better to do at the moment. Maybe I can get some information from them about what's happening at Walling. I write back and suggest Yakiniku Hanabi in Takadanobaba, safely two stops down the loop line from Walling, and we set a time.

The first few days of the week I spend halfheartedly trying to track down Kumanaka, since he's gone MIA for both me and Mizuki. This isn't the first time that this has happened, so I'm more annoyed than anything. A few years ago, my mother was down for a month after a job went south. He was gone the entire time but resurfaced five weeks later after only one message from her. I don't inspire the right amount of terror for us to have an ongoing working relationship at the moment, so my search gets me nowhere.

Next, I fill my time surveilling Funabashi's house. Thursdays at 2:30 p.m. are when his wife does a grocery run, so I make use of the opportunity to search their house for blackmail. Disappointingly, his finances are in order, he and his wife seem genuinely happy, and his kid has been keeping up his grades in school. Their actual laundry is even immaculately clean. What a desperately boring family.

By the time Saturday rolls around, I'm looking forward to the dinner. Igarashi already has a table for us when I arrive. He's dressed in normal work clothes, something I wouldn't have expected since it's Golden Week and the office is closed. When he spots me, he stands and bows. I give him an odd look and slide into the chair next to him, my back to the wall. There's only one other group in the restaurant on the far side of the space, near the door.

Chiyo is right behind me, looking flustered even though she's made it two minutes before our meeting time. She's also dressed in a suit, carrying a nylon briefcase in the crook of her arm. "Sorry, sorry!" she says, also giving a full bow before sliding into her seat. "I missed the train at twelve after and had to wait until seventeen after for the next one."

Since this is a *yakinuku* restaurant, there's a small grill set into the center of the table. With the place mostly empty, we have our waitress's immediate attention. Her uniform is immaculate except for one button missing second from the top, forming a loop in the fabric. I order us a plate of skirt steak to fry at the table, and several bottles of Kirin to share.

"So, the most important thing," Chiyo starts, "did you see the disaster last night? Six runs in the ninth? Wah, how could such an edge case have happened to us?"

Igarashi looks down at the table and raises his shoulders. "That's what you get for rooting for the Tigers. Last week, the Giants won their series."

Our drinks arrive, and Chiyo immediately grabs a bottle to pour for me. I pass the favor along and we cheer, then take a sip in unison.

I follow up the drink with a dry look for Chiyo. "What Igarashi is saying is that your decision to root for the team from Osaka is making them lose."

She looks pained but responds, "My loyalty cannot be bought."

"We're not disputing your loyalty," Igarashi says, "only your judgment."

Chiyo makes a show of looking hurt, her nostrils flaring and actual tension showing around her eyes.

Enough for now. I clear my throat. "If she chose where to put her loyalty, it wouldn't mean much, would it?"

Igarashi freezes for a second, then says, "Fair enough."

Our platter of meat arrives, bright red slabs marbled with fat. Chiyo grabs a pair of chopsticks from the cup and, hiding a small smile, starts moving servings to the grill set in the middle of the table.

"How have things been at the office?" I ask to break the silence.

Both of them give me a dramatic sigh and look at each other to see who is going to respond first. Chiyo takes the lead and says, "Well, we miss you."

"Both you in the personal sense and you in the business sense," Igarashi adds.

"Oh?" I ask, raising my eyebrows and keeping the rest of my expression neutral. They don't seem to be aware of my role in causing my situation, so the less I add the better.

Chiyo bites her lip. "We've been looking into everything since you know...and there isn't going to be enough income to keep everyone anymore and, well, we're the two newest in the office..."

Igarashi continues the thought. "We're thinking that we're fucked." He looks into the bottom of his glass before taking a deep drink. "And we just bought a new house."

"You and Chiyo?" I ask. "Isn't your wife annoyed?"

"Ha ha," Igarashi says. "Here I was thinking our luck had turned when we finally found a buyer."

I should start a list of all the people I've hit with splash damage this month. "Well, finding a new job would suck, but at least none of us are invested in the insurance business itself."

Chiyo pushes her hair back out of her eyes and starts to say something before stopping with a frown and a head bob.

"Really? Insurance?" I ask.

She shakes her head back and forth a few times before speaking. "It's just that we live in this big scary world, and here's this thing that has your back if anything goes wrong." She gives me a sheepish look. "I think it's nice."

Igarashi raises his eyebrows. He isn't nearly so much of a sap. "I'm in it for the money, same as they are. Insurance companies don't want to be there for you. They don't want to pay out. It affects their bottom line."

"That's why we have to sell really good policies that plan for the risk."

Such a charming view of the world, but I can't let this go completely. "Most of the Walling policies have been fake."

She shakes her head. "You're still helping people."

Most often bad people, I think but don't say. Myself included in that.

Igarashi pulls a piece of beef off the grill. "Such a sales pitch, Chiyo-chan. Too bad you're still just making tea. We all know how bad you are at that." He takes a bite, and then uses the communal set of chopsticks to replace the meat on the grill.

"Right?" she asks, with a mock sigh. "Good thing that's not my dream, huh?"

I'll take that bait. "Okay, then, what is?"

"You know, right? I've almost finished my actuary program," she says, flashing a smile and a small v-gesture with her fingers.

I couldn't be more surprised if she'd said her dream was to become an elephant. "An actuary."

Igarashi gives me a look. "She passed the five qualifying exams last year. Don't you remember?" He turns to Chiyo. "Are you taking the secondary exams soon?"

"They only give them once a year, so next December I had planned to take them. Assuming I can afford it. When hiring season rolls around, office ladies who were recently fired get first pick of jobs, right?" she asks lightly.

I'm still lost by this development. "An actuary? I don't even know what that is."

"Managing risk, plotting tables, modeling," she says. When she sees my expression, she adds, "Spreadsheets and statistics and math."

"Huh," I say, and have to wash it down with more beer. "I really don't know anything about this business. You are a claims processor, aren't you, Igarashi?"

He laughs. "Yeah, for now. It's a pretty quiet job at this agency. As you said, there are so many empty policies on the books that we don't get many claims. And frankly, I'd prefer to avoid finding another job that'll likely have mandatory overtime."

"How about you, Kenji-san?" Chiyo asks, between bites. "What's your dream?"

There's a question. I've never really been in a position to have one. Sarcasm about Mos Burger aside, there aren't many job postings for my particular skill set.

I could make a killing as a phantom thief, I'm sure. But that would mean taking on a complicity that I've never had. Working in this business, we've served as the means, not the decision-makers. In doing so, we've operated in the gaps between proper organizations. You don't blame the knife; you blame the wielder.

I could also find a gullible *yakuza* group to join, if I were willing to replace everyone I know with a loyalty designated for me. Pass.

Or this. At least what shreds remain of what this was.

I flash her a smile. "Protecting the weak and helpless, I guess."

Chiyo giggles into a closed fist. "Like Mister Wiggles!"

"You know, we're not helpless," Igarashi says, all polite speech but a hint of edge to his voice.

He's right. They aren't, but seeming like they are makes them an even more valuable asset.

Igarashi sets down his chopsticks and sits back to look at me. "I'm also not about loyalty for the sake of it."

My own words in Mizuki's voice burn in my ears. I don't say them. "You shouldn't be. But we can take care of each other. If I have the opportunity, I'll make sure that the office stays funded. I just need something on Funabashi or else he's not going to let me do it."

He breaks eye contact first, looks at the table as he nods. "Okay, then. Just remember that I have more on the line than you do."

With a suddenly serious expression, Chiyo leans in and clears her throat. "Excuse me. I am in too. This is my moment too."

"Okay. If you two find me leverage, I'll make this happen." My words are an eerie callback to my phone call with Kumanaka from two weeks ago.

Chiyo breaks the moment by clapping. "Perfect!"

I meet Igarashi's eyes again evenly. "We're in this together," I say solemnly. "Now, the important question. Are we getting team pennants made?"

He tries to hold a straight face, but fails. "We're probably screwed either way, right?"

"That's the spirit," Chiyo cheers, raising her glass.

I follow her lead. "Okay, we're doing this. But," I glance over at Chiyo, "you know, being attached to the insurance industry is really crazy, right?"

Igarashi lifts his glass as well. "Here's to being crazy together."

ASAGAWA KENJI

Working out this arrangement with Chiyo and Igarashi should have helped me sleep—it's the first time in over a week that I've had a solid lead, a plan of where to go from here. Instead, I'm lying on top of my futon cover, thoughts racing.

Like Igarashi said, they have a lot more to lose than I do if things go south. And not just them, Mizuki and Kumanaka and Yuri and even goddamn Rina. It's one thing to say that I've got this, and another to be carrying someone's still-beating heart around in my pocket, hoping I don't trip climbing unfamiliar stairs.

I don't have my mother's contacts, her entire history of work connections, except for a handful whom I've met and maybe what I'll be able to glean from the dead briefcase. I'll need someone to help me decode those, even to hold each page while I read.

Having seen his reaction to the Toyama-gumi info, Green is probably happier not knowing what my mother has been doing. It'd be better to find someone else, someone with an investment in the outcome. Someone I can trust to help and not see another better opportunity down the road.

My thoughts are lost enough that I almost don't hear my port buzz. It's Mizuki. Calling me at 4:30 a.m.

"Kenji-kun?" She's trying to keep her voice even and failing.

"What's wrong?" I ask, sitting up and running into the limit of the cord that's charging my port. With one foot, I hook the pair of pants from the floor.

"Rina is still having problems with her work..." Her voice drops off as she fishes around for what to say.

"I offered to help, but she made it clear that she doesn't want it."

"It's Soseki. He was here and so angry. He went to the bar where Rina works. He said he was going to sort things out, but I don't think... I—"

Oh, shit. The other problem that's been hanging out there. "Send me the address."

* * *

The location is within walking distance, a spot typical of bars in Kabukicho: back door off a back alley off a back street. The service door in an even tinier gap between buildings is locked, but the mechanism isn't anything special. There are muffled noises just behind it, so I don't open it yet.

To the left, there's a small window, pebbled glass, which is unlocked. I ease the window open a crack and look through the space using my port as a camera vantage point. Kumanaka is on one knee, his meaty hand resting flat on a tabletop. There are three thugs, sleeves rolled up and away from their blood-spattered and tattoo-covered forearms, taking turns hitting him around the head and shoulders. Another one, his suit still impeccable, is leaning up against a countertop covered in boxes browsing something on his port. No knives visible.

If I'm going in there, this is not the door to use. Even with only fists one against four is not going to end well. What I need is something they value more than their likely well-deserved chance at retribution.

I quietly slide the window closed again. The bar next door is properly closed for five a.m., so I make use of their back entry to climb up to the third floor and out a window. From there I hang from the sill and drop down onto the roof of the second floor above where Kumanaka is. The lock on the roof entry is as simple as the back door below, and in under a minute it swings open into darkness. This floor is empty of people, and consists of two rooms and a set of stairs. There's a safe under the desk in the front room, one that would have locked properly had a quickly stowed envelope not caught as it swung shut. Hello, leverage.

The envelope contains a stack of 10,000-yen bills, a large enough amount to get their attention. There are also a few sheets of whatever formulation of L is the drug of choice this week, maybe Love? I fold the sheet in half and tuck it in my pocket, avoiding contact with my skin. I scrounge a metal garbage can and start a small fire with a packet of tissue, a stack of terrycloth towels, and matches from on top of the desk. Together, this isn't anything worth dying over, but I doubt their next level up on the Toyama chain would be happy if it disappeared either.

The stairs lead down to a landing between the two rooms, the doors on either side shut. The door to the front opens silently, revealing a small space of three tables and four chairs at the bar, all covered in broken bottles, with whisky, *sake*, and even some *soju* pooled in the shards. There's a fire extinguisher but no sprinklers, not in a place designed for excessive booze and smoke. This bar is large by Kabukicho standards, where access to drinking at the smallest space possible is a matter of pride. Nonetheless, the cost of all this high-end liquor is well in excess of what I have in my hand.

"Is he down?" one of the punks in the other room asks.

Moment of truth—I don't have to be here. I could have arrived too late. With my mother out of the picture I could keep this money and use it as a seed to take the business in a different direction. I could even give the money to Mizuki to help pay their way going forward.

His hand reaching up to cover hers. A moment of intimacy that I wasn't meant to see.

I hook my foot around the closest chair and pull it out from under the table. The legs make a loud scraping noise across the floor, and the hot metal garbage can makes a distinct clatter when I drop it on the seat. Immediately the door from the landing to the back flies open.

"What the shitting fuck?" The man in the suit has a mouth on him, but he stops when he sees me waving the stack of 10,000-yen bills over the smoking fire. "Isn't that Asagawa's kid?" he asks the thug behind him.

I put my foot up on the seat, next to the can. "You haven't been taking very good care of your things. This chair, for example, is rather shaky." To demonstrate, I rock the chair enough to pull two of the legs off the ground, the smoke bending as the can slips a few centimeters toward my leg and closer to the alcohol pooled across the floor.

Thug-in-charge laughs, but with a bit of a sneer. "Trying to prove how crazy you are, Asagawa?"

I shrug. "With accelerants it isn't the liquid you have to worry about. It's the fumes, and"—I pretend to see the floor for the first time—"there is an awfully strong smell in here."

One of his underlings with a horned mask and snake tattoo on each arm pushes forward to come into the room. Full-suit puts his elbow out and stops him.

They could try to rush me, but with the position of my foot on the chair there isn't much they can do without risking a full fire. He'll kill time until we either come to a compromise or he thinks of some way to subdue me without risking this bar and potentially the entire line of connected rickety little buildings.

Now that I have their attention—"To answer your question, my mother would have already burned this place down on principle, but crazy hasn't ever been one of my personal goals. I think we can avoid that, if you prefer."

His underling is less than impressed and wants me to know it. "You're a little shit who thinks he can talk big and we'll accept he's wearing his mommy's shoes."

"I'm trying to be polite, and you want to toss insults back and forth." I peel off one of the bills and dip it into the garbage can. The green- and rose-colored printed bill takes quickly, the corners bending inward. If it wouldn't mean risking a larger fire, I'd wave the bill around a bit to add to the drama. I drop it into the can instead. "You four have something that belongs to me. I want him back."

"This fucker?" the leader asks, gesturing behind him. "I think he's a bit worse for wear."

"Your property is too." I tap the heel of my left shoe, the glass crackling underneath the thick sole. "Like I said, I think we can work out a deal."

"Yeah?" For once, the leader seems genuinely curious what I have to say.

"First, we stop acting like thugs, and apologize for inconveniencing each other. I give you back your property"—I wave the packet of bills in the air and use it to gesture toward the back room—"and you give me back mine. Later," I pause again for effect, "you send me a bill for the mess he made. And, like a respectable member of the community, I pay it."

A grunting laugh again, this time heavily tinged with sarcasm. "You don't have that kind of money."

"Where do you think her ledgers went?"

I didn't say I have them, but Necktie takes it to mean I do. He glances back behind him, and I can see the calculation going on in his head. As it stands, he runs the risk that Kumanaka bites it and then he has a body to deal with. Even if I don't pay, foisting off that potential headache would be the easiest resolution. "Okay. We'll try it and see how this goes." He turns his head and grunts to the goons behind him, "Throw the shithead out the back."

The underling who has been at his elbow disappears. There's the sound of sliding and some muffled cursing, the kind I know well from dragging Kumanaka's goddamned unconscious body around.

As a gesture of good faith, I toss the envelope of money at the leader's chest. He catches it and neatly tucks it away in a pocket of his jacket. From the same pocket, he pulls out a card case and then brandishes one single business card. "If we are going to act like businessmen, then—"

I shake my head. I'm still alone in a restaurant with four *yakuza* who might get ideas. "I'm young, not stupid. You can send me your card with the bill." I pull my old Walling card from my coat pocket and set it on the table next to me. It's the only card I have with a legit address. "Asagawa Kenji, of the Asagawa-gumi. Pleasure to meet you."

"Ota of the Toyama-gumi," he says. I doubt he's much up the hierarchy, but I'm surprised he has enough status to claim membership in the main organization at all. By my count that puts me as an organization currently of 1 negotiating with a group of more than 50,000. Perfect. "Pleased to meet you, Asagawa"—he pauses for much longer than is necessary, before finishing—"-san." The honorific hangs there awkwardly.

I wonder what he would think to know how much time I spend in an apartment where his *kumicho*'s daughter is screwing a *gaijin*.

Taking my foot off the seat of the chair, the weight drops back onto all four feet with a thud. "I apologize for the inconvenience, Ota-san."

Ota eyeballs me and finally manages, "I am sorry as well that it came to this shitty situation."

"Send me the bill, and I trust we won't ever inconvenience each other like this again."

He nods and leans against the doorframe. I'm not leaving my leverage no matter how much Ota claims to be polite. I grab the backrest and drag the chair with me as I back up to the front. Unlocking the door without looking doesn't go as smoothly as I'd like, but when it clicks, I slide the door open in its track and back outside into the cool morning air.

I close the door in front of me, thankful that this is hopefully the last I see of these four. For their part, once I released the chair Ota seemed to lose interest in me entirely. Not sure if that is a relief or an insult.

There's still a not-small chance of an ambush in the back alley, so I take the long way over another building roof coming from the other direction. Kumanaka is alone, leaning on his side in a pile of trash bags. His face is covered in blue and red bruises, cuts, and enough fresh and scabbing blood that he must have been there a while. Mixed in with the mess on his shirt is caked-in vomit, the small particles clinging around the buttons of his shirt.

I drop down on both heels in front of him. He also has a large patch of L stuck on his neck, the higher dose stuff. No wonder he was making even worse decisions than usual.

"Hey, asshole," I say.

A groan, and his right eye opens just enough that I can see the pupil, wide and dark. He's conscious, just barely.

"You are here, alone in this alleyway." I say it evenly, feeling calmer than I have in weeks. Months maybe. "If you don't get help, I don't know if you are going to make it." I pull out the strip of Love that I pocketed from the safe upstairs. "In fact, you could easily die of an overdose here in this alleyway, and my life would be easier for it. Everyone's life would be easier."

He draws up one side of his mouth, a mixture of saliva and blood spilling out the opening and trailing down the lapel of his coat.

I continue, "It's up to you to decide. If I do this, if I help you now, you belong to me." I reach out and grab his flaccid head, my fingers and thumb pressing into his cheeks, hard enough to make them tingle. His skin is feverishly warm in my hand. "Do you want my help?"

He tries to jerk his head away, but I just pinch my thumb and index finger tighter and after a moment he stops struggling.

I lean in and drop my voice. "Do you want my help or not?"

He says something quietly, too quiet to hear, then tries again. A noise comes out that sounds affirmative, as filtered through clenched teeth.

I release his face with a gesture that is more forceful than necessary and push my right hand into his armpit. He starts shaking as I pull him upward—is he going into shock? My feet planted, it's a heavy task to yank his full weight up from the ground and his arm over my shoulder so I can walk him toward the street and toward help.

Three of his fingernails next to my face have the blue splotches common to L addicts. His whole body is boiling hot against my side, and he smells even worse than he looks.

It's at this point that I realize he isn't shaking, but laughing. In my ear he manages a gravelly wet-sounding series of words: "Fucking Asagawa family."

"You know," I say, "I'm not always a fan of yours either."

* * *

"When do you need to go back to the hospital?" I ask.

Mizuki is next to me, kneeling proper, with a book of go puzzles in her hand. She's been looking at the charts of black and white pieces for the last hour, her free hand tapping the *kotatsu* surface silently more often than not.

The windows of her living room are open, a grayish light streaming through. It's been threatening to rain all day. The kind of weather where most people would carry an umbrella and never get around to using it.

She looks over, keeping her eyes focused on the tabletop. "If you don't mind, I think I may bring him some lunch soon."

Kumanaka had a concussion, a few broken ribs, internal bleeding, extensive bruising. Nothing we haven't had before, but the hospital always makes a big deal of keeping people for longer than necessary. Weeks longer in this case.

"Of course," I say. I have plans this afternoon myself. "Could you...?"

She reaches in front of me to the sheet of m-paper that's supported at an awkward angle on the *kotatsu* by one of Yuri's phonebook *manga*. With the overhead light on and the angle, I can read the text as long as I pull myself up into a partial kneel. A soft touch, and she advances the text ahead.

I give her a halfhearted smile. "Too far."

"Excuse me," she says, and pushes the text back down a few lines.

There isn't much in the m-paper documents that doesn't have a password on it, so I'm trying to get through these as quickly as possible to check them off. There are a few names I recognize, here and there a connection I didn't know about. Things like a Maeda-gumi group in Ueno that's been importing motorcycle parts from a Chinese factory and reselling them at wholesale to a local club. That's cutting into Toyama-gumi profits because of the location, but not in an area where they are particularly invested. Or someone from a Kubo group came under suspicion and was called into the police to see if he'd crack and give out information on his buddies. He avoided the conflict by ending up in the hospital himself. And so on.

That reminds me—"Were you ever contacted by the police?"

"Hm?"

"About my mother. Did they ever speak with either of you?"

Mizuki shakes her head. She has a sunburn across her nose and cheeks, just starting to peel. "I didn't speak to them. It's possible that

Soseki did since they would have known there was a connection from years ago."

"They never did contact me." I lean back on my hand and eye the *kotatsu*. A terrible thought occurs to me. "She was arrested, right?"

A slight strained sound escapes before Mizuki swallows it back. "It was in the paper. Not directly, since they obscure the names, but there was an article referencing the arrest."

We haven't talked about that day she closed the door in my face, and by unstated agreement we aren't going to either. We also haven't been talking about the fact that she's been doing a part-time job handing out plastic fans with ads for foot cream outside Meiji-jingumae station. There aren't many employers looking for a middle-aged housewife with limited work experience.

I grunt and nod.

"Kenji-kun," she says, interjecting a smile. "I think you may underestimate how difficult you are to reach."

Apparently, even for people with my number. The two messages I've sent to Date Hatsumi in the last few weeks have gone unanswered. She was in a weird mood the last time I saw her, and she must have decided it was time to ghost. Maybe she's embarrassed after sharing her childhood sob stories.

We were careful about condoms, so I know it's not that. I snort. The idea of more "fucking Asagawa family" members running around this city probably keeps Kumanaka awake at night.

There having been no calls from the police is probably a good sign that they didn't track my mother's finances back to Walling. Funabashi has one of the numbers that's still in my pocket and I'm sure would have had great enjoyment in giving it out if faced with the opportunity.

"True," I say. "I'll need a new public number going forward, maybe plain business cards." That'll be my next task after we get the Walling situation in hand. Kumanaka isn't out of the hospital until next week, so it's not holding things up yet to handle first things first.

The front door rolls open, and Rina's voice announces, "*Tadaima.*"

Mizuki responds with a "welcome home," but doesn't turn or get up. Behind her back, Rina makes a line for the stairs, glancing over long enough to see that I'm here too and give me the finger mid-step.

"Rina, be nice," Mizuki says, even though she can't have possibly seen the gesture.

I respond with a friendly wave, the kind I know will really piss Rina off, but she keeps going up the steps without acknowledging either of us further.

My port says it's approaching late morning, around when I had planned to head over anyway. I put my hand across the face of the m-paper to close it out, and then slide the sheet back into my bag.

"Are you going already?"

"Yes, I have an important meeting," I say, understating the scope. As I move to get up, I slide a plain rectangular envelope onto the table by her elbow. It's almost the end of my personal savings, and exactly what their bank book records show is due for their mortgage next week.

She looks down at it but doesn't otherwise acknowledge that it's there. Once I leave, it'll still be there for her to open.

As has become the new normal, she instead escorts me to the front door and gives me the creepy low bow. "Thank you, Kenji-kun."

I take the Odakyu line to Shinjuku station and stop off at my apartment to leave the folder of m-paper. If I ended up arrested, no need to gift wrap a connection to my mother.

From there, I follow Yasukuni-dori back under the train tracks, and then turn off into Nishi-Shinjuku. The clouds are still making the sky gray, but bits of blue are starting to peek through here and there.

Everyone in the front office at Walling keeps their heads down when I enter and make for the back office. Funabashi stands up out of protest as I elbow the door shut behind me.

"I think I made myself clear—" he starts.

"Very, but I didn't," I say, projecting casual confidence as I drop into the chair in front of his desk. "Feel free to sit down."

Funabashi continues to stand. We are going to be having a rude-off: If he's higher ranking, then I'm rude for sitting. If I outrank him, then he's rude for ignoring my suggestion to sit.

I continue, "I'll get to the point quickly because I don't want to waste your time. You had a surprisingly large payout day before yesterday when an insured shipment was lost at sea. I now have, well, a significant amount in a bank account that I control. The office has a minimal amount to cover utilities and basic petty cash for the upcoming month."

Funabashi keeps his mouth and cheeks an empty mask. He's not as successful around the eyes. His mind is racing as he tries to think through this and cut me off. "I can report this to the authorities," he manages finally.

I nod thoughtfully. "I appreciated your lecture last month. It really was my failure that I didn't know much about the insurance business. I didn't want to continue to be negligent, so I made sure to study up."

One of my first improvements around here will be a better security system. Breaking Chiyo in after hours to read through all of the recent records was far too easy, and the fact that we were able to do so for weeks is an embarrassment.

I continue. "Isn't it fascinating that insurance companies were originally created to cover shipping vessels, something so fundamentally untraceable? The insured item goes missing, and the absence of that item is the proof you need to pay it."

This is really too satisfying, but I mostly manage to keep it out of my voice. "More to the point, this branch of Walling Insurance Company Ltd. has been skipping over the very important step of submitting some of these policies to the underwriters for actual coverage. Instead, you've been selling who knows how many mysterious policies and making supposed payouts from your own accounts. I know you are so very diligent in keeping up appearances, but somehow, you've missed that tiny little detail that would have cut into certain people's profit margins. How naughty. But then you have so many artificial policies on the books that won't ever require payouts, I imagine it's easy to forget steps." I pause. "You can sit if you want."

He slowly sinks into his chair. It's a small victory, but it only says we are on equal footing for now. He meets my eyes with surprising directness. "What are you proposing?"

"A continued working relationship. For now, I will forward what is needed to run the office and pay out on policies on a monthly basis."

At that he reverts to his previous contempt. "Even with everything, you don't have the income to keep this office running for more than a few months."

By his tone, he's not inclined to drum up new business and contribute to a shared success. He'll do what he can to put responsibility for every last yen of expense on my shoulders. He doesn't know about the bill from Ota of the Toyama-gumi that is coming either. I'm going to have to figure out income and fast.

That said, I'm not going to concede this to his face. "If that happens, we'll have another conversation."

He nods, looking suddenly more confident in the situation. Banking on my imminent failure is a risk he's willing to take. "What about your mother's associate?" he asks, emphasis on the word mother.

"Kumanaka has also decided to take up my offer of continued employment. He will be added back onto payroll effective immediately."

Under a small frown, Funabashi simply says, "I see."

He's not excited to continue dealing with Kumanaka. Something we have in common.

One more related point that I need to make: "I understand that you may harbor some hard feelings toward any staff who may have processed this payout, so I want to be clear that they are now my employees. As far as I am concerned, they're hard workers who deserve the lifetime employment that they were promised. The only person on probation is you."

Leaning back in his chair, he actually snorts at the last comment. Waiting for me to fail is the easiest path for him. Short term, I'm in a hostage situation—if I fall behind, he will use that as his excuse to start firing people. Long term, he'll try to find alternative revenues so that he can cut me out. Unfortunately, my only means of keeping him from reporting me the way he did my mother is his own reliance on continued employment at Walling and his desire to maintain that squeaky clean self-image.

This is the best I'm going to be able to do right now. I stand. "Thank you for your understanding, Funabashi."

He stands as well and gives me a bow that is just barely deep enough to qualify as respectful. "I look forward to working with you for the next few months, Asagawa-san."

Yeah, I bet. "As I've said before, I look forward to a long and fruitful working relationship."

In the main office, Igarashi gives me a look from the corner of his eye but doesn't stop what he is doing at the computer. The less obvious we make the connection the safer it is for him, at least until I solidify control. Outside the office, I send the same message to him, to Chiyo, to Mizuki: "I've got you."

For now, at least.

DATE HATSUMI

Family name registries are considered sensitive documents these days, only accessible by those listed in the document, the police, and select government officials. But once I knew what to ask for it was easy to cash in a favor. Now, fresh from the town hall in Nikko, which oversees administration for Ashio, Tochigi Prefecture, a copy of the Asagawa family record is in my hands.

> *Mother: Asagawa Yukina* 朝川雪凪 *(F),*
> *Children: Asagawa Takeshi* 朝川健 *(M), Asagawa Kenji* 朝
> 川健二 *(M)*

First observation: She might be terrifying, but Asagawa Yukina is not very creative. The names she gave her two kids are literally written using characters that mean "healthy kid" and "healthy kid #2."

Second: The Asagawa family registry was created on the birth of Takeshi and is conspicuously missing mention of their father. Normally a new family name registry is started when a couple gets married, listing the parents and basic details like date of birth. Their children are added as they're born, a cycle that continues from generation to generation, spawning a daisy chain of records. The format here indicates the births happened outside of marriage.

To say there's a push for the proper stability of marriage doesn't even begin to cover it. These registers are usually required for finalizing entrance to schools and employment, and abnormalities like that can be enough to get an offer rescinded on the grounds that you aren't respectable enough to represent the institution.

Back when I was still in school, a member of the Wa Party was running for re-election after a successful first term. He'd gotten married while serving his first term, and during the next campaign an opposition staffer pulled her parents' family name register. There, they discovered that the politician's mother-in-law had been born outside of marriage. This tenuous connection was enough to sink his reputation and cost him the election.

These days, the laws that restrict access to the family name register are meant to minimize cases of discrimination, some from genetic links extending back through family lines to feudal days. But when you're required to submit the copy of your registry to an institution yourself there isn't much to be done to stop the practice. I don't know if Kenji has ever tried to find employment outside of his group, but there's a good chance he'd find his opportunities limited.

Looking at his birthdate, Kenji is too young to have had any part in what happened seventeen years ago. His brother is a few years older, so there's a slight possibility he might have a partial memory of something. Minoing Asagawa Takeshi turns up a handful of potential matches but no obvious leads: an accountant in Saitama, a dental technician in Itabashi, a construction worker in Yokohama, and an employee of Minotaur itself.

Which puts this line of inquiry at a bit of a stop again. I'm going to have to try another tactic.

Luckily, I have time today before I need to get this article in. I change trains, and head toward the other side of the city.

Garden Mansion Taito is a much less impressive building than the name would imply. A plain shade of gray-ish green tile, a FamilyMart that takes up most of the first floor with four floors of apartments above, three balconies per floor. The word garden is in the name because there's a small park across the street. I can see why Green might have picked this building if he was going for the best of the cheap options that would rent to a *gaijin* with a dog.

Kenji said he broke into Green-san's apartment. But the big question is why this particular building in the first place? How is another one. The apartment doors are on the back side of the building, so I'll have to take the elevator to look at that aspect.

It's a Friday morning, and Green-san and Misora should both be at work, giving me an opening.

First, a stop at the FamilyMart, partially because I'm thirsty and also to rule out any goofy convenience store-*yakuza* connections that might have caused interest in the building.

The high school student behind the counter calls out "*Irasshaimase*" as I enter. I beeline toward the beverage case at the back past the print on demand service kiosk and the periodicals, each popping up suggestions for publication websites. Taehyun's smugly perfect face is plastered across a row of celebrity mags for his award win last week. There's one inset photo of Eika on the cover of *Kira-Kira*, her smile broad and for all appearances genuine even as she's stretching in a heavy sweater. She finds wool unbearably itchy.

I grab a bottle of Pocari Sweat and circle around for a pack of Xylitol gum. Everything looks exactly as I'd expect for this particular chain. If there's anything that would interest Kenji, it's hidden away from my prying eyes.

While I'm paying, I consider pressing the young girl in the black uniform jacket on whether she's seen a tall blond foreigner or his orange-haired friend. When I was in high school, I spent my fair time standing behind one of these counters myself. Part-time work wasn't allowed by the school, but I wanted lunch money and did what I needed to in order to make that happen. I decide against asking. After all, there's not much she could tell me besides beverage preferences anyway.

Next to the FamilyMart, an unremarkable glass door leads to a small lobby filled with nothing but a neglected palm and a bank of mailboxes in front of the tiny elevator. On the handwritten label for 401 is the name Green, a match to the address on the lease that Misora sent me. I look through the other cards for anything that stands out, and one catches my eye: 501 - Ascent Services. A generic business name that is, according to standard numbering, in the apartment directly above Green's.

After seeing Kenji climb into the ceiling at One Eleven, a balcony could as easily be a means of ingress as a door. There is a significant distance between the railings on each floor that makes sideways less likely, but climbing one floor down might be possible for someone who is—what was Himura's phrase?—batshit insane.

The mouth on the mailbox for 501 is large enough for my hand. I fish out a thick stack of envelopes—by postmarks, at least a full three weeks' worth. I flip through it, keeping it in order. Every single piece seems to be junk and the address isn't even triggering a MinoSo page suggestion.

"Well, isn't that strange," I say to the empty room.

I shove the bundle back into the mailbox and ride the elevator up to the fourth floor. The hallway is open to the air, three apartment doors and the exit to the emergency stairs. Green's door looks like the others, but I can hear his dog barking from inside.

The fifth floor is identical, except for a handwritten sign taped to the 501 door that says "Ascent Services."

"Well, hell," I say to the door. "What's your story? Are you something or are you not?"

I knock, not expecting an answer. All the same, waiting to hear if anyone comes to the door is suspenseful enough that I can feel icy anxiety thread down through my legs.

When no one responds, I lean against the wall next to the door and slide down into a squat, keeping my gray dress pants off the dusty floor. I pop a piece of Black Black gum in my mouth, the menthol rising up through my sinuses, and pull my headphones on to think.

> *Wood supported, crown inverted, roots free*
> *The house is wrong, the house is crying*
> *But inside we're so right yeah*

The *sakabashira* in Monster Party is an old ghost tale about what happens if one of the pillars in a house is installed upside down from how the tree grew. It's an invisible wrongness, at least until the wood itself starts shaking and misfortune befalls the family. The only options are to fix it or move and let it be someone else's problem.

The likelihood that there's something here is small, but I don't have a lot of leads. Do I really want to let this go?

> *The well so dark*
> *You came from deep*

I don't. I don't want to do this either.

> *To make a cry*
> *To kill us, to warn us*
> *You're jealousy, baby*
> *La la la*

My curiosity is going to win out in this round.

The locksmith who arrives forty-five minutes after my call is a middle-aged man, heavy around the middle and balding on top. His uniform shirt is neatly pressed, and the patch on his shirt is embroidered with the label "Naito."

"I apologize for the inconvenient wait," he says, not sounding particularly sorry.

"Thank you for coming so quickly, Naito-san," I say, bowing a few times. I know I look flustered, but that's only going to sell my story more effectively. "I'm so sorry... I don't know what I was thinking leaving the key behind..."

After another trip to FamilyMart to use their printer kiosk, the signs on the mailbox and door now match the name of my press club with more professional signage than was there before. I have one of my business cards together with my ID out with both hands to show him.

He takes both items and looks them over carefully. His wrinkled mouth moves back and forth a few times, and he hands both items back to me. "Sorry for the inconvenience, Date-san, but do you have more documentation that this apartment is owned by your organization? The police have asked us to be careful since there have been a number of reported break-ins in the neighborhood."

As I feared might be the case. I give him a few more apologetic superficial bows as I pull out my port. Hopefully the bowing is making it less obvious that my hands are shaking. "Of course. Will this work?"

On the screen is an image of Green's lease, only I've altered it in Pixelpush so the apartment reads 501 and the name of the lessee is my press club.

This time he barely skims the information before handing it back. "Do you only need the door opened?"

"Yes, if you could," I say. "Again, I'm so sorry for being such an inconvenience."

He grunts, squats down to look at the lock without responding. I'm getting the feeling that he's tired of hearing the same song and dance from everyone he interacts with when he has a job to do.

"I'll just, um, let you work," I say and will myself to shut up.

A minute or two working on the lock, and he swings the door open. I refrain from peeking through the door as he writes up an invoice and I pay him with a pair of starched 10,000-yen bills. There goes the new pair of headphones I had my eye on.

He's already halfway to the elevator before I think to thank him again. On second thought, the less I give him to remember, the better.

Inside, the air is so very quiet compared to the city noise outside, silent enough that I can hear my heartbeat heavy and fast in my ears. I step out of my shoes and up into the hallway. It's a short space with a series of four rooms branching off to the sides and in all of them except the bathroom there is stack after stack of boxes.

Two message notifications pop up in my lenses, overlaying the hallway:

Asagawa Kenji { Hey)

AK { What are you up to?)

I fumble with pulling the port from my pocket, to answer or to turn off notifications or to something, I don't know what, and when my fingers fumble, the device goes flying across the floor.

Shit.

The hallway narrows suddenly, and the floor is hard against my butt. At first, I'm not clear what's happening but then I recognize the breaths and shaking hands and numbness creeping up my legs as having congealed into a panic attack. I haven't had one of these in a few years.

He doesn't know. He can't know. A coincidence.

I sit there on the imitation wood floor and will myself to take full breaths, a few sips of Pocari Sweat. I don't know how long I have here but it's not much. If there is something to find, this is not the way to fucking find it.

Finally, I push myself up onto my knees and crawl over to my port. It's face up, the screen still on, so I can't have taken too long. I close out of the message app and gesture to turn off messages on my glasses. I can't deal with this, with him, with the moral implications of what I am doing right at this moment.

My hand on the wall, I stumble up into a walk and drag myself forward to the largest room.

All I am going to focus on right now is looking through these boxes.

* * *

The files here belong to the business Walling Insurance Co., Ltd., a branch located in Nishi-Shinjuku, with a normal, if generically corporate, website. The boxes are meticulously organized. Ordered by date, there are files for every piece of income and payment, stretching back twenty-eight years to the earliest documentation of the branch opening.

At first glance, everything is so ordinary that my instinct is to assume I'm in the wrong place, at least until I find a copy of the payroll from March, which includes Asagawa Kenji as Assistant Manager, Sales and Services. The job title is even more boring than the card he gave me. If this were his real job, he wouldn't have needed to hide it with something else. I'll take this as confirmation that the business is a front, at least for some of the employees.

Also, he makes almost as much as the actual assistant manager, which is close to twice as much as I make. There really is no justice in the world.

With that in mind, I start going through the boxes in more detail and one thing quickly becomes obvious: While all of the policy documents are filled out with the same level of detail, maybe every fourth one has been completed with a fake name. I can tell because the names are all classical writers, poets, that sort of thing. Someone thinks they're clever.

I dig around until I find the box that holds the records from that spring quarter seventeen years ago. These forms are recognizably the same as the modern ones, but on thinner paper and completed in blue ink instead of using a computer. In that month, there were three payments under the names of famous haiku poets: Matsuo Basho, Tachibana Hokushi, and Ome Shushiki.

I set the three forms next to each other, willing them to give me something more, a hint of whether they have any meaning at all to my search, but they're nothing more than dates and numbers, the details lost to time.

As I stare, I realize that I've stopped chewing my gum because my jaw is locked.

One of these amounts might be what someone paid to end my dad's political career and deprive a whole class of people property rights. Is there a price tag I can stomach someone having spent to ruin lives?

Hell.

Okay, that's enough wallowing in pity right now. For now, I can just take photos of the poets' payments, the payroll from that quarter, maybe the payroll from this March as well.

When I take my port out from my pocket there are several missed calls on the screen, all from my mom. After the first one, she left a message. I hit play.

"Hello, this is Chikamoto. I'm a friend of your mother. We called an ambulance—"

This is her grocer friend. This message shouldn't be a surprise. This isn't the first time this has happened.

She is okay. She has to be okay.

I'm not paying attention to the message. I replay it, and this time I catch the name of the hospital. I've been there before. I try to call him back, but there's no answer. She might be resting soundly, and her port tucked safely in her purse. She might not be.

Shit, shit, shit. I probably can't come back here, so I take photos of the documents with shaking hands even though it means I'm a garbage human.

She has to be okay, I keep repeating to myself.

I've been to this hospital before. Yushima is the station I usually use; can I get there easily? I tap the air in front of the two stations on the route map, and my glasses run a line between the two with an estimated time. Yes, the Chiyoda line goes right there, that's not far, thank fuck. Plunk down my pass on the turnstile, stand in the crowd pressed directly over a teenager illicitly eating chocolate almonds, get off at Yushima, and then book it.

By the time I make it to the hospital, my throat is raw, and my damn bag has been slipping off my shoulder so much I almost threw it into an alleyway. As I'm entering the doors under the words Kato Hospital, my port rings again: Chikamoto-san.

"I'm here. Is she okay?" I ask without preamble.

"Date-san, yes, yes. She's resting now, and the doctor should be back soon with more information."

So, you don't know if she's okay and we don't know anything, I want to yell into the phone.

"Thank you," I say instead. "What floor?"

He tells me. I take the elevator and find Chikamoto-san looking frustratingly calm. He's still wearing his green apron, some kind of food product smeared across the hem.

"Thank you for taking care of my mother," I say, dropping down into a repeated series of bows. It's not enough, but it's all I have right now.

He returns the gesture and starts to say something, but the doctor comes up instead. Chikamoto-san respectfully steps back to give us a chance to talk.

The doctor is tall, with a set of permanent frown lines between his eyes. "You're Date Tetsuyo's daughter?" he asks, looking down at me.

My glasses suggest a MinoSo profile, so I glance at the icon long enough to pop up more details on his background. Northeastern Medical and Dental University. Tomorrow might be the start of Golden Week, but what kind of fucking train station kiosk does this hospital think they can run here?

I shift my bag on my shoulder and give him a bow as well. "Yes, that's me. How is my mother?"

"Are you married?"

"I'm not," I say, confused. The MinoSo popup fades, and I let it go because I clearly need to pay more attention to wherever this is going.

"Do you have any older siblings?"

"There's only me." I shift my weight to the other foot. Where is this going?

He clears his throat and tilts his head. "Your mother is not well."

Tell me something I don't know, dipshit. But I can't say that out loud, not to a doctor. "Yes, she hasn't been for a long time."

The doctor pulls a folder from under his arm, flips it open, and scrolls through the record. Almost absently, he asks, "Then why don't you live with her? Don't you care about her well-being?"

My whole body freezes, and I'm stuck staring at the no-tech glasses he's wearing. There are fingerprints all over the lenses—how can he even see?

I can't tell him that she's embarrassed about this, about everything. That six years ago she kicked me out because she didn't want me to see it. That I've been working on the one thing I can do, even if it probably doesn't mean a damn.

Finally, I manage, "I've been working to support her however I can."

Chikamoto-san comes up next to me and makes a gravelly noise with his throat. "It's a difficult situation. Date-san's mother is a very independent woman."

Now there's a dilemma. Should I thank Chikamoto-san for the support, or sucker punch him in the nuts for cutting in like his words mean more than what I can say for myself?

If Noah were here, would this doctor be more likely to talk to him because of his gender or less because he's not Japanese enough? Now there's a question.

The doctor from the bargain school looks up at the man wearing a nametag from the corner market, the man with no familial relation to my mom, and nods like he's said something sage. "It's true."

They both bob their heads together for a few seconds, basking in their communal agreement. Dropping the file back under his arm, the doctor continues to talk to Chikamoto-san. "This time it is only dehydration."

I can't even trust that what he's telling me is true or the whole story. Sometimes when the outlook is bad, terminal even, a doctor won't tell the patient or the family, to save everyone the worry. But at least it's good news on the surface.

The doctor continues, "But I hope that in the future this one will think more carefully about her mother's health."

Dropping forward, I give the doctor a few bows, partially so I don't have to worry about my searing core of anger burning through my blank expression and causing a scene. "Thank you for your help, Isha-sensei. Is she receiving intravenous fluid?"

The doctor continues talking to Chikamoto-san as if he asked the question. "Yes. She will need to be in the hospital for a few days. She had to be sedated for her own safety, so it would be best if someone were here when she wakes up."

If only this process were anything other than standard operating procedure at this point. Knowing how terrifying my mom finds the world these days, I don't understand why she doesn't take care of herself better to avoid this. Except I do understand, at least in that way that I try to and still can't really.

Chikamoto-san looks over at me expectantly. Why is this even a question?

I need to get my article done but I'll just have to make that happen here. "Of course I will stay."

Both of them say their niceties and excuse themselves, leaving in opposite directions. Since they don't expect her to wake for a while, I pace the hallway for a bit, staring at a text document consisting of the one sentence I've managed to write. Briefly, my finger hovers over Noah's name before I close out from messages. I can't put any more of my family's dysfunction on his shoulders.

Finally, I take the time to look for a vending machine. The one on this floor is stocked with nothing but toothbrushes and sundries, so I have to head down to the main floor. A normal vending machine is across the street from the entrance. The sun is still up but at an angle that casts the wall in shadow, leaving the blue and red buttons as glowing polka dots.

I pop some change into the slot and select a can of Boss Coffee Rainbow Espresso Blend. When I pick the can out of the return, it's Pokka Milk Coffee. Crap coffee—too sweet by half.

How is that even possible? This isn't even the right brand of vending machine for Pokka. I hit the button for the Boss coffee again, then again, and a third time. Then a fourth and a fifth. Then I hit the side of the machine with the flat of my palm.

Of course nothing happens.

I throw the can unopened into the recycling bin next to the machine.

"Fuck." There's more change in my wallet, but why the hell would I trust this damn thing to give me anything I want when it's demonstrated it can't be trusted. "Shit," I say to the machine again.

My hand fits into the opening of the recycling receptacle well enough that I can fish the Pokka back out. It tastes as bad as I expect, which is to say I can drink it.

Back upstairs, a nurse informs me that my mother is awake with a look that says I shouldn't have disappeared. I nod and bow and make nice because what else can I say.

Knocking softly on the doorframe, I peek my head in. "Hi, mom."

She's lying there, small under the blanket. I pull up a chair from the corner and lean in to take her hand. Her eyes move to look at the gesture and then follow the line of my arm up to my face.

There's no spark of recognition.

"You're on a lot of medication right now," I say. "So, you probably don't know what's happening. I'm your daughter. I'm here."

Her attention drifts back down to our hands, and she frowns, pulling her hand back away from mine.

"Mom, please don't—"

I close my eyes and let go. "Why do you do this? This is exactly what dad did, just slower."

After the accident he recovered physically, but he couldn't live with the failure, the debt he incurred registering for the race, the hounding by reporters excited to paint him as a victim, the loss of status. And then he did exactly what whoever set the accident would have wanted him to do.

If he'd died in the accident, he would have been a martyr. But no one talks about someone who did something so embarrassing as kill themselves. He's not even someone people bring up in polite conversation anymore.

Has anyone ever done so much for a person by dying without accomplishing anything?

My throat tightens. And here I am, following his exact path: Not doing what I can with what I have, but waiting and waiting. For what?

I force myself to lean back in my chair, and cross my arms. "You might not want me here, but you're stuck with me. I don't give up even when I really want to. I'm inconvenient that way."

My mom doesn't respond, just closes her eyes again. I sit as she drops off to sleep, then watch her chest rise and fall for minutes more. Eventually, I just lean forward and rest my head on my hands and silently refuse to cry.

FUJIWARA EIKA

Archival footage: DBW advertisement 5 (15-second clip)

Fujiwara Eika is wearing a black suit with a fitted skirt as she scampers into a messy living room. She looks around, frazzled, first peeking into a closet, then moving pillows piled on the floor. Still not finding what she's looking for, she pushes her hair back out of her face before noticing something off camera.

Smash cut to her stepping into a pair of heeled dress shoes. A giant pink lychee is standing behind her, holding out a fabric briefcase by the door. Eika reaches for her bag with a smile.

Pink title card that reads "Kinoshita Diet Breakfast Water."

* * *

Gushiken-san approves a lavender suit for my second spot on *NHK Discuss!*, saying it'll help differentiate me from the dark colors of the others behind the table. This time we pull my hair back in a low bun to increase the formality, bangs styled toward my left side for a hint of softness. My makeup is simple and well-blended to not stick out on the high definition format.

The first half of the show goes well enough: a discussion of new recycling policies with Ito Yasuhiro in his pompadour smirking from across from me at the other end of the table and Koike Nenosuke sternly arguing against from between us to my left.

After we return from commercial, Ito starts by reminding the audience of the new topic. "Again, we are here to discuss developments in the plans for the Hokkaido mine. Koike-san, before our break, you mentioned there have been some delays. Could you outline these developments since our last show?"

The screens behind us shift to show images of mountains blending into the red and gray *NHK Discuss!* logo.

"Yes," Koike-san says, "there has been what many are seeing as an unnecessary delay: the local authorities have started an impact analysis for a hospital that's distant from the proposed project. This red tape has even caused smaller bids to come in for access to the land."

I lean in a bit to make space for myself to speak. "This is only a temporary delay as we pursue appropriate precautions. The local government is partnering with the University of Tokyo's Center for Applied Magic. Their researchers will analyze data on the magic potential of children born near previous mines in the area."

To be honest, I'm overselling the progress. But we do have an agreement from the local officials to cooperate with whichever research proposal on this topic we pick to fund, and Shimizu-sensei has at least one person readying to meet our deadline at the end of this month.

From there, hopefully we can encourage more research on the science instead of just statistical correlations. "This work is an important first step in determining the impact of environmental factors on birth potential."

Koike-san makes a noise in the back of his throat and shifts a gray-clad elbow on the arm of his chair. "Yet the scope of the Fujiwara Heavy Industries proposal is causing a much higher bar for scrutiny as compared to what these alternative smaller projects would be asked to complete. We've already seen that artisanal mining projects in other parts of the world have been shown to be highly irresponsible, with individual miners causing much higher levels of erosion and chemical contamination due to their lack of resources and long-term thinking."

"That's not a fair comparison," I say, keeping my face pleasantly neutral. "Artisanal mining in African countries is usually for gold, not coal, and much of the proceeds are going to local warlords. Of course, those actors would be less concerned about environmental impact."

"Now, Fujiwara-san," Koike uses a tone of voice normally reserved for small children, "you can't make such assumptions when we don't have any information about these alternative proposals."

Ito jumps in to add, "It certainly would be helpful if we could peek under the skirt of those proposals, would it not, Fujiwara-san?"

Limiting my reaction to a press of my lips together, I nod. "Yes, more details would be helpful in understanding the other proposals. However, at this point, there is no indication that the local authorities would choose to approve these options over the Fujiwara Heavy Industries proposal."

"Your family's proposal, you mean?" Koike looks at me directly this time, his eyes dark. "Isn't it an awkward position for you to be in as a primary shareholder of the corporation and the one causing the most problems for this project?"

With a dry chuckle, Ito taps his notecards on the table. "It does seem like you are tied up in trying to please two sides. How do you manage?"

This is starting to feel less like a discussion and more like *NHK Ambush!*

Best to keep my answer bland. "As with all of the important corporations that form the backbone of our nation, we are committed to careful planning that is sustainable for the future. My work with Replenish is a part of that vision."

"And yet it sounds like you've been scrambling to keep the support of your family. Recently, there was a leak that Helios is finalizing plans to share proprietary Power Grip technology with Fujiwara Heavy Industries. This is an invention that was developed in the lab where you have been working part time." Koike raises his eyebrows in a biting salute.

What? Did Mi-chan go around me and make a deal to sell some other tech she made to FHI?

"I couldn't comment on anything so speculative."

"Truly, you must not think much of the viewership of this program if you think they can't see this sweetheart deal as the attempt it is to make up for your organization's meddling in Hokkaido." Koike tilts his head. "Curious that this technology is going into use without the long-term impact studies that you claim are needed for other tried and true methods of resource usage."

I start to speak, but Ito uses his moderator authority to interrupt. "Another point to discuss as the situation develops. Sadly, we are out of time, so we'll have to end here. Let's thank both of our guests for bringing both their expertise and perspectives to our discussion today. I am Ito Yasuhiro, and this has been *NHK Discuss!*."

After the cameras are off, Koike stands slowly and turns to look me in the eyes, maliciousness tinging his professional smile. "Congratulations on the sale."

Back in the preparation space, my manager is looking understated. "That was rough. But you did what you could. The good news," Gushiken-san says, scrolling on her port, "is that you steered clear of anything that might alienate Kinoshita. And the reactions on MinoSo are mostly split between surprise and frustration at how they treated you."

I dig through my bag for a bottle of lemon DBW. This is the time for some alcohol or some caffeine, but on this stupid medication I shouldn't have either. I thought it was supposed to help me focus, and look at this. "I haven't heard anything about the deal he's talking about, but if it does happen, he's going to make it sound like I did know and hid it. We both know that's coming."

To that, my manager has no consolation.

* * *

The last planned pose takes twice as long as intended, but finally the photographer lets me down from my seat on top of the model chocolate bar. I can't rub my eyes like I want without smearing my makeup, so instead I stretch my arms and massage the back of my neck. This was only a half-day shoot, and still it feels like it's been forever.

This time Gushiken-san gives me a smile and thumbs up. "Nice work today."

We both know this short photo shoot was important for expanding my base beyond DBW. It would have been expensive if this project were to run over with Golden Week starting tomorrow, and keeping up a reputation as reliable is critical for being on the list to call for next time.

"Thank you for your hard work," I say. "And you have a whole week off now. I hope you're going to get some rest and have some fun."

Gushiken-san gives me a stern look. "Speaking of, you need to take some time yourself."

"Yes, of course." My port is buzzing in my bag, so I dig around for where it might be, somewhere under the papers and my wallet and a drink.

"I'm serious. You need to get some rest, or you're not going to be any good to anyone."

That's true enough, I think, as I lift my port to read the message.

Date Hatsumi { E—my mom)

DH { She's in the hospital agian)

DH { How many fuckign times is she giong to do this)

My stomach drops, and I immediately message back.

(Where are you? Which hospital? } Fujiwara Eika

The response is nothing more than a few words: Kato, near Ochanomizu.

Of course it'd be a Kato Hospital.

This studio offers a few guest parking spots, so I have my car for once today, and I'm thankful for it. It saves on waiting for a pickup service. With most traffic going out of the city for the holidays, my drive in is relatively open and I'm there in less than half an hour.

Ha-chan is in the room with her mom, head bowed, when I arrive. I let her have space and sit down on a bench in the hallway to wait.

I'm not sure how long passes, but next I'm waking from a light doze as Ha-chan sits down next to me.

"You own a T-shirt?" Ha-chan asks, her cheeks red and forehead pale.

I look down at the brown T-shirt with the words "chocolat grandeur" in an elaborate font. This shirt was probably supposed to be returned before I left, but at least it's not worth much on its own. "I had a commercial this morning."

"Eat grand. Eat grandeur," she says, voice thick. "It's good to see you."

"How is she?"

"She's supposed to be released tomorrow, so probably as fine as possible," Ha-chan says. "There's a vending machine outside that probably needs a bandage."

I smile at that. "I'm sure it had it coming. Have you eaten?"

"I'm not hungry."

"I'll find something for you." I move to stand.

Hatsumi reaches out toward me, but stops just short of catching my wrist. "Really, it's okay. Can you just...stay?"

"Of course." Sitting back down, I ask, "Do you want me to call Noah-kun?"

She shakes her head, looking pained. "I can't... no, please don't."

Instead, we sit for a few minutes in shared quiet. There's the sound of movement down the hall and a clock clicking through the seconds.

"How have things been with Johjima-san?" Ha-chan asks suddenly. She doesn't include the words "this time" but the history is underlying her question.

I exhale through my nose, feeling a pit open up in my stomach at the memory of that awful night. I haven't told Ha-chan or Mi-chan about it, and don't plan to. What can I say, though, that will close down this topic? I'd rather not answer any follow-up questions she might have, either.

"Nothing to report," I say lightly, shrugging it off. "I think he expected the dates to be a little more fun. And he was probably embarrassed after everything that happened at the party."

She clears her throat judgmentally. "Well, and you obviously owe him sex since that earthquake happened."

"Ha-chan," I say sternly, uncomfortable with how close she is to the truth.

"Yeah, yeah," she says. "I know."

We sit in silence for another minute. I pray Ha-chan can't see the flush coloring my cheeks. I cheat a glance over at her, but her gaze is firmly on the floor. The fluorescent lighting bounces a sickly yellow undertone off the tile.

Ha-chan shifts in her chair once, then again, and then sighs. "I slept with Green-san's friend Kenji."

"Oh," I say. "Did you have fun?"

Tipping her head back, she looks at me out of the corner of her eye. "I guess I must have since it happened more than once."

"That good?"

She winks and then shrugs. "Knowing him, it wasn't for my benefit. I bet he just didn't want a bad report getting back to his friend."

"Is it serious?"

"No, it wasn't." Her face darkens. "Enough about me. I saw the show—Koike is such an asshole."

"I don't even know what he was talking about," I say. "But if Helios did make that deal, it's going to look like I did."

"All just a way to distract from whatever shady backroom shit he's doing too." She frowns, her face regaining some of its normal vigor. "You know, sometimes I wonder if he's going to be getting a kickback from the property bill passing."

"What kind of deal?"

She leans forward and rests her elbows on her thighs. "That'd be the question. As you'd expect, people are pretty hush-hush on motivations. But I could ask around more, see if anyone is willing to give me more from public records." She looks over at me suddenly. "You know, I'm not sure if it ties in, but I've been watching this project in Roppongi, a headquarters for the Mining Bank of China. It's being arranged through the Kubo-gumi."

"That's the bank that's funding the Hokkaido project. It's a big investment, and I think Kimiko-*oneesan* was having problems getting a domestic bank to back it. Not that they wanted me to know." I bounce my leg a few times. "It's so good to see renewables grow, but this is a hard transition."

She nods and we stare at the floor for a while. I can see in the reflection of the overhead lights where the cleaner missed a spot by the wall.

"Do you remember that literature test we both crashed on back in year twelve?" Ha-chan asks finally.

"After we spent the night at BG7?" I ask, hiding a yawn.

"Yeah, that one," she says, as if that wasn't every other weekend. "I wish I could remember more from that chapter. I ran across a couple of haiku poets being used as cover names in some paperwork I think might be related to what happened with my dad. I'm trying to think of whether there's some obvious connection between poets and what happened."

It pains me to see her cycling through this over and over. I can't tell if she's making progress on what she describes as an investigation, or if she's just hurting herself by not moving forward.

But I've also seen the wedge that Mi-chan's pushback on the topic has driven between them over the years.

Softly, I ask, "Which poets?"

"Matsuo Basho, Tachibana Hokushi, and Ome Shushiki."

Wracking my brain, I let a falling sound escape my throat. The only one that comes to mind is the haiku by Basho, so I recite it. "The old pond: A frog jumps in, the sound of the water."

"Ei-chan, I think everyone knows that one."

Vaguely, I can remember the class we spent on it, something about the frog implying spring, and questions about why Basho chose to use the particularly antiquarian term for the amphibian. Neither of those facts seem like they'd be useful.

"What kind of connection do you think it is?" I ask. "Something with the history, or maybe how it's written?"

Leaning back, Ha-chan taps the tops of her thighs, like her mind is racing. "I wish I knew. It's a code, some reference to a person who paid for something to be done," she says. "Wait. Old pond..."

Digging her port out of her pocket, she taps the screen a few times and then shows me a page for the *NHK Discuss!* episode. In the description, it lists the guests, including Koike's name. "Old. Pond. The character for 'sound' is in his given name too. You think?"

"Yes, get him arrested for me, please," I say. Watching Koike, that smug expression on his face, being marched off in handcuffs would make my year. "But in all seriousness, does it make any sense?"

"Yeah, probably not. We're talking about someone in the political arena, not someone who would have an underground organization on speed dial." She sighs and runs her free hand through her hair. "Enough on that. How has Noah-kun been doing?"

Yes, that is an easier topic. "He's been doing well. Though I think he's a bit sad about his friend Corbin-san leaving to go back to America."

I don't get to say more, though, because a young girl down the hallway is squealing, her eyes huge and her hand gripping her mom's arm. "Oh, my god. Is that Fujika?"

Not now. Not here.

I glance over, and Ha-chan's face is frozen, trying to keep the anger from showing through. My stomach twists with guilt but I know she understands too.

I stand and walk over, projecting a cheery smile. "And what are your names?"

They only want an autograph and a little distraction from whatever has brought them to the hospital on a Friday afternoon, so I'm able to return to the bench quickly. Ha-chan's posture is tight and she doesn't say anything as I sit down again.

"I'm sorry," I say.

"Don't apologize," she says, her voice thick. "It sucks, but I know you're always one viral MinoSo post away from losing the fanbase you need to make Replenish possible."

We sit in silence for another few minutes, but now the air is tense. My port buzzes and I pull it out to read the message, just for the momentary distraction.

> *Toyama Misora { Eika-chan, I forwarded you an important email. Call when you've read it, I'm in the lab all afternoon.)*
>
> *To:* 藤原英華 *<fujiwara@replenish.or.jp>*
> *From:* 東山美空 *<toyama.misora@helios.co.jp>*
> *FWD: RE: Production delays - Project Q77719v2*
>
> *FYI. Let's discuss.*
>
> *M*
>
> *Forwarded message continues below.*
>
> *To:* 東山美空 *<toyama.misora@helios.co.jp>*
> *From: Prototype Team 3 <prototype_3@helios.co.jp>*
> *RE: Production delays - Project Q77719v2*
>
> *Toyama-bucho,*
>
> *I regret to inform you that all prototype production, including Project Q77719v2, has been paused due to the prioritization of the new Gamestasis module. We anticipate returning to your project in 3-4 weeks, and sincerely apologize for any inconvenience caused by this delay.*
>
> *Suzuki*
> *Team 3*

Turning to Ha-chan, I start to explain but her face is blank. She says, "Whatever it is, you can go. I'll be fine here."

I know it's a lie, and I leave anyway.

* * *

I arrive at Helios late enough in the afternoon that Mi-chan's team members eye me with undisguised dread. I feel another pang of guilt. They're all trapped here until she leaves, and my presence usually indicates a multi-hour research session.

"I'm just here to chat," I murmur to Araki as I pass his workstation on my way to the inner lab. He has young children, and I'm sure he's eager to be home with them on a Friday evening. "I'll try to get her to relocate to her office."

He gives me a deep bow of gratitude. Sugihara must have been eavesdropping, because she starts to slowly slot her desk instruments into their individual cubbies. If either of them discerns any worry in my voice, they don't let on.

The light outside the damper room indicating work in progress is switched on, so I press the buzzer and wait for someone to let me in. When the door clicks open, I see Mi-chan is alone at her workbench, one hand on a powerbank while the other manipulates whatever she's examining through her lab lenses.

"Do you need a boost?" I ask. That is always the barrier for her, and while I hate to see her overwork herself, I know how frustrated she gets if she runs out of power in the middle of a process.

She lifts her lenses. "Thank you, but no. Cameron charged it up for me before he left."

"Where is Cameron-san?" I ask, feeling a little twist of concern at the casual way she talks about him now. I hope she's more cautious in front of others, but it's probably just the stress affecting her.

"At his ward office, arguing against some fine he was issued. The timing is a shame, too, because it would have been helpful to have him here for this conversation." She peers at my face. "Eika-chan, your nails."

"I—oh." I pull my left index finger away from my mouth. I can't be seen on *NHK Discuss!* with a raggedy manicure, they will absolutely zoom in on it. "Maybe we could take this upstairs," I suggest, remembering my promise to Araki. It would be nice to distract myself with a cup of tea. I rushed to Helios specifically to have this conversation with Misora face-to-face, yet now that I'm here, I find myself wanting to do anything to postpone it.

Once we're settled into chairs in Misora's office, though, I'm out of options. "They didn't keep even one production team off the Gamestasis?"

"They did, but that queue is backed up longer than Team 3's wait time."

"So, we're just stuck," I say, despair tightening my chest.

"We have to pause one project," Misora corrects. "But I've been wanting to talk with you about this other idea Cameron and I have been working on, an idea that evolved out of the failed test on the first battery. It's only a concept at the moment, but I think the potential is—"

"Only a concept?" I interrupt. My voice begins as a whisper, but slowly, shakily, I gain volume. "Mi-chan, I can't start over with something new."

"It's not starting over, it's in addition. Cameron and I will work on this idea he had for a port redesign, and in the meantime, you can keep your focus on the environmental work. Let the tech dev cycle run its course." Her tone is firm. It's clear she thinks the discussion is over.

"I'm sorry, Mi-chan, I am, but no. I've started reading the FHI board minutes like you suggested, and things don't look good. Even with a major cash infusion from the Mining Bank, liquidity is a real issue right now, and my budget is a juicy target."

I can feel hot tears welling up in my eyes, and I blink rapidly, willing them away. We've overcome countless obstacles to create this technology that could help so many people, only to land here, in a queue behind a video game system. "*Oniisan* was already muttering about cuts, and that was when he expected us to have a product to unveil at Syphon Expo. If Isao learns of this new project from one of the Helios board members, he'll know something is wrong with the battery, and he'll take that to the FHI board."

Misora runs a hand over her face. She stares past my shoulder for a moment, eyes wide and unfocused in that way she gets when she's turning over an idea. Finally, after a beat, she sighs. "Well, I have a solution, but you won't like it."

* * *

By the time I leave Helios, Friday night traffic has clogged the expressways down to a crawl, and Ocelot tells me that what should be a fifteen-minute drive will take more like forty. But it's okay, it gives me time to think. I turn on some ambient wave sounds and ease out of the Helios ramp toward Kyukaigan-dori.

Mi-chan is right, I don't like her idea much. Farming out our project to Toyama-gumi wasn't what I had in mind when I asked Misora to support my work at Replenish.

And Hideki of all people... I didn't even know this was the kind of work he's able to do, although it makes sense, I suppose. In high school, Misora once made an offhand joke about how much easier it would be for her to do precision work if she could shine light out of her hands. A few weeks later, Hideki had rigged a pair of gloves with small LED lights stitched along the knuckles. Misora thought they were silly, and mocked them to me and Hatsumi, but I remember how earnest he looked when he gave them to her, puppy dog eyes reflecting the pulsating strobes of the BG7 dance floor.

But what he did to her was far worse. That text message is still seared on my memory.

They're sending me to Osaka. I hope you fucking die, Misora.

Ocelot chimes, and the map on the car's screen fades away in favor of the bowing cat. I'm home. It's before seven, so the valet is still on duty. As I get out of the driver's seat and hand off the spare fob, my port rings—an incoming video from Noah-kun.

Oh, no. I forgot all about him.

"Evening, Eika-san!" He has to be itching to leave for the *izakaya*, especially when I was supposed to meet him over at the Replenish office hours ago, but he manages to hide it. After a day like today, I envy his youthful energy, all bright-eyed and freshly scrubbed. Am I only a few years older than he is? Today, it feels like decades.

"I'm so sorry, Noah-kun," I say, entering the lobby with a nod to the doorman.

"It's okay," he says, a gracious fib. "I spent the afternoon looking over those FHI financial documents like you asked. Is now an okay time?"

"Yes, I'm alone," I reply, selecting the *Door Close* button once I'm inside the elevator. "What did you find?"

"Well, not much, really. Nothing that looks shady to me, although I'm not an expert—I've only taken one forensic accounting class. There is one project that's bleeding money, but it's more than they could fix even if they swept our entire budget."

"Okay, that's good to know." The elevator has arrived at my floor. "Thank you, Noah-kun. Are you heading down to Watami now?"

He nods, dimples blooming on his cheeks as he smiles.

"Have fun." I return the smile, crinkling my nose at him. "Don't drink more than I would."

A polite cough covers his chuckle. "Never, Eika-san."

DATE HATSUMI

Today is not a great day in Natsuki-chan's life. She seems to be mad at her dress, the breakfast, and her dad for not picking her up. Maybe the table too—it can be hard to tell with kids that age what the real subject of their ire is.

As such, Mori-shicho is splitting her attention between answering a message with one hand and wiping snot with the other. I have questions to ask her but it's not happening over screaming, so I'm shoveling rice into my mouth. With my mom still in the hospital, this is the first hot food I've had in the last 24 hours.

"Shicho-san, would you like me to try?" asks Sadame from the corner.

The mayor sets the slimy tissue on the floor and sighs. "Yes, you are welcome to do what you can. Today is hard, isn't it, Na-chan?"

Sadame swoops in and picks up Natsuki, throwing her up in the air. For a second, the little girl's face freezes in confusion, then breaks into a smile. Sadame does it again, and the crying is replaced with laughter. Even Mikio, who normally has infinite patience for child hijinks, relaxes his shoulders at the break in noise.

Mori-shicho briefly closes her eyes. "Thank you, Sadame."

The poor girl is smiling at the praise, but she has probably solidified her role as a caretaker. Juro is going to be getting the real projects, and in a few years, Sadame will be wondering why she never quite advanced the way she expected.

The mayor looks down long enough to hit send on her message, and then turns her attention to me. "You probably can't wait for this fun."

Mori-shicho's ability to function is built on the help of others, including the funding that supported her run and now the help of others who don't know what they are sacrificing to keep her going. "Someday maybe," I say without emotion. "Will there be time for a press conference later, or is the handshake event likely to take up the afternoon?"

"With what is happening today, I don't think there will be much interest in what I have to say." She gives me a conspiratorial smile, just a little joy she thinks is shared between the two of us.

There's a major announcement scheduled today: the Japanese Industry Alliance, speaking for its more than 1000 members, is coming out in support of the NRPO.

All I can think is how disappointed my father would be to see me return her smile. I do it anyway. "It's true."

Mori-shicho starts to look back down at a notification on her port, but I clear my throat to get her attention.

"I am hoping to get your comment on a story I was given by the press club. I humbly apologize for the sensitive nature of the article, but the topic was out of my hands." A lie. It took weeks of me pressuring people to bring them around and approve this story.

She's frowning now, but I continue. "With the likely passage of the NRPO, there have been some reports of landlords using technicalities in leases to renegotiate lease terms early."

It goes without saying that the new terms are worse, with higher rent and fewer protections. After all, being in another culture with a potential language barrier makes them vulnerable to this kind of exploitation.

"And what might this story have to do with Suginami ward?"

I sigh, pretending I'm reluctant to share. "Unfortunately, a few of the earthquake victims from the Grace Court 5 buildings are among those who have been impacted. They've only been in their new homes for two months and they are already being asked to negotiate new leases."

There's a click as Mori-shicho sets her port down on the table. She fixes me with a blank mask of an expression and says blandly, "Sadame, Mikio, could you give us a few minutes? I need to give an interview."

I don't think I'm going to be invited to breakfast anymore.

* * *

I'm standing across the desk from where Goto is hunched in his chair, hands carefully set in his lap. He has large hands and feet, and he always seems keenly aware of them. "The article was late."

With the amount of time I spend at the press club office, it's surreal to be in the office at the *Nihon Times*. The walls are painted pink, the sickly kind, and the air smells vaguely musty.

After all that work getting it through the press club approvals, and burning my good will to get Mori-shicho on the record. I finished it sitting at the damn hospital, I want to say. I should still be there with her until she's released.

But I don't because asking for sympathy on these things only makes me look weak. "Fifteen minutes. You could have put it in."

"Maybe. But today it's old news."

"Bullshit," I snap, then regret it. He's going to be more likely to see sense if I don't piss him off. "Sorry, but that doesn't make sense, Goto-san. The property bill vote isn't until next month. It's still current."

"Hatsumi," he says. For as long as we've known each other, we've never been on given name terms. "You know we can't run this. The timing of this is not right. It's not something we can do right now."

"The Civics press club approved it." When that happens, it means all the relevant staff at the major newspapers have decided it's relevant, timely, and appropriate for a particular paper to run. At that point, the jump to print at an individual paper should be nothing more than a formality.

Goto's right hand tightens around his left wrist. "There are stakeholders, you know... It's not possible."

Oh, I see.

Back in primary school, I once found him on a bench nursing a split lip and muttering, "She told me to do it." It took coaxing and a *mikan* from my lunch bag before he would say more, that it was from some kid whose homework he'd done. He hadn't done it well, and the kid hadn't taken the low grade kindly. What made it strange was that back at that age, Goto was known as a pretty good student.

Later, I found out that before doing the homework, he'd run to the teacher to tell her everything. Rather than deal with an angry rich parent, she'd told him to do it poorly and she'd take care of the rest. She'd graded it fairly for the work, and Goto got a punch for his troubles.

He's always wanted approval from someone above him.

"We can't?" I try to keep my voice steady and almost succeed. I'm not giving form to the real question: who bought you?

I don't know why this surprises me so much. After all, it was the only way this could have ended. I chose my priorities and let Goto slide into the job where he makes the decisions about what to run, not me.

"You understand, I'm sure. There isn't anything to be done."

I swallow my emotion and let his statement hang in the air.

Goto takes my silence for agreement instead. "I'm glad you understand. With everything." He clears his throat. "On another topic, I, uh, heard that you were talking to the crimes desk. About the Asagawa organization."

Slowly, I nod. We might not be close, but he's known me long enough to know why I'd be digging for information from that department. Everyone in my class knew what had happened when it did, and as much as I try to keep my research under wraps, people talk.

He rubs one of his hands across the fabric covering his knee. "I found out something you might like to know. Their head, Asagawa Yukina, she was arrested. Gun possession. Isn't that good to hear, after all these years?"

My back goes stiff, and my legs feel light.

"Gun possession," I repeat for lack of anything more substantial to say. That's the charge that organized crime uses when they lack the evidence for other actual crimes. It's an effective workaround since prosecutors are pressured to keep up their 99% conviction rates and they aren't going to bring charges they know won't stick.

Is this what you think I'll accept as payment for playing nice?

My mind drifts to Okada and his spite. Looking back, I can't help but wonder what he saw about me. Was he simply jealous of my connections and opportunity, or did he think of me as this? He never knew the stories Mori pushed and I ignored. He'd have only seen me eating her food and then writing about her work on the homeless, the thing that is going to get her re-elected.

Goto is still talking. "Average sentence of seven years. If they have proof she fired it, maybe a life sentence. That will be satisfying, won't it?"

And yet, this is such a hollow offering. None of what Goto said proves that Asagawa Yukina had anything to do with the accident. I have the copies of the three payments to Walling Insurance, a lead for sure, but those might mean nothing in practice.

Even if they do, the person I want is who gave the order.

"When is the trial?" I ask, feeling a calmness suddenly.

"It's not set yet. You know how these things go, it might be a while before that happens."

Indeed, I do.

* * *

It doesn't take long to get permission to meet, but the paperwork is tedious. My first appointment is canceled by way of an automatic message two hours before the scheduled time. The prisoner is too excitable to make the visit advisable at this time. I dutifully follow the procedure to set up another one for next week.

Finally, the day comes, and as much of a fool as it makes me, I take the train out to the prison.

The uniformed official who checks through my things and leads me to the room is professional, but I can tell she's suspicious of anyone who would be here to visit. Hard to say if it's because of the particular person or my role as a member of the press. The judicial system has had a number of scandals in recent years as they've refused to release details on prison conditions, limited access to detainees, and even have been reported to complete executions without notification to the families of the scheduled date.

Two chairs are placed in this room, one on either side of the plexiglass, with a series of small holes to allow some sound to pass through. The guard warns me to remain back from the divider, which means that I will need to talk loudly. As there will be a guard in the room on each side of the divider throughout the meeting, this is all designed to guarantee that we will not be passing information without our supervision hearing it.

There's no air conditioning in the facilities, so the room is steamy hot, and sitting there as I wait is officially miserable. Being limited to just a notebook and pen, no ports or AR glasses allowed, slows time immeasurably. There is a small window on the wall opposite, and the air in front of it has a lazy amount of dust particles dropping through the beam of light. I fidget and drop my pen, pick it up, and roll it back and forth across the paper.

Finally, the door on the other side of the room opens to admit a different officer and Asagawa Yukina. She carries herself with ruler-straight posture, her hands held in front of her hips as if they were restrained even though they are free. She's wearing a pair of loose knit pants and a T-shirt in two different shades of dark gray, not a uniform—a visible sign that she hasn't been convicted yet.

When she sits, she keeps her eyes on the floor and for a moment beyond as the attending officer takes his place by the door. Her hands remain in the same formal position by her hips and she's sitting on the edge of the chair, a ready stance. As soon as the officer's footsteps stop in a click, she flicks her gaze up to meet mine with an intensity that makes the room feel cold and distant. This was a bad idea.

"Since you requested this, we both know who I am. Who are you?"

"Nice to meet you. You can call me Idachi," I say, trying not to shift in my seat anymore. The "Date" pronunciation of the two *kanji* in my family name is extremely common, enough that if she'd seen it written she wouldn't need to ask. This is an ancient, bordering on obscure, alternate pronunciation that doesn't contradict the paperwork

I submitted. "Thank you for taking the time to talk."

"My cell will still be there when I get back."

A constellation of bruises is running up the pale skin of her right arm and under her shirt, coming out along her neck and culminating in a black eye. All recent. By the report, she's been in custody for nearly a month.

I have plenty of questions of my own to fill the thirty minutes, but I can't not ask, "Are you okay?"

"You have a soft heart." Her mouth twitches in a way that indicates some kind of amusement. They don't look as similar as I would have expected, but her expression isn't that far off from a particularly cutting one I've seen on Kenji.

That sentence was not a compliment, and I'd rather she not have any kind of thoughts on who I am or what I care about.

She continues, "I engaged in a disrespectful amount of eye contact and had to be restrained for my own safety. I now understand my error and hope to be rehabilitated successfully. I hear that if I'm lucky they will train me in the respectable trade of assembling chopstick wrappers in preparation for my eventual return to society. That's not why you're here." The entire phrase is delivered so evenly, without particular emphasis or emotion, that I almost miss the implied question in the last sentence.

This woman, Yukina, has caused a lot of suffering to other people, I remind myself. In other circumstances, she wouldn't hesitate to hurt me.

First, establish the timeline. "I hope that you can help me with a research project. I am looking to confirm some details of candidate Wada Isamu's run for governor of Tokyo about fifteen years ago. Do you remember where you were in May of Heika 31?" I ask, using the traditional calendar numbering system.

The small bit of useful irony here is that what I'm asking about, what changed my life so much, was hardly even a crime. No one died directly, just a small bit of technical mishap with the stage lighting that wasn't ever able to be properly explained. It's hardly even worth the time for a prosecutor to look at, especially not when they have a gun charge to use.

Still, even asking is giving this woman the opening to ask for something in exchange for information. The old adage about the first to make an offer usually losing applies here.

Asagawa Yukina takes a second to think, not dropping her gaze from me. The room is still stuffy as hell. "Tochigi City. We returned to Tokyo in September of that year. But you're wondering about June."

"I am hoping to explore the timeline during the entirety of the election season."

"The entirety of June 23," she says, confirming she has the information I want. The guard behind her doesn't react, so it's clearly not a date that has somehow permeated the public consciousness.

I close my right hand around my pen to keep my fingers from shaking. I bet she'll notice anyway. I may as well have come in here naked.

"Okay, then. Related to Wada Isamu's campaign that season: I received a tip that on June 23," I say, quoting the date on the record labeled Basho, "someone contracted with a Walling Insurance for services related to the election. I am hoping to clarify the details and timeline."

"I was in Tochigi City with my family at the time." The sun is shifting enough that the light is aimed at me directly, putting her face in shadow. As if I need more of a disadvantage in this conversation. "Speaking of which, how old were you at the time, Date Hatsumi?"

The floor drops out, and for a moment I'm falling. I bite back the reflex to deny. She's not stupid, and wishing she were isn't going to change that.

Asagawa Yukina continues as if she were reading from a dictionary. "They kept you out of the papers after the election, but you and your mother were featured on TV during some of your father's early rallies. You do look like him, around the eyes."

Even though it's deadened coming from her mouth, the tone is the same soft mockery I've heard several times before. I see your child in you too, I want to shoot back.

Shifting in my chair, I line up the core of sunlight behind her head so I can at least see her eyes again. It's a mistake. Does she always look like this? The tiger cubs were maybe understated in their warning. I can see her doing almost anything without worry or fear or any emotion really.

I try again. "My interest is in exploring Koike-san's groundbreaking work during that electoral season. If you don't remember, I don't want to trouble you any further—"

"Here we ponder our mistakes through quiet and contemplation. You're the first person I've talked to in a week."

Goddamn it, she's trying to play off my sympathies. It doesn't make hearing that any less horrific. "It sounds like time for contemplation is not entirely uncalled for in your case."

"I know exactly why I'm here," she says, the corners of her mouth curling up into a rictus of a smile. There's sweat beading up on her forehead and temple. She doesn't seem to notice.

I'm having a hard time tracking what the timeline might be on her organization. She knows about the events, and the payment matches the timeframe. Is she lying about when she was in Tokyo, or did she take over an existing organization when she came here?

Either way, she's trying to sell me the illusion of innocence. "There are those that would assign you responsibility for actions of another, then."

"Those with power will do whatever they want to those without it." Her eyes flicker to the side where the guard is standing.

"Doesn't that make you angry?"

"The only reasonable answer is more power. Then you can do what you want." Her eyes burrow into me. I don't want to know what she is thinking of doing to me in this moment. "If you want a start, talk to the person named Kumanaka Soseki."

"Bear middle?" I ask to verify what characters are used to write it. That name seems familiar—where have I seen it before?

"Center of bear. Or eaten by one."

Was that an attempt at humor? "And you think he would be helpful in establishing this timeline?"

"At the time, he did contract work with Wada's election campaign, supplies and other things as needed. He would have any records. He may still be connected with that insurance company that you mentioned. Or not. Professional loyalty has become outdated these days."

The sweat on the side of her face has reached the edge of her jawline and she reaches up to wipe it away. The officer in the room shouts something, probably words, but through the plexiglass all I hear is the sound of his voice. She drops her hand immediately.

It's too late. The officer is there, demanding she stand, whisking her out of the room. As she goes, the upturn on her mouth under lowered eyes makes me wonder if she did it intentionally.

I'm left alone on this side of the plexiglass, just me and my notepad with the characters KUMA - NAKA in the corner. My shirt is soaked against the plastic chair. I think that was the name of the other assistant manager at Walling.

Today, well-respected reporter Date Hatsumi got herself in for more than she expected. When asked for comment, she...

She...

Hell. I need to find a bathroom. I'm going to throw up.

FUJIWARA EIKA

Archival footage: DBW advertisement 6 (15-second clip)

 Fujiwara Eika is leaning over a railing, eyes closed, the light of a sunrise kissing her face. She opens her eyes and looks over to her right, blushing.

 A young man is looking in the opposite direction. He has a shaggy haircut and is wearing a navy cardigan over a horizontally striped blue and white shirt. His eyes open widely and a blush blooms across his cheeks.

 Smash cut back to Eika's face as she pushes her hair over her ear coquettishly. The camera pulls back to reveal that she's sharing the morning with a giant peach in front of the water. The young man is nearby, stopped on a bicycle, watching in shock as Eika smiles at the peach.

 Peach title card that reads "Kinoshita Diet Breakfast Water."

* * *

How did my emails get to be such a mess again? There's at least three hundred, and I haven't responded to the blurb request for Syphon Expo. I do need an assistant, especially since wrestling with the combination of complex *kanji* and informal language in fan mail is beyond Noah's ability. Maybe Gushiken can help on that front.

My port buzzes twice, and I see it's Noah calling. He took a late lunch and was supposed to head over to FHI to pick up the mail afterward. A seed of worry wiggles its way into my gut; what did Isao do now?

I answer on video. "Hi, Noah-kun! Is everything alright?"

He's sitting on a bench in the atrium at FHI, golden light streaming in behind him and reflecting off his hair. "Hi, Eika-san! Sorry to be inconvenient. You're still at the office, right?"

"You're not a bother. Did something happen?" I ask.

"Well, no. That is what's strange." He puts his hand up to show confusion. "There hasn't been any mail this week."

I frown and make a *hm* sound. "That is strange. Did you ask about it?"

"I did. At least, I thought I did. The woman working only gave me the 'no' gesture." He's holding his port with one hand, so he brings up the other arm in a firm half of an x to demonstrate.

Unfortunately, some people don't want to deal with trying to communicate across a language barrier, even one as low as with Noah. I'm glad to see he doesn't seem particularly upset about being given such a rude response.

"Don't worry, Noah-kun. I'll contact them and see what's going on." My port buzzes in my hand again, and I see there's an incoming call from Isao. "Speaking of, there's another call, I think this might be about that. Come on back and I'll figure it out."

"Sorry again, Eika-san," Noah says as he disconnects.

I hit the button to connect to the other call, and Isao's angry face glares at me. "Good afternoon. Are you working hard, *oniisan?*"

"Your pet *gaijin* has been hassling the mail staff."

"He's been what? How?" With smiles and friendly apologies?

Isao adjusts his tortoiseshell frames with one hand. "He's been told several days in a row that there is no mail and yet he keeps making FHI staff take time to repeat this. He's also currently taking up space in our atrium that is reserved for clients."

"I think he may be leaving now," I say apologetically. "He called me because he was surprised that there wasn't any mail. We had been receiving several pieces a day before this week."

"So I heard." His tone softens, sounding almost corporate, as he continues, "You must understand that this organization cannot continue to support your vanity projects indefinitely. Even small expenditures over time impact the bottom line. We have a fiscal responsibility to our shareholders."

Sorting out a few pieces of mail in the thousands that arrive every day? "I'm sorry, I don't understand."

"We have notified the post office that your organization is no longer located at this address. We ask that you kindly cease taking up the time of FHI staff with unnecessary interruptions."

"I'm sorry," I repeat. "You returned our mail?"

He smiles, just enough to pull the corners of his mouth up. "If you need help with locating anything that had been misrouted, I suggest you contact the post office for assistance."

The call disconnects, leaving me staring at the screen of my port in shock.

What a petty thing to do.

Okay, so we'll need a redirect request put in to the post office. That's probably easy to do in person, or maybe online. I'd better do it myself since it'll involve some specific language.

Would there have been anything we needed in what might have come through? The utilities were all set up to this address. The rent is an automatic payment. There's probably nothing to be done about one-off letters. Returning the junk mail might be for the best, anyway.

One thing, though—we haven't received the research proposal from Shimizu-sensei, even though the deadline was on Monday. I thought she was going to be sending it by email, but maybe she sent it as a paper document instead.

Somewhere I have her number. I search through the notes on my port but it's not there. After a few minutes of trying different apps, I resort to digging out her business card from the case at the bottom of my purse.

The line rings a few times and then clicks as she answers. "This is Shimizu."

"This is Fujiwara Eika, following up on the research proposal deadline," I say. "I think there may have been an issue with the mail."

Dead silence for a moment, then she says, "There were no submissions to forward."

My stomach sinks as my mind races. "I thought your grad student was interested."

"I'll be honest with you, Fujiwara-san. After you talked about this project publicly, there was significant pushback within the department. I can't in good conscience put a postdoc in that position. They have their futures to think about."

I grip the edge of my skirt and force myself to keep talking, even though I want to curl into a ball of shame. I should have realized this might happen and kept this secret until it was done. "Was it my brother? On the advisory board?"

"Not just. There is skepticism in this department already on Santos and Monteiro. That you politicized the topic only made these attitudes more prominent."

"You were sympathetic. Surely you can—"

"I am an assistant professor," Shimizu-sensei says, like this explains her hesitancy in full. "I cannot afford to be pushing for something controversial like this pre-tenure. I'm sorry."

Again, I'm left staring at my port. This time, I notice that there's a slight reflection in the glass front, and I can see the puffiness threatening to take over my face.

I select another number and let it ring. Please, Mi-chan, be available.

The call connects surprisingly fast, before I can even formulate what I want to say.

"Eika-chan, what now?" She sounds tired and annoyed.

There's been so much lately that I can't blame her for being exhausted by this roller coaster. I'm sick of the ride that seems to be stomach-flipping drops day after day. If only I didn't think this work was so important.

"Mi-chan, has Isao been trying to cancel the project with Helios?" As I finish the question, Noah walks into the office, starting to call out a greeting. When he sees I'm on the phone, he switches to a wave.

"Not to my knowledge, but there are a lot of conversations that happen above my pay grade. At the last board meeting I attended, he was trying to limit funds to my department, though—he opposed the cost of creating Cameron's position."

"But it all depends on the project making money, doesn't it?"

"Everything depends on making money," she replies, a wry note to her tone.

"He's been going around pulling on threads to keep Replenish from accomplishing anything. He just blocked the research project we were working on with Todai."

"So... is the battery all you have?" she asks.

"I can start new projects, but not on the timeline I need to keep funding," I reply, feeling panicked. It would help to see her, to talk this through in person. "Mi-chan, are you at Helios?"

"I'm on my way back there."

"From—?"

"Daikan-Yama."

She's never one to be chatty, but this is reticent even for Misora. "What's in Daikan-Yama?" I probe. It's odd for her to go somewhere in the middle of the workday.

A long pause. "Hideki," she finally replies.

Suddenly, a roaring in my ears, nerves and excitement and fear all bundled together. "Mi-chan!" I exclaim, voice too loud. Noah looks up from watering the monstera plant and gives me a quizzical smile.

"Does this mean what I think it does?" I demand, breathless, then cover the microphone. "Maybe the battery," I murmur to Noah. His smile turns into a full-on beam—he knows how much this means to me.

"Yes, but before you get too excited—"

"Toyama Misora! Why didn't you tell me first thing?"

"Because it's untested," she says, "and I didn't want you to get your hopes up until we know the issues from the last version are all ironed out."

"Can you bring it by?" If she's going to Helios from Daikan-Yama, it's on her way. The sale of the Powergrips to FHI probably wasn't her decision, but she could have warned me before I face-planted on *NHK Discuss!* I feel a little bit like she owes me.

"Eika—"

"Please, Mi-chan?" I beg. "Fifteen minutes. I just want to see it and celebrate with you and Noah-kun."

"Fifteen minutes." She ends the call.

"Do we still have that bottle of champagne?" I ask Noah. When we moved into this office space, I held a welcome reception, and the small group of friends and supporters I'd invited managed to take down almost two cases of Veuve Clicquot. It was such a special night, fizzy with possibility, so I'd saved one bottle as a memento. This seems like the perfect time to crack it open.

"We do! Do you...?"

"Sparkling water for me." Bubbles will make it feel like a real celebration, even if we have to use mismatched teacups.

Misora arrives in her usual quiet-yet-purposeful way, somehow already standing beside me in the kitchen by the time I hear the door to the suite open. "I see you've brought out the good stuff."

"If not now, when?" I reply, pushing cups across the counter to her and Noah. "Trade you."

From her bag, Misora withdraws a reusable silicone baggie with a cheap burner port inside, laying it next to the cups.

If I'm being honest, it's anticlimactic. Helios products, even prototypes, are always nestled in a bed of foam that's fitted into a branded black and silver box; this baggie is a sad reminder that we had to have the battery made via alternative channels.

Misora's port—her actual one, not the burner—emits a staccato burst of buzzes.

"I have to take this. Can I use your office?"

I nod.

"Thank you. Don't mess with that battery." Her demeanor shifts as she answers the call. "Hello, Papa. Yes, of course, it's always a good time..."

Once my office door has closed behind Misora, I reach for the bag with the battery, causing Noah to let out a nervous titter from above the rim of his teacup. I think Mi-chan intimidates him.

"Don't worry, I'm not going to 'mess with it,'" I say, fixing him with my biggest, most winsome smile. "I just want a quick video of you using it. I promise I won't post it on MinoSo, but I have to capture our big moment!" I wish Cameron-san could be here to celebrate, too. We all worked so hard. But at least I'll be able to show him the video later.

The port is light in my hand. I know it's partly because it's a throwaway, but it's hard to believe there's a battery in it at all. I flip it over, peering at the tiny silver Syphon panel on the back. The port is off, so what's the harm? I slide my fingertip over the panel, feeling the faint grooves against my skin. So much thought, so much hard work, and it's finally here. Euphoria washes over me, rushing a bright flush to my cheeks.

"Eika-san?"

The heat inside me rises, and I register that it's a genuine heat, a physical one. Feeling unsteady, I lean against the counter, but the waves of heat keep coming, faster and faster.

"Eika-san?!"

The floor is distant but also tilting up and toward me.

An impact and everything goes dark.

CAMERON GREEN

"Green-san, do you have a free moment?"

"Toyama-bucho and I are supposed to have some bench time this afternoon, but I'm available until she's ready," I reply, following Li to her workstation. We've just finished our weekly staff meeting. Across the room, Sugihara and Matsuda retreat to their desks, while Araki catches Misora for a follow-up question.

I perch on the stool next to Li's bench. "What's up?"

She smooths a sheet of magipaper across the work surface. "I did some calculations on the maximum power load that an interconnected network of miniature Syphon nodes could handle."

"And?" I dare to let myself get a little excited. For a few weeks now, Misora and I have been working to re-engineer a port so that, instead of having a single large battery, it has many smaller, integrated ones spread across the surface. Any risk in using an L-based uptake model will, theoretically, be mitigated if it's spread across multiple points. But the idea will only have legs if Li can confirm that these much tinier energy draws can supply the same juice that today's high-power apps require.

"You will need to do the biostats and generate some data on how much power is pulled via the hand, broken down by MAR score in increments of ten."

"Alright, I can do that. But... you think this could work?"

Her wire-rimmed glasses slide down her nose as she nods. "Yes. I'm not sure if it will reach MAR scores as low as your initial design, but it should still be accessible to downslopes who fall below the industry standard."

"I'll take it." I try to catch Misora's eye, because she'll want to hear about this, too, but she has wrapped up her conversation with Araki and is now—what else?—on her port. She gives me a curt wave and then, still listening to the person on the other end of the line, she leaves the room.

"I guess my bench time is canceled," I say to Li with a wry smile, stretching toward a bit of solidarity. Of all my colleagues, she's been the toughest nut to crack.

"Yes."

"Always great to chat with you, Li-san."

I'd chalk her brusqueness up to the language barrier, but her Japanese is better than mine. At least she no longer makes an awkward comment about my height every time she sees me.

When I get back to my desk, there's a message from Misora waiting.

> *Toyama Misora { I have to run an errand. Tell Nozomi to reschedule our bench time for next week.)*

I want to ask if she's going to come over later tonight. Since our strange non-fight a few weeks ago, things are superficially back to how they were, but it all still feels off-kilter. I wouldn't take back what I said to her, but just once I wish she needed me half as much as I always seem to need her.

> *(Will do } Cameron Green*

* * *

Compared to the jam-packed rush hour trains and the sticky air outside, my apartment feels almost glacial. Panzer makes the executive decision to keep his walk short, and we both sprawl in the living room afterward, basking in the cool breeze coming from the minisplit unit above our heads. I definitely forgot how hot and humid Japan can get, and it's not even full summer yet.

I turn on the TV and click to the auto-saved programs in my regular streams. Reilly had a match last night, Munich time, and I managed to avoid seeing the score today. I figure I might as well watch it, but I'm barely into the first period when there's a knock at the door.

I pause the game and switch the TV over to Gamestasis mode. Asagawa already seems irritated that I know Eika, Misora, and, by proxy, Taehyun—no need to clue him in on the fact that my baby brother is a midfielder in the Bundesliga. Though if he bothered to ask, I'd tell him that the byproduct of living in mere proximity to wealth and fame is an ego in constant state of bruised deflation.

To my surprise, Asagawa is dressed in a dark suit and tie. Even with the jacket draped over one arm and the sleeves rolled up, it's more formal than I've ever seen him. "Who died?"

"It was about time for a new job," he says. "Need some actual insurance?"

"From you?" I raise an eyebrow at him. "No, thanks. Being a rational person, there are other salespeople I'd trust first. Wall Street bankers, Nigerian princes. Maybe even an actual alligator."

"Suit yourself," he shrugs. Then he pulls a pair of chintzy-looking slippers from his bag, the decoration on the toe box a vague gesture at a traditional white-on-indigo pattern. He drops them with a loud clap onto the hallway floor, then adds, pointedly, "You're welcome."

"Okay...?" I'm contentedly barefoot, and in any case, these are at least two sizes too small for my massive *gaijin* feet. I silently demonstrate this by putting my left foot next to one of the slippers, dwarfing it.

"Guest slippers. They're a thing."

"For the hallway?" He can't wear them on the living room *tatami* or in the bathroom, so they are of decidedly limited utility.

"There's laminate in your kitchen."

It's been a long day, and I cannot be bothered to argue. "Make yourself at home," I say with a sigh, knowing I'll regret it later.

"Got anything cold to drink?" he asks, stepping up into his victory slippers.

"You can look," I reply, going back into the living room and checking the charge on each of the GS controllers. A quick boost on the Syphon brings them both up to nearly 100%. Asagawa spends more time at the fridge cooling down than he does choosing a beverage, but he eventually ambles back with two cans of Asahi Super Dry. He leaves the slippers at the door to the room, then flops on the sofa, exchanging one of the beers for a controller.

"Giving me the bad one again?"

I'm about to reply when my port, face down on the *kotatsu* table, starts to vibrate against the Formica top. I lunge for it, hoping to see Misora's name and photo even though I know this isn't her signature ring pattern.

Incoming call: Reilly Green

"I should answer this, it's my brother," I say to Asagawa, crossing past him to go into the kitchen and nearly tripping on the damn slippers. Into the microphone on my port: "Are you spying on me? I had just started watching last night's game."

Reilly groans. "Don't bother. We lost."

"Hey, spoilers," I say without much actual ire. I guess he's saved me the time. "What's up?"

"Check your messages!" As he says this, my port vibrates, so I pull it away from my ear to look at what's just arrived on my screen. It's a photo of Reilly and his girlfriend, Karolin, both beaming.

Well, not just his girlfriend anymore, judging by the eye-popping diamond that's dwarfing her hand.

"Huh. Did you change your hair?"

"Cam."

"Kidding, kidding, I'm kidding." I turn to roll my eyes at Asagawa, because even if he can't understand the words, he'll get the tone, but he's on a call of his own. I need to stop being shitty. "No, for real, congratulations, Ry! To both of you. This is great news."

Reilly starts giving me the play-by-play of his proposal, but it's hard to hear around the primal scream of my own thoughts. First Vanessa's baby announcement, now this.

"So, will you?"

"Will I what?" Asagawa is gesturing that he needs to cut out early.

Story of my life.

"Cam, sheesh, are you even listening? Will you be my best man, I asked. We want to get married this Christmas in Minnesota."

"Sorry, I had a friend over, and he's just leaving. Yes, yes, of course I'll do it. It would be an honor."

What else can I say?

I'm seriously such an asshole.

* * *

With Asagawa gone, I let myself wallow. I delete Reilly's match from my streams and cue up an old NHL game from SportsNorth Classic. Then I chug the rest of the Asahi before switching to straight Patrón. Partway into the bottle, I send a series of alternately whiny and truculent text messages to Vanessa.

(Seriously? He's been with carolyn like 6 months)
Cameron Green

Vanessa Green (Karolin)

(Whatever) CG

(Must be nice to br Ry, always the chrmed life) CG

(Moms favorite. World fuck9ng Cup) CG

Second string, and he only got notable field time in the disastrous match against Sweden, but still. Even if he'll never be a superstar, he's making ten times my salary to chase a ball down a patch of grass.

Incoming video call: Vanessa Green

"Good, save me the typing," I say once her image appears on my screen.

"You need to stop this right now." She narrows her eyes at me. "Have you been drinking?"

I shake the bottle of tequila in front of my port camera, sloshing the contents up the sides. "Some. As much as I want to, too, since she isn't coming over tonight." I am, thankfully, still sober enough not to utter the words "whisky dick" to my sister.

"Jesus, Cam."

"I told her I'm falling for her, Ness, and it was like it didn't even register. Far as I could tell, she gives zeeeero shits." Unfair to Misora, as it isn't exactly true, but I'm not in the mood to offer a nuanced narrative.

"Oh, Cam," Vanessa says, her expression shifting from shock to pity, which is worse. For a moment, she turns to the side and mouths something. Drew must be just out of frame.

"Tell Dr. Mukherjee hello from me," I say, a little too loud.

With obvious reluctance, Drew steps into view, taking a seat next to Vanessa on the couch. "I see you're a belligerent drunk," he observes.

I shrug and pour myself another shot, though I don't drink it. I'm using the same tactic that Misora's friends deployed at my ill-fated birthday party: letting the alcohol say all the things I couldn't get away with otherwise.

"Cam, I know the last year has been hard," Vanessa says. "Your whole life was upended, and it sounds like things here haven't gone quite how you'd like. But don't take it out on Reilly. Don't ruin his moment."

Every moment has been Reilly's moment. Or Vanessa's. I stare at the screen, looking not at my sister's face, but at the drape of Drew's arm around her shoulders, the squeeze of her hand on his knee. They don't even know they're doing it—they just create their world of two wherever they are.

Two, soon to be three.

"I have to go," I say, ending the call before Vanessa can protest.

Vanessa Green { Ask her to be your plus one for the wedding. She might surprise you.)

Ask Misora Toyama to be my date to my little brother's wedding in the U.S.? It's a batshit idea, and Vanessa would think so, too, if she knew who Misora was. And yet—the mental image is a pleasing one. I would look a lot less like the family loser with Misora by my side.

I drop my port back onto the *kotatsu* and slouch into the couch cushions. The hockey game, muted, is still playing on the TV. I've watched this one before, not just live when it happened, but several times since. Minnesota is playing a penalty kill, and then—there it is, the short-handed goal by Matti Koskinen. Thrilling in the moment, yes, but somehow even more satisfying on replay, because you already know the outcome. Everything will end well.

A long buzz from my port, followed by two short ones. Misora.

> *Toyama Misora { Sorry to disturb you when you're hanging out with Asagawa, but I really need you. It's stuff with Eika again. Would you do me a favor?)*

> *(Anything } Cameron Green*

* * *

I've been at Helios early in the morning before, but not this late at night, especially on a Friday. I shake out my umbrella and stash it in one of the receptacles in the entryway so I don't drip across the lobby. Motion sensor lights illuminate my path to the elevators.

The air in the hallway is circulating yet stuffy, as if the cooling system can't keep up with the unseasonable humidity from outside. I use my own AppKey to operate the elevator and enter the windowless suite containing our team lab space. Walking past the desks guided only by the beam from my port, I pause at the door to the inner lab and thumb open the instructions from Misora's message.

The AppKey she sent works immediately, causing a panel next to the door to slide open and reveal a keypad. I punch in her code: 04022030. A click, and the lock disengages. I'm in.

Moving with deliberation, I check each of the machines. Misora was certain she'd left herself logged in on one, but they're all properly shut down for the night. I'm not thrilled to have made the long trip down here for nothing, especially while semi-buzzed. But even communicating by text message, Misora seemed so stressed out, so exhausted by the endlessness of Eika's problems. This was the least I could do for her.

(It's done } Cameron Green

* * *

I don't wake until late morning, and when I get out of bed and step into the hallway, it's straight into a puddle.

"Oh, damn it, seriously?!"

Panzer is cowering in the kitchen, and as soon as I see his hangdog expression, I feel terrible. "I'm sorry, bud," I say. The tequila must have conked me out—if he whined at me this morning, I slept right through it.

I clean up the mess and throw my wet socks into the wash before taking Panzer outside. As we amble around the small park so he can sniff every rock, flower, and tree, I scroll through my notifications. It's mostly spam or listservs, but there's already a calendar hold from Reilly for a full week in December with the subject "BACHELOR PARTY + WEDDING." And a reply from Misora, sent earlier this morning:

Toyama Misora { Thank you. I owe you.)

Since that first night at BG7, I've always been the one who owed her. I'll ask her how Eika is, what happened, and whether she's really okay—but first, I allow myself a moment of indulgence.

For once, Misora was the one who needed me.

Panzer strains a bit, eager to sniff harder at a bush that's just out of reach. Smiling, I pat his soft side and unspool another foot of the leash.

I know exactly what I'll ask for in return. Vanessa's right; maybe Misora will surprise me.

PARK TAEHYUN

Archival footage: Hello, Seoul! *Interview (1-minute clip)*

The longtime host of Hello, Seoul!*, the morning show that is every housewife's staple, is seated in one of two matching wing chairs across from a young man. He's in modest attire, and though his hair is still cut in sharp military style, he's strikingly handsome in a way Gangnam's best plastic surgeons can't replicate.*

Cha Eunbi looks first at the camera. "Good morning, and welcome to Hello, Seoul!*. We're wrapping up our four-part series about the terrifying events that occurred in Hwacheon County this January. If it weren't for the courage of our soldiers, the Hwacheon Dam, a vital national asset, would have been damaged by North Korean saboteurs. Today, we're joined once again by the Hero of Hwacheon himself! Park Taehyun, thank you for coming back to our studio."*

Taehyun nods, half-bowing from his seated position.

"I hope it hasn't been too difficult for you to speak with me about your experiences," Eunbi continues. "I know from KBC's MinoSo feed that our audience appreciated your candid account of how a simple ice-fishing expedition took a frightening yet ultimately valorous turn. The last time you were here, you told us you were unsure of what you were going to do after your honorable discharge from the military. It's my

understanding that this has changed. Do you have any news you'd like to share with our viewers?"

"Yes. I am humbly grateful to you and your viewers for all their support. I credit the gracious letters I received while I was in the hospital with my full recovery. The women of the Republic of Korea are undeniably the finest in the world." As he speaks, Taehyun's demeanor subtly shifts, and he slowly brings a soft smile up to full wattage. "Thanks to their—and your—encouragement and support, I am delighted to share my next venture. I am being sponsored by KBC, JeJuice, and the entire family of Apogee products to join the new cast of We Live... With a K-Pop Star *this fall."*

In the corner of the screen, the JeJuice mascot, a cartoon Jeju weasel, pops up and dances with an anthropomorphized orange.

Eunbi beams again at the camera. "Truly a fitting end to the story of our newest hero. We'll look forward to those new episodes this fall, beginning Chuseok *weekend here on KBC."*

* * *

It's only about ten when I get home, but I did a lot of damage in just a couple hours—to both my liver and my wallet. One more round and I probably could have won back a lot of my losses, but I've got to watch my spending. If Misora ends things, as it seems likely she will, I'm going to have a deluge of new expenses.

The entry lights are on, as are the ones in the hall and living room. Huh. Misora hasn't been home on a Friday night in ages.

"Hello?" I call. My voice is thick, and I can tell the word is blurred at the edges. It's possible I drank more than I thought. No response, so I head down the hallway. The *shoji* doors to the *tatami* room are slightly open. That's odd. "Misora?"

There's the outline of a person in the futon, her black hair peeking above the covers. I guess she's sleeping in here tonight, though it's very early for her to have gone to bed. Maybe she's sick; if so, it's just as well for her to stay out of our room. I pull the doors closed and walk down the hall to our suite, eager to rinse off the smoky grit of the club.

In the outer bath, I yank off my clothes, grimacing at the stench of my shirt as it passes over my nose. Sweat and vodka—I'm getting too old to live like this. I slide open the door to the inner bath, where we have both a marble tub and a multi-jet shower.

It takes a moment to register what I see.

Misora is in the tub, fully clothed. She's slid down into the bath, and her eyes are wide open, staring at the ceiling in glassy stupor as the water laps under her nose. A livid bruise of indigo and deep violet skitters over her cheekbone and down the left side of her face.

"What the hell, Misora?!" I burst out as I bend down to pull her from the lukewarm water. She seems to register my presence, at least enough to push with her legs and propel herself up over the edge of the tub, but then she just stands there, shivering. Up close, I notice that her eyes are red-rimmed, and some of the tiny blood vessels near her nose have burst, leaving spidery lines.

I've never seen her this way, face slack, trembling and silent. Thick anger twists in my stomach like a snake as I wonder who did this to her. I have a thousand questions, but first, it's clear I need to help her. Reaching for the hem of her T-shirt, I pull it up over her head, then unbutton and help her out of her jeans, too.

I hear myself inhale on a sharp hiss. The pale landscape of her body is marred by bruises, bright in their freshness. Vivid handprints mark both of her forearms, and a stained bandage covers most of her torso. As she sways a little, I catch her gingerly by the upper arms, afraid of disturbing any invisible wounds. I can feel myself getting flushed and clammy.

"What happened?" I growl.

She finally meets my gaze, and when she does, her face crumples, and a strangled sound escapes her throat. "Oh, god, Taehyun—"

I half-expect her to push me away, but when I pull her against my chest, she doesn't resist. Instead, she presses her face into the skin of my shoulder, her breaths coming in shudders. I realize she's sobbing, a verb I never would have associated with Misora.

"Hey, hey, it's okay," I say. I stroke her hair as she cries, my shoulder slick with her tears. Eventually, her breath steadies, and she leans against me in silence.

I try again, tone gentler. "What happened? Who's in the other room?"

"Eika."

I wait for more.

"Did you know she was using L?" she whispers.

"Oh, god." I resent the implication, but now isn't the time. My mind races, trying to link Misora's wounds to Eika's secret habit. Did they have a physical fight over it? A comical thought, if Misora weren't so obviously injured.

A shiver wracks her body, and I step back a bit to look her over again. I had basic first aid training during my stint in the army, and I can tell that while whoever patched her up meant well, they were working with mediocre supplies. The gauze doesn't even have a magitech adhesive, when such a thing could be easily found at any hundred-yen store in greater Tokyo.

"Can you walk?" I ask. When she nods, I continue, "Go in and sit at your dressing table, I'll be right back."

I bring her water and a bottle of painkillers, and then I patch her up, cleaning the wound and applying an m-bandage. As soon as it seals against her flesh, Misora sighs with relief.

"Better?"

"Yes." For the first time, her eyes look clear. "Thank you."

"Do you need anything else?"

"Only rest."

I help her out of her remaining clothes, careful not to bump her many bruises, then tuck her into her side of our bed. In the moonlight, she looks frail and doll-like. A doll who's had half her pretty face punched in.

"Stay with me. Please."

I climb in next to her, and she presses herself into my body, still trembling. For a long time, I just hold her, letting her soak up my warmth. It's strange to be with her like this again, after our months of existing in parallel. She's both familiar and foreign.

"Taehyun, are you awake?" she whispers. There's an urgency in her voice; she sounds more like herself.

"Yes."

Her mouth finds mine, and her hands, still ice cold, aren't shy, either. She moves quickly—faster than I would have thought possible given her aching shuffle from the bath to the bedroom—to position herself on top of me. At first, fearful of her injuries, I hesitate to touch her back, but the insistence of her kiss is the permission I need.

My answer to her has always been yes, whenever she's wanted to hear it.

* * *

When I wake up with a pressing need to pee, it's still dark, just a hint of false dawn peeking out over the edge of the bay, so I use the flashlight on my port to guide my way. In the dim light I can barely see Misora, now back on her own side of the bed, curled into a tight ball.

As I walk into the bath, my foot lands in the sodden pile of Misora's wet clothes, still heaped where I dropped them last night. I scoop them up. Uniqlo T-shirt and jeans, men's size small. There's no way these belong to the towering American, nor to Razan, either.

It's a struggle to think through the blunted waves of hangover pounding my skull, but I'm clear enough now to grasp that something more significant than too much L happened last night.

But what?

Setting the clothes back into their puddle, I snap several pictures of them. Once I've used the toilet, I creep down the hall to the *tatami* room to look in on Eika. The sun has risen enough now to spill wan light across her face. She's not battered like Misora, but she's paler than usual, almost gaunt, with dark circles under her eyes. It's consistent with an overdose.

"Eika," I whisper. When she doesn't move, I try again, louder. "Eika."

Still nothing, so I snap a few photos of her as well. As I do, there's a flicker of guilt that I quickly suppress. Whatever happened last night, Misora has gone to some trouble to hide it, and capturing this evidence seems worthwhile. Who knows what might be useful to the *chaebol*.

Back in our bedroom, I try to get a few pictures of Misora. I have to keep the flash off, and the light is poor, but even in the grainy pixels you can make out the bruises on her face. I crawl back under the covers on my side.

My blackmailer has turned me into a blackmailer too.

By the time I resurface from heavy sleep, blinking in the midday light, Misora's side of the bed is empty. There's an hours-old message on my port:

> *Toyama Misora { Out for a while. Please check*
> *on Eika.)*

I scramble out of bed and into the bathroom. The clothes are gone, and the tile is pristine and dry. Did I hallucinate it all?

> *(Are you alright? } Park Taehyun*

> *TM { Of course.)*

I check my photo roll.
No. It happened.

DATE HATSUMI

THE TOKYO CITY ONLINE FORUM
>*News of the Day*

Landlords Use Expected Bill Passage to Take Advantage of Immigrant Tenants

When Lin Shu-chen moved to Japan this winter to begin a graduate program in economics, she expected case studies to be her biggest challenge. Yet in the last few months, she has found herself on the brink of homelessness twice, first as a former resident of Grace Court 5 after the March 23 earthquake and now as a victim of the rising anti-immigrant sentiment.

"I wasn't home when the earthquake happened, so I was safe," explained Lin. "But my apartment was in the middle of the collapsed end, and I lost all my things. In early March I'd used most of my savings on the key money and deposits, and also buying furniture. I was able to ask my family to send money so I could find another place to live, but now my new landlord canceled my lease and is saying I have to pay double rent for next month."

When contacted for comment, Mori Umeko, mayor of Suginami-ku and member of the Civic Action Party, described recent work in relocating the refugees. "It was a major effort to find new homes for the 162 residents impacted by the March *events," said Mori, adding that she couldn't comment on those who had moved out of the ward.*

Yet in follow-ups with the relocated tenants, this writer found that while all but 3 Japanese residents remained in the ward, every one of the 34 immigrant residents had been relocated to another part of the city. Of those relocated, 28 have now experienced rent increases in anticipation of the likely passage of the National Resource Protection Ordinance, a bill with combined support of the Japanese Reform Party, the Civic Action Party, and the All Nippon Party.

Click the link below for a guide to common tactics being used by landlords and contact information for Helping Hands, a non-profit dedicated to providing low-cost legal assistance.

- Sakabashira

* * *

The chicken and vegetables are simmering, so I sit down and take a sip of beer.

My mom reaches the end of the printout and looks up. "This is on the internet?"

She's looking thin but she's there again, behind her eyes, and that's all I can ask. I nod. "Not under my name, but I imagine a few people know it's me. I only changed a few lines from the version I submitted to my editor, after all."

"I'm so proud of you," she says. "Your father would have been too, you know."

"Maybe," I say. "I'll just be glad if this helps some people. It's worth being stuck in the front room with cold tea for now if it just does that."

I guess I'll find out at some point if Goto and his patrons, whoever they are, pay attention to the *Tokyo City Online Forum*. Or, on the opposite side of the equation, if anyone even reads it at all. Now that I've found a new creative way to try throwing away my career, I don't know which would be worse: too much attention or too little.

My mom takes a sip of her own beer and then volunteers, "Mayors don't last forever."

"We can only hope."

"You should invite Noah-kun over so we can celebrate this weekend," my mom says as she stands, the printout still in her hand. For once, I don't try to stop her from hiding my writing away somewhere.

I grunt noncommittally about her suggestion. It's been a month since I last talked to him. I haven't had the guts to reach out since Eika told me that Corbin-san left.

My port buzzes and I lean over to look at the screen on the table. The notification is nothing important, but it reminds me that Eika messaged me earlier and I haven't responded yet. I open the thread.

Fujiwara Eika { How did your meeting go~?)

What do I say? That after a decade of looking I finally have my first solid lead? That I may have an actual path to finding out what happened to my father, mere weeks before another property bill is going to pass?

(Well, my chance of being murdered
went up } Date Hatsumi

(That was a joke...I hope } DH

There's a sound of glass clinking as my mom starts washing at the sink, and I look up. Her arms are moving rhythmically as she works through a stack of plates, and she's humming lightly under her breath. I can't say anything to her yet since I don't want to get her hopes up.

At least I can share this news with Eika.

(But yeah } DH

(I think I found it } DH

(The link } DH

ASAGAWA KENJI

I'm sitting cross-legged on the *tatami*, my knees pressed against the front of an open box. Flipping to the next page in the open folder, I read the header of the policy out loud. "January 23. Policy renewal annual."

Chiyo is seated on her knees next to me, notebook and pen in her hands. I hand the sheet off to her, and she looks it over. "This sweet old lady. She was adding a rider to her policy for her son's model train collection."

"That much?" I ask. "Sounds like you took her for a ride."

It's not a particularly funny joke, but Chiyo giggles as she hands the page back.

The next page in the stack I recognize by date and amount. "The Pinking Custom Shoe and Repair job. Can you explain how we did work for these guys unpaid?"

She covers her face with her fingers. "Ah, that was, uh, maybe me. They paid, but I checked the wrong box on the form when I was taking notes. Funabashi-shacho was so mad."

"Chiyo-chan," I say in a deep tone, drawing out her name for the drama. "You know that mistake got me stabbed."

"Whaaaat?"

I tap my shoulder and then my left palm, the spots where the awl went in. "They weren't so happy to be asked to pay a second time."

It also started the long path to here. I'm not sure how I feel about that part.

"I am so sorry." She leans forward into a half-bow, the soft curls of her hair falling over her face.

"No need for a production about it." I lean back and raise an eyebrow. "But don't do that again if you can help it."

"I promise I'll do my best!"

We're only partially through January from this year so far. There have to be at least a hundred boxes in this office, filled with what might be useful leverage and potential connections. Even with Chiyo's help, this takes too long to find anything genuinely useful.

Which reminds me, I need to have these moved before Funabashi gets any ideas. As soon as I have the money for deposits and key money. "Do you or Tomohiko usually bring over the records?"

"She does. I don't think she trusts me to do it."

"Hm, I can't say I blame her," I say, tapping my shoulder again. "In case you forgot—stabbed."

She whimpers and drops into a bow, this time hands on the floor.

"Relax. It's a joke."

"I know, but I feel so bad." Chiyo raises back up and tucks her hair behind an ear. A blush blooms across her nose. "I just wish I could make up for it somehow."

In the heat of this stuffy apartment, she's unbuttoned her suit coat and the white shirt beneath is thin. Her skirt is riding up her thighs, a line of thread running up her leg and disappearing under the hem. She knows exactly what she's doing.

I wouldn't be in this position without her help, both deliberate and accidental. All of which she's been doing mostly for the thrill of chasing something she shouldn't have.

It'd be so easy to ruin her life.

She'd enjoy it too, at least at first.

But I don't have time to make those kinds of mistakes right now, not when Kumanaka and I barely made 10,000 yen between us this week.

"I think that's enough for today," I say. "Next time, Igarashi better get his lazy ass up here. We had enough payouts that I want to know the details on."

She nods silently, keeping her eyes down. I close up the box and lift it back onto the stack. When I take the notebook from her, I can't help but frown. For all these hours, not one of these names is a useful lead. "Thanks for your hard work today."

Her voice is quiet as she answers. "Of course, Kenji-shitencho. Thank you for your hard work too."

Once I'm sure Chiyo is gone, I take the stairs down.

Even though it's creeping into evening, the air is heavy. I might as well be standing in a bowl of ramen as I wait for Green to open the door. I reach up to knock a second time, and this time he swings the door open before I can. He hasn't bothered to turn the overhead light on, leaving the hall dimly illuminated by the doorway to the living room. A cool burst of air conditioning flows out from his dark apartment.

Green accepts the guest slippers with about as much appreciation as I expected: none.

I follow but veer into the kitchen. Opening the fridge, I lean my arm against the freezer door and with my free index finger tug the tie knot loose and use my thumb to pop the collar button open to take in the even cooler air. There are a few stray cans of Asahi Super Dry on the top shelf. I'd prefer some tea, but he only ever has beer in his fridge.

Crossing back, I leave the slippers in the hallway and drop down on the couch, positioned directly in the path of the air con. On the floor, the dog is lying with his belly up. Even a visitor isn't enough for him to leave his position tonight.

We barely start to talk before Green holds up a finger and digs his port out from his pocket. "I should answer this—it's my brother," he says, standing. As he crosses past me toward the kitchen, he's already speaking English.

Leaning back, I take a sip of beer. Panzer shifts on the floor, his tongue hanging out. A creature without any concerns. Lucky bastard.

One of my ports starts to buzz in my bag. Toyama-gumi HQ.

I'm not technically overdue on payments to Ota yet. What the hell.

"Asagawa-san," the voice says to me. "I have a job that I need kept discreet."

* * *

By the time I arrive, there's a light drizzle, just enough to cut the humidity and bring the air down to a more normal temp for May. With the kind of high-end residents who live in Azabu-Juban, I would expect the neighborhood to be infested with police, but this building is off the main streets. There are no obvious cameras on the outside and not even good lighting by the entrance. While there is a window for an attendant at the front, the space is unused under dust and behind a messy stack of discarded mail flyers left by residents.

The open-air hallway on the second floor is deserted, my footsteps silent on painted concrete.

When I reach for the handle to the apartment, Toyama-hime opens the door. Her bloodshot eyes snap into focus on my face, though her face is pale between dripping strands of hair. Threads hang bare on the sleeves of her shirt, in patches that look almost burnt. Her right arm is looped around her stomach, hand clutching the seam on the opposite side. She half-hides a wince as she steps back up out of the *genkan* so I can enter.

Closing the door quietly behind me, I say, "No one was outside, and there was just one car parked by the building."

From her high position, Toyama-hime stares me down for a second. I step around her and up into the room.

"In there," she says.

From where I'm standing, I can see through the apartment all the way to the balcony door at the far end. In between is an office, or at least what's left of it.

The room looks like a tornado hit, starting in the center. In front of me is a glass-topped table, the surface a spiderweb of cracks. Around it, lighter chairs are tipped over, fabric burst and charred. The smell of smoke is in the air, and charred plants barely hang from single attachments to the ceiling.

I take a step forward. The kitchenette to the right is largely untouched.

I can't say the same for the two on the floor at my feet.

Now why did Toyama-hime, princess of the underworld with the full might of her family and organization at her fingertips, call me?

With what happened with Asagawa-san's data drops, I can't rule out that there was more released than what got Takamine fired, something that made someone in their organization truly mad. But putting someone so high and relatively untouched on the board seems like a significant gamble, all for something that could be more easily solved by one loyal low-level thug with a knife.

Toyama-hime herself is obviously not beyond her own schemes, but I don't think I've pissed her off enough to warrant anything targeting me.

Intent eyes and perfect posture aside, I can see her far hand trembling just at the edge of my peripheral vision.

Okay, yeah, I wouldn't want Toyama Razan to know I'd fucked up like this either.

"I take payment up front," I say, holding out my gloved hand. An envelope drops into my hand, and I tuck it into my bag.

The room is chilled, so it's no hardship to put a hat on my hair and step back into my shoes for now. This isn't the kind of scene where I need to be worried about offending someone. This is the kind where I don't leave evidence behind. The kind where I'm dodging the crosshairs of both the police and the Toyama-gumi.

"This is—"

"I don't need a story," I say, with what approaches a soft tone. Keeping this as businesslike as possible is my best chance of having a tomorrow. "Or the truth. What are the police going to find when they look at these bodies?"

"Body," she says, kneeling down to touch the closer of the two. There's hair covering the face there, but even from several steps away, I recognize the glimmering blue earrings from our phone call last month: It's Fujika on the floor.

At a closer look, the celebrity is breathing evenly, so I cross around Toyama and squat down next to the other. There are scorch marks on the carpet around this body, and a second separate scorch mark closer to the plants.

The eraser end of a pencil from my bag functions as a tool to turn his head up slightly. His muscles still move freely. Pupils dilated and dull, this *gaijin* is definitely dead but hasn't been for long.

His skin is pale blue between splotches of red bruising. The markings extend across his face like lightning, down his arms, on what I can see of his abdomen where his shirt with some kind of bold text has pulled up and away from his baggy shorts. He smells like piss in the way that happens when there's not a person there to mind anymore.

I let his head roll back, dark curls hiding the unresponsive eyes. "Who is this?"

To my side, Toyama-hime stands. "Her assistant."

His hands are curled up like dead cockroaches. Using the end of the pencil, I lift a digit to take a closer look—there aren't splotches under the nails like you'd find with long-term L use, so this must have been an unlucky first-timer. There's also no patch on the neck. I pull up the edge of his shorts. None on the inner thighs. Did Toyama remove it?

I sit back on my heels. "Her family isn't going to want the publicity of an investigation. We'll want to separate the problem from her. Find a logical alternative."

"Yes, something logical," Toyama-hime says, voice flat like we're talking about ordering delivery. "A drug charge could ruin her reputation."

"People like her don't have consequences. He's a foreigner. It'll be on him." There's no reaction, so I continue. "We can move the body, but everything in this room would still be evidence." It'd be impractical to get full rolls of carpet both in and out tonight with the number of hands we have.

She's standing straight, chin up, her body unnaturally still and arm still loosely looped around her stomach. Whatever is under there, it's hurting her, and she doesn't want to show it.

Neither of these two on the floor are going anywhere soon. "I brought a first aid kit. Let me see."

She looks at me for a long moment, then nods, pulling her shirt up enough to uncover a burn on her abdomen. Deep red, like a *hanko* stamped across her pale skin. The pain is a good sign that it hasn't gone so deep she needs medical attention.

I gesture to the chair closest to the entrance, the only one that's upright and out of the mess. She makes her way to it and sits on the edge of the seat, her feet tucked back all neat.

In the kitchen cupboard, I find an almost empty bottle of whisky and some Okinawan rum. I carry the rum back over, and Toyama-hime takes it, our fingers brushing. She's hot, more than a fever, and the temperature difference in the air conditioned room causes a prickle up my forearm.

I get out the first aid kit from my bag so I can swap to a different kind of glove.

"You didn't bring—" she starts, then catches herself. "Of course, no, you wouldn't. Thank you."

She opens the bottle and gulps some down. Then she tucks the shirt up and grips the edge of the chair while I pat the burn with a sterile wipe and cover it with a bandage. She has to bite down on the collar of her shirt to do it, but she keeps silent as I work.

Toyama's stomach is just as fiery as her fingers, and by the time I'm finished I can feel the echo of the heat up both arms. Shifting my weight back on my heels, I close up the first aid kit and put it back in my bag.

"Looks like he was using. That what a lab's gonna find?" If only the rich had better things to do than dabble in the deep end. The least that flighty playgirl could have done was OD by herself.

"The speed of the temperature overload would have variance...and the follicle sampling... Yes, it will be in his system." Slowly, Toyama nods. "If you can handle the immediate problem, I can handle the room. What's here, having it cleaned."

"Then we'll move it. I can call someone with a vehicle—"

"No, no other people. Eika has a car, it should be outside."

"Okay. I can drive," I say. "I can make some space on timing, depending on when we set it up for this to be found. But you'll want an alibi for both of you, just in case anyone thinks to check for a connection."

"I have one."

Of course she would. She can order one up as easily as she can order new carpet on the sly.

"When does it need to be for?" she asks.

"Depends on where I drop it. Somewhere out of the way gives you time, but an alley near clubs would invite fewer questions." I stand and turn to look at the body again. "Any idea if anyone was expecting him somewhere?"

"No," she leans forward and, with effort, stands, "His port would say."

It takes some looking, but I find the port in the space under a desk. When I pick it up using a small towel, it's still in working condition.

"We can't use a fingerprint to open it, not now. Know his passcode?" I ask, not expecting it to be that easy.

Toyama shakes her head, staring at the device in my hand. Then a flicker of horror crosses her face before it clicks back into a neutral mask. "I can open it," she says eventually.

Kneeling down next to the body, she gestures at me to slide the port under his hand. Her fingers tremble as she puts them over the dead digit and closes her eyes, concentrating on something I can't see. After a few seconds, there's a click as the port unlocks.

She snatches the device out by the towel and stands in one awkward movement. She flips through screens, then says, "No plans on the calendar or in the messages."

"Good. That gives us room. After thirty-six hours, the lab tech won't be able to tell the difference of a couple hours, at least as long as we get him into place in the next hour or two."

Flipping the towel back, she presses the charging panel against her arm. I frown, and she catches the expression.

"In case they look at when the port ran out of power," she clarifies.

As she does that, I dig in my bag to retrieve the other item she wanted. I hand her the bag of new clothes with the explanation that I'd bought men's to avoid being memorable, and she takes the bag with the port she's charging to the bathroom.

In the cold empty room, my stomach feels warm, like I was the one who drank the rum. I clean the rim and the fingerprints from the bottle and return it to the cupboard.

I take another look at the body and verify that whatever patch of L was on him when he died is gone. There's still that sheet of Love in my bag from Ota's office, so I peel off two and put them on his neck. This amount would be barely enough for a high for Kumanaka, but since this doesn't look like a long-term addiction, this is around the right amount for the OD. It's still her family's product—in this city it'd be more suspicious if it weren't.

When Toyama returns from the bathroom, I'm using a box cutter to slice out a square of carpet. She hands me the port, still encased in the towel, and I push the device into his pocket. Then I roll up the carpet, tape it, and then wrap it again in a large plastic sheet from my bag. In the end, it looks like the kind of uncut sushi roll you'd eat for *Setsubun*, if you were inclined to eat building materials.

We find Fujika's car keys in her purse and Toyama identifies her vehicle near the entrance. In two trips, I carry the bodies down through the dark and mercifully empty street, one that I lay in the back seat and one that I drop in the trunk. I put the bag with Toyama's ruined clothes in the trunk too.

When I start the car, Fujika's port connects and startles both of us with a sudden burst of music.

Toyama hits the volume button down click by fast click, finally leaving us back in silence. Then she gives me directions, and we remain quiet until we arrive at the gate for the underground parking at her apartment building. There's probably a key on her port, but we both know she's not handing that over to me even now. Instead, she gives me the code and I punch it in with my gloved hand.

When we take the elevator, I switch from a carry with both arms to having Fujika draped over my shoulder like she's drunk. It's more awkward, but better in case anyone gets on. No one does, not in this space that money built.

The hallway is indoors, the floors covered in carpet. When we reach the door, she opens it with a key and has me wait outside while she checks for the Flower Boy Ramen Chef.

He isn't there, so I switch back to a two-armed carry and walk through what might as well be a hotel lobby to a *tatami* room that is larger than the upstairs of my mother's house. Toyama slides open the closet door so I can see where she keeps a futon before stalking back out. I set Fujika down long enough to unfold the mattress, and then move her body on top of it.

Toyama is standing in her living room, back to a wide wall of windows overlooking the expanse of the city, every bit the queen of her space even in a misfitted pair of jeans and T-shirt. "Bring her car back when it's done."

"The key will be in the car, unlocked."

We look at each other, something passing between us. Toyama and I have never been friends, but in this instant, we have an understanding.

In the elevator, watching the floor number count down, I wonder how long it will be before Toyama's feelings turn to hate because I saw her when she was weak.

In that glimpse of the future, I understand Asagawa-san's actions better than I ever have.

From Fujika's car, I call Kumanaka and tell him to drive over, give him the garage code. Toyama might not want another person involved, but this will be safer than Fujika's license plate showing up in the neighborhood near where the body is going to be found.

As I wait, I look at the leather everywhere: the upholstery, the steering wheel. The envelope of cash in my bag is enough to keep things for us all floating for a bit, but it's nothing like the money that went into this.

Sweat is starting to stick between my back and the seat, so I turn the car on to use the air conditioning. The car connects to Fujika's port up in the apartment, kicking in the music.

I turn the volume down but stop before clicking the power off completely—by my hand the screen is slowly filling up with messages.

Date Hatsumi { I think I found it)

DH { The link)

DH { the woman I talked to was impressively suspicious)

DH { But some of what she said did match up

with our guess)

DH { Also, side question—have you ever heard the last name Kuma-naka before? Bear middle?)

DH { Talk about a fitting name for a shady dude)

There aren't any messages about this in the conversation above, just screens and screens of one side complaining about work and invitations to parties from the other. So, I tap the screen to pop up a keyboard and start to type myself.

(haha that's so funny } Fujiwara Eika

(tell me more } FE

TOYAMA MISORA

My eyes are gritty, the lashes stuck together. As I lift a hand to rub away the sleep, pain shoots through my shoulder. Enough light is seeping in around the partially closed blinds that I can see Taehyun sprawled on his back next to me, chest rising in even breaths. I roll onto my side and then carefully shift into a sitting position.

My head throbs, tenderness radiates across the skin of my arms, and there's a crisp, fiery pulsing in my abdomen. I'm surrounded by a maelstrom: chairs upended, carpet shredded, the ashy remains of the plants.

Eika and Noah on the floor. It all comes rushing back in a tsunami of horror.

The thought of his name causes a sob to rise in my throat, but I swallow it down. I still have so much to do—for both my own protection and Eika's.

I dress in long sleeves and long pants to hide the majority of my bruises, then head into the bathroom to figure out how much makeup my face will need to be similarly concealed. The clothes Asagawa bought are in the wet pile where Taehyun dropped them; I shove everything into a plastic bag and mop up the puddle. I'll toss it in a random dumpster on my way to Replenish.

The last thing I want to do is go back there, but I have to be on time to meet Yoshida.

Checking her pulse again and again, just to be sure. It's there, weak and thready. Shaky relief. Then checking him. Nothing, no matter how much I might wish otherwise. I go into the bathroom and vomit. Some part of my brain, the darkest and cruelest part, thinks about how the ramen I ate with Hideki tastes just the same in both directions.

The walk to Replenish is painful, my clothes rubbing on my aching skin, but it's better than having a ride logged with a car service, and it's not like I can take Eika's Mercedes. I have about forty-five minutes before Yoshida is supposed to arrive, so I let myself in with Eika's key and survey the damage.

Sitting on the floor in the rubble. A rough edge of the melted carpet digs into my thigh through a hole in my ruined skirt. With shaking hands, opening my port. Four names in my priority contacts.

Fujiwara Eika. Obviously not.

Date Hatsumi. Oh, god. Oh, god, no. The bile rises in my throat again, but I swallow it down, pressing on.

Park Taehyun. He's the only one who's done something like this, who might understand what this is like. But that was with the army, and he was lauded as a hero. No, I can't call him either.

Lastly, Cameron Green. Oh, no. He can never know what I've done. Never.

And yet—seeing his name gives me an idea. Two, actually. One for an alibi, and another for who I might call to help.

I wipe down every surface I touched the night before and stash most of the incriminating debris in garbage bags, ready for Yoshida's crew to take for incineration. The charred remains of the dummy port I slip into a special case—I'll lock that in the safe at home.

When I see a shadow behind Yoshida in the doorway, I fear he's brought someone from Toyama-gumi, but it's only his wife.

"This will take most of the morning," Yoshida tells me. "Minyoung and I will finish the cleaning, and then I'll bring in some of my old pals from Dai Construction to do the repairs and install new carpet and furniture."

It's not ideal, not when Dai is a Toyama-gumi firm, but that's the risk I took in calling on Yoshida for help. Besides, by the time his friends get here, I'll be long gone. I hand him an envelope of cash, thicker than the one I gave Asagawa last night.

"This is for this month. When I can, I'll set up an account to auto-pay Shigeru's school."

Yoshida bows, and Minyoung's eyes well up. "*Kamsa hamnida*," she whispers. She starts to reach for my right hand, but I snatch it away, grasping it with my left behind my back and returning Yoshida's bow.

In my rush to leave, I forget to say goodbye.

* * *

"Is Eika awake?"

Taehyun hops up with one foot on either side of the treadmill deck, letting the belt continue to run, and pulls out an earbud. "Huh?"

"I asked if Eika is awake."

"Not yet." He stops the belt and wipes his face with a nearby towel, peering at me with what might be genuine concern. "What happened last night, anyway?"

I say goodbye to Papa and step out of Eika's office. Noah is frozen in the entrance to the kitchenette, mouth agape as Eika's body convulses on the floor.

"What happened?" I demand. I already know, and the knowing is horror. I inhale, and the scent of ozone crackles in my nostrils.

Rushing to Eika's side, I grab the port from her hand, swallowing a scream of agony as the power rocketing out of her engulfs me. If Cameron was a firehose, then Eika is a waterfall.

"Eika and a friend of hers had a little too much fun at BG7 last night. They were both already double-patched when I got there."

Taehyun takes a drink of water, eyeing me over the edge of the bottle. "And you?"

I lift a hand to rub my cheek, wincing as my fingertips brush the edge of where Noah punched me. I force a wry smile and deliver the lie, hoping he won't probe at it too much. "Have you ever tried to unpatch someone in the middle of their fun? Believe it or not, Eika fights dirty."

The pain is endless. It is mitochondrial; it is molecular. It is all that I am.

Desperate for relief, I crawl across the floor, fumbling blindly for the monstera plant. It bursts into nothingness the instant my hand brushes a frond.

I can't contain this. Too much longer, and it will claw me apart from the inside. Already, I can feel the heat pushing out from my core, seeking equilibrium in the air-conditioned room.

Me.

Eika.

Noah.

I make a choice.

"She's scrappy," Taehyun agrees, mirroring my smile. Thank god. "Why don't you look in on her, and I'll order us some lunch."

He's being too nice, nicer than he has been in weeks. Of course he is: my night of hell was his return to normal. I am so grateful for his help, and for how readily he accepted my story, but oh, do I ever hate him for it, too.

"Thank you, Taehyun."

Eika doesn't stir at the sound of the door, so I slip in quietly and walk over to her bag, intending to return her office key. As I undo the clasp, I notice a little packet of banana yellow pills wedged between her wallet and a tube of gloss. Unable to stop myself, I reach for them and read the label.

And then I drop the pills and barely catch myself from falling to the floor. My heart hammers, my breath stops, and even though I haven't eaten since yesterday, I feel like I could vomit again.

The rush of sudden understanding doesn't make anything better. There's no satisfaction in completing this puzzle. I thought I was numb, that I had nothing left in me, but as I stare down at those fucking pills, the ordinary ADHD prescription that surely interacted with the synthetic L in the battery that I TOLD EIKA NOT TO TOUCH, I feel fresh tears sting my eyes.

"Mi-chan?"

My back is to her, but I can see her warped reflection in the window. She's so tiny under the fluffy duvet of the futon, her hair mussed and mascara streaky.

Me.
Eika.
Noah.
I made a choice.

And she has no idea. For just a little longer, I'll let it stay that way. I rub furiously at the tears with balled up fists, willing them gone, then turn.

"Eika-chan, thank goodness. I was so worried about you."

INTERSTITIAL

Assistant to Fujiwara Eika Dead from Overdose

The assistant of celebrity and Replenish Initiative founder Fujiwara Eika was found dead on Sunday in Roppongi from an alleged overdose of the synthetic drug L. The Tokyo Metropolitan Police Department has announced that they will release additional details later today.

Fujiwara's talent agency, Astral Entertainment, released a statement that they have temporarily discontinued the use of her image for all promotional materials during the investigation. The Kinoshita Group has also pulled all related commercials for the products Diet Breakfast Water and Chocolat Grandeur from airing, and NHK has removed all episodes of Let's Challenge *and* NHK Discuss! *featuring Fujiwara from their website until a decision is made by prosecutors on whether to bring any criminal charges against the celebrity.*

Neither Fujiwara nor the Replenish Initiative have released formal statements at this time.

Comments

I didn't think she was such a druggie :/ Fake-a, not Fujika

-Naoki384 (3 min. ago)

My daughter has her poster, how awful
                              -SailorRibbon (4 min. ago)

Take a look at these clips of her high (link)
                              -thesenpai (4 min. ago)

I read this junkie was Canadian. What other foreigners
is she working with?
                              -r47632198743924 (5 min. ago)

lol, what a way to go
                              -TanakaofTokyo (5 min. ago)

anyone see what that Johjima guy was saying on MinoSo?
                              -Malingerance (5 min. ago)

FruitMan didn't deserve this
                              -RedAppleRiot (5 min. ago)

POSTSCRIPT

This story is supposed to be a puff piece, eloquent prose to permanently elevate the people behind the Daejeon Magical Accords. I'm supposed to sell these people, sell us, as a neatly packaged product for all ages.

If only there were something flattering for me to write.

Was there a point to Noah's death, something that made it all worth it in the end?

What a question to ask, as if a neatly wrapped narrative makes tragedy justified. He was a person, not a price paid for a brighter future. A life lost isn't a step on the path of progress, as much as people might want to appease their own guilt with such a frame. When you swim in sewage, no one stays clean.

Yet fighting against this current is the only way upstream.

-Sakabashira

APPENDIX: PEOPLE

Organized by the perspective in which they first appear, then by family name.

CAMERON GREEN

Green, Davis – Cameron's father
Green, Reilly – Cameron's younger brother
Green, Vanessa – Officer at the U.S. Embassy in Tokyo; Cameron's older sister
Ichikawa Masanobu – Primary Investigator on Drew's project, University of Tokyo
Lindholm-Green, Leanna – Cameron's mother
Mukherjee, Drew – Post-doctoral researcher, University of Tokyo; Vanessa's husband
Nygaard, Ingrid – Cameron's girlfriend
O'Connell, Chuck – Cameron's coworker
Panzer – Cameron's dog
Shimizu Ikumi – Assistant Professor, Magical Analysis, University of Tokyo

FUJIWARA EIKA

Fujiwara Isao – COO of Fujiwara Heavy Industries; Eika's older brother

Fujiwara Kimiko – CEO of Fujiwara Heavy Industries; Eika's
    older sister
Fujiwara Yuuto – Cello player; Eika's younger brother
Gushiken Hina – Eika's manager at Astral Entertainment
Ito Yasahiro – Host of *NHK Discuss!*
Johjima Haru – Director of Emerging Market Strategies,
    Johjima Pharmaceuticals; Eika's friend
Kato Mitsue – Nobel Prize winner and professor emeritus,
    University of Tokyo Hospital
Kato Sayuri – Physician, Kato Hospitals
Koike Nenosuke – Director of the Strategic Assets Agency
Lambert, Noah – Intern at Replenish Initiative
Yokoyama Fusanosuke – Johjima Endowed Chair in Applied
    Magical Sciences, University of Tokyo

ASAGAWA KENJI

Asagawa Takeshi – Kenji's older brother
Asagawa Yukina – Head of the Asagawa-gumi; Kenji's mother
Bunya Tomohiko – Senior Office Lady (OL) at Walling
    Insurance
Funabashi – Manager of the Nishi-Shinjuku branch of Walling
    Insurance
Igarashi – Claims processor at Walling Insurance; Kenji's friend
Kumanaka Mizuki – Kumanaka Soseki's wife
Kumanaka Rina – Oldest daughter of the Kumanaka family
Kumanaka Soseki – Member of the Asagawa-gumi
Kumanaka Yuri – Youngest daughter of the Kumanaka family
Mr. Wiggles – Chiyo's pet snake
Noguchi Chiyo – Junior Office Lady (OL) at Walling
    Insurance; Kenji's friend
Ota – Lower level boss of the Toyama-gumi
Takamine – Client of the Asagawa-gumi; middle management
    at a supply company

TOYAMA MISORA

Akanishi Nozomi – Misora's assistant, Helios
Araki – Engineer, Experimental Magitech, Helios
——— Fumiko – Assistant to Toyama Rei, Helios
Li Xiaohui – Engineer, Experimental Magitech, Helios
Matsuda – Engineer, Experimental Magitech, Helios
Okamoto – General Counsel for Helios
Sugihara – Engineer, Experimental Magitech, Helios
Takahashi Saburo – Lawyer for the Toyama-gumi
Toyama Razan – *Kumicho* (head) of the Toyama-gumi; Misora's
    father
Toyama Rei – CEO of Helios; Misora's mother
Watanabe Daichi – Youngest son of Watanabe Yusuke; member
    of the Toyama-gumi
Watanabe Hideki – Middle son of Watanabe Yusuke; member
    of the Toyama-gumi
Watanabe Kaihei – Eldest son of Watanabe Yusuke; member of
    the Toyama-gumi
Watanabe Yusuke – *Wakagashira* (second in charge) of the
    Toyama-gumi
Yoshida – Manager of Banana Garden 7

DATE HATSUMI

Date Hideaki – Former mayor of Suginami-ku; Hatsumi's
    father. Deceased
Date Tetsuo – Proprietor of Used Books; Hatsumi's mother
Eguchi – Pledge to the Kubo-gumi
Goto Naoki – Hastumi's boss, *Nihon Times*; former classmate
Himura – Younger member of the Kubo-gumi
Inoe Nozomu – Boss of Kubo-gumi sub-family (tiger father)
Juro – Senior assistant to Mayor Mori
Mori Mikio – Mayor Mori's husband
Mori Natsuki – Mayor Mori's daughter

Mori Umeko – Current mayor of Suginami ward; member of the Civic Action Party

Okada Arata – Reporter for *Sekai Shimbun*; member of the press club covering the Civic Action Party

Sadame – Junior assistant to Mayor Mori

Terrell, Corbin – Noah's friend

Wada Isamu – Former governor of Tokyo

Yamada – Senior member of the Kubo-gumi

PARK TAEHYUN

Choi Kyunghee – Taehyun's mother

Hong Minho – Taehyun's reality TV co-star

Kim Hyori – Taehyun's sister-in-law

Oh Soojin – Taehyun's co-star on *Flower Boy Ramyeon Chef*

Park Aejung – Taehyun's niece

Park Kijung – Taehyun's nephew

Park Taeyong – Taehyun's older brother. Deceased

AUTHOR'S NOTE

Elements of this story started more than 20 years ago—not as a book at all, but as a role-playing game among teenage friends. Although the game itself never fully captured our imaginations, the characters certainly did, lodging themselves in the backs of our minds even as we were each busy with the thousand other things that comprise the transition to adulthood. Through graduate degrees, international moves, and wedding planning, these characters remained, awaiting their turn to take center stage. Some were more patient than others, as you might expect.

We started putting pixels of ink to digital paper in earnest during the summer of 2016, this time drafting a fresh story woven from the accumulation of our interim experiences. What we never imagined was that the magic ban—something we once joked was too draconian for even the U.S. to contemplate—would soon look tame compared to the rolling political cataclysms that followed in the real world. The World's Worst Birthday Party was the first sequence of scenes we wrote, and it became the linchpin of the book: the socially awkward center from which all the other events would unfurl.

There is a special kind of joy in creating a world positioned as a funhouse mirror of our own, where magic—and the way it shapes the lives of its haves and have-nots—can serve as a stand-in for the problems that plague life here in the Darkest Timeline. The experience of our own reality certainly shaped the way we interpreted the characters' lives and problems. We hope you found your time in the

Syphon Continuity to be both relatable and a reprieve.

No story, not even one with two authors, comes into being without support, especially when it devours half a lifetime of labor and love. A deep debt of gratitude is owed to our beta readers: Stephanie Rosen, Nicholas Bobbie, and Jeff. In addition, K. would like to thank her significant other and parents for support through long nights of writing and long years of work with uncertain ends. S. would like to thank her partner, her family, and her dearest friends for understanding when she needed to focus on writing—and when she might desperately need a distraction. Thank you for swimming against the current with us.

ABOUT THE AUTHORS

A. Sherman Karlsson is the pen name for two Minnesota-born women in a trenchcoat who have maintained their ongoing creative collaboration since their teens despite multiple transoceanic moves and many years of graduate school.

They have wide ranging interests, including cat herding, games, creating elaborate continuities of the mind, and reading voraciously as an escape from the horrors of this timeline. Both lurk somewhere in the greater Midwest, missing their home state terribly.

www.ingramcontent.com/pod-product-compliance
Lightning Source LLC
Chambersburg PA
CBHW020000120726
47903CB00004B/1076

9 798999 923905